Seven Crows a Secret Yet To be Told

Vernon Oickle

Seven Crows a Secret Yet To Be Told
© 2023 Vernon Oickle

Cover design: Rebekah Wetmore
Author photo: Heidi Jirotka
Editor: Andrew Wetmore

ISBN: 978-1-998149-20-9
First edition September, 2023

MOOSE HOUSE
PUBLICATIONS

2475 Perotte Road
Annapolis County, NS
B0S 1A0

moosehousepress.com
info@moosehousepress.com

We live and work in Mi'kma'ki, the ancestral and unceded territory of the Mi'kmaw people. This territory is covered by the "Treaties of Peace and Friendship" which Mi'kmaw and Wolastoqiyik (Maliseet) people first signed with the British Crown in 1725. The treaties did not deal with surrender of lands and resources but in fact recognized Mi'kmaq and Wolastoqiyik (Maliseet) title and established the rules for what was to be an ongoing relationship between nations. We are all Treaty people.

Also by Vernon Oickle

One Crow Sorrow
Two Crows Joy
Three Crows a Letter
Four Crows a Boy
Five Crows Silver
Six Crows Gold – available from Moose House

Life and Death after Billy
Friends & Neighbours: a collection of stories from the Liverpool Advance
Busted: Nova Scotia's War on Drugs
Queens County
Ghost Stories of the Maritimes (volumes 1 and 2)
Dancing with the Dead
Great Canadian Ghost Stories Volume II (co-author)
Disasters of Atlantic Canada: stories of courage and chaos
Canada's Haunted Coast: true ghost stories of the Maritimes
The Editor's Diary: the first 13 years
Angels Here Among Us
Red Sky at Night
South Shore Facts and Folklore
I'm Movin' On: the life and legacy of Hank Snow
Beaches of Lunenburg-Queens
Nova Scotia Outstanding Outhouse Reader
Red Coat Brigade
Ghost Stories of Nova Scotia
Kiss the Cod!
Strange Nova Scotia
Newfoundland and Labrador Outrageous Outhouse Reader
Where Evil Dwells
How to talk Nova Scotian: the Bluenoser's book of slang
The Nova Scotia Book of Lists
My Nova Scotia Home
We Love Nova Scotia: a people's portrait
More Ghost Stories of Nova Scotia
Queens County: a history in pictures
The Second Movement: Nova Scotia's outrageous outhouse reader No. 2
So you think you KNOW Nova Scotia?

One crow sorrow, two crows joy;
three crows a letter, four crows a boy;
five crows silver, six crows gold;
seven crows a secret yet to be told;
eight crows for a wish;
nine crows for a kiss;
ten crows for a time of joyous bliss.
eleven crows for good health;
twelve crows for improved wealth;
thirteen crows beware for it's the devil himself.

- One version of a common
Nova Scotian folk rhyme

This book is dedicated to my good friend, Marci.
Your support and encouragement mean more than
you will ever know.

This is a work of fiction. The author has created the characters, conversations, interactions, and events; and any resemblance of any character to any real person is coincidental.

Seven Crows a Secret Yet To Be Told

The past is prologue

1760

Perched atop the tallest pine trees in the pristine, unspoiled forest, they watch the thing not far offshore.

They've seen these creatures before, but only in recent years. Now these strangers are invading their land.

Black eyes narrowed, vigilant, bright, they watch as the head of the monstrous beast with three spear-like white fangs cuts through the choppy water, heading to an unknown destination.

They have no idea what these creatures are or what purpose they may have here in this wild land, but they sense that their world is changing forever.

Strong and proud, the majestic black birds have lived here with their families since time began. This is their world and they are in tune with nature. They have lived in harmony with the peoples who share it with them.

Their feathers collectively ruffle as an instinctive understanding passes through their minds—this new wind blowing into their world is bringing people and issues they have never before seen or know how to deal with.

Observing the floating beast, with its white sails scratching the pure cerulean sky as it snakes along the coast, the birds occasionally send out scouts to investigate.

They will do so today, for they know the beast looming on the horizon is different from any of the others they have seen.

They sense the connection. One among those strange beings on the monster vessel is different from the others.

These shining, night-black birds know at this moment that they will have to adapt. They will have to live among these new people.

But most of all, they will have to find allies.

The Present

Vernon Oickle

1: At the end of the shadows

"One life ends; another begins."

It has been thirteen and a half years since his family was wiped out in a bloody crime that left him an orphan, but Alex Goodwin remembers these words his mother often spoke whenever there was a death in the community. He was a curious youngster and, as such, he asked a lot of questions.

"People die."

He remembers her being blunt. She understood that, despite his age, the young boy's wisdom stretched well beyond the date on his birth certificate, and she knew he would see through her if she tried to sugar-coat the truth, especially when it came to the natural order of things.

"While that makes us sad," she told him, "we also have to understand that dying is part of life and it is a fate that no one can escape. We will all die someday, but you will not have to worry about that for a very long time."

Her words, which are especially poignant on this, the anniversary of their deaths, seem prophetic now. *Truer words were never spoken*, he thinks.

As he kneels in front of the tombstone that marks the graves of his mother, father and brother, those memories pierce his heart.

"If only you knew," he whispers, his words falling on the light summer breeze that blows through the quiet cemetery, and are quickly whisked away to a listener who suddenly emerges from the shade of a large, nearby oak tree.

"She knew."

As the skinny woman with fiery red hair who is the spitting image of his mother remains in the cover of darkness at the edge of the shadows, Alex keeps his back to her. He doesn't have to look at her to know who she is.

"I wondered when you'd say something, Aunt Zoey," he says, reaching out to touch his mother's grave marker, a silent gesture to emphasize his love for her.

"How long have you known I was here, Alex?"

"Ever since you arrived."

"I forget." She pauses, carefully considering her next words. "Those birds tell you everything."

"They do," he replies, springing to his feet and spinning around to face her. "Especially Augustus."

"Ah yes, Augustus, the fearless leader of the flock." She slowly approaches her nephew. "Where is the ole wise one?"

"He's here. You just can't see him and he will only show himself when he wants to."

He studies her. "Where have you been?" he finally asks. "It's been almost six months since your last visit and not a word from you. You could have been dead for all I knew."

"Here and there."

"Here and there? Where exactly is here and there?" He squints at her. "Don't you think I deserve a better explanation than that?"

"That's not important," she answers and he can tell she is being evasive. She says, "I want to know how you're doing."

She studies her teenage nephew. He towers over her like the ancient oak that sheaths her with shade.

"Alex, I swear to God that you are getting taller every time I see you. And your hair. Wow. It's almost snow white now. There's hardly any black left except for a few streaks here and there. I have never seen anything like that before on someone so young."

"My height and the colour of my hair are not important."

She feels his intense glare cutting through her body.

"I want to continue learning and, now that I'm sixteen, I know I'm ready. I want to know everything. I *deserve* to know everything." He pauses, then adds, "You owe me that much."

"Yes, I do. And yes, you are ready." She studies him. "But honestly, Alex, there is nothing more I can teach you."

"Yes, there is." His tone becomes sharp. "You've taught me a lot, but I am ready to know the secret of Alexandria Gorham, the woman who started all of this. You really haven't told me much about her, other than the fact that we are related. I need to know more."

"I will tell you, Alex, but not today and certainly not right now."

"Why not today?"

"Because, right now, we have more pressing matters to discuss."

"I don't know what you're talking about, Aunt Zoey, but from my perspective there's nothing more important at this point than knowing the truth about my family's ancestors and who I am. After all, you are the one who told me how special we are, and that this 'thing'—this so-called 'gift' that has been passed down to us—began with Alexandria Gorham making some sort of spiritual pact with the crows several hundred years ago. And since that shit still haunts me today, I think it's time for me to finally find out what it all means."

"And you will, I promise. But right now I want to tell you about something else that concerns you and me and this whole town."

"I can only imagine."

"Don't get snarky, Alex," she says, her posture becoming defensive. "You're too smart for that and we don't have time for any teenage petulance."

He glares at her, but he learned many years ago that it is a waste of time to argue with his aunt. "So, then, what's so important that you've come here and bothered me on this sacred day? You know how important this time is to me, or have you forgotten what today is?"

"I do know how important today is and," she shakes her head, "I have not forgotten anything. I miss her, too. She was my sister, after all."

She reaches out as if to pull him in for a hug. He backs away. "Come on, Alex, what gives?"

"Nothing. It's just that you blow into my life without any notice and, if I'm lucky, you stay for maybe a few days, making all the right gestures and telling me how important I am to you. Then, all of a sudden, you disappear again without warning or any goodbyes.

Then you're gone sometimes for months and I never hear from you. And then, when you do show up again, it's never with an explanation about where you've been. You come back with all this crap about events that are going to disrupt my life or threaten the existence of this entire town. Honestly, Aunt Zoey, it's all becoming a bit much."

"I know, Alex."

She pauses, studying his face. She is amazed at how mature he has become since the last time she saw him. "And right now, honey, you may not understand, but everything I do, it's for your good. My number one priority is to keep you safe. You have questions, and I get that. You *should* have questions, considering everything you've gone through in your young life, and I promise you'll soon have all the answers you want. But not today."

"So, what is it this time? The end of the world? Is it Armageddon? Is Satan rising from the bowels of the earth to enslave all of humankind?"

"Sort of."

"Sort of?" He chuckles. "Now if that's not being elusive, then I don't know what is."

"I don't welcome your sarcasm, Alex."

"And I don't welcome your interruption of my life whenever the urge hits you."

He pauses, takes a deep breath and then continues, "I certainly don't welcome all of your bloody secrets and all of the shit you bring into my life whenever you decide to show up."

"Come on, Alex. The melodrama doesn't become you."

"What would you know about that, or anything else about me?"

"A lot. And right now, I know you are in danger."

She stops short and glances around the sprawling cemetery where the family tombstones that commemorate the generations are organized in neat rows. There are several hundred of them in various shapes, sizes and colours, all marking the final resting places of those who came before them and fought for the cause throughout this town's history.

"He's close, isn't he?" she asks, her eyes scanning trees and grave sites.

"Who? Augustus?" Alex sighs. "He's always close. He's number seven. He's their leader, so that means he's always close to me."

"Yes." She nods. "There is that special bond you two have. It's stronger with him than any of the other crows."

"He gets me. It's a thing."

"I know it is and it's an important thing. It's part of the gift you have inherited."

"So, then, if you know about him and you have something to tell me, you'll have tell me with him close by. We don't keep secrets from the crows. You know that. You are the one who taught me that."

"Yes, I know I did."

Glancing around again, she adds, "I would just like to know where he is."

"He's close and he's watching" Alex assures his aunt. "Now, will you please tell me everything I want to know?"

"Yes." She shudders at the thought of being watched by something as powerful as the large black crow. "I will tell you everything but can you meet me later today?"

"Where?"

"Let's say seven o'clock at my place."

"Why your place?"

"Because we'll be safe there and no one will see us."

He considers her suggestion, then asks, "Are you going to let Samantha and Kate know you're back in town?"

"Eventually, but not right away."

She squints at him as if trying to get a better understanding of the intuitive young man who stands before her. "They don't care for me very much, so I don't think they need to know right away that I'm back in town. What purpose will that serve?"

"It's not that they don't like you, Aunt Zoey. It's just that they don't understand you and they worry about me."

He scans the graveyard for any signs of these unwanted observers that she's clearly worried about. "I hate keeping secrets from them. When my mom and dad died, they stepped up and cared for me. But where were you? I would not have gotten through these past thirteen years without those two women. They took me in and loved me like I was their own son. I owe them a lot."

"Yes, you do, and I am not arguing about that. But they don't understand that you have a larger role in all of this. You know it. I know it and the crows know it."

She reaches out again as if to take his hand. He pulls further away.

"Sam and Kate will come to understand that, and sooner than they think."

"There you go again," he says. "What the hell are you talking about?"

"Not now," she insists. "We'll talk later at my place."

"Fine, but I want answers."

"I will tell you everything you need to know."

"Everything?"

"We'll see," she answers, turning to walk away.

"We'll see? That's all you have to say to me?"

"That's it for now." She nods and adds, "I hope you find peace today, Alex. We'll talk later."

"Jesus Christ," he whispers while watching as the mysterious woman who has popped in and out of his life over the past thirteen years leaves the historic cemetery.

"What in the hell are you up to now?" he says, turning to the nearby oak tree, where some rustling leaves have caught his attention.

Suddenly, the large black crow emerges from its hiding place and perches on the tip of an outstretched branch just above the boy's head.

"Augustus, what do you think that woman is up to?"

The bird, its smooth black feathers reflecting an iridescent greenish-purplish tone in the mid-morning sunlight, bobs its head as if it understands what the boy is saying.

"You know, don't you, Augustus?" he studies the bird's reaction. "I know you know, and if you could talk, I would demand that you tell me right now."

The crow releases a low, guttural caw and is immediately joined on the tree by six of its brethren.

"Don't go looking for help. I'm not mad at you, my friend. Honestly, right now, I'm not even sure that I'm mad at Aunt Zoey," he says, as he approaches the oak tree. "I'm just pissed off that I don't know all of her secrets. If this, whatever it is, involves me, then you'd think she would tell me sooner rather than later. But instead of telling me the truth, she spews more secrets. It's as if she likes to play games with me."

The largest crow freezes on the branch, it's beady, pellet-like eyes locking onto the boy's clear blue eyes.

"Yes, Augustus," he says. "I know she means well, or at least I think she does. And I guess she's only looking out for me, but why does it always have to be more secrets?"

Augustus lifts his massive wings and suddenly springs from his perch. His eyes focused on Alex, the bird circles the young man three times.

Alex knows the crow is trying to tell him something.

Landing next to him, the crow holds eye contact for a full minute. Spellbound, Alex shivers. He doesn't know exactly what the crow is trying to tell him, but he feels the cold right into the marrow of his bones, like a knife through his skin.

"Something bad is coming," he whispers to his black-feathered friend. "Something really bad."

2: Tough conversations

"Hunter? Alex? Are you boys home?" Samantha Henderson calls out as she enters the modest but cozy two-level house that she shares with her wife, Kate Webster, and their two adopted sons. "I'm just home for a little bit and then I've got to go right back out again."

"Hi, Mom," Hunter, a tall, slender young man with wavy brown hair answers as he enters the living room from the kitchen. He is carrying a tuna sandwich on oat bread and a glass of pomegranate juice, his new obsession as he vows to eat healthy. "What's up?"

"I've had a busy morning," she says breathlessly.

He can tell she's been rushing about.

She half-laughs. "It's the story of my life these days, isn't it? And I have meetings all afternoon, so I've got to leave again in about forty-five minutes. Where's your brother? I want to make sure he's doing okay."

"You mean the white-haired wizard?" He chuckles at his stab at humour. "I guess he's up in his room. He went there as soon as he got home about an hour ago and I haven't seen him since, not that I ever expect to see him."

"Hunter! For God's sake, what have I told you about making fun of his hair?" she snaps. "It's not funny and I don't want to hear any more of that, especially not today. Do you hear me?"

When he doesn't respond, she asks again, "Do you understand?"

"Yes, Mom," he says, knowing he has crossed a line. Plopping into a well-padded sofa that's stationed near the window, he asks, "So, what's up with all the meetings today?"

"Council has some zoning decisions to make about a possible new development on the north end of town, and this afternoon we're receiving the engineering and traffic flow reports, so it will be a long session. That reminds me, what do we want to do for supper tonight? Kate won't be home, as she's in Halifax doing some research for an upcoming trial. I was thinking that maybe I'd pick up pizza on my way home."

"Yes, she told me about that trial last night. Sounds interesting, but you don't have to worry about me doing anything for supper. I've got work tonight at the store until eight and then I'm hanging out with Ally for a while."

"That's all you better being doing with Ally, young man." She glares at her oldest son.

"For God's sake, Mom. I'm 20 years old and just finished my first year of university. Give it a break already."

"I'm just saying that I want you guys to be careful, Hunter." Her tone becomes urgent. "You've got your whole life to have sex. You don't want to mess up your future by getting her pregnant, do you?"

"Come on, Mom. Don't you think we've outgrown this conversation? Ally and I have been dating for over three years. We know what we're doing, so sooner or later you will have to trust us." He glares back at her and adds, "Trust me."

"I trust you, Hunter. It's your hormones I don't trust."

"Please God, rescue me from this overbearing woman, will you?" He stares back at his mother with a clear message to drop the subject. "Don't you have to talk to Alex or something? I think he needs your interference in his life right now more than I do."

"Some day you'll thank me for being such a caring mother and looking out for what's best for you."

"I appreciate it, Mom, and you are the best, but believe me when I tell you I have no desire to be a father right now. Ally and I have plans for the future that will include kids someday, but that's a long way down the road."

"I am glad to hear that."

He smiles and speaks calmly. "Ally loves kids and someday she'll be a great mother, but she wants to get her teaching degree first and then a job before we even consider that. We'd also like to get married before babies come along."

Samantha bends to his level on the sofa and gives him a hug. "Maybe it's all the shit I've seen in my lifetime, but I just want you to be careful."

He smiles and winks. "Now you be careful or you'll make me spill my juice."

After quickly setting the glass on a nearby table, he hugs her back and gives her quick kiss on the cheek. "I'm always careful. So, go see to Alex. I've got to eat this sandwich and get to work before I'm late. If you make me lose this job because of your nagging, you'll be the one picking up the extra tuition costs."

"Okay," she says with a chuckle. "Fair point. But please give me a call if you're going to be too late tonight."

"Yes, Mother." He nods. "I promise."

"Good. Thank you." Turning to ascend the stairs, she adds, "I love you."

"I love you, too." He laughs. "Now please leave me alone."

Moving down the dimly-lit hallway on the second level, Samantha notes that the door to her younger son's bedroom is closed, a sign that he's having an off day. *Understandable,* she thinks, *considering what the day is.*

"Alex?" She knocks softly. "Alex, it's mom. Can I come in please? I just want to talk to you for a minute."

"It's not locked." His voice sounds like a whisper through the door.

"Hey buddy," she says, cautiously entering the darkened room. She notices that the curtains are closed and the lights are turned off. "Are you okay? I've been worried about you all day."

Alex, who is sprawled on his bed, gazing aimlessly at the ceiling, is slow to respond, but finally answers. "I'm fine. Just laying here thinking."

"About what? Do you want to talk about anything?"

"No, not really."

She pauses, then begins again, choosing her words carefully. "Hunter tells me you were out this morning. Were you at the cemetery?"

He turns to her and says, "I was."

"Are you okay, Alex?"

"Yes, Mom. It has been thirteen years, so I've learned to deal with things. I just go the cemetery to talk to my birth mother." He pauses and then continues, "I know she's gone but I can't shake the feeling that she hears me whenever I talk to her, and I feel closer to her there than anywhere else."

"She will always be with you, Alex. I believe she is right here watching over you." Motioning toward the bed, she asks, "May I sit down?"

"Sure." He slides his feet over to make room. "It makes me feel good just to tell her things."

"Like what?"

"You know. Things that are happening around town and stuff like that."

"Do you ever tell her about us?"

"Sometimes, yes, but mostly I tell her I'm doing alright."

"And are you? Are you doing alright? Are you happy here?"

"I am....I love you guys very much."

"And we love you too, Alex, very much." She grabs his left foot and gives him a little shake. "Forever and for always."

Taking a deep breath, she looks into his blue eyes. "Alex, I want you to know that you can talk to me about anything no matter what. Nothing is off limits."

"Thanks, but I am good for now."

"Okay, then." She sighs. "If you're sure."

"I'm okay. I promise."

"All right then." She returns his smile. "It looks like it's going to be just you and me for dinner tonight, buddy. Kate is in Halifax and your brother has to work. So, what do you say about pizza?"

"Just pepperoni with extra cheese?"

"If that's what you want."

"That would be fine."

"Okay, one gourmet pepperoni and extra cheese pizza coming right up for supper, but I should tell you I could be a little late."

"Any idea how late?"

"I don't know, maybe around six. Why? Is that going to be a problem?"

"Not really, but I have to be done by seven."

"Why? What's happening at seven?"

He hesitates as he knows if he tells Samantha the truth about who he's going to meet, she will be upset. Inhaling deeply, he finally says, "I'm meeting someone."

"Can I ask who?"

"You can ask but I really don't want to tell you." He squints at her and he can see the worry immediately enter her eyes. "You'll be mad."

"Who, Alex?"

Reluctantly, he answers, "Aunt Zoey is back in town and she wants to talk to me."

"For Christ's sake," she blurts out, jumping off the bed. "When did she get back?"

"I'm not really sure but I just saw her today."

"At the cemetery?"

"Yes."

"Of course, only she would disturb your solitude on an important day like this. She has no compassion. She doesn't think of anyone else but herself."

"It wasn't bad, Mom. She didn't say anything to upset me. Honestly. She just wanted to let me know she was back."

"That's it? I don't believe it. When she's back in town, it usually means one of two things—either she's up to something nefarious or she wants something." Samantha exhales and adds, "Either way, it's not good for you when she's around."

"We just talked and she wants to talk some more later on."

"About what?"

"She didn't say. I think she just wants to catch up." He pauses and adds, "You know, find out how I'm doing."

"God damn it, Alex. You know what she's like. She blows into town and stays for a little while, usually just long enough to fill your head with all kinds of bullshit about your *purpose* and your *destiny* and you being the *chosen one*. She's crazy."

"I don't think she's crazy, Mom." He sits up on the bed but remains calm. "She just wants me to know about my family's past and about my legacy. And I need to know that stuff."

"There's always more to it than that."

"See, that's why I didn't want to tell you about her being back because I knew you would be mad and try to make a big deal out of it."

"It is a big deal, Alex, for you and for the whole family," she says, trying really hard to contain her disdain for the woman who seems to bring nothing but trouble every time she enters his life. "Her short stays are always disruptive and she causes you so much pain. I hate what she puts you through and I hope you won't see her."

"I have to. She's my aunt and she's my only biological connection to my birth mother."

He smiles reassuringly at his adopted mother, the woman who took him in after the tragedy. "I love you very much and nothing will ever change that, but I cannot shut her out. I won't do that."

Samantha remains quiet and studies the lanky, teenage boy who has taken the place of the vulnerable child she raised upon the wishes of her best friend, Lily.

"No," she finally says, recognizing that it wouldn't be fair to ask Alex to sever ties with his aunt. "I suppose I can't expect you to do that, but I want to be with you with when you go to see her."

"I don't think you should." He shakes his head. "Not this time."

"I don't like this, Alex." She hates that he has put her in this position. "You don't have any idea what she's trying to pull you into."

"Please try and understand, Mom. We are just going to talk."

"If I can't be there, can you at least tell me where you are seeing her?"

He really doesn't want to tell her, but finally says, "Her place. But please promise me you won't go there."

"Why don't you ask her to come here?"

"Honestly, because you'll be here and you guys don't get along. I know you don't like her, but she would never do anything to hurt me."

"It's not that I don't like her. I just don't trust her."

Samantha, sensing that she is losing this argument, sighs heavily but persists. "I really believe I should be there with you to hear what kind of nonsense she's putting into your head."

"Not this time, Mom. Please. I have to do this alone. Aunt Zoey and I have a lot to talk about without anyone interfering."

He smiles at her again and it's a smile that melts her heart. "We are just going to talk. That's all."

"How long will you be there?"

"I don't know, maybe a couple of hours."

"If I ask you to be home by nine, will you listen to me?"

He nods and accepts her compromise. "I promise I will be in this house by nine."

Turning to leave the room, she says, "I will hold you to that promise, young man."

"I'm sure you will." He chuckles and adds, "I have no doubt of that."

"And if you're not home by nine o'clock sharp I will come looking for you."

"I expect you will."

Reaching the door, she says, "I'm not kidding, Alex."

"I know, Mom." He nods. "You are being serious."

"Very serious." She studies him and says, "I will be worried about you."

"That's one of the reasons I love you so much." He adds, "You are always looking out for me."

"I love you too, Alex, and now I have to get ready for an important meeting. If I could cancel it, I would do so and I'd spend the whole afternoon with you."

"But you're the mayor and you can't cancel because they need you there."

"They don't always need me there, but I do have to be present for this meeting."

"Go on, Mom. I promise you that I am fine and I will see you for supper. We can talk further before I go to Aunt Zoey's."

"Okay, my love. Call me if you need anything, no matter what, and leave a message if you can't get through. I will call you right back."

"Yes, Mom," he says, as she leaves his room, closing the door behind her.

Jesus Christ, she thinks, bracing herself against the door. *What in the bloody hell does that woman want from him now?*

3: The assignment

"Graham Security Services," the friendly receptionist answers after the second ring. "My name is Maria. How may I help you?"

"Hi Maria, it's Samantha Henderson here," Samantha says, as if the young woman will immediately recognize the name. Stepping into her office and closing the door behind her, Samantha quickly makes her way to her desk, puts her cellphone on speaker and asks, "Is Cliff in, please? I need to speak with him right away."

"Just a moment, Mayor Henderson. I'll check to see if he's free."

"Thanks." Samantha slips into the black swivel leather chair behind her desk, opens her laptop and begins reviewing the agenda for this afternoon's meeting. There's a lot riding on these deliberations and she knows she must be prepared.

"Madam Mayor," the distinctive gravelly voice of retired RCMP Corporal Cliff Graham says a few minutes later. "What can I do for you on this fine June afternoon?"

"Hi Cliff," she replies, closing her laptop, turning off the speaker and placing the phone next to her ear. Even though she's alone in her office, she feels it's best to be cautious. "Nice to hear that you are your usually sunny self this afternoon. I was going to ask how you're doing but you sound like you're doing well."

"I am," he says and she can practically hear him grinning. "What's not to like about this beautiful early summer day?

"True," she nods. "It is a beautiful day. A little on the hot side, but I'll take it. Thanks for taking my call, Cliff. I hope I didn't pull you away from anything."

"Nope," he answers. "Just doing some paperwork so I'll take a phone call any day to escape that torture. I hate doing paperwork." He chuckles and then asks, "So, what's up with you? I sense something is not right in your world."

"You are very perceptive, my friend. How do you do that?"

"Years of police work combined with the wisdom of old age. Seriously, though, what's wrong? How can I help?"

Samantha sucks in a deep breath and exhales forcefully. "She's come back."

"I'm sorry, Sam." He pauses. "I need more. Who's come back?"

"Alex's aunt. Zoey LaCroix showed up at the cemetery this morning when he was there visiting his family. You know, she has always had a way of just showing up unannounced and throwing everyone's world into a tailspin. Well, that's what she's done again."

"Must be serious if you're also using her married name. What does she want?"

"I don't know." Samantha can feel her frustration bubbling to the surface. "I have not spoken to her and I don't ever want to talk to her. Besides, Alex wants me to stay away from her. I told him I would, for now at least, but only because he made me promise."

"Okay, so then, what do you *think* she wants?"

"Alex says she just wants to talk, but after everything she has put that kid through over the years, I don't trust her. Maybe I'm being overly suspicious and I should give her chance, as Alex suggests, but I can't shake the feeling that she's up to something. Usually when she shows up out of the blue like this she brings trouble with her and that's what I'm afraid of."

"You have good reason to be suspicious, Sam. She's a mysterious one, that's for sure."

"Yes, mysterious. That's a good way to describe her and I can think of a few other choice words to describe her that wouldn't be so nice."

"I'm sure you can, after everything she's put you through," he agrees. "So, what can I do?"

"How busy are you these days?"

"Things are steady. We're conducting a few shoplifting and senior fraud seminars over the next few weeks throughout the region and we've got our regular clients, but I might have a bit of time on my hands. What are you looking for?"

"I'm not really sure, Cliff, but I was thinking maybe you could keep an eye on Zoey while she's in town and possibly check into things for me, on the QT of course." She pauses as if perhaps reconsidering the assignment. Taking a deep breath, she adds, "I'd like to know what she's been up for the past six months since she left town, but I don't want Alex to find out that I'm keeping tabs on his aunt. That would really upset him."

"I think I can manage that, but how deep do you want me to go?"

"As deep as you have to go just as long as you're discreet."

"Discretion is my middle name."

"You know I know that, Cliff," she replies. "Whatever you do, she can't know that I'm checking into her or there will be hell to pay."

"Got it." Even though she can't see him, she knows Cliff is nodding and grinning, two of his habits that she has observed over the years. "Stay on the down-low."

"Yes please, and let me know as soon as you find anything."

"What are you expecting to find?"

"Honestly, I have no idea. But if experience has taught me anything it's that I should expect surprises when it comes to that woman." She sighs. "There is always so much cloak and dagger with her. I know she is Alex's family, but I hate it that she gets into his head and gets him all wrapped up in her crap."

"For sure, but he's a smart kid. He knows what he's doing."

"He does, yes, but it's not him I'm worried about. It's Zoey. She's very good at manipulating Alex and getting him to do whatever she wants, even if it's not always in his best interest. She sucks him in by playing with his emotions about his family's past. I worry about what effect her crazy crap has on him long term."

"Don't sell the kid short," Cliff tells her. "He's a strong young man, Sam. We've seen him survive some pretty heavy shit over the years. Is it possible that you're over-reacting?"

"I don't bloody well think so." She is surprised by her friend's comment. "How can you even think that after everything we've seen and been through over the years?"

Cliff knows he's hit a nerve. He has learned over the years that you have to tread lightly around Samantha Henderson when it comes to anything connected to Alex. "Easy, Sam," he says. "I don't mean anything, really. All I'm saying is that maybe you could cut her some slack for the boy's sake."

"For the boy's sake? That's why I'm worried. I just don't trust anything she does. I can't. I have to protect Alex, no matter what."

"Of course, you do." Realizing he may have crossed a line, he says. "I get it: Deep dive. Lay low. Report immediately back to you."

"Yes, please do."

"What about Kate? Are you going to tell her what you're doing?"

"Not a chance." Samantha's response is quick. "This investigation is just between you and me and it's important that it stays that way. Kate won't understand that I'm just trying to protect Alex."

"Got it. Do you have any idea where Zoey is?"

"All I know is what Alex told me. He says she's staying at her place and he's meeting her there after dinner."

"Okay, we'll start there."

"I am trusting you with this, Cliff," Samantha adds, glancing at the smart watch that was a Christmas gift from Kate. "Just you and me. No one else."

"I totally understand," Cliff replies. "I will be in touch as soon as I have anything to tell you."

"Okay, Cliff and thank you. I'm counting on you." Realizing it's almost time for her meeting to start, she adds, "Now I have to go or I will be late for my meeting."

"All good, Sam. We'll talk soon."

Grabbing her laptop and cellphone, she pauses for a second to reflect upon the recent conversations she's had with Alex and Cliff. *Am I doing the right thing?* she wonders. *Maybe Cliff is right. Maybe I should cut her some slack.*

Heading toward the door, she thinks, *No. I have to know what's going on. If it's nothing, then I won't have to worry, but if she's up to something I have to be prepared and I have to protect Alex. That's all that matters.*

4: A black bird and a boy

Tap. Tap. Tap.

What the hell? Alex's eyes pop open. Glancing at the time on his phone, he sees it's now 3:17. *Jesus. I must have fallen asleep after Mom left for her meeting.*

Staring up at the nondescript white ceiling, the blank, white space reminding him of the void that sometimes seems like his life, he sighs heavily. *Now what am I going to do? Mom won't be home for a while yet and it's too early to go see Aunt Zoey. I need to find a hobby or a job, maybe. That's what I need, a job. But what the heck would I do? More to the point, who would hire me in this town?*

Tap. Tap. Tap.

Hearing the steady tapping again, he rolls to face the window; the blinds are still closed tightly. He stares at them as the bright light spills around their edges, but he knows the origins of the sound without looking.

"I hear you," he says, speaking softly while slipping off the bed and planting his sock-covered feet on the cool hardwood floor. "I know you're there, Augustus. You just woke me up so give me a few seconds to come around."

Slowly shuffling to the window, he pulls the cord, carefully raising the blind and allowing the warm sunshine to spill into the room, breaking the darkness that he often embraces. He blinks several times and squints in the bright light.

"I see you, Augustus," he says to the large, black crow delicately perched on the windowsill. "I wasn't ignoring you." He cranks open the window, allowing the hot air to rush in and hit him in the face. "I fell asleep and lost track of time. What's so important that you had to wake me up?"

The crow stares at him, blinking occasionally.

After studying the bird, Alex remarks, "I know you're worried about me. Everyone's worried about me, but really, I am okay."

The bird emits one low, but very distinct, guttural caw.

"I'm telling the truth, Augustus."

The bird bobs its head as if checking the boy from head to toe.

"Are you happy now? I told you I was okay but no, you had to see for yourself. You don't have to be afraid. I'm not going to do anything drastic."

Leaning closer to the window screen, he says again, "I promise you that I am fine. I talked to Mom earlier and told her about Aunt Zoey being back in town."

He pauses and then continues, "I know Aunt Zoey didn't want me to tell Mom, but I felt I had to. As I expected, Mom wasn't happy about that and she asked me not see Aunt Zoey this evening. But what am I supposed to do? She is my family, after all."

The bird quickly bobs its head as if agreeing with everything his human companion is saying.

"I know you don't like Aunt Zoey either, but I do think I have to see her. You know we're all connected and I think it's important that I hear whatever it she has to say. How can I know what to anticipate if I don't hear her out?"

The crow squawks again.

"I have no idea what she wants to tell me, but I can't just ignore her. She was my mother's twin sister and she knows so much about the family that I feel obligated to see her and learn whatever I can from her," the boy answers. "What if it's something really important?"

The boy locks eyes with the crow. "What if she has something urgent to tell me?" his whispers.

The bird blinks.

"I know. I know. This wouldn't be so hard if Mom hadn't objected so much," he continues, talking to the crow as if he were talking to another human. "I know she's just worried about me but if she would try to get along with Aunt Zoey, this would be so much easier for me. So, old wise one, what do you think I should I do?"

The crow caws lightly as Alex continues to listen intently, as if he might actually understand what the bird is saying.

"You're not being helpful, Augustus," he finally says with a sigh. "I need answers, not more questions. I'm sure if you could talk you would tell me I have no choice but go to see Aunt Zoey. Well, that's what I think, too. She's the one who knows all the secrets so she's the one who can help me understand what I'm supposed to be doing. I need to know what my role is, and if she can help me understand that, I have to go and hear her out."

The crow suddenly releases a loud and piercing cry, as if it's calling out an alarm.

"What's up Augustus? What's wrong?"

Looking toward the trees Alex notices the afternoon sun has disappeared behind the clouds just as a murder of six more large crows lands on the trees that surround the house. "You've called for reinforcements. Why? What's happening? Is something wrong? Should I be worried? What are you trying to tell me?"

The bird bobs its head and continues eye contact.

"Yes, I know seven crows are here to watch over and protect me. That's what the legend says. As Aunt Zoey keeps reminding me, I know that's your role and that my role is to be the guardian of the secret. But what's the secret?"

The bird remains silent.

"Trust me, friend, I am glad you are here to watch over me. I really am, but it would be better for me if I knew what was happening."

With that, the largest of the seven crows suddenly springs from the windowsill and takes flight with the other six immediately following.

"Where are you going, Augustus?" Alex calls out as he watches the seven majestic black birds disappear from his immediate line of sight. "I was really hoping you would be able to shed some light on this mystery for me, but I guess maybe not."

Turning from the window, Alex stops as a sudden movement on the upper end of the property near the street catches his attention.

What the hell? he thinks, seeing a tall, slender man quickly duck behind a hedge that borders the property. He wishes he had been able to get a better look, but the watcher was too fast. *Who in the hell is that?*

Alex immediately pulls back from the window and quickly closes the blind. Knowing that Hunter has gone to work and he's alone in the house, he wonders if he should call his mother to tell her about the man outside the house.

But why get her worried while she's at her important meeting? He backs away from the window and sits on the edge of the bed, trying to figure out what to do. *It's probably nothing. Maybe I was just seeing things and there wasn't really anyone there. Just my imagination running wild.*

"No," he whispers, reviewing the image in his head. Alex is sure he saw a man outside the house. "I know there was someone there."

Could have been a reporter, he thinks.

It wouldn't be the first time that a reporter has tried to get pictures of the only survivor of the massacre that shocked this town thirteen years ago, especially on the anniversary of the crime.

He's managed to avoid that level of public scrutiny as much as possible over the years. *But that's probably exactly who it was. Why can't they just leave me alone?*

He's lost in his thoughts when his phone snaps him to attention. The distinctive sound confirms that he's just received a text.

"God damn," he blurts out. Grabbing his phone off the bed, he sees he's had several texts while he was sleeping. A couple from his friend Ozzie and this one from another friend, Bree.

"What'cha doing?" she writes.

"Not much," he quickly replies.

"Me neither. Want to hang for a while?"

"Not sure I'd be good company right now."

"Come on, Alex. Don't do that. We could watch a movie."

"I don't know."

"For God's sake. Let's just watch a freaking movie. I'm not looking to talk or anything else. Just thought you might like to hang."

He briefly hesitates then answers. "K. Come over."

"See you in 10. Bye."

"K."

He likes Bree Hamilton. She's smart and funny, but best of all, she never asks him any questions about the past. He first met her in grade five after her family moved to town when her mother, a nurse, took a job at the local hospital. Her mother works with his uncle Charlie, who's a doctor at the same hospital, while her father is an RCMP officer.

Scrolling down, he reviews the messages he's received from Ozzie Merrick, another good friend from school. Alex met Ozzie two years ago when he moved to town with his father and younger sister, Dani. While Alex doesn't know the whole story, he knows they came to town after Ozzie's parents divorced, so his father could take a job with a local accounting firm.

Even though he considers Ozzie to be a close friend, he remains guarded around the boy who is the same age as he, but who asks a lot of questions, especially about his past. Alex doesn't like to discuss such things with people outside of the family. And then, there are times he doesn't even like to talk about those things with anyone whatsoever. It usually depends on his frame of mind at the time of the conversation.

"Got any plans for today?" Ozzie asks in his first message.

"Are you avoiding me today?" He follows up with a second text about fifteen minutes later, after Alex had failed to respond because he was sleeping.

"Want to do something?" A third text follows a short time later.

Better write back to him or he'll be pissed, Alex thinks. *He's pretty sensitive.*

Alex types, "Bree is coming over to watch a movie. Want to come over?"

The other boy immediately answers, "What were you doing? Thought you were mad at me or something worse."

"Sleeping," Alex answers, thinking his friend should just chill a bit. *Not everyone responds to text right away.*

"I'll be right there."

Tossing his phone back on the bed, Alex scans the room, his eyes coming to rest on a picture on his desk of his former family. Making his way across the room, he resists the urge to peek out through the blinds to see if the mysterious man is still lurking about outside. He decides he really doesn't want to know.

He picks up the picture and studies the three faces smiling back at him through the glass—his brother Carter, who was only seven years old when he died; his father, the black-haired, wealthy businessman Josh Goodwin; and his mother, the feisty-redhead Lily Pittmann. She looks so much like his Aunt Zoey that it sometimes hurts to see the remaining sister alive.

"I miss you guys so much," he whispers, lightly touching the glass as the tears roll down his cheeks. He's fighting hard to forget the pain but to this very day he reluctantly remembers the horrific events that shattered his world thirteen years ago. The memories are still very fresh.

"I'm doing okay with Sam and Kate, but I wish you were here. There's so much going on and so much I want to tell you."

He's lost in his memories when a sudden and loud knocking at the front door brings him back to the present.

"Frig," he tells himself, returning the photo to its place on the desk. He shakes his head. *Shit. There will be no more of that today.*

Assuming that the knocking means one of his friends has already arrived, he bolts from his room and quickly darts down the stairs.

"Coming," he yells.

5: Surveillance

Could be a long one, Cliff Graham thinks as he hunkers down behind the wheel of his black Chevrolet Silverado 1500 and grabs the cup of black coffee he just bought at the local café. He prefers the local brew over anything served by the chains that are taking over the marketplace.

Shouldn't be drinking this stuff, period, and especially not at this hour of the day. He longs for the old days when he could drink barrels of coffee and not worry about how it was going to affect his body.

Besides, it'll make me want to pee. He grins, finding humour in his own stupid joke. *It's hellish getting older, but it sure beats the alternative.*

Surveillance isn't his most favourite part of being a detective, but as a former RCMP officer with years of investigative work under his belt, he understands that it's part of the process. *It comes with the territory.*

Sipping his coffee, he thinks, *Besides, it helps to pay the bills, and sometimes you hit pay dirt.* He sighs. *So, let's see what secrets you're hiding, young lady.*

Samantha Henderson asked him to keep an eye on Alex's Aunt Zoey LaCroix while she's in town, and that's exactly what he intends to do. *A deal is a deal and she's counting on me. Is Sam being paranoid? Maybe. Is she worried over nothing? Based on this woman's sketchy past, I would say not one god-damned bit.*

Parked down the street from Zoey's house on the heavily trafficked street just off the centre of town and main business district, Cliff has a clear vantage point where he can observe the comings and goings. So far, he hasn't seen any activity near the house, but he sees lots of people going about their business, shopping and attending their appointments.

Busy for a Friday afternoon, he thinks, as people rush in and out of the nearby buildings. *I thought most people would be heading out of town to enjoy the long weekend, especially since it's supposed to be hot for the next few days.*

"Oh well," he says aloud, "not a big deal." He turns his focus back to the task at hand.

Looks like I'm going to be busy for a while so it won't matter to me what anyone else does, he thinks, staring at the historic home with the exposed cedar shakes and red shutters that he believes was built some two hundred years earlier by the Gorhams, Zoey's ancestors.

Marvelling at how well the structure has withstood the ravages of time, he thinks, *Nice place. With the current price of real estate around here, I bet she'd make a killing if she sold it today. Be a shame, though to see it turned into something else, like more offices. Wonder how she can afford it? Can't be cheap to keep a house that old looking in such good condition. The taxes alone would cost a small fortune.*

As he scans the well-maintained yard, sudden movement on the left side of the house catches his attention.

"Je-sus Christ," he says. Several crows have perched on the lawn, not far from the house.

"One. Two. Three," he counts out loud while the birds prance around the yard, pecking at the grass, looking for food. "Four. Five. Six. Sev...Wait. Where the hell is number seven? I'm sure you're here somewhere, you black devil."

Craning his neck for a better vantage point, he continues to scan the yard until he sees that a solitary larger crow has taken up position in a tree just outside the living room window.

"There you are. Seven." He sighs heavily. "What the hell are you doing here?"

Even though the birds appear to be focused on the house and could be oblivious to his presence, Cliff isn't making any assumptions. "Are you guys here watching me or keeping an eye on the woman? I really don't trust you—not one bit."

"Christ," he blurts out when his ringing cellphone jolts him from his musings. Quickly glancing at the screen, he sees it's his daughter Carly calling. "Scare the living daylight out of me, why don't you?"

Pressing the green bottom to answer the phone, while keeping his eyes glued on the crows and the house, Cliff takes a deep breath and says, "Hi, honey." He steadies his breathing and adds, "What's going on today?"

"Not much, Daddy," she answers. Her sweet voice always makes him feel good. "Just calling to check in and to see how you're doing."

"All good, honey. How are things in Halifax? What's more important, how are my grandbaby girls today?"

"They are perfect."

He can feel her pride all the way from Halifax. He loves how she's taken to motherhood; but, then again, he isn't surprised. She has always had strong motherly instincts.

"Believe it or not, they are both still napping."

"Lucky you."

"For sure, so I thought I'd take advantage of the downtime to give you a quick call."

"Well isn't that nice. Honestly, honey, not much happening here these days. I'm still working, but mom should be home."

"Yes, I was just talking to her and that's why I'm calling you."

"Oh, what's going on?"

"So, I was thinking that, since Leo is working this weekend and it's supposed to be really hot, wouldn't it be nice if me and the girls came down to visit you and mom, especially with it being a holiday?"

"It sure would, sweetie. We haven't see you in a while, but I may be working this weekend. You know we always love having you and the girls around." He pauses, then asks, "What did mom say?"

"She said she was okay with it, but that I should ask you because she knew you were busy."

"You don't need my permission to visit, honey. We love to see you any time."

"I know, Daddy, but I like to check before showing up at the front door, just in case you and mom might have plans."

"Plans? Us? Nothing exciting." He chuckles as he watches the crows flit around the yard, occasionally pausing and turning their heads in all directions, scoping out the immediate area. *It's like they are gathering intel*, he thinks. *They really are like little feathered soldiers—or spies. Freaky!*

To his daughter he says, "We always like it when you and the girls visit, you know that, so why don't you come along? If I have to work for a bit, you can visit with mom."

"That's what mom and I were thinking, too," she giggles. "Actually, I've got us all packed. Once the girls get up from their naps, I'll get them ready and we'll be on our way."

He laughs. "So, if you and your mother had this all planned, why even bother to ask me?"

"Because," she says through a laugh, "we don't want to make decisions without your input."

"Sure, I know how it works. Just let me or mom know when you're leaving the city so we know you're on the road."

"I will. See you in a couple of hours, Daddy."

"Okay, honey. Drive carefully."

Scrolling down his favourites' list, he dials his wife, Julie, whom he married twelve years ago for the second time. She answers on the second ring.

"Jewels?"

"Who were you expecting to answer my phone, Cliff?"

He rolls his eyes. *She thinks she's being funny.* "Just got off the phone with Carly. Looks like we're having company this weekend."

"Yes, I told her to come. Is that okay with you?"

"No problem, but I just want to remind you that I will probably be tied up all weekend with this new case I'm working on."

"Yes, I remember, but Carly sounded so lonely when she called and I got the feeling that she really wanted to come down."

"Oh," he pauses. "I didn't get that feeling from her, but you're better at that sort of thing than me. Do you think everything is okay?"

"I'm not sure, but I sense something's not right. If I had to guess, I would say it has something to do with Leo," Julie says. "She really doesn't see him all that much and she said Leo has to work all weekend."

"Hmmm. Well, his job does keep him pretty busy."

"I just got the feeling she needs to be around other people and maybe she needs someone to talk to."

"Well...,"

He notices the crows are suddenly very agitated. *What gives, fellas?* he thinks, as he watches the larger bird on the tree branch emit a series of loud caws and cackles. *It's like he's giving marching orders to the others. What are you doing?*

Several of the birds quickly take off from the ground and disappear around the back side of the house, out of his view.

"Well what, Cliff?" He hears his wife talking.

"Oh," he answers, "I was just going to say that if she needs to talk, it's probably a good idea that I won't be there. You know me, if something is going on, I won't be able to keep my mouth shut."

"Oh, sweetheart. You're so funny."

He knows she's trying to stifle any conclusions that he may already be drawing based upon what she just told him.

"I'm sure everything is okay."

"I hope so." He nods. "But the real reason I was calling was to tell you I don't know how late I'm going to be this evening. I will keep you posted."

"Okay. I've got to run to the grocery store. If we're going to have company for the weekend, I've got to get a few things like milk and eggs. I also want to get a few treats for the girls. They love ice cream and we're out. You ate the last of the chocolate the other day, even though you know you aren't supposed to have it."

"I was hungry and it was hot." He pauses and then adds, "There really wasn't all that much there."

"Right," Julie says with a chuckle. "That container was nearly half full."

"Ice cream won't hurt me."

"You will find out when you go for your check-up in six weeks. I really have to stop buying that stuff. If it's not in the house, you can't be tempted to eat it. Anyway, do you need anything?"

"No, I don't think so."

"Okay, let me know if anything comes up."

"Will do. Let me know when the girls arrive."

Best thing I ever did was marrying that woman, not once but twice, he thinks, turning off the phone and tossing it on to the passenger seat just as it begins to ring again. He sees it's Emily Murphy returning his call.

She's his go-to person on the force when he needs some investigative help. He's worked with Emily on some of the most-high-profile cases in this town's recent past, including a maniac serial killer who was targeting young girls, and the heinous murders in which young Alex's entire immediate family was killed.

Reflecting upon how far this young woman has gone in the force, he presses the talk button and says, "Sergeant. How are you doing? Thanks for returning my call."

"No problem, Cliff. Always have time for one of our own, especially one as important as you.

 So, what can I do for you Cliff? My guess is that if you're calling me, you need my help with something."

"In fact, I do. It's about this new case I'm working on. Actually, maybe it's an old case or at least it's a continuation of an old case, or something like that."

He pauses, keeping his eyes on the black birds in the woman's yard. The remaining five have once again become quiet, going about their sentry duties. "If I tell you it involves the crows, you'll know why I called you."

"Oh, Jesus, that's not what I wanted to hear today. What are they up to now?"

"I have no idea, but I can tell that something is brewing and my gut is telling me it's something major. They're pretty restless right now."

"Major? Like what?"

"I don't know, but it involves Zoey LaCroix, Lily's twin sister, if that's any indication."

"Zoey? Didn't she cause enough trouble the last time she was in town? I thought maybe she'd stay away after everything that happened."

"You'd think so, but she has returned."

"What does she want?"

"I don't know, but that's where I need your help."

"How?"

"By my calculations, Zoey has been gone for about six months and no one seems to know where she has been. I'm wondering if you might be able to help me figure that out. I'd like to know what she has been up to and if it's going to be a problem for folks around here."

"I can, but it could take me a few days, especially with a holiday thrown in," the sergeant says. "I'll do some digging and get back to you."

"That would be fantastic." He pauses. "Hold on, hold on, what do we have here?"

"What do we have where?"

"Just wait a second, Sergeant," he answers. "Someone is going into Zoey's house and I want to see who it is."

"Sure, go ahead and take a look"

Craning his neck to get a clear view of the slender built man walking up the front walk way, his breath catches in his throat as the man turns and looks around as if he's doing a quick check of the immediate area.

Just like those bloody crows, Cliff thinks. He notes the last crows —four in the yard and the larger one in the tree next to house—go about their business, seemingly unphased that a human has just entered their zone. *They have to see him, but why aren't they scared off by him? I bet if I walked up to the house, they'd be out of there in a second. People have that effect on those bloody birds, so why not this guy? Do they know him?*

"Now this has just gotten really interesting," he says.

"Cliff? Are you talking to me?" Emily asks.

Cliff continues to observe as the visitor knocks gently on the heavy wooden front door. He waits a minute and then opens the door just a crack and quickly slips inside, turning to see if anyone is behind him.

"Oliver Lewis. Of all people," Cliff whispers. "Now what in the hell do you suppose he's doing meeting with that woman?"

6: An ominous message

"I'm coming for you!" the note says. Scrawled in bold red ink, its messy block letters suggesting someone wrote it in a hurry, the message has left Alex shaken.

"And this is all there was?" Bree asks, holding the piece of thin white paper up to the living room window and scanning it for any other clues that may be hidden there.

"Yes." Alex nods. He has become desperate. He's anxious, not sure what to think of the strange note. Observing the slender brunette with the sharp wit and personality that could lighten up any room as she studies the hastily scribbled message, he adds, "But what does it mean?"

"You say it was tacked to the front door when you opened it a while ago?" she asks.

"Yes. About half an hour ago. After I texted you and Ozzie to come over, I heard a knock at the front door. I was expecting to see you guys, but when I opened the door, this is all there was."

He drifts for a minute as he tries to piece the evidence together. His friends can see that he's worried.

He continues, "I didn't see anyone around so I have no idea who would have put it there or why, but I have to admit, it scared the shit out of me."

"Freaky," observes Ozzie, the sixteen-year-old with the razor-thin physique, pointy nose and dark-framed glasses, who, besides Bree, is his closest friend and confidant.

"Come on, Ozzie. It's more than freaky," Bree says. "It's scary."

Looking directly at Alex she adds, "This sounds like a threat to me. I think you should show this to your mom or somebody else you trust."

"I can't do that," Alex quickly answers, pulling back from the others as if he's been insulted. "Mom's already freaking out because Aunt Zoey showed up this morning out of the blue, and now this. Mom would lose it."

"I think she needs to know, Alex. But if not your mother, you have to talk to someone," Bree counters.

He knows she is right but he shakes his head. "I just can't."

"This is no joke," she tells him, waving the note at him. "It seems pretty serious to me and I'm worried for you."

"I don't know, Bree," Ozzie says. "Maybe it is a joke. We don't find it funny, but there are some sick fucks out there in the world. Who the hell knows what motivates some people?"

"But what's so funny about this, Ozzie?" She squints in his direction, her frustration at his lack of urgency clearly evident in her tone. "And on this day of all days. Who in their right mind would do something so sick to Alex on this day?"

"A lot of people," Ozzie says with a shrug. "Some people don't care how other people feel. I could see some twisted freak asshole doing something this fucked up just for kicks. He's probably out there laughing at us right now because he got a rise out of you two."

"I don't know. This is a line that even sick people wouldn't cross," Bree argues. "I think there is more to this note than we think."

"I'm with Bree," Alex says, his voice cracking. He knows she makes sense. He pauses, then adds, "But I haven't told you guys everything."

"What do you mean?" His friends ask in unison.

"Alex takes the note from Bree. "Just before I found this, I saw someone from my bedroom window. They were out in the yard, sneaking around the house."

"Oh my God, Alex," Bree gasps. "Are you sure?"

He nods, fighting hard to keep his nerves under control.

"Why didn't you tell us sooner?"

Alex can see the panic in Bree's green eyes, the fear written on her face.

She asks, "Do you know who it was?"

"I have no idea." He shakes his head, thinking back to the slender figure he saw. "But it was definitely a man, and when he saw that I had spotted him, he ducked behind the hedge."

Ozzie says, "This is some serious shit. Now I agree with Bree, and you know how much I hate to agree with her about anything, but I think she's right. You have to tell your mother about this. What if you're not safe, Alex?"

Considering his next words, Ozzie adds, "What if everyone else in this house is in danger? At first, I thought maybe the note could be a joke, but it sounds pretty serious when you put the two things together."

"Who would want to hurt me...us?" Alex asks, staring at his friends as he feels the ball of anxiety rolling in the pit of his stomach, gaining momentum.

"Come on," Bree answers. "Some people don't need a reason, they are just bat-shit crazy. You, of all people, should know that."

"Mom and Kate will both lose their minds if they find out about any of this," he says, exhaling with a force. "Why the hell is this happening?"

"I don't know, Alex, but what if you don't tell them and something serious happens to you?" she points out. "Maybe if you tell them, they can help you find out what this is all about and stop it—whatever it is—before it happens."

"Again, I hate to admit when Bree is right, but I do believe she's right about this," Ozzie says. "What if something happens to one of them, or Hunter, because of this and you could have prevented it? How would you feel then?"

Alex shrugs. "I hadn't thought of that," he whispers. "I'd feel pretty shitty."

"Yes, you certainly would," Ozzie says with a nod. "And you'd feel guilty because you'd think you were responsible."

"Honestly, Alex, considering everything that has happened in your past, you shouldn't be surprised when something like this happens," Bree points out. "You have to tell them."

"Yes. I guess maybe I do."

"No maybes," Bree replies, reaching across the sofa where they are seated and taking his hand. Squeezing it gently, she says, "It's a definite 'yes', you do."

"Okay. Okay." He nods. "You guys win. I will tell Mom when she comes home, which," he glances at his phone, "could be any time." He sighs. "You guys should be going."

"No, man," Ozzie says. "I think we should stay until she gets home. It's probably not a good idea for you to be alone right now, not after everything you just told us."

"You really don't have to worry. I'll be all right," he says, his tone conveying his anxiety.

"This time, I have to admit that Ozzie is right," Bree tells him, squeezing his hand again. "We're staying put, so don't argue with us."

"Okay, you guys win. I appreciate the company."

Just as Alex finishes his sentence, he hears the front door open and Samantha suddenly appears in the living room, carrying a box of pizza from their favourite shop in town.

"Well, hello, guys," she says to her son's friends when she rounds the corner to the room. "I didn't know we were having guests, but we have plenty, so you are welcome to stay for pizza."

"Mom, you're home early." Checking his phone again for the time, Alex continues, "It's not even five thirty yet, and I wasn't expecting you until six."

"We finished early."

"Oh, how did it go?"

"Pretty good, I think, but we'll see," Samantha says, then asks, "So, who wants pizza?"

"No, but thank you," Ozzie quickly answers, springing to his feet, his skinny frame barely leaving a dent in the cushion of the large padded chair where he had been sitting for the past half hour. "My dad is expecting me home. He's taking my sister and me out for dinner tonight. He promised Dani a night out, now that school's done for the year. I can't back out on them."

"Well," Samantha says with a smile, "some other time Ozzie. You know you're always welcome here for dinner with us." Turning to

Bree, she asks, "How about you? It's pepperoni and extra cheese, Alex's favourite."

"I'd like to, Mrs. Webster, I really would, but not tonight," she answers with a smile.

Alex knows that his friends are clearing out to give him and his mother some privacy so they can talk.

"Are you sure?" Samantha asks, glancing towards her son. "I'm sure Alex would love the company."

"Yes, I'm sure," Bree says, quickly. "Mom is planning a dinner tonight for some friends and, since they have kids, she asked if I could be home to help entertain them, the kids, I mean."

"Got it. You can't disappoint your mother," Samantha replies. "Well, some other time then. The door's always open."

"Thanks, Mrs. Webster." Turning to Alex, Bree adds, "Will you call me?"

"Sure, but it could be later."

"That's all right. I'll be home."

"Okay, then. Later," he says, watching his two best friends as they leave the house.

"Nice kids," Samantha says as the door closes behind the pair. "I'm glad you have them as friends. You all seem to get along so well."

"Yes, me too." Turning to face his mother, Alex takes a deep breath, swallows and says, "Mom, there's something important I need to tell you."

"My God, Alex. You sound so serious," she says. Taking a seat beside him on the sofa and placing the pizza box on the coffee table, she asks, "What's going on?"

"Well, mom..." he pauses. "It's just that..."

Seeing that her son is struggling to find the right words, she asks, "Did something happen while I was out this afternoon?"

"It's kind of embarrassing," he finally whispers, turning away from his mother's gaze. "But I need some girl advice."

Despite promising his friends that he would tell his mother about the note and the man he saw lurking around the house, Alex has decided to keep the information to himself. He's certain she would lose her mind if she found out, and would absolutely forbid him from seeing his Aunt Zoey this evening, even though there's nothing to suggest she's involved with any of this. He does not want to take that chance, and knows the perfect subject to distract her from anything connected to Zoey.

"Girl advice?" She sounds surprised. "From me? Do you think that's a good idea? Maybe you'd rather talk to your brother about that. You might feel more comfortable with him."

"No." Alex shakes his head. "I'd rather talk to you. Hunter can be a jerk sometimes."

"You know, Alex. He doesn't mean anything by the stuff he says. He's just joking around. You know what he's like." She studies her youngest son. "Yes, he can be a pain in the ass at times, but you know he really loves you."

"I guess so." Alex nods.

"No guessing. I know he does and I know you feel the same towards him."

"Okay, then, but I really don't want to talk to Hunter about this. You're always after me about being honest with you, so now I'm looking for advice. Do you want to help me or not?"

"Of course, Alex. You are right. Sorry." She smiles. "Who, then? As if I have to ask," she says with a wink. "Bree. Right?"

"Yes, Mom. Bree. Who else?" He sucks a deep breath between his teeth and then blurts out, "How do I know if she feels the same way about me as I feel about her?"

"Do you think she does? Has she ever given you any indication about how she feels?"

"I'm not sure. Maybe." He glances toward the floor, as if he has suddenly lost his nerve to speak, but adds, "I think so. But like I said, I'm really not sure."

"Well, honey. I'm not really an expert on relationships, but I think it's pretty clear she likes you a lot. You guys have known each for many years and I can tell you are close. Do you think you like her as more than a friend?"

He nods and shyly turns back to face her. "Yes, I'm sure I do." He smiles. "I think I've known it for a long time."

"Have you thought about telling her how you feel?"

"I have thought about it—a lot—but I'm afraid of how she'll react. What if she doesn't feel the same way about me? I'm afraid of losing her as a friend."

"I know this is hard, but what if she feels the same way and she also wants to be more than just friends?" Samantha smiles at him and, speaking softly, says, "If she's a good friend, you won't push her away by telling her the truth. The truth could actually make you closer. It's just important not to pressure her in any way. If you do, you may push her away. Just be up front with her. Bree is a smart, beautiful young woman. I bet she'll know just the right words to say that will put you at ease."

Suddenly, this talk about 'the truth' has made Alex uncomfortable. "I'm not sure, Mom. I think I have a lot more thinking to do before I tell her anything." He sighs. "Thanks for the advice. I really appreciate it."

"I'm not really sure how much help I've been, but you know I'm always here for you, honey, anytime you want to talk."

"I know, Mom. Now, let's have pizza. I'm starving."

"Okay, buddy," she says, rising from the sofa. Bending to kiss the top of his head, she adds, "You get us some drinks while I run up and change. I'll just have water, please."

"With pizza? Geez, Mom, way to live dangerously," he jokes, heading to the kitchen.

He knows he dodged a bullet this time, but he also knows that at some point he will have to tell her what's happening.

Just not tonight. He swallows and contemplates his next move. *Maybe tomorrow.*

7: Visions of blood

"What took you so long?" Zoey asks as Oliver eases the door closed behind him. "I was expecting you an hour ago."

"I came over just as fast as I could," Oliver answers. He can sense the tension between the two has already started to build, and he's only just arrived. "I told you when you called that I had to finish the job I was working on and then I would come by. I couldn't just drop everything and come running just because you called. I don't answer to you, remember?"

"No, you don't, but you do answer to them," the wiry red-head answers, quickly spinning around and heading down the main hallway to the kitchen, strands of her long hair flying about her head as if having a life all their own.

Oliver follows slowly.

In the kitchen, Zoey looks him up and down, her eyes narrowed. "Let me get you something cold to drink. It's hot out there and if you've been working as hard as you say you've been, you must be parched."

"Don't be a smartass, Zoey, or—"

"Or you'll what? Leave?" She pauses to give him time to respond. She then adds, "I didn't think so."

She suddenly notices how thin he has become since she saw him last time. Not that he was ever really large, but the change in his size is striking. "You look good, Oliver," she says. "On a diet?"

"Thanks, and nope. Most days, I'm just too busy to eat," he answers. He's always skeptical of her compliments, as he knows they often come with ulterior motives. "Now, can we just get on with it?"

"Why don't you come in and sit your ass down?" She smiles, deciding it's time to break the tension between then. "I just made some fresh iced tea. It's great on a hot day. I love iced tea."

She pauses, then asks, "Do you like iced tea, Oliver?"

"No, not really." He takes a deep breath. "But I could use a glass of cold water."

He follows her to the kitchen despite his reservations and the gnawing in his gut telling him he should turn and leave while he can. He has been down this road with this woman before and each time he's made the journey, he's lived to regret it.

I should probably just get the hell out of here, he thinks. *God knows what kind of shit she's got cooked up now. Whatever in the hell it is, I'm sure it's not going to end well for me.*

"Sit right there at the counter and I'll get it," she says, grabbing a tall glass from a shelf next to the sink and filling it with cold water from the fridge. Plopping a couple of ice cubes in the glass, she adds, "We have a lot talk about."

"We sure do." Oliver pulls out a barstool and sits at the counter as instructed. "Like where in the hell you've been for the past six months?"

"I'm not going to get into all of that right now."

"I don't fucking get it, Zoey." His pent-up anger erupts. "After what happened the last time between us, I thought we said we were always going to be honest with each other."

He glares at her. "I thought we had something real."

"We did say that and, yes, we did have something going." She pauses, carefully choosing her next words. "But that was then; this is now and things have changed."

"What in the hell gives, Zoey?"

He studies her, waiting for some sort of explanation, but she doesn't bite so he continues, "You were gone all that time without one god-damned word. What the fuck were you doing that was so important that you couldn't even call me? You couldn't even text? That only takes a second, for Christ's sake."

"I was busy. Focused."

"Focused? On what?"

"I was doing their business and I was only focused on that."

"Their business? What are you talking about?" He knows his words are wasted on her, but he persists. "What kind of business?"

"I can't tell you that, Oliver, but let's just say it was important."

"More important than me?"

"Well, Oliver." She looks him squarely in the eyes as she finally hands him the water. "If I'm being perfectly honest with you, yes, more important than you."

"I fucking don't believe this."

He refuses to take the glass so she sets it on the counter in front of him.

Her gaze hardens. "You asked me and you wanted me to be honest, didn't you? So, I'm being honest." She leans up against the butcher-block counter, her bony fingers clenched so tight he can see them turning white.

"I'm not going to lie and tell you something just because you want to hear it. I like you very much, Oliver. In fact, I'm pretty fond of you, but I—*we*—don't have time right now. There's too much at stake and I cannot allow personal feelings to change my perspective or my mission."

"Mission? What mission?" He's seething now. "There you go again; all cloak and dagger. What the hell are you talking about?"

"You'll learn more about all of that when the time comes, but right now, let's talk about the boy."

"That's what this is about?"

She nods. "He's the only thing that's important right now."

"Of course, he is." He glares at her, then adds under his breath, "It's always about him."

"Yes, it is—and you know that. He is my *raison d'être*."

"Can't we talk about something else first?" Oliver asks, studying her face for any sign that she may actually care for him. "Can't we talk about us? I haven't seen you in a long time and I'd like to catch up. I'd like to know where we stand."

"There is no *us*, Oliver, at least—not right now."

He hates how brutally honest she can be at times, but he has learned over the years that when it comes to the boy, that's all she can see. Her words leave no mystery about their relationship.

"Everything else can wait," she says.

"Including us?"

"Yes."

"Of course, it can." He's pissed and he wants her to know how angry he is. "It's like nothing else in this world matters to you other than that kid."

"He *is* all that matters." She glares at him. "When the crows saved you from dying fifteen years ago, they didn't bring you back from the brink of death because they liked you. They did it because they had chosen you for this mission. They knew way back then that you had an important part to play in all of this, and you almost blew it thirteen years ago."

"I've proven myself many times over the years since then. I have made my remittance."

He attempts to calm his anger and, lowering his voice, says, "I don't know what you want from me, Zoey. I've given my entire life to protecting that kid. I had nothing to do with what happened back then. I wasn't even in town when all of that happened."

"That's the point, Oliver. You were supposed to be here."

"After everything that happened to me back then, I needed the space to regroup," he says. "I needed to find myself again, but I came back."

"You did, but it was almost too late," she counters. "They trusted you to protect him and you were off some place half-way around the world doing God knows what with God knows who."

"Don't go there, Zoey. You have no right to do that. You are not one for pointing fingers when it comes to people not being here."

He watches as her grip on the counter becomes more intense and the skin on her hands becomes even whiter, if that's possible. But he continues to push. "I came back just as soon as I heard what happened and I have been here ever since, watching over the kid and doing whatever I had to do to keep him safe. I've been here while you've been the one off chasing whatever ghosts that you've concocted in your head."

"You know what I was doing."

"Do I?"

"Enough of this, Oliver." She releases the counter from the death grip she had maintained for the last several minutes and backs away from him. Slamming her right fist on the counter as if to prove a point, she says, "We have a job to do and we better be on our toes because trouble is coming." She clenches her teeth. "Something really bad is going to happen."

He wants to continue this argument, but instead he takes a deep breath, snatches the glass of water from the counter and gulps down several mouthfuls. The cold liquid goes down hard and he stifles the urge to spit it back out.

"Okay. Okay," he finally says, sitting the glass back on the counter. Seeing she is clearly distraught, he decides to take a softer tone with her. "I will let it go."

He sighs, then adds, "But we will pick it up again after all this settles down. So, tell me what's coming down so I can help you deal with this."

"That's just the thing, Oliver."

She starts to cry, which he knows is unusual for this woman who always puts on a tough façade no matter how bad things get. She never shows her emotions, and if she's visibly upset then he knows whatever she's holding back isn't good.

"I don't know what's coming." She quickly wipes away the tears. "I just know it's going to be serious."

Heaven forbid that she shows any vulnerability, he thinks, pushing back from the kitchen counter and making his way around the island to get to her. "Tell me what's happening and we'll work it out together," he says, reaching out to embrace her.

"Don't," she snaps, backing away.

"Come on, Zoey. I was just going to give you a hug."

"It always starts with just a hug from you." Putting up her hands to fend him off, she tells him, "We don't have time for that right now." She stops and looks him in the eyes. "We can't afford any distractions. Time is not on our side."

Retreating like a dog with its tail between its legs, he says, "Okay, Zoey, if that's the way you want to play it. I'll be cool." He takes a deep breath. "So, tell me everything."

"It started a couple months ago while I was away. I started having visions of Alex being in danger. At first, I see him lying on the floor but I don't know if he's dead or not." She pauses and studies Oliver's face for a reaction, then says, "I see him covered in blood and the crows are swooping around him. It is obvious they are trying to protect him."

"Protect him? From what?" Oliver has learned over the years to trust her visions.

"I really don't know."

She brushes away the tears that are continuing to trickle down her cheek. "I can't see the threat. I can sense that there is someone else there with him, but I have never been able to see who it is. I'm scared, Oliver. I know Alex is in danger and I don't know what I can do to protect him."

"Have you talked to him yet about any of this? He's a smart kid and he should know what's going on."

"I just got back in town yesterday and I saw him this morning. He's coming by in a little while so we can talk."

"Are you going to tell him about your visions?" Oliver waits for her to answer, then asks, "Don't you think you should tell him?"

"Yes, I should and I will." She breaks down again and sobs.

He's never seen her like this. He's not used to her showing any vulnerabilities.

"I'm scared, Oliver," she repeats. "Scared because I don't know what the threat is. I don't know how to help him."

"Take a deep breath, Zoey," he says calmly, moving closer to her again, expecting her to back away. When she doesn't, he pulls her into him. "I'm here to help you and Alex. We'll figure this out together and then we'll deal with it, whatever it is."

"I don't know, Oliver," she says, her voice trembling. "I've never felt anything like this before. The feeling of death is very powerful with these visions. I believe it's all a warning that Alex is in serious danger." She swallows and adds, "That he is going to die."

"Don't jump to conclusions. We've faced threats in the past and we've dealt with them. We'll deal with this one, too."

Stepping back and staring into her eyes, he adds, "Now, I need you to tell me everything you've seen and whatever else you know. We can only help him if we work together. That other person you see with Alex, can you tell if he's there to help or is he the one posing the threat?"

"I don't know. None of that is clear." She shakes her head. "But there's a lot of blood."

"Can you tell for sure if the blood belongs to Alex?"

"No, not really. But he's covered in blood, so I just assumed it was his."

"Maybe the blood belongs to the other person," Oliver suggests. "Maybe it's the other person who is in danger and Alex was there to help. Is that possible?"

"I hadn't thought of that." She contemplates Oliver's suggestion. "I suppose that's possible."

"You know how your visions work, Zoey. Sometimes the answer isn't obvious."

"True."

"So, let's just think about this. Were there any clues that might help us figure out who that other person might be? For starters, was it male or female?"

"Based on the build, I've always assumed that it was male."

"Are you sure?" he prods.

"Honestly? Now that you ask me, I'm not one hundred percent positive about that." She considers what Oliver has said and nods. "I guess it could have been either."

"Good. We're making progress."

"How? We still don't know anything more than we knew a few minutes ago."

"Let's think about it some more." He remains calm. "Can you tell when this takes place? Is it summer? Winter? Fall? Look around. Are there any trees? They might help to identify the time."

"I can't really say for certain *when* it is, but I get the feeling it's hot."

She thinks for a second and adds, "So I would guess it's in the summer or late spring, perhaps. Or even September. We do tend to have a lot of hot weather in September these days."

"So, then, whatever it is, it's likely to happen sometime in the next few months while it's hot."

"Or tomorrow!" she suggests. "It's supposed to be really hot tomorrow."

He pauses and studies her, then adds, "Yes. I suppose it could be tomorrow."

"We are no further ahead." She throws up her arms in frustration.

"Let's try this again." He speaks softly, his voice soothing. "Close your eyes and remember the last time you had a vision. Now, what do you see? What do you hear?"

She closes her eyes, then answers, "I see Alex covered in blood."

"Is he still alive?"

"I can't tell for certain." She shrugs, her eyebrows knotting as if she is in pain. "I see the other person but I have no idea who it is. I see the crows swooping around Alex. They are trying to protect him."

"Good. That's very good." He pauses to let her concentrate. "Look at the surroundings. Are they in a room?"

"Yes." She nods. "A room."

"Is there anything in the room that might tell us where it is? Furniture or paint colour? Are there any pictures hanging on the walls? Are there lots of windows or maybe there are no windows? What's on the floor? Tiles or hardwood?"

"I can't see anything. It's all kind of hazy."

"That's okay," he tells her, trying to convince her she's doing great. "We'll figure it out."

"How?" She opens her eyes and stares at him. "How are we going to figure it out?"

"We will. Trust me. Close your eyes and let's continue. Concentrate on the sounds. Do you hear anything that might be a clue?"

"All I can hear are the crows. They're calling out. They're angry and they're scared."

"Listen carefully. Try to block out the crows if you can. Is there anything else?"

"They are very loud," she says, her voice almost a whisper. "Very loud. It's almost like they are crying for Alex, maybe trying to coax him to get up. 'Get up, Alex,' they're saying to him. 'Get up!'"

"What else do you hear? Go further into your mind. Dig deep."

As Zoey becomes quiet, Oliver can see that she's concentrating.

Suddenly, she says, "Wait!" She's excited. She's had a breakthrough. "Wait, wait, wait. There is something else but it's not clear what it is."

"What else, Zoey? Come on. You are doing great. What else is there?"

"I don't know what they are, but there are definitely other birds in the room and they are fighting with the crows."

"This is an important clue. What kind of other birds?"

Her eyes snap open. "I don't know, Oliver, but this is bad."

The tears start to fall again and she trembles as if moved by an invisible force. "It's really bad. I have no idea what's going to happen, but Alex and the crows are in danger."

He pulls her close and he feels her trembling. "We'll help them," he whispers. "We will protect them. It's what we do."

8: A warning

Samantha quickly answers her cell when she sees it's her darling Kate. She has been monitoring her calls this evening, keeping the line open in case Alex calls, but she also needs to talk to her wife, and the sooner the better.

"Kate. Am I ever glad that you called. We need to talk," she says, the words spilling out of her mouth with urgency, as she intended.

"Hi, honey, nice to hear your voice too." Kate senses this must be serious because Samantha usually greets her with a more loving tone.

"Sorry, honey, yes, good to hear you too." Samantha tries but cannot stifle her worry. "I wish you were here."

"This is taking longer than I thought it would, so you shouldn't expect me much before eleven or maybe even later."

"Really?" Samantha sighs. "Your research is taking you that long? Must be an important case."

"It is. And it's one hell of a lot of work. I was in meetings all afternoon with a couple of other lawyers, and this evening I've been meeting with clients. We're planning our strategy for the trial in a couple of weeks, but we've taken a short break for a quick dinner. So, what's up? I got the sense from your texts that it's something urgent."

"You sound tired, Kate," Samantha says. "Do you really think you should be driving home tonight after a long day? Why don't you stay in the city for the night and then drive home in the morning? I really need to see you, but that would be the safest thing to do."

"Normally I would do that, but I have an early meeting in town tomorrow, even though it's Saturday," Kate says. "I would just rather come home and sleep in my own bed, with you."

"I get it, but your safety comes first."

"I promise I'll be fine." Kate knows that, despite whatever she says, her wife will still worry about her driving home alone and so late at night. "It won't be the first time I've pulled an all-nighter. Now, what's going on that you needed to talk to me right away?"

Samantha sighs heavily. "I need to bring you into the loop about something serious."

"I don't like the sounds of that," Kate says. She can feel her wife's stress all the way to Halifax. "This can't be good."

"No, it's not good." Samantha shakes her head. "And no, you won't like it."

"What is it?" Kate asks, bracing for the worst. "I can only think of a couple of things that would get you this stressed out like this, and most of them involve our kids. Is something wrong with one of the boys? Did something happen to one of them?"

"Well, it does involve one of the boys, but nothing has happened to him." Samantha pauses, searching for the best way to say this. She finally adds, "Not yet, anyway."

"Jesus, Sam."

Kate's reaction is predicable. Samantha knows that, while her wife doesn't openly declare her affection for their sons as often as she does, Kate still loves them very deeply.

"Sorry, honey," Samantha says, telling herself to remain calm. "I have to tell you that Zoey LaCroix has come back into our lives and she's already reached out to Alex."

"No fucking way."

"Yes way," Samantha responds. "She showed up today, of all days."

"That freaking little bitch."

Samantha can feel Kate's anger over the phone and she can only imagine how twisted and red with anger Kate's face has suddenly become. She knows her wife is pissed because she's also pissed.

Kate says, "I thought we had an agreement with that woman that she wouldn't come back, or if she was coming back, she'd give us a head's up so we could prepare Alex. Did you hear anything from her before she showed up?"

"Nope, not a word," Samantha says. "But Alex told me she showed up at the cemetery this morning while he was there visiting the graves. He said it totally caught him off guard, and me too. That was the last thing I was expecting today."

Searching for answers, Samantha takes a deep breath and asks, "You didn't hear from her, did you? Maybe you were afraid to tell me or something because you knew how I'd react to such news."

"Are you kidding?" Kate pauses, then adds, "That bitch wouldn't dare to contact me, not after what she did the last time. I don't want to talk to her ever again. I have no room for her in my life."

"I know you don't, but I do think we have to make an effort for Alex's sake."

"You make the effort," Kate snaps. "I'm done with her. She's only interested in one thing, and that is what's best for her. In the long run, it's all about her."

"Easy, honey." Samantha tries to calm the waters. "I know how you feel Kate and, trust me, I feel that way too, but we have to think of Alex and what's best for him."

"I *am* thinking of Alex, and what's best for him is for us to keep him as far away from that woman as we can," Kate says. "I don't believe anything she says and I don't trust her as far as I can throw her. I never will."

"Oh, believe me, honey, I'm not saying we shouldn't keep our guard up around her, but I don't think we can simply ignore her while she's in town." Samantha tries to be reasonable. She thinks that's what makes her such a good politician. "She's here and she's going to want to spend time with Alex, regardless if we like it or not."

"I hate that idea, but I know you're right."

"On that note, then..." Samantha pauses, takes a deep breath and says, "I have to tell you that she wants to see him tonight."

"What? I hope you told her no God-damned way. We need time to think this through."

"I haven't been talking to her since she showed up," Samantha says. "Alex has asked me not to see her right now."

"Since when do you do what Alex asks you to do?"

"Come on, Kate, there's no time for that right now."

"Sorry, honey, it's just that that woman brings out the worst in me." Kate tries to stifle her anger for her wife's sake. "What did you tell him?"

"I asked him not to see her, but of course that didn't sit too well with him."

"I wouldn't expect that it would."

"He's going to meet her around seven, regardless if we like it or not."

"Christ. I hate this," Kate says. "I hope you are going with him."

"He won't allow it."

"He won't allow it? You are his mother, Sam. You tell him what's going to happen. You can't allow him to control you like that."

"I can't do that, Kate. If we play hardball with him, we'll only be playing right into Zoey's hands. You know she'll always be the wedge between Alex and us. If I fight with him over seeing his aunt tonight, he's going to push us away and end up with her. We can't have him end up with that crazy woman. Lily would never forgive us and I could never live with myself."

"She is crazy, isn't she?" Kate says. "So, what then? What are you going to do?"

"I've given him permission to go and see her this evening, but only if he promises to be home at nine-sharp."

"Did he agree to that?"

"He did. I think he knew that was the only way that I would agree to let him go," Samantha says. "I think he knows that he's pushing the envelope with this and there's not going to be much leeway this time as far as his aunt is concerned."

"I don't know about this, Sam." Kate sighs heavily. "Will he do as you ask?"

"I have to trust that he will." Samantha pauses, then adds, "There is one more thing."

"There always is when it comes to that woman."

"I was thinking of asking Cliff Graham to do some surveillance on her while she's in town. I want to keep a really close watch on her."

Kate pauses and considers her wife's suggestion. "I'm not so sure about that, Sam. That would really be crossing a line. If you do that and Alex finds out about it, there will be hell to pay. I would hold off on that for a bit as you could be opening a whole new can of worms that might only lead to more trouble. Just sit tight on that idea."

Too late, Samantha thinks, but says, "Okay, if you think I should wait on the surveillance, I will. But I am going to ask him to do some digging for us. I want to know everything she has been up to since she left town six months ago, including where she's been and who she's been seeing. I figure the more we know about Zoey the better prepared we'll be for what's going down with her."

"Okay, I can live with that. Cliff's a good investigator. I have no doubt that he will find out whatever he can about her," Kate says, reflecting on her past dealings with the retired RCMP corporal. "I have never trusted that woman ever since she showed up at our back door thirteen years ago on Christmas Eve, so let's see what he finds out."

"Me neither and she's proven our suspicions were right, many times over."

"There is definitely something off about that woman," Kate says. "I don't know about you, but I never experienced any of that weirdness with Lily. Did you? You were closer with her than I was."

"No, I certainly did not," Samantha says, thinking about her deceased friend. "Remember, I didn't even know Zoey existed until she showed up at our house after the murders. We should have known right then that something was off with her. She had never laid eyes on her nephew and she didn't even ask to see him that night, after everything he had just been through. All she wanted was her grandmother's family bible and photo album. On hindsight, that was a clue right there, but we missed the signs."

"It was, but we were giving her the benefit of a doubt because she had just lost her twin sister," Kate says. "I figured she was in shock or something."

"I've thought about it a lot, and I could never understand why Lily never told anyone she had a twin sister," Samantha says. "She never even told me and I was supposed to be her best friend. She could have trusted me with that secret."

"You *were* her best friend. She left her son with you to raise because she trusted you and knew you would love him as she did," Kate says. "We both do. We'll never know why Lily kept the secrets about her sister, but I think we've figured some of it out on our own."

"We kind of have, haven't we?" Samantha knows, however, that they are never likely to find out the full truth about Lily and Zoey. *Whatever it is, Lily took that secret to grave with her,* she thinks.

"We know she's weird," Kate continues, "that's a given, but we also know that in a lot of ways she's like Alex. She seems to have a special bond with the crows around this town. Maybe the bond is not as tight as what Alex seems to have with the black birds, but the bond is there nevertheless. I mean, they share the same bloodline, so it's conceivable she has some of the same abilities that he's demonstrated."

"Yes, it's quite clear that they are connected—Zoey, Alex and the crows." Samantha reflects on Kate's observation then asks, "But for what purpose?"

"God only knows."

"Let's hope that whatever it is, it's not anything that will cause Alex any harm," Samantha says, thinking now that maybe she should have tried harder to prevent his meeting with his aunt.

"Or Zoey, for that matter," Kate adds, "because, for as much as I'm always suspicious about her motives, I wouldn't want anything bad to happen to her."

"No, me neither," Samantha agrees. "She is Alex's aunt, and he would be devastated if she suffered any harm."

"He would," Kate agrees. "So, honey, for as much as I would really love to be there with you right now, I have to be going. It's almost time to get back in there with my clients. Are you going to be okay?"

"I will be when I know that Alex is back, safe and sound, in this house."

"I will try not be too late, but don't wait up for me," Kate says.

"You get some sleep. Sounds like you're going to need it."

"Sleep? Not likely. Not right now at least," Samantha says, wishing her wife was here with her. "Promise me you will be careful and if you are feeling too tired to drive home, please promise me you'll just get a room and stay the night. I will miss you but I would prefer that you be safe."

"I'll be fine but, yes, if I think I'm too tired to drive home, I will call you," Kate promises.

Samantha disconnects the call, just as pangs of deep remorse suddenly rip through her gut.

What the hell? She shivers as cold chills race up the middle of her back and come to rest at the base of her neck, while the tiny hairs on her arms spring to attention.

"Jesus," she says aloud, moving to the thermostat to check the temperature. *Moderate*, it reads. *There's no way it should be this cold in here with a freaking heatwave outside.*

Looking at her phone screen as she goes to the closet to find a sweater, she sees it is seven o'clock on the button.

He should be there by now. I hope that woman doesn't fill his head with a bunch of crap. She shudders at the thought. *Not again.*

She's lost in thought when a loud thud at the living room window draws her attention. Racing to the front door, she swings it open and, without thinking there might be danger, switches on the flashlight option of her cellphone and makes her way to the living room window.

"For the love of God," she says spying a large owl sprawled on the grass under the window. Seeing the bird's lifeless, mangled body, its brown and white feathers soaked in blood, and its remains stretched out in the waning light of the early evening, she backs away from the bird. She knows it is dead, its neck clearly broken. "In the name of all that is holy, what in the bloody hell is going on around here?"

Samantha Henderson has lived in these parts her entire life and she has heard all of the legends about forerunners and omens and signs of death. She knows that this dead bird is a warning.

"Jesus," she whispers, gasping to catch her breath and regain her footing.

As if on cue, she hears the unmistakable guttural calls that she's come to immediately recognize after years of dealing with the black birds.

Crows.

Scanning the yard, her eyes come to rest on the three pine trees that tower near the outer edge of the property. A quick count of the flock reveals there are seven crows perched brazenly in the trees.

"Oh my God," she cries, racing back inside the house and slamming the door behind her. "Oh my God. What is happening?" Still struggling to catch her breath, she sobs, "Someone is going to die."

9: So many secrets

One hour and seventeen minutes, Cliff thinks as he observes Oliver Lewis leave Zoey's historic home, turn down the street and quickly disappear around a corner.

He notes the times Oliver entered and left the house, places the pad of paper on the passenger seat and considers the length of time Oliver spent visiting Zoey. *That's a lot of talking for two people to do. Must have had a lot of catching up to do.* He grins at what he's thinking. *Or maybe you were doing something else.*

Cliff chuckles like an immature teenaged boy. *Oliver, you old dog. Good for you.* He chuckles again.

He's about to call his client just as his phone screen lights up. He sees that the incoming text is from Julie.

"Hey Cliff," the message starts. "Just wanted to let you know the girls have arrived and are getting settled in. They say hello."

"Give them all a hug for me. Tell them I'll see them soon," Cliff types, taking his time with the small keyboard so that he doesn't make any mistakes. 'Fat fingers' is always his excuse, or at least that's what he tells people even before they comment on the typos in his messages.

"I will. Any idea how late you are going to be?"

"Not sure."

"Was wondering what to do about dinner."

"You guys go ahead and eat. I'll grab something when I get home."

"Are you sure? We can wait for you."

"I'm sure. Go ahead. The girls are probably hungry."

"Okay. We're going to make some burgers and salad. I'll make extra for you."

"Sounds good. See you as soon as I can."

"Bye, Cliff."

"Over and out," he types. It's his typical conversation closer whenever he texts.

"Now, Sam," he whispers to the empty truck cab while scrolling through his favourites' list. "Time to bring you up to date."

He's about to dial Samantha Henderson's number when he sees a teenaged boy heading down the street.

Alex Goodwin. There you are. He knows it's Alex because Samantha had told him that her son was going to see Zoey this evening.

"Seven-o-three p.m.," Cliff says, making note of the time on the pad of paper beside him. *You're a punctual kid, I'll give you that much.*

Pressing Samantha's number, he waits for her to answer.

"Hi Cliff," Samantha says just as Zoey LaCroix opens the front door and quickly ushers the boy inside. When he doesn't answer immediately, she asks, "Are you there?"

"Ah, yes, Sam. Sorry," he finally says. "I was just watching your boy. He just got here and has now gone inside the house."

"I'm glad to hear he made it okay. I'm so worried about him. I really don't trust that woman," Samantha says. "I hope I did the right thing by letting him go there tonight."

"How were you going to stop him?"

"I don't know, but I'm not really sure I tried all that hard to prevent him from going." She pauses, then adds, "Now I'm worried about what that woman could possibly be up to and what kind of foolishness she's going to put into his head."

"I'm sure you are, but, based on what you told me earlier, I don't get the feeling that he was going to let you stop him from seeing her," Cliff reasons. "Sounds to me like you did the right thing. After all, she is his family and they say blood is thicker than water, or something like that. I'm sure he'll be fine."

"Let's hope so, but when it comes to Zoey, I am always waiting for the next shoe to drop. She's proven herself to be untrustworthy over the years since she came into our lives and Alex refuses to see it. Bottom line is that I just don't like her and you know, Cliff, I always give everyone the benefit of a doubt, but my patience has worn pretty thin with her."

"Are you okay, Sam?" Cliff pauses to give Samantha time to think about his question. Then he adds, "You sound 'off'. Is something bothering you, other than that woman, I mean?"

"I don't know." She takes a deep breath and exhales. "Yes, I guess so. There is something, but you are going to think I'm crazy for believing in old wives' tales."

"No, I won't," Cliff assures her. "After everything I've seen in my thirty-plus years of living in this town, I know enough not to dismiss anything I hear even if it sounds far-fetched. Now, Sam, what's going on?"

She is slow to answer, but then she begins. "It's the crows, Cliff. They are at it again, and this time it has something to with owls. The thing is, I think it has something to do with that woman showing up in town again. Just the timing of it. I mean, they have been quiet for a really long time and now, on the very same day that Zoey arrives back in town, the crows are suddenly coming after us again. More to the point, I think they are coming after Alex."

"Why do you think that?"

"Because," she sighs heavily, "an owl hit our window and died a little while ago, and I know that, according to old superstitions, that means someone in the house is going to die and it's going to happen within three days."

"Not necessarily," Cliff cautions. "Doesn't the superstition also say that the death could be someone you know, which means that it's not necessarily someone who lives in the house—unless the bird got into the house. It didn't, did it? Get into the house, I mean."

"No, or I would me really freaking out," she says. "It hit the living room window and it looks like it probably died right away."

"So, there you go. Maybe it does mean that someone is going to die, but maybe you shouldn't jump to any conclusions."

Recognizing the fear in her voice, he quickly adds, "And let's use common sense. People are dying all the time. We humans have simply created these old wives' tales to explain things we can't understand. Isn't that how all superstitions are born?" He pauses.

"Take a deep breath, Sam. Just breathe."

She takes a minute. *Cliff, of all people, making sense*, she thinks, and says, "You are right. I need to slow down and consider all the facts. But there is one more thing."

"I can only imagine."

"No, you can't."

Cliff can tell that his friend is struggling to find the strength to continue. "Are you going to be okay?"

"Yes, yes, I just need to calm my nerves." Samantha takes a deep breath and continues. "When I went to investigate the dead bird, there were seven crows lurking around the yard and, I can't say for certain, but I think they killed that owl."

"Jesus, that is creepy." He was going to tell Samantha about the seven crows he saw at Zoey's house, but he thinks better of it, deciding not to add to her stress. *Why give her something else to worry about?*

"It sure is, but I don't think you called me to discuss crows and dead birds." She wants to change the topic. "Got anything for me yet?"

"Not really a whole lot, but we're working on it. I just wanted to check in to let you know I am still on the job. But I do have one piece of juicy information that you might find interesting. I know I sure did."

"Now I'm curious, Cliff. What have you got?"

"I'm not really sure it's anything too startling, but did you know that Oliver Lewis and Zoey LaCroix were good friends?" He pauses for a second to let that little tidbit sink in, then adds, "How good, I couldn't really say, but I can tell you that he spent almost an hour and a half with her this afternoon, and I can only imagine what they were doing."

"Really?" Samantha wasn't anticipating that piece of news. "Now that *is* interesting, but maybe we shouldn't be too surprised. I'm sure that, after all of these years in town, they must know each other, but I never saw Zoey as someone who Oliver would hang around with. She's really not his type."

"I know." Cliff shrugs even though Samantha can't see him. "I know that you are going to say 'typical guy' when I tell you this, but my first thought was that they were getting it on."

"Yes, Cliff. Typical man." She laughs.

Happy he lightened her mood, he continues, "But if they were just shooting the breeze, as they say, what could they possibly be talking about for all that while?"

"That is a very good question. Maybe they are good friends and were just catching up."

"Maybe," Cliff nods. "But then again—"

"Then again," Samantha interrupts, "when it comes to Zoey, you just never know. But I do know someone who might be able to shed some light on the subject."

"Who?" Cliff asks.

"Oliver's best friend."

"Let me guess, Kate's brother, the famous Dr. Charlie Webster."

"Yes, the one and only Dr. Webster," Samantha says. "He and Oliver are pretty close, so if anyone knows what's going on with those two, Charlie will know about it. I'll talk to him and let you know what I find out."

"Okay. Sounds good."

"Anything else?" she asks.

"It's a bit too early for any details yet, but I've got my people working on it and I'll let you know just as soon as I hear anything."

His phone rings. "Just a minute, Sam. Someone's calling."

Cliff sees that it's Sergeant Emily Murphy. "Hey Sam. I've got an important call coming in. I'll get back to you when I have something."

"Okay, Cliff. Thanks for the info," she says.

"Bye." He presses the answer button and takes the new call. "Sergeant," he says to the caller. "What are you doing calling me on a Friday evening? Didn't they tell you that summer's here and during the summer months the weekends start on Friday afternoon? You can leave early, you know."

"In what lifetime?" She laughs. "Come on, Cliff, you know this job doesn't work that way."

"I do. What's up?"

"I have an initial report on Zoey LaCroix I want to share."

"There's no grass under your feet, is there?"

"I know a few people, Cliff."

"Yes." His chuckle is deep, guttural. "I bet you do. So, did you have any luck?"

"Actually, I did. For someone who has always seemed to be so secretive, so elusive, she didn't try all that hard to cover her tracks. All I did was ask someone to put her name into the system and there it was, everything I was looking for right in front of me. We had no trouble tracing her travel itinerary for the past six months, so I can tell you where she's travelled to, but—"

"Oh, I hate this part," he interrupts. "There's always a 'but.'"

"In this case, there's a big 'but', because while I can tell you where she's gone, I can't tell you what she was up to while she was there."

Cliff sighs heavily. "Well, tell me that much at least. It's a good start. Where did she go?"

"Okay," Emily says. "When she left town almost six months ago, she got on a plane in Halifax and, after a six-hour layover in Toronto, went to Vancouver, where she stayed for about a month. Unfortunately, we don't know where she went when she got there, and whatever she did, she paid for everything by cash, so there don't appear to be records of any electronic transactions, but we'll continue looking. Unfortunately, we can't look too deep at this point because this isn't an official case and I'd need to make it official to delve into her personal records like that."

"It's not official yet."

"What do you mean, 'not yet'?" Emily asks. "Are you expecting something to happen?"

"I don't know, but if experience has taught us anything it's that, when it comes to that woman, we should always be expecting something to happen."

"True, but I can't do much more digging at this point without an official status."

"I understand. She was in Vancouver—or wherever—for about a month and then what? She was gone for almost six months. She had to be somewhere."

"She was in South Africa for almost two months and then she spent a month and a half in Australia. On her way back to North America, she stopped in Mexico for a week or so, then flew to New York and was there for a while. From there, she flew back to Toronto and then on to Halifax. We know she showed up in town yesterday, so that's where her journey ends."

"That's one hell of a sight-seeing trip."

"It sure is, and it must have cost her a bundle," Emily observes. "Travel to any one of those locations wouldn't be cheap. Where would she get that kind of money?"

"I have no idea and, beyond that, what was she doing in all of those places? Where did she eat and sleep? Did she meet anyone? Did she make any calls while she was away? Are there any cell-phone records you could look at that might tell us something?"

"Come on, Cliff. You know I can't tell you any of that."

"I know, I know." He shrugs. "And I suppose she didn't use any credit cards or anything the whole time she was gone, just like in Vancouver?"

"Not once, that appears evident," Emily tells him. "The only electronic footprint she left was for her travel, which is pretty much impossible to hide these days, even if you tried. Other than that, it's one big—"

"Mystery." Cliff interrupts.

"Exactly. And I will admit, now I'm intrigued."

"Me, too." Cliff sighs. "This is all very interesting. Thank you for your help and for getting on it so fast, but I'm not sure how useful the information really is to me right now other than raising more questions."

"Sorry, but it's all I can find without breaching any privacy laws. In fact, as you know, I've already crossed a line, but I did it for you."

"Will you keep looking?"

"Of course, quietly, but like I said, since this isn't an official case there isn't much more I can do. You know, if you can link her to a crime or any kind of criminal activity, then we're off to the races." She pauses, then asks, "Can you?"

"No." Cliff sighs again. "No, I cannot and I hope I don't have to."

"Well then, unless there's something more I can do for you right now, I am going to say goodbye and head home."

"No, Sergeant," he answers. "There is nothing right now but thank you for your help. It's greatly appreciated."

"You are welcome. If we find anything further, I'll be in touch."

"Appreciate that," he says. "Over and out."

Hmmmm. So, young lady. He stares at the historic home. All is quiet on the outside, at least. *What have you been up to, Ms. Zoey LaCroix? Why so many secrets?*

10: More fowl business

Trying to digest the information that Cliff has shared with her, Samantha Henderson cringes. She can't even imagine Oliver and Zoey together. *I can't wrap my head around that. Come on, Oliver. Of all people, why her?*

Even though she has no idea what the two would have been doing for an hour and a half, she finds it hard to picture them being intimate, as Cliff implied. She cringes at the mere thought of that possibility.

Not for one second. Oliver would never get caught in her trap, would he?

"No way," she says, flipping through her phone to find Charlie's private number. Hitting dial, she thinks, *He's too smart for that. Or at least I think he is.*

Charlie answers quickly. "Hello."

"Hi, Charlie."

"Hey, Sam. What a nice surprise," he says. "How are you doing? Everything okay?"

"Oh, yes," She lies. "Everything is perfectly fine and we're all good."

"Okay, glad to hear it. But if everything is fine, then why are you calling me on a Friday night?"

Samantha can sense his angst and she wonders if maybe this phone call wasn't such a good idea.

Before she can answer he adds, "You don't usually call me. Are you sure Katie is alright? Did something happen to my sister?"

"No, no, Charlie. Just relax. I didn't mean to get you worked up. I promise your sister is okay. She's still stuck in Halifax on some case, and she's going to be pretty late getting home, but she was fine when I talked to her a while ago."

"Good." Samantha can feel the doctor's relief over the phone. "So, what can I do for you, then? I can't imagine you were just calling to check in on us."

"You know me too well." Samantha chuckles. It's a forced laugh but she hopes it sounds sincere. "But now that you mention it, how's the family?"

"We're all good. Rebecca is doing a shift at the hospital tonight and me and Liam are holding down the fort. Trying to keep an eleven-year-old entertained isn't easy, especially when school's out. But they are going away tomorrow, so I'll get a break."

"Oh, I remember those days." Samantha chuckles again. "But make the most of it while you can. Give it a few years and Liam won't want to be around you. He'll be too busy hanging with his friends, but I'm sure you know how it goes. You were a teenager once."

"Jeez. I hope that won't be the case. I kind of like the little gaffer, so don't ruin it for me."

"I hope so. You made him after all."

"That's what Becca tells me anyway." He laughs.

"Charlie Webster. Rebecca and your sister would kill you if they heard you talk like that."

"I know, but they know what I'm like." He laughs again and Samantha can tell he's enjoying the chat. "But seriously, how can I help, Sam?"

"Well, honestly, Charlie, it's about Oliver."

"Oliver? What the hell is that idiot up to now?"

"I am not really sure but—and here's the real question—what do you know about him and Zoey LaCroix?"

"Zoey LaCroix? What the hell does she have to do with Oliver?"

"That's what I'm hoping to find out."

"She's not even around these days, so why bring her up?"

"Well, actually, she is," Samantha tells him. "She showed up this morning right out of the blue and talked with Alex at the cemetery."

"What?" He pauses and Samantha understands he needs to let

the information sink in because that's how she felt only a few hours ago when she learned of Zoey's return.

He finally asks, "What does she want, and what does she have to do with Oliver?"

"I don't have an answer to either of those questions, but the two were together earlier today and I just find that suspicious. Have you ever known the two of them to be friendly or hang out together? Has Oliver ever mentioned Zoey to you?"

Charlie considers her question for a minute and then responds, "No, Sam. Not that I can recall, at least no more than anyone else around here."

"That's what I thought, too, but it appears they are closer than any of us knew."

"Well, I don't really see Oliver all that much these days because we're both busy with our jobs, and when I do see him it's usually over a quick beer down at the pub to catch up." He pauses, then adds, "We never talk about that woman. We have no reason to discuss her."

"I just don't get it, Charlie. Something doesn't add up because he was at her house for an hour and half today so they were doing something."

"God, Sam. That really doesn't sound like Oliver. Maybe he was checking out her place. Maybe she wants to hire him to do some work for her. He is a good contractor with an excellent reputation. That's very possible, you know."

"I guess so, but she just got back into town and in one day she's already going to do some renovations?" Samantha asks. "I know you don't want to think anything bad about your good friend, but that really doesn't sound practical to me or very likely. It just doesn't make sense."

"No, not really, does it?"

She can practically see him shaking his head. *He and Kate are alike in so many ways*, she thinks.

"I can't help but think there's something more to it than that," she says. "When it comes to that woman, I have to be careful, especially where Alex is concerned."

"Of course, you do. He's already been through so much and you don't need her disrupting his life now that he seems to be in a good place."

"About that, Charlie." She takes on a softer tone. "I really don't think Alex is in a good place. He may put up a good front, but I can see he's still hurting."

"He's gone through a lot, Sam. I know it has been thirteen years, but he lost his entire family that day. That would not be easy for anyone to deal with, and especially not a young kid like Alex was when it happened."

Sounding more like a doctor than her brother-in-law, he continues, "I am sure those events haunt him every day and I am also sure they will continue to follow him for his entire life, which is actually better for him than burying them away. When you experience such a trauma, it's healthier to face your pain than to hide it. But you and Katie have done a good job helping him through all of that. I know it wasn't easy for any of you."

"It wasn't, but I would do it all again for Alex. And for Lily." She pauses and quiets her emotions. "I have no regrets."

"For sure, but Alex is a brave, strong and smart young man. I don't think he will let Zoey suck him into anything, and if Oliver is somehow connected to her, then maybe that's a good thing that he's there if Alex is going to be around her," Charlie suggests. "I know Oliver and I know he would not let anything happen to Alex. He's like a member of the family."

"I know you are right about that, but it still doesn't explain why they are sneaking around with each other behind everyone's back."

"If you were seeing a crazy woman, would you want the whole town to know about it?" Charlie asks.

Samantha ponders Charlie's question. "Maybe not so much."

"I know you have your reasons not to trust that woman, but maybe this is all perfectly innocent and it's nothing more than two friends catching up after six months." Charlie gives it a few moments for his words to sink in, then adds, "I'm not saying that's what it is, but it's a possibility, isn't it?"

She is reluctant to agree but finally concedes. "I suppose that is possible—but again, I can't let it go that easily."

"I know you can't and I'm not suggesting you drop it," Charlie says. "I wasn't planning on seeing Oliver any time soon, but I suppose I can give him a call to check in with him. Actually, it has been a while since we chatted. But I will have to be careful. If I go in too hot and start asking a bunch of questions about Zoey, he's going to know something's up."

"I understand, Charlie, but I would appreciate whatever you can do."

"I'm not promising that I'll be able to find out anything useful, but I'll try." He adds, "Just remember, Oliver isn't the kind of guy who talks much about his personal life, not even with me. But I'll see what I can find out."

"Thank you. And one more thing, Charlie. Can we please keep this conversation between us?" Samantha asks. "You and I both know that your sister would be pissed at me for coming to you with this, and she would be pissed at you for agreeing to help me."

"Absolutely. I don't need Katie on my ass right now."

"I understand that, better than anyone."

"I'm sure you do." He chuckles but Samantha knows he's being serious. Maybe it's the lawyer in her, but his sister can be a tough nut, especially when she believes she is right about something.

"I know she loves Alex and would do whatever she had to do to protect him, but I think sometimes she believes I go overboard and jump to conclusions too quickly without considering all the facts." She catches herself before saying something about Kate that may upset her brother. She then says, "I know I can be impulsive, but I can't take the chance when it comes Alex and that woman."

"You don't owe me any explanation, Sam," Charlie tells her. "I've known Katie my entire life and I've learned to pick my battles with her. I love Alex too, but this isn't a battle I want to have with her so I promise this is just between us."

Glancing at her cell, Samantha says, "Speaking of your sister, she's calling right now."

"You better take it. I will let you know what I find out after I talk to Oliver."

"Okay. Thanks. Give Liam a hug for me."

She disconnects the call, takes a deep breath, presses the talk button and says, "Hey, honey. Everything alright?"

"Yes, dear," Kate Webster answers. "All good."

"What's up? I wasn't expecting to hear from you for a few more hours yet."

"I cut my meeting short and I'm heading home," Kate tells her. "I just wanted to let you know I was on my way. Just heading to the car as we speak."

"Did you finish everything?"

"No, but after we talked earlier, I got to thinking that I should be home with you and the boys, so I reviewed a few things with the clients and then suggested we could pick it up early next week. We'll arrange a Zoom meeting after the holiday. So, I'm done for now and I'm heading back to my car as we speak."

"They were okay with that?"

"They had no choice. Truth be told, I think they were a bit relieved," Kate says. "Everyone was tired and it's the long weekend so they were all anxious to get on with their plans."

"Honestly," Samantha says with a sigh, "I'm glad you're coming home. I'll be happy to have you here."

"Are you doing okay? You sound stressed or worried. Did something happen since we talked?"

"No, I'm just a little on edge because of the situation with Alex. I'll just be glad to have you home."

Kate says, "I'm on my way, honey. The traffic should be light by now, as everyone left the city several hours ago and headed to the country. I should be home in about an hour and a half, give or take a few minutes."

"At least the weather is good so the roads are clear."

"Yes they...holy shit. Just a minute, Sam."

"Kate? Honey?"

She can hear Kate's breathing intensify and her footsteps pick up the pace, as if she is running. "Kate? Kate? What's wrong? Talk to me, Kate."

"Hold it a minute, Sam," Kate blurts into the phone, her tone urgent. "Are you fucking kidding me?"

Samantha panics. "What's wrong, Kate? Are you okay? Please talk to me."

Finally, Kate says, "I am okay. But I'm not sure about my car."

"Your car? What's wrong with your car?"

"You are not going to believe this, because I fucking well don't believe it myself."

"What is it?"

"The god-damned grill's all busted. I don't know anything about cars, but it looks pretty serious to me."

"What? How did that happen? You must have hit something."

"I don't think so. I'm sure I would know if I hit something."

Samantha considers another option. "Did someone hit you while you were parked there all day?"

"I can't tell for sure, but I suppose that's possible."

"Look for a note," Samantha suggests. "Sometimes people leave a note if they hit a car and can't find the owner. Do you see a note anywhere? Maybe around the windshield?"

After a moment, Kate finally says, "No, I don't see a note. Give me a second, honey. I want to have a closer look."

"Be careful, Kate."

"There's no one else around," she tells Samantha. "This parkade is pretty desolate right about now. It's a late Friday evening on a hot long weekend. This is the last place anyone would be hanging out."

"It's not always people you have to watch out for."

"I know." Kate pauses, then suddenly declares, "It's sometime owls."

"Owls?" Samantha is stunned by her wife's unexpected declaration. "What about them?"

"Actually, to be more precise, it's only one owl." Kate pauses. "Jesus, this has to be one of the weirdest things I've seen. It looks like I hit an owl somewhere along my drive in this morning and the damned thing is still stuck in the grill. It's dead, of course, but it's just hanging there, the poor thing. It's gross and sad at the same time." She adds, "It's a good-sized bird and it caused considerable damage to my grill, but, for whatever reason, I didn't hear it hit."

"You didn't see anything this morning?"

"Nothing. I got out of my car when I got here, grabbed my stuff and went directly to my first meeting. I was in a hurry and I just didn't notice anything."

"Jesus, Kate." Samantha exhales forcefully. "What are you going to do? Can you drive the car? *Should* you drive the car?"

"I'll have to call CAA and see if they can send someone. I don't want to take a chance on driving it before I know what's wrong because driving it may cause more damage or I may break down somewhere between here and home. I can't risk it."

"No, you can't," Samantha tells her. "Do you want me to come and get you?"

"Jesus, no, I don't think that will be necessary. Let's wait and see what CAA says first."

"Okay, if you're sure, but this isn't good." Samantha swallows and says, "It's another sign."

"Another sign? What do you mean?"

"Not right now, honey. We'll talk about all of that when you get home."

"Are you sure you're okay, Sam? You don't sound okay."

"Yes, I'm fine," Samantha insists. "I'm just worried about you being stuck there all alone."

"Don't worry about me. I'm calling CAA right now and I'm getting in the car to wait for them."

"Lock all of the doors."

"Yes, honey, I will lock all of the doors. But please don't worry."

"You know that's not going to happen."

"I will keep you posted."

"Call me as soon as you know something."

"I will. I love you."

"Love you, too."

Samantha hears the connection end. "Jesus," she cries, thinking about the events that have unfolded this evening. "Why are you doing this to us again?" She sobs, "Why us?"

11: Vigilance is the best weapon

It has been close to a year since Alex was inside his Aunt's Zoey's house, but, looking around the kitchen, which seems to be the usual hang out whenever he visits, he quickly concludes that not much has changed. Everything is just as he remembers it, except for a stack of books neatly piled on the kitchen counter, books that he does not recognize.

They look old, he thinks. He can't clearly see their titles.

Noticing where her nephew's eyes have landed, Zoey says, "Yes, Alex, those books are pretty old but we will get to them later."

Instructing him to take a seat at the kitchen counter, she asks, "Can I get you something? A cold drink perhaps? Water? Soda? You name it, I'm sure I have it."

"No. I'm fine, thanks," he answers, sliding his tall, lean body onto a stool, one of three stationed at the counter. He takes the one closest to the door in case he wants to make a hasty retreat. "I'd just like to talk, please. I promised Mom that I would be home by nine and I won't break that promise."

"I understand," Zoey nods. "And just for the record, Samantha is not your mother. Not your biological mother at least."

"I know that." He studies his aunt, squinting in the dim glow from the two pendant lights that hang above their heads. He's trying to gain a better understanding of the woman who bears an uncanny resemblance to his biological mother, but he hasn't been able to get an accurate read on her.

He sighs and says, "If this is going to be another sermon about me and the family that raised me, then I am going to leave right now. I really don't feel like having that conversation again."

"No. No. I admit it bothers me when you call her 'mom', but of course you don't want to talk about any of that. Understood."

She tries to maintain a calm tone. "Sorry, but I get all worked up when I think about what happened to my twin sister. It's hard, you know, because I didn't get to see much of her while she was alive and now she's gone." She pauses and then adds with the anguish that she usually hides from him, "I miss her."

"None of us will ever see her again," he says, wondering where all of this is coming from. He believes it has something to do with this day being the anniversary of his mother's death, but he can't be sure as his aunt is usually very stoic and is always the ultimate picture of masked emotions. "We all miss her," he says, "but I can't talk about her right now. So, let's talk about the real reason why I'm here tonight. Like I told you this morning, I feel it is time that you told me everything about my past and my family history. I have a right to know."

"Yes, of course you do." She forces a smile and, approaching the counter where he's sitting, leans in close. "Again, I apologize if I upset you. That wasn't my intention."

"I'm fine." He too forces a weak smile. "Now, can we please get to it before we run out of time?"

"Yes. But first, I want to let you know that I have asked a special friend to join us."

"A friend? Who?" Alex is surprised and feels ambushed by this latest development. "I thought this was just going to be between you and me—just the two of us."

"It is between you and me, but it's important that he be here as well as he's also a part of this. We need him." She takes a deep breath and adds, "More to the point, Alex, you need him."

Zoey motions to whoever is in the shadows of a nearby hallway, waiting for her cue and Alex is surprised when Oliver Lewis slowly, but deliberately, enters the kitchen. Oliver had left the house earlier to clear up some things at the job site, but returned later through her back door and remained hidden so Alex wouldn't see him until the time was right.

"Oliver?" Alex is confused by the man's presence. "I was not expecting to see you tonight. What are you doing here? Aunt Zoey,

I'm confused. Why Oliver?"

"Because," she tells him. "He's important to you."

"He's a friend of my mom's and my Uncle Charlie's and"—while staring at Oliver he adds—"while I like him, I wouldn't exactly say he's important to me."

"Ah, but he is, Alex," Zoey answers. "More important than you know."

"How? Why? What do you mean?"

"It will all be very clear to you a few minutes," Zoey tells him. "But I wanted to let you know he was here."

"I don't understand."

"You will," she says, "but all you need to know right now is that Oliver is your protector."

"My what? Protector? What's he protecting me from?"

Pushing away from the counter, he adds, "This is crazy. I think I'm just going to leave. Maybe Mom was right after all and this was all a big mistake. Maybe I should not have come here tonight."

"Just wait, Alex," Oliver speaks up. He keeps his distance from the boy but adds, "Please let your aunt finish what she has to tell you. Once you hear everything, I promise that you will understand."

"Why are you here, Oliver?"

"She will tell you." Stepping back even further from Alex and his aunt as if trying to remove himself from the conversation, Oliver says, "Let her talk. I'm just going to stand right here and I won't say a word. But, Alex, you must hear what she has to say. It's very important."

Sliding back onto the stool, Alex nods and becomes fixated on Oliver. "Okay. I'll hear her out, but only because you asked me to."

"Thanks, Alex," Zoey says, folding her arms around her slender body and taking a deep breath. "I want to take you back a few years to a woman named Clara Underwood. She was my grandmother. Your great grandmother."

"I've heard of her, but I never met her."

"You wouldn't have. Clara died when you were very young, but she's important to your story. She's important to all of us." She takes another deep breath as if gathering her thoughts and continues, "You see, Alex, Clara was a guardian of the crows and, as such, the keeper of their secrets."

"Guardian? Keeper of what secrets? What are you talking about?" Alex is suddenly confused and lost. "I want to hear the truth, not some fantasy story that you've concocted. I was hoping that we had moved beyond the games."

"Believe me, this is not a fantasy story. It's all true and it is *your* story. You see, Clara and my mother, along with your mother and me, and now you, are the main players in this story," she says. "We are all direct descendants of a woman named Alexandria Gorham. She came to this town with her family a couple hundred years ago, when it was just a young, fledgling settlement, and she became the vital link between our family and the crows that turned the skies black around these parts. That link has endured over the centuries."

"I've heard all the legends about her being a witch or something, but I don't know anything other than those stories."

His reaction is predictably negative, as Zoey imagined it would be. "Most people don't know the true story and many don't even know that she was a real person, but that's all about to change," she tells him. "What I'm about to tell you will help you understand everything that has taken place and everything that will happen."

"I'm listening." He nods at her. "I am listening."

"Good. As I said, Clara was a keeper of the secrets and she knew everything there is to know about the crows around here. She had —as some people would say—an unusual bond with the black birds." She considers her next words and then says, "We all have a bond with them. You have a special bond, even greater than the one I have. Your connection runs very deep and you might not believe it, but it is a real thing."

Alex glances at Oliver as if he's looking for a way to understand what his aunt is telling him. Oliver remains silent so Alex continues to listen.

"These secrets have been passed down through the family for generations, and they have now ended up with us." Nodding toward the books, she explains, "Each keeper maintained meticulous notes in the family Bible, which was first owned by Alexandria Gorham. They also kept a photo album into which pictures of each guardian have been added. After photography was invented, of course. I'm in there. You're in there. You'll see, because these books are going to you. They are now your responsibility."

He looks puzzled but remains quiet.

"It's a lot, I know," she continues. "When the senior keeper dies, these books and any other family records are passed onto the next keeper in the chain. Clara was a keeper and so was my mother, as were your mother and I, as we were twins. But here's where it begins to fall into a grey zone. My mother and my sister, Lily, didn't accept the charge they had inherited and they shirked their responsibilities. As a result, my grandmother was forced to keep the books until her very end, at which time they had to go to someone in the family. The logical choices—since my mother was dead by then and would not have wanted them even if she had been alive— were Lily and me. So, even though your mother had no idea what she was getting, Clara willed the books to us."

Alex says, "I think I've seen the books."

"I'm sure you did. Your mother received the Bible and the photo album," Zoey says, "and they were in your house until she died, at which time I was able to retrieve them with Samantha's help. But there were three important books that were part of the official family record. The third," which Zoey points to in the pile on the counter, "is the actual journal of Alexandria Gorham. Everything in there is written by her hand and it tells you everything about her life and her connection to the crows. When Clara died, she willed that book to me, which I humbly accepted. I cherished the books for what they meant to our family. I wish your mother had done the same with her gifts. I wish she had studied them. Instead, she just put the Bible and photo album on a shelf and forgot all about them."

"Wow, really?" Alex is intrigued by what he's just heard. "I bet that journal would be interesting to read."

"It is very interesting and it's also yours. As the next guardian, you get to keep all of the books."

He considers everything she just told him, then says, "So, I have a couple of questions. If my mother, as you say, shirked off her responsibilities because *her* mother didn't believe in the family bloodline legacy, why would Clara leave her two of the books and why didn't you feel the same way as my mother?"

"Good questions. I'm not really sure why Clara left Lily those books, because my sister had made it clear over the years that she did not want anything to do with them or the family legacy. Maybe it had something to do with her being the older twin. As for me, when I got old enough, I went to visit my grandmother many, many times. As often as I could. I didn't care what my mother said and I listened to everything Clara told me. I drank it up, so I was expecting to receive all three books. You can imagine my surprise when I only got that one, for whatever reason. The reason was only known to Clara and she took that information to the grave with her."

"Another question," Alex says. "If you and I are guardians and keepers of the secrets, as you say, what is a protector and what makes Oliver a protector? He's not in the family bloodline—or maybe he is and I just don't know about it."

"No, he isn't one of the family." Zoey shakes her head. "He was chosen by the crows to protect you and he has been doing that over the years, even though you never knew it."

Alex's confusion continues to grow. "Protecting me from what?"

"Everything and anything that could possibly do you harm, especially after your family was so horribly killed. He's been there every step of the way. Watching from a distance and waiting, and now it is his time because, while we have not figured it out just yet, we do know there is a major threat brewing and you are in serious danger. I told you that this morning."

"Danger? From what?"

"I wish I knew. I'm working on figuring that out as quickly as I can."

"I don't understand."

"I know it's a lot to take in, but I'll try to explain." Zoey takes a deep breath and says, "As guardians, we have special abilities."

"Abilities? You mean, like super powers? Because if that's what you mean, I can tell you that I don't have anything like that, although over the years I have done things that I can't explain."

"No, Alex." She shakes her head. "I wouldn't call them 'powers', because that makes it sound like we're comic book characters. By 'abilities', I mean our natural senses are extremely powerful. Our hearing. Our smell. Our vision. Even our sense of touch. They are sharper than most people and that gives us the ability to be more in-tuned to nature and our surroundings. And there is one more thing."

"What's that? Don't stop now. You have to tell me everything."

"Okay, but this is the one that may be the most exciting and also most difficult to accept," she says, choosing her words carefully. "Those of us who are guardians also have the heightened ability of foresight."

"Foresight? I don't understand. What is that?"

"It means that sometimes we can see things that haven't happened yet. Call it a premonition or intuition. It's like receiving a vision from the future. Some people have them and they don't even realize it, like thinking about a song playing on the radio and then it plays. Or thinking of someone they haven't heard from in a long time and then they get a phone call from that person right out of the blue, or maybe even an unexpected visit from them. Most people just take that sort of thing in stride, without a second thought. But for us, it goes well beyond that. Our visions are extremely powerful and they always come true. I had my first vision when I was fourteen years old. If you haven't had any visions yet, I am positive that you will start having them someday soon. I know this because the bond is especially strong with you."

Alex shakes his head. Unsure of what he's just heard, he says, his voice almost a whisper, "I haven't. Not that I know of. And that's the second time you've said something about me having a special bond with the crows. What does that mean?"

"I mean that you are the fiftieth descendent of Alexandria Gorham. You are the golden one and your link to the crows is very strong. I've seen it. It runs deep with you. The crows are connected to you in ways that even I don't understand."

"I guess so, but I've never thought it about it before." He pauses and adds, "It all seems very natural to me."

"It would seem natural because it is natural," she says. "It's part of who you are."

"This is a lot to comprehend, Aunt Zoey."

"I know, Alex, but you will soon come to understand. I'll help you."

He pauses, reviewing everything his aunt just told him. "This danger you're talking about, what have you seen?"

She glances to Oliver, as if seeking his reassurance that she's doing the right thing by opening up to her nephew. He nods and she tells Alex, "I believe someone is out to hurt you."

"Why would someone want to hurt me? Better still, who? How do you know?"

"Like I said, I don't have all of the answers right now."

"So, what did you see?" He knows she's hesitating, holding back. "You have to tell me all of it. We've come this far and we can't stop now."

She exhales, forcefully and says, "Okay, Alex. This will be hard to hear, but in my visions, I see that you are lifeless and lying on what I think is a floor or something made of wood, somewhere, and you are covered in blood. It's a lot of blood but I can't be sure that it's all yours. There is someone else there in this place with you, but I can't make out who it is and I can't tell if they are the one who hurt you or if they are trying to help you. I can't see where you are, but I can tell you for certain that the crows are there and they are in a frenzy—they are trying to protect you."

"Shit, that doesn't sound good."

"It's not good and the thing is, I'm scared that it's real." She exhales. "I wish I knew more but I'll get there."

"So, these visions you have. Do they always come true?"

She hesitates. Alex can see she is reluctant to answer.

"Please, just tell me," he says. "Do they always come true?"

"Yes," she nods, fear creeping into her expression. "Unfortunately, they always come true."

"If that's the case, what can we do about it? Can we stop this from happening to me?"

"We *are* going to stop it. That's my mission and it's Oliver's mission. We are not going to let anything happen to you, I promise. We have to be vigilant. We have to be ready for just about anything and everything that comes at us. That's what Oliver is here for. To be ready when it happens."

"No offence to Oliver, but why would the crows choose him to be my protector? If this danger is real, shouldn't my protector be someone with some sort of special abilities of his own?"

"This is not like in the movies, Alex," she answers. "The protector doesn't have any special powers, but he will do whatever he has to do to protect you from harm. The crows saved him from death fifteen years ago because they knew that he would have a role to play in all of this someday. It appears that day has finally come."

"So, you are telling me he's ready for this whatever it is that's coming?

"He is." She nods. "He knows what he has to do."

"And that is what, exactly?"

"Whatever he has to do to ensure your safety."

Turning to Oliver, Alex asks, "You're okay with all of this? It doesn't sound good to me."

Oliver nods, but says nothing.

Zoey, however, speaks up. "He knows his role and he's had a long time to prepare for whatever comes along. The thing you have to understand, Alex, is that, without the crows, Oliver would have been dead many years ago. He owes the crows, and he accepts that it's time to pay his debt, for the good of the family and to save you from whatever harm is out there."

"I have no idea what any of that means, but what if I'm not okay with this? What if I don't want Oliver to risk his life to save me? Because it sounds like that's exactly what he may have to do."

"You don't have a say in any of this, Alex. As the golden one, you just have to accept it and we will do the rest—Oliver, me and most importantly, the crows."

He's overwhelmed. He sighs and says, "I don't want any part in this."

"This is happening to you because of your birth line. You can choose a lot of things in life, but you cannot choose your family or anything that comes with them. It's part of the legacy." She is forceful and blunt. "You must accept this, Alex. It will be easier for you if you do."

"I think I want to go home now."

"Of course," Zoey tells him. "You can leave anytime you want, Alex. You are not a prisoner here, but please know my house will always be a place of sanctuary for you. You will always be safe here. I can help you face whatever is coming."

"I can't digest all of this right now," he says. "I need to let it sink in."

"Of course, you do. Go home. Think about it. Call me. Text me. Or come back if you want to. I'll always be here for you."

"Not always." He stares at her and then says, "You're not always here. Actually, you go away a lot."

"Yes, well, about that." She hesitates and then says, "There are important reasons why I travel so much. That's when I'm off doing research."

"On what?"

"Crows. I have devoted my entire life to studying the crows, trying to learn everything I can about them, so I go wherever I have to go to find information. I've learned a great deal about them—their habits, their strengths and weaknesses, their family hierarchy, their allies and, most importantly, their enemies. Crows cover the globe. Did you know?"

He shakes his head.

"I've seen them in some pretty exotic places. But you need to know that when there is any kind of danger to you, I will always be here and, right now, I am not going anywhere. I will be here as long as you need me."

"We'll see," he says, sliding from the stool. "I have to go now."

"Okay, I understand, but,"—she goes to the stack of old books and pulls one from half way down the pile—"I want you to take this with you and read it."

"What is it?"

"Alexandria Gorham's journal," she explains. "Once you read it, you will understand much more. This will help to explain a lot of things."

"You're just going to let me take it? Isn't it valuable?"

"It is very valuable, but it belongs with you so, yes, you can take it. You can take all of the others as well, but I didn't think you'd want them this evening. Start with the journal. You can get the rest of them some other time."

As she hands it to him, he marvels at the old book with the dark green cover that has clearly seen the passage of time. "Thanks."

He shudders as a sudden surge of energy jolts through his body when he accepts the hard-covered book. He imagines it is like how an electrical shock would feel if he stuck his finger in a wall socket.

"What's wrong?" Zoey asks. "Are you okay?"

"Yes," he answers, almost breathlessly. "I'm fine." Rubbing his hands over the book's cover, he adds, "Now I have to go. My mom will be expecting me."

"Alex." Oliver finally speaks up. "I can't let you walk home alone. Come with me. I will give you a drive."

"That's not necessary. I've walked these streets all alone many times since I was a kid and I've been fine. Nothing's going to hurt me in this town."

"Remember, Alex," Zoey says. "Things are different now. Vigilance is our best weapon. Oliver will drive you."

Heading toward the door ahead of the boy, Oliver says, "Let's go, buddy. My truck's just down the block."

"Well, if you guys insist," Alex says. "But you really don't have to."

"We do, and get used to it," Oliver says.

"I can tell you right now, Oliver, I will never get used to it."

He chuckles. "I did, and once you learn to do that, it will make your life a whole lot easier. Trust me on this."

"If you say so," Alex says, following Oliver out the front door and down the cobblestone walkway that was installed some two centuries earlier. *If you say so.*

12: An invitation

"Thanks for the drive, Oliver," Alex says as he opens the truck door to get out.

Once he's out of the truck, he turns to face the man he's known almost his entire life. Oliver is tall and slender, and kind of wiry, with short chestnut-coloured hair and a beard to match. Alex doesn't think he looks like much of a protector.

"You know, I'm not really sure how to digest everything Aunt Zoey told me tonight," he says. "It's a lot."

"It is a lot." Oliver nods in agreement. "Feel free to call me anytime you need to talk."

"I will."

"And Alex," Oliver says. "I know you're probably afraid after what you just heard, but I hope you know we will do everything we can to protect you."

Alex studies the man's face, looking for any clues that might reveal anything about this person he thought he knew for all of these years, but clearly didn't. "How did you get here, Oliver?"

"What do you mean? Here with you in this situation?"

"Yes. How did you become my 'protector'?" Trying to push aside his skepticism, Alex says, "If all of this is real, and you guys seem to believe it is—"

"Oh, please understand Alex, it's real. Don't be mistaken about that," he says. "It is very real. You should believe everything Zoey told you."

"Okay, Oliver. It's real." Alex studies the man's reaction, his rigid body movements signalling just how tense the situation has become. "So, then, how did you get here?"

"It's a really long story, but like your aunt told you, fifteen years ago I was dying and the crows saved me from certain death."

"Dying? How?"

"I had brain cancer." Oliver's answer is very matter of fact. "But somehow, the crows worked their magic and performed a miracle. I don't know how they did it, because the doctors had told me there was nothing they could do for me, but the crows cured the cancer and, I am happy to say, it has never come back. After that, I had this special connection with them. It was like I knew what they wanted me to do without them telling me. I know it sounds strange, far-fetched, but that's how it happened."

"I understand what you're saying about the crows." Alex nods. "I have that same kind of connection to Augustus."

"Augustus? Who is that?"

"He's a crow. A big crow, and he's their leader." Alex takes a breath and explains. "He showed up at my window one day many years ago and we connected right away. I can't explain it, but he has been with me ever since and now, after all these years, it's like I can hear everything he's thinking. I don't how it happens. It just does."

"Zoey has told me about your abilities," Oliver says. "And of course, I've seen things over the years, but I've never questioned them. I know that, when it comes to the crows, you just accept whatever happens."

They study each other. They suddenly feel closer than they've ever felt.

Alex considers telling Oliver about the mysterious note he received earlier today, and about the man he saw lurking outside the house. However, even though he knows he probably should tell him everything, he decides not to. He's not quite there yet.

"Well," he finally says. "I guess I should go in and face all of the questions."

"Your mother means no harm, Alex. She's only worried about you," Oliver tells him. "I know she loves you very much."

"I know she does and I'm thankful she's in my life." Alex pushes open the truck door further. "I guess I will see you soon."

"Good night, Alex. Call me if you need anything." He quickly adds, "And I mean any time."

Oliver smiles and Alex suddenly feels safe in his presence, more so than ever before or around anyone else that he can remember. He can't explain the feelings but he is glad to know Oliver is on his side.

He closes the truck door and watches as Oliver drives away.

Don't know why, but I suddenly like him a whole lot more than I did a few hours ago, he thinks, darting up the front steps.

Inside, he finds Samantha in the living room, on the sofa. "Hi, Mom," he says, telling himself to remain calm no matter what she asks.

"Hi, Alex," she answers, glancing up from a report she's been trying to read all evening, even though her mind wasn't on it. "Was that Oliver Lewis who just dropped you off?"

"It was. I was walking home after I left Aunt Zoey's when he stopped and offered me a ride," Alex tells her. "Since it was getting close to nine, I took him up on the offer because I didn't want to be late. I hope that's okay. I knew you and Kate would trust him."

Samantha knows her son is lying, as Cliff told her that Oliver was at Zoey's house all evening. "Wasn't that nice of him," she says.

"It was." Alex smiles and takes a seat next to her on the sofa. He hates lying to his mother but he knows that if he tells her they were all at the house for the past few hours there will be lots of questions. "I like him," he adds. "You've known him a long time, haven't you?"

"I have." His mother nods. "For many years. I like him too."

"How did you meet him?"

"Through Kate, actually," she answers, putting the report aside. "Your Uncle Charlie and Oliver have been very good friends for a very long time. He's a good guy. He's kind of like one of the family."

"Seems like it." Alex agrees and smiles. "Were you waiting for me?"

"I was but I was also waiting to hear from Kate."

"What's going on with Kate?" Alex asks, happy to change the subject.

"She had some car trouble on her way home from Halifax and

had to call CAA."

"Is everything okay?"

"It is. CAA came and dealt with it. Didn't turn out to be anything serious, so she's driving it back to town. It will go into the garage on Tuesday." Glancing at her watch, Samantha sighs heavily. "She should be home just about now."

"I'm sure she'll be pulling into the yard any minute."

"I hope so." She studies her son and then, while trying to remain calm, asks, "So, how did things go with your aunt? What did she have to say?"

"Everything was fine, I guess." He sighs, thinking she's about to launch into a long spiel about his aunt. He's not ready to have it out with her this evening. His mind is still reeling from everything he heard earlier. He needs time to put it all into perspective.

"Fine? You guess?"

"Yeah." He nods. "I mean, it wasn't anything special. We just kind of got caught up since she had been away for a long time. She told me about her vacation and stuff like that."

"I see. And nothing else? Wasn't she going to discuss your family background with you, or something like that?"

"We talked a bit about that, but she said she was tired after her travels and didn't want to get into it too much because it would take a while. She said we'd do that another time, after she was rested and we won't have to rush through it."

"You were there a long time to just be talking about her travels."

"I guess." Alex smiles, hoping she'll drop the subject.

Nodding toward the old book resting on her son's lap, Samantha asks, "What you got there?"

"Aunt Zoey gave it to me to read. It's all about my family's past. She said if I want to learn about my family, I should read this before we talk again."

"Well that sounds interesting. Can I read it after you're done?"

"I guess."

"You guess? Is it a secret?"

"No. I mean, yes, you can read it when I'm finished with it." He hates it when she trips him up like she's just done right there.

"Aunt Zoey says it's all about my ancestor, Alexandria Gorham."

"Sounds interesting. I've heard stories about her." Studying her son, she asks, "Alex, are you okay? Please be honest with me."

"Yes, Mom," he answers, resisting the urge to tell her to stop asking so many questions. He adds, "I am fine. I really am. I had a nice evening catching up with my aunt and that is all that happened."

"Okay, Alex. If you say so."

"I say so." He slides closer to her and gives her a hug. "I appreciate that you're only asking because you are concerned for me, but everything is okay."

Returning the hug, she says, "I just want you to be safe, Alex. That is my number one concern right now."

She wants to confront him about lying to her, but she stops herself. *This is not the time*, she thinks.

"I know Mom, and I am okay." He pulls away. "Now, if you don't mind, I'd like to go upstairs. I told Bree I would give her a call when I got home."

"Sure, Alex. Go ahead and talk to Bree. Tell her I'll see her soon."

"Okay. Let me know if you hear anything about Kate," he says, while starting up the stairs.

"Oh, Alex, I almost forgot. Ozzie's dad called earlier. He wanted to invite us all over for a family barbecue to celebrate July 1 on Monday. He's having a little get together and thought we might enjoy it. Wasn't that nice of him? He said he should have the pool open by then, so if it's hot, we'll all be able to go for a swim."

"What did you tell him?"

"I thanked him for the invitation, of course, and told him that as far I knew we didn't have any plans, but I would have to talk to you and Kate and then let him know. So, what do you think? Should we go?"

"If you want to. I know these things are important to you, as the mayor, I mean."

"Not as important as you. What's wrong? Don't you want to go? I thought you would enjoy spending time with Ozzie. Something happen between you two?"

"No. We're good."

"What, then? I thought you'd be happy about this, especially with the pool."

"It's just that there's something about Ozzie's dad that rubs me the wrong way."

"How do you mean?"

"I don't know. I just get a weird vibe whenever I'm around him." Alex pauses and then adds, "I can't explain it, but he's a little off."

"I've never noticed anything."

"Must just be me, then."

"No, Alex. If you're going to be uncomfortable, then we won't go. I'll just tell him I'm busy with council stuff and that will be the end of that."

"No, Mom. It's okay," he insists. "See what Kate says, then we can decide."

"Fine. We'll discuss it again." She smiles at him. "Now, don't keep Bree waiting."

She knows I was lying to her, doesn't she? He thinks as he flops onto his bed. *Of course, she does. She knows everything, damn it. She didn't buy anything I said about Oliver and Aunt Zoey. How does she do that?*

Even though it's almost nine-thirty, Bree made him promise he'd call when he got home, so he finds her number on his phone and hits *talk*.

"Hey, Alex." She answers on the first ring.

"Hey, Bree. You must have been sitting on your phone." He chuckles. "I don't think it even had chance to ring."

"I was waiting for your call. So, how did it go? Tell me everything. Was your aunt nice?" Bree fires her questions at him and adds, "I find her kind of weird, but not necessarily in a bad way. In a fun and quirky kind of way."

"It was fine, I guess. But I'm not really sure." He likes how Bree gets right to the point. "Aunt Zoey told me all kinds of weird things about me and my family, stuff that I'd never heard before. It's a lot to digest."

"What kind of stuff? Can you tell me about it?"

"I will, but not right now. I have to wrap my head around it before I can share it with anyone else, but I can tell you it has to do with the crows and our family and some kind of special bond we have that goes way back in time. It all sounds very fantastic to me, but Aunt Zoey insists everything she told me was true. She did share some interesting stuff, as well, about my ancestor Alexandria Gorham."

"You told me before that you thought you were somehow connected to that witch," Bree says.

"Well, it seems I am a direct descendant of hers, and we don't know that she was witch. All of that stuff that we heard as kids could just be stories."

"No shit?"

"Apparently not. Aunt Zoey even gave me a really old book that she says is Alexandria Gorham's personal journal. She said if I read that, it will tell me everything I need to know about her."

"Interesting."

"I guess, but I'll know more about her once I read the book."

"Can I see it?"

"Sure. I don't see why not. I'll show it to you the next time you come over. It's very old, so we have to be really careful with it."

"I can't wait." He can feel her excitement even over the phone. "I love this kind of stuff. It's all so mysterious."

"I know you do. So, let me ask you a question. Mom just told me that Ozzie's dad invited the whole family over to their place for a barbecue on July 1. Did he invite you guys?"

"I don't think so. Mom never said anything, but I'll ask her later. Why? I think that sounds nice. They have a pool, you know."

"I do know that." He chuckles. "I've been to Ozzie's house before and we've actually been in the pool, remember?"

"Duh, of course I remember." She laughs. "Don't you want to go? Ozzie's our friend and it sounds like fun. I love summer barbecues."

"It's not him." Alex exhales. "It's his dad. I can't really explain it, but there's something I don't like about him. I've never really felt comfortable around him, so I'd feel better if you were going to be there, too."

"Well, maybe he'll call and invite us."

"Hope so." Alex sighs. "Well, it's getting late, Bree, and it has been a really long day. I think I want to go to bed."

"Okay, Alex, but one more thing." He knows what's coming. "Did you tell your mother about the note on your door? Please tell me you did."

He exhales again and says, "I was going to, but then we got distracted by other things."

"Alex." He detects the urgency in her voice. "You can't keep that from her. It's very serious."

"I know and I will tell her tomorrow, but there was just so much going on today that I didn't have a chance."

"Promise me that you will tell your mom," she insists.

"Yes, Bree. I promise I will tell her first thing in the morning. Okay? Are you happy now?"

"It's not that I'm happy, Alex, it's that I'm relieved because I'm worried about you. You have to take this more seriously. I hope I'll see you tomorrow?"

"I hope so too." He smiles.

She pauses, then says, "Since tomorrow is Saturday, why don't we go hang at Pine Grove for a while? We haven't done that for ages."

He considers her suggestion. "Okay, that sounds nice. What time?"

"I'll swing by before lunch and meet you," she suggests. "How about around eleven?"

"Okay, sounds good. I will be ready. Are you going to invite Ozzie?"

"I probably should, don't you think?"

"I guess so."

"Okay," she agrees. "I'll shoot him a text when we get off the phone. Bye, Alex. See you tomorrow."

"See you tomorrow."

Pressing the talk button to end the conversation, Alex sighs. *Sooner or later, Alex, you have to tell her exactly how you feel about her. But what if she doesn't feel the same way? Then you might ruin your friendship.*

Moving to the desk to plug his phone into the charger, he glances out his window. In the early summer moonlight under the open sky, he catches the glimpse of a figure near the same spot where he saw the man earlier today.

"Fuck," he says aloud. "Fuck, fuck, fuck."

He quickly closes the blind and then the curtains. He shudders when he thinks about what his aunt told him. *Who in the fucking hell are you? What do you want?*

Hurrying back to his bed, he turns off the lamp. It was only a quick glimpse but he is certain there was a man out there and it's freaking him out.

I should tell Mom. No. She'll lose it and that won't be helpful. Holy hell, what should I do?

Looking for Oliver's number, he's about to press *talk*, then thinks again. *Maybe I'm seeing things. Maybe all of this talk about danger and needing a protector has made me paranoid.*

Returning to the window, he slowly pulls the curtain back, opens the blind just a crack and peers through. He sees nothing.

Fuck. What the hell? He is relieved, but confused at the same time. Now he isn't sure if he really saw someone outside.

Maybe not.

He returns to the bed and, even though he knows Oliver and his Aunt Zoey stressed that they now have to be vigilant because of what she's seen in her vision, he decides to wait before telling anyone. He needs to be sure about this before he turns his world upside down.

But first thing tomorrow, Oliver is going to hear about this and about the note. If he's my protector, he should know.

13: A murder of crows

The flock grows restless. There is suddenly great turmoil in their midst.

One of the elders is missing. The older bird went scrounging for food this afternoon and failed to return.

The Seven can sense that something foul is afoot.

They smell it. It hangs in the air.

Danger.

She's back, and even though she is one of the long chain of guardians, they wish she would have stayed away. Her return means danger is close.

They know that whenever she's around, their world tips and goes off kilter.

They don't expect anything to be different this time.

We can protect the boy.

Their thoughts are linked. They are one.

But they feel something is different this time.

They sense that a new threat has come, something dark. Something ominous.

The 'others' have returned after all of this time and they threaten the boy, the chosen one.

He must not be harmed.

They will protect him...at all cost.

~

Jesus. What time is it? Alex wonders, flopping around in his bed. Sliding out of bed and planting his feet on the hardwood floor, he knows it is still very early in the morning.

He makes his way to his desk and retrieves his fully-charged phone. The screen lights up. *2:47 a.m.* it glares at him.

Shit. So much for sleeping late on a Saturday. I'll never be able to get back to sleep, so what the hell am I supposed to do now?

"Are you out there, you fucker?" he whispers, making his way to the window and pulling the blind apart. Making a small crack just large enough to look through, he presses forward and peers outside.

The front yard is well lit as it basks in the glow of bright moonlight.

No one. He sighs heavily. *Thank Christ. But at least you're there, aren't you?*

Under the bright moonlight, Alex can see the crows perched on the branches of the trees that border the front yard. The black birds remain still, almost like statues, sentinels standing duty, the bright moonlight glistening off their sleek, black feathers.

"I'm happy to see you guys," he says.

Quickly counting the crows, he adds, "Seven."

He knows that when there are seven, his friend Augustus is with the flock. He knows the others will protect him, but he feels safest when the leader is near.

"Thank you, my friend, for being here."

The crows remain still, as if they are frozen in place.

Letting go of the blind, Alex backs away from the window, feeling a little more at ease in knowing that the crows are outside. He knows they will remain in their place as long as they sense a threat.

Spying the book that his aunt had given him on the desk, he picks it up and returns to his bed. *This will help me pass some time*, he thinks.

Rubbing his hands over the dark green cover, he suddenly feels connected to his past and his destiny, in a way he has never felt before.

Alexandria's Secret

XIV: The New World

I was a slender, freckle-faced girl of eleven when we set sail from England in the late spring of 1760, just as soon as the winter winds stopped blowing and the ice retreated from the channels.

"We are going on an adventure unlike anything you have ever experienced before," Papa told me. He was so proud and happy for the family. He also told me it would be nothing like any place I could ever imagine.

Papa said our destination was the New World, where we would start a new life filled with riches and bounty beyond our wildest imaginations and our grandest dreams.

I didn't know much about this place to where we were headed, but I believed Papa when he said we would never again have to buckle to the will of the aristocrats, those powerful and rich men who looked down their noses at us as though we were inferior beings. And their wives and children, well, let's just say they were the worst kind of snobbery one could ever encounter.

In the social construct of old England ruled by King George II, we were considered less than third-class citizens and were relegated to the poverty-stricken, rat-infested and disease-riddled quarters of the city. Although I may have been a child at the time, I was old enough to understand that class and wealth can create a great divide between men who should be considered equal in the eyes of their Creator.

I saw those powerful merchants, and politicians with money and influence, grind the weak and destitute under their thumbs and I vowed that I would never become a victim to such oppression. I would never be a slave to the rich and powerful, nor would I ever subject another human being to such atrocities.

My father, Benjamin Gorham, was a blacksmith by trade, and he laboured on the docks from the time he was orphaned as a young boy of twelve until he could break free of the chains of poverty that had bound him to his lowly existence. Somehow, he found a way to take control of his destiny and, in time, he became the man he had always dreamed of being.

He met Martha Sinclair in Liverpool on the River Mersey when she was fifteen and was assisting the parish ministry with aid to the poor. He said he fell in love with her the instant he laid his eyes upon her fiery red hair and emerald green eyes. He knew in that moment that he would have her as his wife and, even though their worlds were far apart, their love eventually found a way.

Papa always said that, with the same colour hair and eyes, I was the spitting image of Mama, and I considered that the ultimate compliment, as she was the bravest and strongest woman I have ever known. Kind and caring, she was the true embodiment of all that is beautiful in this world.

Eventually, after overcoming the many obstacles that had conspired to keep them apart, they married, had children and tried to provide us all with a good life. But these were difficult times, filled with struggles beyond compare.

Miraculously, we survived and, through the course of time, Papa and Mama found a way to escape the oppression that existed under the King's rule. Somehow, mercifully, they managed to scrape together sufficient funds to buy passage on one of the newly-built military vessels heading to the Colonies. It would be a one-way voyage.

I remember well the day we left. The fog was as dense as pea soup and the light mist that hung in the air was thick with the smell of salt. The sun had not fully risen as we made our way to the docks and the dampness clung to our outer garments as if it were an additional layer.

"Bring only the things you can carry," Papa had told us, since he had been told there would be limited room on board the ship.

We carried little with us except clothing and some provisions for the voyage, and Mama carried a black, leather-bound Bible. It was the King James Version and she had it with her always.

There were six of us in total making the voyage. Papa, Mama, my three brothers and I set sail from Hull, England on *H.M.S. Rose*. Built in 1757, she was a fine navy frigate used to scout the coastline of hostile countries. Sleek and quick, *The Rose* soon became legendary for her exploits along the coasts of the Americas, and she was our bridge to this new life that Papa so coveted.

While civilian passage was, on occasion, allowed on such vessels, it was not a routine practice and could only happen if the ship's captain allowed it. Fortunately, Papa knew James Wallace, the captain of *The Rose*, and it was with his good graces that we boarded his ship with our meagre belongings on the morning of May 21, 1760.

Papa never did tell us how he knew Captain Wallace, and even though Mama coaxed him many times to explain how it was possible that he secured our passage on one of the most impressive vessels in His Majesty's navy, he refused to tell her.

"Captain Wallace owed me a debt for something I did for him when we were both in our youth," was the only explanation Papa would provide, or at least the only one to which we youngsters were privy.

What that favour was, we never did find out. Papa took that secret to the grave with him. Even on his death bed, as he lay drawing his last breath, he would not confide it to anyone, so we can only assume this secret had dark undertones. But we shall never know.

Papa was a proud and God-fearing man, so it is safe to assume that, if he would not tell us, then it must have been a serious debt. I also conclude that whatever favour Papa had been required to perform on behalf of Captain Wallace to earn the privilege of sailing on *The Rose* must have come with a steep price.

I believed it must have been something illegal, but I dared not share my theory with anyone. I feared that if, indeed, Papa had done something against the law on behalf of Captain Wallace and the truth were ever revealed, he would most assuredly have been hanged, for justice was harsh and unforgiving in my time.

We did not know much about where we were headed in this New World, but Papa said we were going to some place named Halifax. "I heard the other men on the docks talking about this place and learned that, if we could reach this destination, we would get a fresh start. It was a place where all men are equal and are treated with kindness and dignity," he said. Papa believed it was the answer to all his prayers and aspirations.

All I knew about Halifax was that it was founded in 1749 and was under the command of Governor Edward Cornwallis, whoever he was. I heard some of the crewmen talking during the voyage and, while I later learned the truth about this so-called great man, the sailors said Governor Cornwallis was powerful and that, someday, this place called Halifax would be an important city in the Commonwealth.

I could only imagine what they were envisioning because, as a girl of eleven, I could not fully comprehend the things about which they were speaking, but there we were on a ship heading to this place carved out of the wilderness.

Although *The Rose* was bound to the New England Colonies, as part of the deal with Papa, Captain Wallace agreed to stop at Halifax for one night to allow his civilian passengers to disembark. After that, I had no idea where we were headed and Papa said we would learn more about that upon our arrival.

It was barely breaking dawn when we left port and I was nervous about what lay ahead. I had never before been on a ship and the idea that I would never again see my home made me weep.

"Be brave, young one," Papa told me on that day. "Think about this voyage as an adventure and as a new beginning for the entire family."

Indeed, it was that. It was all of that and then some.

XV: First contact

Although *The Rose* was designed for speed, it still took almost two and a half months for her to sail across the Atlantic Ocean. We weathered several storms during the voyage and ran into many hardships, including disease and near starvation as rations were limited and quarters below deck were tight and poorly ventilated.

There were four of us born to Benjamin and Martha Gorham. Their firstborn, Jonathan, was a month shy of his sixteenth birthday when we set sail from England. Samuel was thirteen months his junior, followed by Seth a year after that; and then there was me, Alexandria.

Mama said I was named after her mother, another great woman who devoted her entire life seeing to the needs of those who suffered in this world from the ravages of war, poverty, starvation and disease. I never knew my grandmother, but Mama said she would have loved me and, in turn, she is certain I would have returned the affection, because she could see my grandmother's example shining through in my kind words and actions.

Mama took great care of her children, nurturing and loving her offspring much like a mother bird does with her chicks. She was kind, tender and always forgiving with never a scolding word for us. In turn, we gave her our unconditional love and affection.

We did not attend school, as in that era formal institution was reserved for the rich and people of influence, neither of which described us. But we were not lacking for an education, as Mama taught us well. We learned to read and write under her tutelage and we studied the Bible with reverence.

The boys learned to use their hands by working the trades with Papa, and I learned the necessities of maintaining a home from Mama. I considered us to be well-rounded and perfectly suited to making our way in this New World.

We were at sea no more than two weeks when the first storm struck. It tossed *The Rose* around as if she were one of the toy boats that Papa used to fashion out of wood scraps that he gathered at the barrel factories down on the docks. With great skill and delicate hands, he made us each one, and when we were still young children we would spend many hours playing with the boats in the brooks and streams that ran near the shack where we lived back in England.

We'd pretend that our boats were part of the King's navy and they'd be engaged in fierce battles with the enemies or fighting the elements on the high seas. Never did we think that, in time, we would actually be on one of His Majesty's ships as the captain struggled to keep us from being swamped by the massive waves that sometimes reached heights taller than the biggest buildings in England.

I had never before seen a storm of such magnitude, but somehow *The Rose* managed to stay afloat. The crew said it was a testament to the ship's design and structure, and to the skilful captain. I considered it either to be good fortune or God's grace, for at the height of the storm I prayed like I had never prayed before. When the seas finally calmed and the dark clouds parted to make way for the sun, I remember thinking that there before us was the hand of God. It was breathtaking and an awe-inspiring sight to behold. The beauty was so heavenly that it made my knees grow weak.

We encountered three similar storms during our journey, but miraculously not a single deck hand was lost during the tumultuous hours, even though *The Rose* was battered like a plaything. However, where one natural phenomenon failed to claim a victim, another had much more success.

We had been warned that trans-Atlantic voyages could be long and arduous. We were told they can be costly in terms of human life, for if one were to fall sick out on the high seas, there was little that could be done to save you. Three members of the crew fell to the scourge that struck about a month after we set sail.

Mama said it was God's way to weed out the weak and frail, but after my brother Samuel became bedridden with the fever and chills, I could see that she feared her words had been a prophecy. She stayed at Samuel's side throughout the day and long night, tending to his every need and trying to coax him to drink water, but four days after he fell to the sickness, he drew his last breath.

Samuel's death caused in me the deepest, most heart-wrenching pain I had ever experienced, and I felt a part of me had died with him. Papa said it was natural to feel that way, but he said that, even though we suffer with great sadness when we lose someone we love, death awaits us all, and that death is the natural destination to which we all arrive.

"It is the natural order of things," he said, in trying to console me in these darkest of times that brought such immense grief for our family. "Some, like your brother, complete their journey quicker than others, but someday we will all reach the Promised Land where we will rejoice and bask in His glory."

That may have been the natural order of things, but it was difficult for a child such as I to comprehend and come to terms with. But Samuel was gone and I had to accept his passing.

As the crew had done for those of their company who had died, we wrapped Samuel's body in heavy linens, secured it with rope, and disposed of it into the sea.

Mama never fully recovered from Samuel's death. It was clear that she felt guilty for mocking God's will and that she felt Samuel's death was His retribution for her sins.

But I'm not sure I believed such a thing, for I could not accept that God was such a vengeful entity that He would take a young boy as some sort of response to a few words uttered by a mother to appease her troubled child. Instead, I chose to believe that Samuel's body simply could not tolerate the strain of the journey and, once he became ill, he could not fight off the infection.

Whatever the reason, it was clear that God had a plan and, as Papa said, what was meant to be was simply meant to be. It was not our place to question His wisdom. Our penance was to accept that Samuel's time on Earth was done. God had called him to His flock and now we were down to five.

Mama mostly remained confined in the lower quarters for the remainder of the voyage, while Papa, Jonathan and Seth assisted the crew where possible. With three crew members having succumbed to the same illness that claimed Samuel, their hands were needed to keep the ship on course and on schedule.

There wasn't much I could do, or at least that's what all the men told me, so I spent the days exploring the ship and tending to Mama's needs. Many of my hours were also taken up observing the actions of the wonderful and unusual sea creatures that often swam beside the ship, but it was the birds that provided me with the most comfort and enjoyment.

Their graceful and majestic maneuvers as they swooped and glided on the cool air currents with great agility and skill provided me many hours of pleasure. I was fascinated to watch from my perch on the deck. Their powerful wings were built for endurance and speed, and I often found myself fantasizing about what it would be like to be just like them and to be able to soar high over the land and sea.

What would it be like to look down upon the Earth and see what they see? I wondered, as I sat at the ship's stern for hours at a time and watched as the wonderful creatures sometimes came close to our vessel, as if investigating this strange creature that had suddenly and so rudely invaded their natural space. What do they think of us? What would they tell us or say to us if they could talk? I wondered.

My brothers teased me for taking leave of my senses. They said that fantasizing about such things proved that my intelligence had slipped with the voyage's long duration. But I didn't care what they said, and I couldn't shake the feeling that somehow the birds were attempting to communicate to me.

If my brothers thought my fantasies were an indication of the level of my sanity, then they surely would have concluded that I had totally taken leave of my senses when I began talking to the birds, but I never told them about that. As a matter of principle, I never told anyone about the first time the birds came to me.

It was one mid-afternoon, as the sun hung high in the clear blue sky and the salt spray from the waves crashing against the ship's hull splashed up onto the deck, that a large, powerful bird, with purple and black feathers so dark that they sparkled an iridescent green under the bright sunshine, landed on the railing.

Initially, I was started by its presence and I will admit that its stature intimidated me at first, but after we had stared at each other for several minutes, I found myself relaxing as I became enthralled by the bird's graceful appearance. In turn, the mysterious visitor watched me, its tiny black eyes, blinking and taking in my appearance.

While I was enamoured by the creature's sleek build, I had the distinct impression that the bird had never before seen anything quite like me with my red hair and green eyes. However, I felt that we had made a connection. But I could not explain why it was that on some level, on some plane, I felt we had established a bond.

The bird stayed until one of the crew members appeared on the stern, and it became startled by the burly man's presence. It flew away, but not before the crewman threw something at it.

As the majestic creature spread its powerful wings and soared upward into the afternoon sky, the crewman warned me that I must be more careful of such things out here on the ocean where dangers can run amok.

The crewman said that there was no way of knowing that bird's intentions and if I was not careful it might pluck the eyeballs from my head and feast upon them, but at no time was I afraid of the bird. At no time did I feel it provided any threat to my well-being.

Truth be told, I feared the crewman more than the bird, for instinct-ively I knew it meant me no harm.

Still, the man told me to take heed of his warnings and said that in the future, I must be more mindful of how close I get to such wild creatures.

While I assured him I would, indeed, take his warning very seri-ously, at no time did I ever intend to follow through with my prom-ise because, for some reason unknown to me, I knew there was noth-ing nefarious about the beautiful black bird.

Nothing, I thought, and I was sure of that.

XVI: By God's grace

It was almost the middle of August by the time we arrived in this strange new land that Papa insisted held the promise of a better life for all of us, but I was just happy to be finally setting foot on solid land once again.

It had been a long voyage from England to Halifax. It was tough going, and at times I wondered if we would reach our destination. Between Samuel's death, extreme hunger, constant seasickness and the discomfort of not being able to bathe properly, I was convinced that I must have committed some extreme sin and the trip across the tumultuous Atlantic was surely my punishment.

Papa coaxed me on during the voyage, telling me to search deep for my inner strength. However, as much as I can recall, I don't think I had ever been so happy in my entire life as I was that day when *The Rose* caught a late afternoon breeze, rounded the point, and sailed into what we were told was Chibouctou Harbour on the rising tide.

Papa was happy, too, probably the happiest I had ever seen him before or since our arrival. His excitement rushed to the surface as we all crowded along the ship's railings so that we could catch a glimpse of this wondrous place that had lured us from our homeland.

Noticing as I struggled to gain a clear vantage point, Papa bent down and picked me up, something he rarely did. He was not a man of outright affection, and such physical contact was rare, indeed, and certainly out of character for him.

"My dear Alexandria," he beamed, hoisting me onto his broad shoulders so that I could get a clear and unobscured view of the burgeoning settlement being carved from the wilderness along the shore of the harbour. "You must see this, my child, as it is the beginning of something wondrous that will someday become the place of great men and great structures."

I will admit it did not look like much to me, nothing more than a settlement of rudely constructed huts and tents, but everyone else on board *The Rose* seemed to think we had arrived in paradise, so I reserved my judgment, thinking it best that I keep such opinions to myself. After all, what did adults want of a child's opinions, and from a female, what's more?

"Welcome to Halifax," Papa declared. He was positively glowing with happiness. "Here is our future. Here is our new life. Are you happy to finally be here?"

"Yes, Papa," I answered with as much enthusiasm as I could muster, considering my weak body and weary mind. "I am extremely happy that we have finally reached our destination."

That much was certainly true.

"But," I queried, "who is General Edward Cornwallis? Will we get to meet him?"

"I hardly think so, my dear girl," Papa quickly answered. "He has long since left this place and gone on to serve the King in other areas of the Empire. How did you hear of General Cornwallis?"

"I overheard some of the crewmen talking about him," I told Papa. "They said he is a great man, maybe the greatest soldier in His Majesty's army."

"Oh," Papa responded, speaking in a softer tone for fear that a crew member might overhear his words. "I hardly think he is all that. There are many who would dispute such a claim."

"Is he important?"

"I suppose he is," Papa said, thoughtfully. He then added, "The government appointed General Cornwallis as Governor of Nova Scotia with the task of establishing a new British settlement, so that makes him important."

"What is Nova Scotia?" I asked.

"This," Papa said, sweeping his hands before his body. "All of this is Nova Scotia."

"But I thought this was Halifax." I was so naïve at that age.

He chuckled. "My dear child," he said, "Halifax is the settlement, and it is located in the new land known as Nova Scotia, much like the city of London is located in the country of England."

"Does Nova Scotia have a king?"

"Indeed. George II is also the king of Nova Scotia," he told me. "We are still loyal, British subjects. You must never forget that, Alexandria. Even though we are in a new world, it is still part of the Empire, and we must still observe the King's laws. Do you understand?"

When I didn't answer, he asked again.

"Do you understand?" he asked, his voice and disposition much sterner than the previous time. "We must respect the crown. Do not forget that, my girl."

"Yes, Papa," I quickly answered. "I do understand."

"Good," he replied, his voice now much softer.

After that, our conversation abated. We stood silently on deck, along with Mama and Jonathan and Seth, as *The Rose* glided through the harbour's choppy waters with grace and precision while Captain Wallace stood on the bridge barking commands to his crew.

With great ease and much precision, he brought the beautiful vessel safely to dock side, and then joined us at the bow as the crew began to secure the ship with ropes. It seemed to me that they were all very skilled at their trades.

"Well, Gorhams," the captain said. "We have arrived. As promised, I have delivered you to your destination, albeit one fewer than I had hoped."

"Thank you, Captain," Papa responded. "Your kindness and seamanship have been greatly appreciated throughout our journey."

"Take fair warning, Benjamin Gorham," Captain Wallace said, his voice heavy and dark, dripping with seriousness. It was as if he was about to deliver some grave news and I shuddered at such prospects. "You may have safely reached your destination, but you must be aware that this is largely an uncivilized land, still wild and waiting to be tamed. You will be wise to step carefully and take good care to watch your backs."

"Indeed," Papa answered, but he did not outwardly show any apprehension about the captain's dire warning.

I, on the other hand, was not so sure about this. Were it up to me, I might have chosen to remain onboard *The Rose* and journeyed with her to Massachusetts, but the decision was not mine to take.

"What do you know of this place, Captain?" Papa asked.

With a steely expression such as you might expect from a seasoned seaman, Captain Wallace explained there was much unrest in Halifax. "Upon his arrival in 1749, Cornwallis was faced with a difficult decision, that being where to site the town. Back in London, planners had ordered the settlement to be located closer to the mouth of the harbour, for close access to the ocean and ease of defence. But the general and his naval advisors had other ideas, which did not sit so well with those back in England. Cornwallis opposed the recommended site due to its lack of shelter and shallow water, which he believed would not allow ocean-going ships to dock safely. He wanted the town located at the head of the basin, where there was sheltered land and deep water for the King's vessels. Still others favoured the other side of the harbour altogether."

"So, what happened?" Papa asked.

"Cornwallis chose the location of his preference and ordered the settlers to lay down foundations halfway up the harbour, in this area that is protected by a defensible hill and where there is deep water. However," Captain Wallace said, "let us just say that the decision has been met with much skepticism back in England. But Cornwallis is his own man, and so here is Halifax."

Noting the growing settlement spreading out along the shore and up the rolling hillside, Papa said, "Looks like an inviting place."

"Do not be fooled by first impressions, Benjamin Gorham," the Captain replied, and I could see his right eyebrow rise and fall along with the ominous words.

"Duly noted, Captain," Papa answered.

"Once the lines are secured, sir, you and your family may disembark at your pleasure. Please ensure to remove all your belongings directly, as we will not be long in this port. We sail with the morning's tide and it is doubtful that you shall ever see *The Rose* again."

"Very well, Captain." Papa nodded as Captain Wallace turned and headed to his cabin. "And, sir, thank you for the passage."

"Your gratitude is duly noted," the Captain replied without turning. "But it may be hasty and misplaced, for I am not sure that I have done you much favour in bringing you and your family to this wild place. But may you go with God's grace and with his Majesty's blessing."

XVII: Monsters in your head

As soon as the deckhands lowered the gangplank and gave us the all-clear sign, we gathered up our things, which admittedly weren't much, and disembarked. For as many challenges the voyage had thrown at us, I was still sad to be leaving the vessel that had been my home for more than two months, but Papa told me to be brave as the end to our long journey was near.

Once we left *The Rose* that afternoon, we never did return to the ship, and we never again saw Captain James Wallace. He and his crew sailed away the next morning into the fog, leaving us behind in this vastly uninhabited and wild land, essentially severing our last and most tangible link to England.

Even though we were relegated to sleeping in a small warehouse on the edge of the docks that night, Papa remained optimistic that we would be fine, and he kept telling us that we were heading off to a great adventure. While I tried hard to temper my fears and anxiety, I will admit that I felt trapped in this strange place, and the unknown seemed like a great monster. The sights and sounds and even the smells were foreign to me.

"There is no need to be afraid," Mama told me that night as we huddled together for warmth on some makeshift beds that the dock crews sometimes use when they do watch duty. Fortunately, Papa had found a foreman who was most generous in letting us stay the night or else we would have been forced to sleep under the stars for we did not have the means to pay for lodging. It was still only mid-August but the cool, damp air blowing in off the Atlantic made for a most uncomfortable night.

"We must have faith in your papa that he is leading us to a place filled with great opportunity. The only thing that matters," Mama whispered, as she pulled the old wool blanket, worn thin from years of use, up around my chin, "is that we are together as a family."

"Yes, Mama," I whispered back. "But are you not afraid of the creatures and monsters that exist here? I hear they are unlike anything we ever saw back in England."

She chuckled softly. "My dear child," she said, her voice soft and soothing, "you have such a vivid imagination for one so young. That imagination may serve you well someday, but for the present you would do well to keep it in reserve, for the only monsters that exist in our world are those that dwell in your head."

I did not believe what Mama said, and I could sense that she did not believe it either, but I did not challenge her. I understood that her words were meant to sooth the worries of her only daughter.

Although I remained timid of the unknown, somehow I did manage to sleep that night, and when I awoke early the next morning, I overheard Mama and Papa discussing the next leg of our journey.

Situated behind a pile of crates as they were, I believed they did not want us children to overhear their conversation, but I strained my ears so that I could listen regardless.

"Do we have sufficient funds to pay for passage for the entire family?" Mama asked. "The captain does know there are five in our party, does he not?"

"He does for sure and, regrettably, no," Papa told her. "We are short sufficient fare to cover the entire expense."

"How much are we short?" she asked him, keeping her voice to a whisper.

"The captain says he can take four of us with what we can pay," he said, and I could hear the sadness in his voice.

"Oh, Benjamin," Mama cried. "Whatever shall we do? We cannot leave anyone behind."

"I do not know, Martha," Papa said.

I could not swear to it but I do believe at this point that Papa was crying. I had never seen him cry, so, in my thinking this confirmed the seriousness of this matter.

"But," he added, "we are not leaving anyone behind. However, we must get to Port Rossignol, for that is where I am to meet Jabez."

"Are you even certain that Jabez will be in this Port Rossignol?"

"I do believe so," Papa answered. "Granted, it is almost a year hence since I heard from him, but according to the last correspondence I did receive, Jabez was to leave Massachusetts in the spring of this year, so he should now be well ensconced within the settlement."

I didn't know much about this Jabez of whom Papa spoke, but before we left on this adventure Papa had told us that he had a cousin named Jabez Gorham who lived in Plymouth, Massachusetts, and who had full intentions of relocating with his wife and children to Nova Scotia. Here, he had told Papa, they could amass great riches in retail, trading and merchandising.

Granted, as a blacksmith, Papa didn't know much about being a merchant, but he insisted this was our passage to the better life that he envisioned for us all. It had been a leap of faith, but Papa decided to take up his cousin's offer. They had agreed to meet in Port Rossignol by the end of this current summer, which was growing near with each passing day.

So here we were in Halifax, bargaining for passage on the fishing schooner that would transport us to this strange place that was to be our new home. From the dock foreman, Papa had learned that there was a fleet of thirteen schooners from Port Rossignol here in Halifax, but he discovered that only one had room to take our family of five.

"What shall we do?" Mama sobbed. "It is getting late into the season and soon the winds of autumn will be upon this place. We have no permanent shelter or supplies, and insufficient funds to reach our destination. I do believe our predicament is grave."

"I fear your assessment is accurate," Papa agreed. "But there must be a way."

"How?" she cried.

"I shall return to the wharves and discuss our situation with the captain of this schooner," Papa said. "Surely, I can impress upon him the urgency we face, and perhaps we can reach an agreement of some sort. Rest easy, my dear wife, for I am certain everything will be fine."

It was clear from where I lay that Papa was saying whatever he could to ease Mama's worries, but I am certain she wasn't accepting it.

"I pray that you are correct," she said, as he made ready to leave. "What shall I tell the children when they awake?"

"Tell them to be ready, because we will sail this afternoon," he answered. "And Martha," he whispered, "trust me."

"Very well, Benjamin," she said as he left the warehouse. "Indeed, I most surely do trust you."

I cannot say exactly how long it was until Papa's return, but I lay in my spot until I heard my brothers moving about. Then I pretended they had awoken me, thus completing my ruse.

When we were ready to eat, we found that, by using what was left of our rations, Mama had prepared for us a light breakfast of something called hardtack, which essentially was a type of hard cracker, and cold beans.

This is what they had served us on *The Rose*, but truthfully, I didn't care much for it. However, considering the constant state of hunger from which I suffered, and appreciating that there were no other choices available, I did not complain about the food. Instead, I remained deeply thankful for every morsel I put into my mouth.

No sooner had we started our meal, then Papa returned and joined us, although he did not eat but little bites. While he tried to put on a brave façade, I could tell he was greatly bothered and, knowing of the burden he was carrying, I could conclude that he was not able to resolve this pressing matter to his satisfaction.

Finally, after swallowing hard and maintaining steady eye contact with Mama, he spoke. "We are to be on the wharf in the early noon, as the ship will sail by mid-afternoon," he announced.

"All the arrangements have been secured then?" Mama asked.

"Indeed, they have."

"How?" she asked again. "How have you arranged for the passage of five?"

"The captain and I have struck a bargain," he whispered, casting his eyes downward, as was often his practice when he was attempting to avoid Mama's glare, for he knew she could see him clearly.

"I am not sure I want to hear this in front of the children," she replied.

"I did what had to be done," Papa said.

"And what was that?"

"The schooner captain has agreed to provide transport for the entire family under the condition that we pay him for four passengers," Papa said.

"And what of the fifth?"

"The fifth member of our family, that being myself, can also make the journey."

"At what cost?" I could see the look of concern cross her face. This adventure had not been kind to Mama, and I could see that the idea of being in this sea captain's debt was not resting well with her. "What did you have to give him?"

Papa sighed and then broke the news. "To secure my passage, I have agreed that, once we reach Port Rossignol, I will sail as a member of his crew for one year. During that time, he will provide me with half my wages while keeping the remaining portion to be paid toward my debt. After a full year, I will be free of my burden. If I work well for him, then I may keep my job at full wages."

"Benjamin," Mama reacted as tears welled in her green eyes. "That is a steep price. What of us? What of your family? If you cannot provide a full wage to cover our expenses, then I fear we will be destitute in a strange place."

"I assure you that we will be fine," Papa told her. "It is only a year. And I will speak with Jabez once we arrive in Port Rossignol. I am sure he will agree to allow us to reside with himself and Mary until I can work this out to the satisfaction of all concerned."

"We left home to escape the shackles of poverty. We did not make this journey at great cost, so that our family could continue to live as the poor back in England," she said. "Were that going to be the case, we may as well have remained there. At least Samuel would still be alive today."

"I understand, Martha," he said. "And I am not pleased about this arrangement either. But, my dear wife, there is no other way."

"Perhaps there is, Papa," Jonathan spoke up.

"How?" Papa said. "I have thought this through, Jonathan, and this is for the best. For the family to remain intact and for all of us to sail on that schooner this afternoon, this is the only option. I see no other way."

"No, Papa," Jonathan said. "There is another way."

"How is that?"

"Allow me to take your place on the crew. I want to do this for you. Please permit me to help the family in this way. They need you at home."

"No, Jonathan," Papa quickly answered. "I cannot allow you to do that. You are still but a boy. I do not wish to burden you with such a debt at this point in your life. You are just getting started."

"You must," my brother insisted. "I am sixteen and a man. Think about it, Papa. If I work on the schooner in your stead, you will be free to pursue your other interests with Cousin Jabez and I can contribute to the family. You must agree to this. You must see this is the correct course of action."

"Benjamin," Mama spoke up. "I do not like this either, but perhaps our eldest son makes sense. He is young and strong. We know he is an excellent worker and not afraid of difficult tasks."

"It will be hard work," Papa pointed out.

"I am able to execute hard work. I did so back in England in the blacksmith shops," Jonathan replied. "And while I mean you no disrespect, Papa, I am years younger than you."

"You speak the truth, my boy." Papa slowly nodded. "But what of the dangers? Working on the open seas can be perilous."

"What isn't dangerous in this strange, new world?" Jonathan said.

It was decided, then. Jonathan was to take Papa's place.

I didn't like it, but I also didn't like the thought of Papa working on the ships. There was no easy solution.

XVIII: Welcome to Ogumkwigeok

So it was agreed. The captain would transport five passengers to Port Rossignol and receive payment for four. Jonathan would remain as a member of the crew for the next year and work to pay off Papa's debt. It was not an arrangement that sat well with Papa, but he accepted that it was truly the best—and only—option available to us.

We left Halifax on the six o'clock tide and I never returned. Whatever became of that burgeoning settlement that General Edward Cornwallis had founded, I can only imagine.

Admittedly, I know very little about sailing or the ships that roam the great bodies of water that cover much of the earth, but I believe the captain of this fishing schooner was a skilled and masterful sailor, for it seemed we made record time. Riding the waves, pushed by a steady wind, we made the voyage in less than ten hours.

None of us slept during the trip. Mama and Papa worried for Jonathan, who was receiving his first lessons in seamanship from the captain's first mate, while Seth and I marvelled at the stars and moon that we could see so clearly in the night sky. The view was breathtaking and beyond description. From our vantage point on the deck, we could also often observe this new land as we passed by, and its pristine beauty often left me breathless.

To say that we were excited about finally approaching our destination would be like saying the globe is round, for it would surely be an understatement of the obvious. And then, finally, before the sun broke over the horizon, a deckhand informed us that we would shortly be making port and I could feel the excitement quicken in my veins.

This is it, I thought as the breeze tossed my long red hair around my head and shoulders as if it were thin ribbons.

While the darkness of the early morning still clung to the land, I stood beside Papa at the bow, watching large stands of virgin timber pass us by as the schooner entered the mouth of the bay and then, veering toward the left bank, seemed to follow an invisible channel further up the river to a series of rickety wharves lined with an assortment of vessels and ships that I did not recognize. There were many docked at this place, that a crewman called Shipyard Point, and I wondered what lay beyond the docks.

"Not much," the crewman answered, his voice gruff and gravelly as if he had swallowed too much salt water from the briny ocean. "Big forests filled with tall trees and wild, savage beasts. That's about all you'll find there. You would be wise to not venture from the settlement, miss. Those woods are no place for children."

Papa was not impressed with the crewman's answer. "Do not frighten the girl," he scolded the deckhand, who limped away to carry out his duties as if he were a wounded dog.

Noting the look of worry on my face, Papa added, "Do not be afraid, Alexandria. There is nothing in this place that can harm you. I am sure that the settlement has been secured and that all beasts of a wild nature are kept at a sufficient distance."

I admit that the crewman's observations did put a scare in me, but I tried hard not to reveal my fears to Papa, for I felt he carried sufficient worry at that time. Instead, I directed my eyes around the settlement and drank in the surroundings.

Granted, there wasn't much to see beyond the docks. But for a collection of huts and buildings, which I assumed were dwellings, storehouses and warehouses, I could not say that I was overly impressed with the place. If this was the land that held so much promise, I concluded that someone had lied to us.

"What do you think, Alexandria?" Papa asked as he put his arm around me and hugged me closer. This was another unusual show of affection from Papa, but I was beginning to like it. *Indeed,* I thought, *this New World may hold promise after all.*

"It is wonderful, Papa," I lied, choosing to hide my true opinion in an effort to preserve his dreams that this was a better place than the one we had left behind.

"Indeed," he said, breathing deeply. "Smell that air," he added, exhaling with force. "It's so clean and fresh."

I did not dare to tell him that I was not yet impressed with what I was seeing, but I decided to reserve final judgment until I had a chance to explore this new place that was to be my home, and to get the measure of its people.

As the deckhands, including Jonathan, scrambled to secure the ship's lines to the dock, the captain appeared at the bow and told us we had reached our destination.

"Welcome to Ogumkwigeok," he said. To Papa he added, "Do not forget our arrangement. I will be expecting your boy the day after tomorrow, when we will set sail on our next trip. We will be gone five days."

"Understood," Papa replied.

I stared at the captain with great puzzlement in my mind until I could resist no longer. "Captain, sir," I finally interrupted as Papa threw me a scolding glare. As a child, it was not my place to interrupt the adults, but my curiosity was bursting to break free. "What is O-gu-m-k...?" I struggled to say the strange word.

"Ogumkwigeok?" The captain chuckled as he looked down at me. "That is what the original peoples call this place. We know as it as Port Rossignol or simply Rossignol, but they call it Ogumkwigeok."

"That would be a strange word," I answered. "Can you tell me what it means?"

"Aren't you a curious young lady," he said with a smile. "In their tongue, Ogumkwigeok means the place of departure."

"Be that as it may," I said, "I shall continue to call this place Port Rossignol."

"As you wish, young lady." He laughed and turned to leave.

"Now, I must be going." To Papa, he added, "This is a small settlement so I have no doubt that we will be seeing each other often."

"Indeed," Papa agreed.

XIX: Putting down roots

Once we had disembarked, it took Papa but a few minutes to locate the residence of Jabez and Mary Gorham. It seemed everyone in the small settlement knew their neighbours and were willing to provide directions to the newcomers, even though we must surely have looked like a band of hoodlums dressed in our rags and wearing weeks of filth.

Like most of the other settlers, Mr. and Mrs. Gorham fled to Port Rossignol not only to pursue their riches in the *New World*, but to also to escape the rising tide of independence that was sweeping through the thirteen Colonies. As fears of war between those seeking self-government and loyalists to the Crown continued to mount, many of the *New England Planters* decided to remove to *Nova Scotia*, where there was little or no such talk.

Finally, we had arrived and now, here we were, standing at the front entrance of the Gorham home, hoping they could provide us with food, lodging and a place to get clean.

What I knew about Papa's cousin came from the brief descriptions that he had provided prior to our departure from England. He had told us that in the *New World* his uncle, Jabez Gorham, produced a son of the same name in 1726. This man, Papa's cousin, married Mary Burbank at Plymouth, Massachusetts in 1750. Six children were born to the couple, four of whom died in infancy.

Although communication between Papa and Mr. Gorham had broken off more than a year earlier, he hoped that his cousin would still be expecting us. As we walked up the gravel path toward the front door of their modest but comfortable-looking dwelling, it was clear that we would soon find out if, indeed, the welcome mat was still out for us.

"Remember your manners," Papa warned Seth and me as he knocked on the heavy wooden door. Jonathan had stayed behind at the schooner to help unload the catch and then to assist with cleaning up the ship's hold. It was expected he would be there for several hours, and he planned to join us later at the house once his duties were complete.

"Yes, Papa," we said in unison.

"Benjamin?" The short and stocky, dark-haired man with spectacles declared as the heavy door opened. "By His Grace, is it really you?"

"Yes, cousin," Papa said as he thrust his right hand toward the man he had only previously met through correspondence. "It has been a long journey, but we are grateful to be here at last."

"Please," Mr. Gorham said, smiling and grasping Papa's hand. "Please do come in. You look exhausted."

"Indeed, we are most weary," Papa answered.

"And hungry, I am willing to bet," Mr. Gorham said. Turning his head, he called, "Mary. Please come quickly, for our guests have arrived at long last."

Seconds later, as we crowded into the front entrance of the single-level house, a short woman in a long black dress covered by a large white apron appeared beside our host. Her black hair was pulled back in a neat bun at the top of her head and she was carrying an infant whom she introduced as James. I do not believe he was yet a year old, but it was clear the woman was with child again.

I would later learn that James was born within weeks of the family's arrival in Port Rossignol, five months earlier. In total, the Gorhams would go on to have six children in this new place, giving them a contingent of eight, counting the two who had journeyed with them from Massachusetts.

"Benjamin and Martha," the woman said with a warm smile. I liked her instantly. "Welcome to our home. We have been expecting you for some time. Even though we had not received correspondence, we had continued to maintain hope that you would find your way here. Mr. Gorham and I have never given up praying for you."

"We are most appreciative of your hospitality," Mama answered.

"Where are our manners?" Mrs. Gorham smiled again. She emanated warmth and friendliness. "Since the hour is still early, we are about to have breakfast. Please come in and Mr. Gorham will show you where you can clean up. Then you must join us at the table."

"We do not wish to impose," Mama quickly said. "You were not expecting company for a meal at this hour of the day."

"Hush." Mrs. Gorham shook her head. "We have plenty to share so please go with Mr. Gorham. And after you will find me in the kitchen."

"Very well," Mama said with a smile. "Again, thank you for your kindness. We do so appreciate your hospitality."

If it had been up to me, I would have dispensed with the washing up. I was dead hungry and, after existing for months with meagre rations, I would have forgiven the dirt on my hands for the chance to immediately have some food with substance in my belly.

However, it was not my choice as Mama ushered us into a small room where they kept their basins, with a supply of water that was maintained at room temperature.

"Scrub up, young lady," Mama commanded, and I knew better than to disobey.

To ignore her directives usually resulted in a harsh punishment, so I used some kind of soap that Mrs. Gorham made by boiling a solution of wood ash and animal fat and then scraping the foam from the top, then letting it stand until it hardened. I did not much care for how it felt on my skin.

I didn't understand the process, but Mama said I would soon learn how to do it because, when we got our own place, I would be expected to help her with such household chores while Seth would be assisting Papa in whatever venture the men pursued.

So much for Papa's dream of this new place giving us a better life,

I thought, but simply nodded.

With our hands scrubbed good and clean, we followed Mr. Gorham into the modest kitchen where there was a wooden table, a water cupboard where several buckets were placed and a cook oven. Mr. Gorham felt we should eat first, and then he would show us the structure out back where he said we could reside for as long as we needed shelter. There, we could change our clothing and get settled.

Good idea, I thought, because the food Mrs. Gorham had prepared smelled scrumptious, and I feared that I would soon faint from hunger if I were not permitted eat.

It was a tight fit, but we managed to squeeze around their table, the four of us along with Mr. and Mrs. Gorham and their two older children who had come with them from New England. At that point, however, it would not have mattered if I had been required to sit on the hard boards of the floor to eat, for I would have perched anywhere provided I had some real food.

And real food we had. I must say, Mrs. Gorham was a tremendous cook. Our breakfast feast consisted of hotcakes, fresh bread, eggs and a healthy selection of berries, which she said grow in ample supply around the outskirts of the settlement. I think it was the best meal I ever had, before or since our arrival at this place. I ate everything our hostess offered until my heart—and my belly—were content.

"Slow down, child," Mama urged as I shovelled in a healthy helping of the food on my plate. "I promise that no one will take it from you."

"Yes, Mama," I mumbled as I swallowed a mouthful and glanced around the table to see if anyone had been watching my display of gluttony.

To my relief, it appeared that no one other than Mama had been watching, not even Papa, so I scooped up another large spoonful and shoved it in as I listened to the conversations taking place around the table.

Papa and Mr. Gorham were talking about some sort of community meeting that would be held later this afternoon for all the residents of the settlement.

"You must come," he said to Papa.

"I am not sure I have a place there," Papa answered. "After all, we only just arrived and are not yet permanent residents of this settlement. I can't feel that I have any right to attend such a meeting."

"Nonsense," Mr. Gorham replied. "You have as much right as anyone else." He pointed out that as soon as we stepped foot off the schooner, we were considered residents.

"For what purpose is this meeting being held?" Papa asked, pulling out his pipe. "May I?" he asked of our hosts.

I considered that to be a good sign, as I knew Papa only smoked when he was relaxed and I hadn't seen him smoke since we left England.

"Of course," Mr. Gorham nodded, pulling out his own pipe and pouch of tobacco. Passing the small, brown leather pouch, he said, "Try this. I brought it with me from New England."

"Thank you." Papa smiled, stuffed a healthy amount of tobacco into the barrel of his pipe and then passed the pouch back to his cousin. "So, what business will be conducted at this meeting?"

"We have a full agenda," Mr. Gorham explained. "We are discussing the settlement's defences and there is a proposal on the table to form a village cooperative where we all store and share a portion of our goods. The idea is to ensure all settlers have sufficient provisions to make it through the coming winter months. Some of our residents are superb hunters and fishermen, while others are accomplished gardeners. Once all the goods are stored in secured warehouses, then we will assign a council to maintain control over the supplies and they will follow a criterion for use, which will be approved by all the members."

"Sounds like a workable plan," Papa observed.

"Indeed. I do believe it has sufficient merit to warrant support."

"Considering our late arrival," Papa said, "I fear we will have nothing to contribute to such a cooperative this year."

"Allow me to worry about that on your behalf," Mr. Gorham said. "Furthermore, I believe we will also welcome your input on another topic up for discussion at the gathering."

"That would be...?" Papa asked.

"There has been considerable talk of late about naming our fine settlement," Mr. Gorham explained. "There are several options on the table."

"What is wrong with keeping Port Rossignol?"

"Because of its association with the French. You know that tensions between France and Great Britain are high, so we must choose a name that will honour His Majesty's Empire."

"Indeed." Papa reserved further comment.

"So, it is settled, then," our host said. "You must accompany me to the meeting. It will be part of your family putting down roots in your new community. Agreed?"

Papa nodded. "Agreed."

XX: A ramshackle shack

Upon completing our wonderful meal, and after Mama and I assisted Mrs. Gorham with the cleanup, Mr. Gorham showed us to the tiny hut that was situated behind their main house, a few hundred yards down a barely-there path and tucked under a growth of oak and maple trees.

I wish I could say that the accommodations were as satisfying as the food we had just enjoyed, but I fear I would not be telling the truth. Admittedly, Mr. Gorham, was apologetic that they did not have more room in the larger and much nicer house, with its planked floorboards and separate bedrooms, but with two adults and three children, he pointed out, they were already crowded into tight quarters.

"Nonsense," Mama told him, motioning toward the tiny structure that was to be our home. "This will be fine for us. I assure you, Mr. Gorham, it will be much more welcome in comparison to some of the places in which we have been forced to reside over the past few months. It just needs a tender touch, that is all. Alexandria and I will have it cleaned up in no time."

"Just for the interim," Mr. Gorham told us, as he opened the heavy, unpainted wooden door that led into an average-sized room that I immediately realized served as the kitchen and common living quarters, as well as the bedrooms. "Just as soon as time permits, Benjamin and I shall undertake a search for accommodations that will be more to your liking. I know of several locations that would be more suitable for a family of five, but they are currently under construction and are not likely to be ready for several months, perhaps not even until the spring. It would be advisable to stake your claim to one as quickly as possible, though, and to lend a hand in its construction, as there is growing demand for private dwellings."

"In the stead," Papa added, studying the structure that had clearly been hastily constructed, "these quarters will adequately serve the purpose."

"Very well," Mr. Gorham said, while he held the door open for us to enter our new home. "I will leave you to sort things out. Let Mary know if you require anything. And Benjamin," he added, "once you have settled things here, please come and find me at the house and I will introduce you to the settlement. You must become acquainted with the villagers as quickly as possible."

Of course, we children were expected to be seen but not be heard, and if we had an opinion on any topic, we were taught to keep it to ourselves. It was a directive I often struggled to follow, and if I had dared to offer my perspective on this current state of affairs, I am certain Mama and Papa would have been greatly disappointed in me, so I bit my tongue to keep myself from blurting out my displeasure at what I saw.

It is true that Mr. and Mrs. Gorham were showing us great hospitality, and I understood we were to be grateful for their generosity in allowing us to stay in this hut. However, in truth, the place was not much more than a shack that, considering the smells that greeted us, may have previously been used for livestock. I reluctantly accepted that it was to be our home for the interim and I hoped that we would be able to relocate to a new residence in good speed.

It was going to be difficult to be comfortable here as the building consisted of only one room with a dirt floor, but at least it would be dry and warm in the harsh weather that was still months away, but would close in soon enough, as Papa said.

A small stone fireplace was located in one corner, clearly added when the building was converted for human occupancy, most likely servants who tended to the main house. Not only would it provide us with a place to prepare meals, but it would also heat the entire structure in cold weather.

Next to the fireplace was a box for placing the wood that we would burn, two wooden buckets with which we would fetch our water from the nearby well that also served the larger residence, and a bench. In the centre of the room was a wooden table built of planks, with a bench on either side. This is where we would be eating and, as Mama quickly pointed out, doing our studies once we were settled.

"But, Mama," I whispered as we crossed the threshold into the hut and Mr. Gorham hurried quickly back toward the main house, "where will we be sleeping?

"Hush, now. We must make do, Alexandria," she answered, and I knew instantly that Mama did not want to engage in any sort of discourse about our accommodations. "We must be thankful for what we have been given. It is not good manners to question another's hospitality. Mr. and Mrs. Gorham are being extremely generous to us, so mind your tone and stifle your questions."

"Your mother is correct," Papa added. "I am sure Jabez will be able to tell me where I may find some straw. We will stuff burlap sacks that I will obtain at the docks. They will make acceptable beds and they will be easily stored during the daytime."

"Yes, Papa." I should not ask another question, so I quickly went to one of the benches and silently vowed that I would stay seated there until Mama or Papa told me it was time to move. I wasn't sure what I would do, but I would move only when they told me to.

Whatever plans I might have had for a leisurely reprieve were quickly interrupted when Mama instructed Seth and me to scour the property in search of wood so that we could start a fire. She asked Papa to fetch several buckets of water, as she wanted us to bathe as quickly as possible.

If we had had a larger supply of clothes, she told us, she would have burned all the clothing we were presently wearing. But since we were short of supplies, she planned to wash what we now wore for use on another day.

I wasn't convinced that she could restore my dress, for it had clearly seen better days, but I also knew that Mama would do her best to make it at least look clean and presentable for a while longer until it could be replaced. She was a determined woman, and if there was a chore to be carried out, I knew she would tackle it and not give up until it was completed to her satisfaction.

Over the course of the next several hours, we carried in a good supply of firewood, and under Mama's direction, scrubbed and cleaned our new accommodations and ourselves. Papa did find some straw, and he also managed to find an armload of burlap sacks that he would turn into our beds.

I will admit that, while I was skeptical upon our initial arrival, at this point I would now concede that the little shack had promise. When Mama said we would be comfortable here, I actually believed her.

It had been a long and adventurous day so far, but even though we were exhausted, when it came time to attend the community meeting, we walked to the centre of the village, along with Mr. and Mrs. Gorham and their children, to the gathering. Papa said that, as newcomers, we should attend so that people could get to know us and we get to know them.

That was fine by me, as I was ready to explore this place and to meet some other children. In London, I was a bit of a loner and spent a great deal of my time with my brothers, but I had vowed that I would work hard to find friends in this new place and I thought this community meeting was a good place to start.

By the time we reached the village centre, where the meeting was being held outside under a make-shift roof, as there was no structure of sufficient size to accommodate the numbers in attendance, the proceedings had just begun.

"That gentleman right there in the centre," Mr. Gorham said to Papa, as he motioned toward a burly man with a full head of dark hair and a thick, bushy beard, "is Mr. John Doggett. He too came here from Massachusetts, as did Elisha Freeman over there"—he pointed to another tall man across the gathering from us—"and Samuel Doggett and Thomas Forster." He nodded toward two other men who were standing on the edge of the crowd.

"And they are?" Papa asked as he studied the crowd.

"They are the village leaders," Mr. Gorham answered. "They were among the first to settle this village and have assumed the role of chief decision makers while we work toward establishing a local council that will do the bidding of the entire settlement. They call meetings and, upon deliberation, make decisions based on citizen input. Any such proceedings are the first steps toward achieving our goal of citizen government, under the King's laws, naturally."

"Naturally," Papa said.

"In the meanwhile," Mr. Gorham said, "these gentlemen have, almost by default, assumed the mantle of governance on our behalf. Just recently, they successfully petitioned Governor Charles Lawrence for sufficient land to establish a township. The governor has granted us ten thousand acres, extending some fourteen miles inland from the ocean shore. That is why we must come up with a name for our new village."

"Next," John Doggett said to the gathering, casting his gaze around the crowd, "is the business of naming our new township, as required by his Lordship, Governor Lawrence. If any man or woman has a suggestion to proffer, they may now step forward and be heard."

"I propose," one man said from the crowd, "that, since we have become known far and wide as Port Rossignol, that we retain that name. It is what the settlement has historically been called, but I propose that we drop the 'port' and just use 'Rossignol'."

Following a general murmur throughout the crowd, John Doggett said, "I am sorry to say that that name has fallen out of favour with the Crown. There also appears to be a general consensus from those gathered here that a different name should be chosen. Anyone else? Speak up now, or the four of us shall take it upon ourselves to choose a name."

There was the occasional mumble amongst those in attendance, but no other adult ventured to offer a suggestion. Then it hit me and, without thinking, I blurted out my suggestion.

"Why don't we call it Liverpool?" I said. It had totally slipped my mind that John Doggett had not asked children for suggestions.

"Alexandria," Papa quickly replied. "Please refrain from speaking. This is not your place to offer an opinion."

"Excuse me," John Doggett responded, glancing in my general direction. "But who offered the interesting suggestion? Speak up and be heard."

"It was nothing, sir," Papa answered. "Just the foolish mutterings of an outspoken child who has been taught to mind her manners but who obviously had a moment of weakness."

"Sir? You are?" John Doggett asked, looking directly at Papa. For a brief moment I feared that, because of my outburst, I might have brought the man's wrath down upon us.

"He is in my company this afternoon," Mr. Gorham quickly said. "This is my cousin from England, Benjamin Gorham, and his family. Martha, his wife, and their children Seth and Alexandria. Their oldest son, Jonathan, is working on the boats at this hour. The family arrived this morning from Halifax. They plan to set down roots here in our fine settlement. He and I are discussing business opportunities at this moment."

"Very well," John Doggett said, nodding toward us. "A pleasure to make your acquaintance, Gorham family. Welcome to our settlement."

"Thank you, sir," Papa said. "I promise my daughter will mind her tongue for the remainder of your proceedings."

"No, indeed," John Doggett quickly answered. "I, for one, would like to hear her speak. She makes an interesting proposal."

"Alexandria," Papa said, with displeasure in his tone, "please address this good gentleman and this fine group of people, but be quick about it."

"Yes, Papa," I whispered, fearing that I have not heard the last of this. I suspected my outburst might have gotten me in trouble. But no matter, I proceeded to speak.

"Sir," I began from the spot where I was standing next to Papa and Mama.

"Wait," John Doggett said, raising his meaty right hand. "Please step to the centre so that everyone may hear you."

I shook my head. There was absolutely no way I wanted to stand before this crowd and speak.

"Come, child," Doggett said. "If you have something worth saying, then we wish to hear it. Come along, now. Step forward and speak."

"Go ahead, Alexandria," Papa said with a gentle nudge. "Do as this gentleman has asked."

Fine, I thought. *If I must, I must.* Besides, I had only myself to blame for opening my mouth when I was supposed to remain quiet. Now I was being made to pay for my impertinence.

I stepped into the circle. I could feel everyone gazing upon me, and while on one hand I felt intimidated, on the other hand I also suddenly felt empowered. *Look at me,* I thought. *I have something to say and everyone is listening.*

Swallowing to make sure my throat was well lubricated, I then began. "In answer to Mr. John Doggett's question about naming this place in the wilderness, I suggest that perhaps we may call this settlement Liverpool, after our beautiful home back in England."

I paused and looked around at those assembled. I am sure they were wondering who this impetuous and slender redheaded girl might be who, until just minutes earlier, had been a stranger to them. *Who is she who dares to speak when children are not supposed to be heard?* That is what I am sure they were thinking.

"In England, our city is known as Liverpool on the Mersey," I proudly said. "And since you have chosen to locate your fine settlement on the banks of this gently flowing river, I also propose that this waterway be dubbed, the Mersey....Liverpool on the Mersey. It would be a fine way to pay homage to our homeland."

"Well," John Doggett replied, "I believe that is a splendid proposal." Glancing around the gathering, he asked, "Are there any further proposals for our consideration?"

He paused and waited.

Finally, he said, "Well, then, it is settled. Having received no additional proposals, from this day hence, our settlement shall be known as Liverpool in the new land known as Nova Scotia."

XXI: 1765

A great deal happened over the next five years as our fledgling village, nestled on the banks of the picturesque Mersey River grew into a thriving town, on its way to becoming one of the most important seaports on Nova Scotia's coast.

We saw our population rise by the thousands, while an untold number of businesses sprang up and flourished, and the wharves were a constant buzz of activity.

Lumbering, fishing and shipbuilding industries were going full steam ahead. Boatyards had started all along the riverbanks and sawmills became numerous, finding an ample supply of raw material further inland.

Indeed, on the surface, Liverpool had become a centre of commerce for importing and exporting; but underneath the riches and successes of our settlement ran a current of discontent, as tensions between the Colonies to the south of us and those loyal to the British Crown continued to mount.

The town was at first sympathetic to the cause of the American Revolution, but after repeated attacks by American privateers on local shipping interests, and growing fears of a direct attack on the town itself, the citizenry of Liverpool turned against the rebellion. Nova Scotia was far closer to the rebellious colonies than was King George in his palace in England, so settlements along Nova Scotia's coastline were prime targets for raiders, and Liverpool was considered vulnerable.

As our village grew and prospered, so too had my personal existence changed and flourished. We spent one winter in that shack out behind the Gorham main house and, while it was rough going at times, we survived. Early the next summer, we moved into our new home, a three-bedroom, two-story residence near the outskirts of town, with plenty of room for Mama to plant her gardens and even to have some chickens and a cow.

My brothers shared a bedroom, but since I was the only female in the household other than Mama, I was privileged to have my own room. I embraced this privilege with reverence.

All was going well with our family by this time. Papa and Jabez Gorham had partnered in a merchandising and exporting venture which brought them both great rewards. As a result, we became wealthier than we had ever dared to dream and, the older I became, those earlier struggles back in England became a distant memory.

Mama, embodying a kind and gentle spirit, took to helping the less fortunate of the settlement by providing sustenance for the poor and hungry; caring for the sick and infirm; and helping with the births of many of the village babies. Mama's reputation as a skilled midwife spread and, rich or poor, women-with-child often sought out her help when it came time to deliver their babies.

Now twenty-one, Jonathan continued to work on the fishing schooners and had long since paid off Papa's debt. It was his hope that he would soon have sufficient capital to acquire his own ship and hire his own crew.

Even though Mama never warmed up to the idea of her eldest son devoting his life to the sea that had already claimed one of her sons, Papa promised Jonathan that, should he be able to raise half the purchase price required for such a venture, then he would loan him the remaining portion.

Papa and Jonathan would be partners in a deal that did not receive Mama's approval. In truth, she was extremely cold to the idea, but, as she often did with such matters, she kept her opinions to herself. But Papa was wise enough to sense her displeasure.

Seth had gone on to work in the sawmills located further up the river, at a place called The Falls. By this time, a Mr. Richard Kempton and his four sons had established a settlement at this place, where the waters of the Mersey tumbled fiercely over the rocks, thus providing ample energy to power the mills.

Seth seemed content to earn his living in this industry and, unlike Jonathan, who seemed to be married to the sea, had his sights locked on a young lady from the village. He courted Elizabeth Wolfe and intended someday soon to make her his wife.

I liked Elizabeth very much, for she was a beautiful young woman, both in physical appearance and in spirit. She was kind and generous, and I prayed that she and Seth would find lasting happiness in each other's love.

As for me, I had no desire to start a family, nor did I have interest in any member of the opposite gender. Now sixteen years of age, I devoted my time to helping the villagers, especially the youngsters, and I was perfectly content in doing so.

Mama had taught her children well and it was my desire to see a school built in the village where children could gain an education, but it was a proposition that received mixed support amongst the other villagers, many of whom rejected the idea out of hand, primarily, they claimed, because of the expense.

At first, I welcomed two or three children into our home, where I would teach them to read and write and do ciphers. Then, about a year ago, as demand increased and our numbers became too large for the limited space in our house, I convinced Papa and Mr. Gorham to provide me with a room in their store where the children could receive lessons. But that, too, was now becoming crowded and we would soon be forced to look for a location that could accommodate our growing numbers.

I understood that, as our settlement grew, so too would the need to educate the children, and I began a lobby for a school to be built that would meet our current and future needs. This would not be easy, as it would require the villagers to pay for the construction and then to cover the expenses for the necessary educational materials and, eventually, a teacher.

As I continued to live with Mama and Papa and had little need for money, initially, I pledged that I would teach with no compensation. However, I understood there would come a day when it would be necessary to pay a teacher's salary, so that reality made the goal of establishing a school that much more daunting, but I was not about to be deterred in my efforts.

Pushing on, I took my proposal to Mr. John Doggett, who was still one of the village leaders. I understood that if I could win his support, then other residents would follow his lead.

He liked the idea and quickly joined my cause. However, it wasn't until he put me in contact with Colonel Simeon Perkins that my dream began to take shape.

A native of Connecticut, Colonel Perkins immigrated to Nova Scotia in 1762, during the Planter migration, and soon became one of Liverpool's leading citizens. He had established himself as a successful businessman, active in the West Indian trade and the fisheries.

Mr. Doggett told me that Colonel Perkins was involved in many areas of local and colonial government, conducting business and entertaining royal governors, naval officers, private captains and wandering preachers in his home. He said that, if there were one person in this settlement who could help me in my efforts to establish a school for the children, it would be the colonel.

So, it came to pass that, with the assistance of Mr. Doggett, I was granted an audience with Colonel Perkins. I will admit to having been extremely nervous about making the acquaintance of a man of such reputation and distinction, though, based on his diminutive physical stature, I might not have been intimidated.

Swallowing my fear and hiding my apprehension, I stood strong before the great man and, with Mr. John Doggett's blessing, presented my argument for the establishment of an institution for education in our village.

I must say, Colonel Perkins listened intently and asked many questions. However, he carefully guarded his personal opinion.

"You do present a compelling argument, Miss Gorham," he observed upon the completion of my dissertation. "Indeed, our children must learn to read and write, for the road to success comes with acquiring such skills. An adequate education will put them in good stead for their future, which ultimately will better serve our community."

"Thank you, sir," I replied. Indeed, it was humbling to receive such a positive response from such an important man. "I am glad you see things my way and you will help make it so."

"Miss Gorham, I did not say that I would help you in your quest," he quickly replied, cautioning my exuberance. "I believe I said you make a strong case that Liverpool requires a dedicated place of education. There is a distinct difference."

"Indeed." I nodded and smiled timidly, mentally scolding myself for being so impetuous and bold. My enthusiasm for my cause had gotten the better of me, allowing me to engage my tongue before my brain. "I truly am sorry for being so presumptuous. Of course, there is much to consider."

"Be that as it may," the Colonel said with a sly smile. He was a cunning man. "You have sold me on the idea and, without question, I will help where I can, but we are aware that some in our village may not consider a school to be a priority. Faced with the growing threat from the upstart Americans, many residents advocate that all our resources be used in defence of our settlement. I do agree with their observations, for I fear attack is imminent. However, long believing in the power of the written word, I also believe that if our village is to have a prosperous future, our children must be well educated, so I will lend my voice to yours and together we will strive to make your dream a reality."

"Thank you, sir." I was beaming. "Your support is most appreciated. I shall do whatever is required to make this school a reality."

"Temper your excitement, Miss Gorham, for we may have a long struggle ahead of us," he cautioned, as he walked me to the front door of his temporary residence. He and his family were using a place in town while their new home was being constructed along the road that leads to the fort, near the mouth of the bay. "We must start slowly and allow our momentum to carry us to fruition."

"I understand, sir," I said as I offered my right hand to him. "But your support has lent credence to my cause and I believe it will come to fruition."

"We shall see, Miss Gorham." He shook my hand gently. I could sense that he was a kind and thoughtful man. "We shall see."

And so, we did see. We worked hard and lobbied for support within the community, especially targeting residents with young children who would benefit directly from such an institution. A little over a year later, we opened the doors to the town's first school, and it was a happy day.

It was a modest structure located near the edge of town, next to the church, nothing more than a simple log cabin with a big box stove in the middle, but the children were exceedingly happy to have a place they could call their own. We started with a dirt floor, but in time some of the men put down planks. and it became a place of education.

The students sat on several rows of benches and we had one large table where they worked. They were most attentive and responsive, soaking up the knowledge as if they were sponges.

My dream of seeing a school open its doors had become a reality and all seemed well in our growing village, for now at least, but I knew one should never take things for granted. However, little did I know of the storms that were brewing just beyond the horizon.

XXII: Law and order

I considered myself most fortunate to have found success in this new Liverpool, but life wasn't easy for everyone in the New World. While many settlers did find riches in this place, others were less fortunate; and for those who struggled, it often became an insurmountable challenge to merely survive.

There was much disparity within our community. The divide between the wealthy and the poor was great, and while many of my contemporaries spent their time fantasizing about their impending nuptials to the rich and handsome suitors in our town, I cared more about the plight of the destitute who had so very little.

I had experienced the oppression and despair that comes with living in abject poverty. My heart broke for those who worked to eke out a meagre existence and suffered with no hope of relief.

It was an event late in the fall of 1766 that confirmed my greatest fear that, despite our claims to be a forgiving and God-fearing society, we were often not above behaving like barbarians with cruel and vindictive motives.

The circumstances of which I speak began one morning in autumn, when Gabrielle Lewis, my best friend in the whole wide world, and I were enjoying our time in the village market, purchasing a few wares for our mothers. Our attention was drawn to a scuffle at one of the nearby booths just down the street from where we had been surveying the goods.

I met Gabrielle, a strikingly-beautiful, brown-haired girl of the same age as I, when she and her family arrived in Liverpool three years after I had come to this place. I loved her very much as any one person could love her best friend, but not everyone shared my affection for her. In some social circles she was considered an outcast.

Gabrielle's mother was English, but her father was French, descended from the Huguenots, and therein lies the predicament, as it was considered inappropriate that such a coupling should ever occur. I did not see it that way, nor did I care that others avoided social interaction with the family, for it mattered not to me what others thought.

In my opinion, the Lewis family were among some the friendliest, caring and most generous people in the whole settlement. To think that I might be forced to give up my friendship with Gabrielle over some antiquated social convention was beyond my comprehension, and I would have no part of that.

She and I were quick to bond and we became inseparable, for she shared my desire to help the destitute. We often took turns with the teaching duties at the school, although some of the citizens did not think it appropriate that she teach their children.

Damn that attitude, I thought, and insisted that, unless the villagers were prepared to raise sufficient funds to pay for a teacher more suited to their liking, they would have to take my word that Gabrielle was, indeed, a fine teacher and a lovely person.

The villagers continued to mumble their displeasure, but mostly under their breaths; and a good thing it was, too, as my patience for such nonsense had reached well beyond its limits.

I am sure the villagers did not take kindly to being put in their place by such an impetuous woman as I, but I was not one for convention. I had long believed that such outdated social constraints were in great need of reform, and I would not be told with whom I could associate.

On this day in the market, as I have written, we were attracted by the ruckus. As we investigated the goings-on, I was horrified to discover that the authorities had apprehended a young woman whom I had seen around the village on occasion.

I did not know much about this woman's personal situation except from what I overheard from the local gossips, but the woman, who mostly kept to herself, had been left a widow after her husband had died more than two years earlier of a fever he developed following a serious injury on one of the fishing schooners. With his passing, his wife was left poor and with the care of three small children, whom she struggled to feed. It was because of this that this woman now found herself in serious trouble.

It appeared that, with no source of income and little to bargain with, the woman had resorted to thievery to secure food for her children. On this day she was caught in the market taking a loaf of bread to feed the trio of starving waifs, who were now lost in the growing crowd of curious onlookers that gathered when the transgression was discovered by the local merchant, who claimed he had seen the theft occur.

"Please, sir," the woman cried as I searched the crowd for her offspring. "Please do not arrest me for stealing bread to feed my babies. They are so hungry and we have nothing to eat."

How had I not heard of this poor woman's plight before today? I wondered.

My heart broke as the authorities instructed the accused thief to remain silent and reminded her that the known and accepted punishment for such a transgression was death by hanging.

They cannot resort to such barbaric treatment of this poor woman, I prayed. Surely, as civilized people we would never resort to hanging a mother whose sole motivation for thievery was feeding her children. Where was the compassion? The empathy?

As they hauled the sobbing woman along the cluttered gravel roads that were lined with villagers and toward the waterfront, where I knew other hangings had taken place, it became clear that, in fact, this poor widow was about to meet her maker, leaving her children as orphans in this cruel and unforgiving world.

"I must stop them," I said to Gabrielle. I could not stand to watch such an injustice.

"Alexandria," she replied, grabbing my arm. "You must not interfere with the execution of justice. There is nothing we can do if the woman has broken the law."

"Is it criminal to want to keep your children from starving?" I answered, as my eyes landed on the man I knew to be the shop owner.

"What are you about to do?" Gabrielle asked upon seeing the direction in which I was gazing.

"I must stop this cruelty," I said, darting toward the merchant.

"Come back," my friend called. But of course it was too late as I had already confronted the gentleman.

"Please, sir," I pleaded. "You must not allow this to happen. This woman's crime was not one of greed, it was an act of desperation and survival. You must have a heart."

"Sorry, miss," he snapped. "She is a thief and she must pay for her crimes."

"But, sir," I continued, "this woman is a mother. What is to become of her children?"

"That is not my concern," he countered. "The law is very clear on this, Miss Gorham."

"It must be someone's concern," I reasoned. "Who will take care of them if she is dead?"

He simply shrugged as he locked the door to his shop.

"Very well," I said, fishing in my bag for some pennies that I knew were hidden in there. "I will pay for the bread on her behalf and you will stop this at once."

"That is not the point," the shop owner said. "It's a matter of principle and she must stand as an example that such crimes will not be tolerated. If we allow her to go free, then we send a message that such indiscretions are permissible. Law-abiding citizens must know their place, and when one strays then she must pay the consequences."

"That is barbaric nonsense," I said, pulling the three bits from my bag and thrusting them at the portly man. "Take this, please, and make them stop before it is too late."

"I cannot," the shopkeeper said before turning and making his way down the street along with the other settlers and getting swallowed up by the jeering crowd. This poor woman's hanging was now about to become a spectator sport and it made me ill to even contemplate the notion.

"Come," Gabrielle said, pulling my arm. "I have located the children. They are huddled near the butcher stall."

So, they were. Three children, the youngest aged four and the oldest no more than ten, hugging tightly to each other.

"Oh my," I sobbed. "We must not let those poor youngsters see this."

Gabrielle said, "I will gather them up and bring them home with me. Mother will know what to do for them. You make your way to the waterfront and put a stop to this madness, if you can."

We quickly went into action. Pushing my way through the boisterous crowd, I made my way to the waterfront, where the authorities had already begun to string a rope over a thick branch on the hanging tree, its bark rubbed bare from earlier executions. There was to be no trial and I knew, to my greatest horror, that it was beyond my power to stop this public lynching.

"Alexandria."

I looked around with tear-filled eyes, for I knew the voice coming from the crowd belonged to Papa.

"What are you doing here?" he asked. "A young lady should not witness such horror."

"I know, Papa," I cried. "Can we not stop this?"

"I am afraid not, child. This is how justice is served."

"This is not justice," I fired back, immediately regretting that I was taking my anger out on Papa. Calming my voice, I added, "Not in a civilized society."

"I understand, Alexandria," he said, putting his arms around me and pulling me close to him. Taking my head in his hands, he turned my face to his chest and told me to close my eyes.

I am not certain what was worse, the sight of a poor, helpless woman being strung up by the neck as her fellow citizens cheered, or the hideous sounds of the begging woman pleading for mercy and asking the authorities to spare her life as the crowd called for her death.

And then, when the act was complete, the silence that reigned over the gathering was deafening.

The silence was the sound of a miserable life unceremoniously being cut short at the end of a rope. It was the sound of vigilante justice being carried out and the sound of three helpless children being left without a father or mother. It was the sound of my breaking heart and the sound of my faith in humanity being snuffed out as if it were the flame of a fire being doused by a bucket of water. After that day, my view of the world was forever changed.

Gabrielle and her family took care of those three children for several days until the authorities came and collected them. The last we saw of those poor little orphans was their tear-stained faces as they were loaded onto a schooner and sent to Halifax, where we understood they would be placed in some sort of foster home. We never saw those children again or heard word of their wellbeing, so we can only guess as to whatever became of the poor, dear waifs.

I would like to say that this incident marked the last public hanging in Liverpool's history but if I did, I would not be telling the truth. However, it was the last time that anyone was hanged from that particular tree.

A few years later a family named Barss purchased the property where that tree stood. The land was promptly cleared, and the tree was felled. In its place, a grand mansion was built right over the spot on the riverbank where that tree had been rooted in the rocky soil.

I have never set foot inside this house, but from what I heard from others who have had the privilege, it is a spectacular place with rich, ornamental trimmings and some of the finest furniture to ever grace a Liverpool residence. It was true opulence, I was told.

According to those same stories, the house came with one other thing—a restless spirit.

Again, this is only hearsay, but from the stories that circulated throughout the settlement, not long after the new owners moved into their home, they began to experience unexplained phenomena such as doors and windows slamming closed by their own power, items being tossed about the rooms on their own propulsion, things going missing, smells that reminded the residents of a woman's perfume, and the one occurrence which surely causes my flesh to crawl, that being the unmistakable sound of a woman weeping.

As word of these happenings spread, we were left with one conclusion, but to speak it seems almost sacrilegious so I choose not to verbalize what most of the residents were freely repeating to whomever would listen.

How does one go on existing in a society where public hangings are not only acceptable, but are openly encouraged and cheered? So much for law and order in a civilized society.

This incident scared me badly and from that point on our world seemed like a much darker place.

XXlll: Unanswered prayer

For me, life was never the same in Liverpool after that senseless and barbaric act of violence against that poor woman. Instead of cheering to see her dangle at the end of the hangman's rope, we would have shown more humanity had we offered her assistance to sever the bonds of poverty that embraced her.

If we were truly God-faring people, as we espoused, then it was our duty and responsibility to take that poor woman and her children under our care and provide for them the sustenance they needed to survive. Instead, we celebrated her suffering as if we relished the plight of another, less fortunate, human being.

I tried hard to forgive the people of this town for what they had done, but once one sees the underbelly of society, it is truly difficult to look the other way. Gabrielle and I continued to run the school and to assist the destitute however we could, but it was not easy for two young females to be taken seriously in this world dominated by members of the opposite gender and where the wealthy wielded all the power.

"We should have done something, Gabrielle," I said to my dear friend one afternoon after the children had been dismissed and we were cleaning up. "We are God-fearing people. Would God not have wanted us to understand our duty was to care for that woman and her children? Why do some people find it so difficult to practice charity? Are they afraid to offer the goodness of their hearts because they are scared the same thing could happen to them? Are they really that superstitious?"

"I guess we are," Gabrielle said, her words filled with a deep angst. "For me, the world seems darker, more foreboding. That seems melodramatic, I know, but I see it all around me. That woman lost her life for trying to feed her babies and, as a result, we have lost our innocence and love for the world."

I shivered as images of that horrific event flashed through my memory. "I have tried to forgive those people," I whispered. "I can't even look at the property where that tree stood. It's like the whole incident cursed me."

Despite our struggles with the inner turmoil we shared, Gabrielle and I remained steadfast in our efforts to help others, and I thank God for Gabrielle's friendship. Without her love and support I fear I would have truly lost my way in this world filled with such discontent hidden within a society that claims to be just and fair.

I took Gabrielle's hand and looked her in the eyes. "Thank you for being here for me and for your understanding," I whispered. "I don't know what I would do without your friendship. You are my anchor."

"And I thank you," she smiled and whispered back.

Gabrielle's guidance and courage gave me the strength to carry on even though my faith had been called into doubt and our collective futures appeared bleak, as we braced for war with the rebellious colonies.

It had now become evident to all who paid attention to such matters, that the 'Sons of Liberty' in Massachusetts and other places were moving to act against the Empire and that war was eminent. The winds of change were, indeed, blowing and they were brushing against our once-tranquil coastline, causing a stench of distrust and deceit within our own ranks.

We understood the growing dissension within the Colonies to be the result of the imposition of the Stamp Act of 1765, imposed by the Parliament of Great Britain. The government insisted it had the right to tax colonists, who were still British subjects, to pay for the cost of their defence against the French and others who might intend ill. Conversely, the colonists galvanized around the position that the tax was unconstitutional. Whilst I was still a loyal British subject, I shared the colonists' perspective on this issue, for it did not seem legal or just that they should be taxed without representation in the British Parliament.

Ostensibly claiming loyalty to the monarch and a place in the Empire, each of the thirteen colonies along the coast to the south of Nova Scotia formed a unifying continental congress and a shadow government to ensure their place in Parliament, but underneath, it was a ruse and war was brewing. The seeds of independence had taken root.

Many of our people had first settled in New England before removing to Nova Scotia, and were divided between those who recognized the plight of the colonists and those who would remain true to the Crown to their own deaths.

As one of strong will, it was difficult for me to remain silent on this issue, but I understood that should I voice an opposing perspective, then I risked being ostracized by most of the community.

As a teacher of the children, I did not think that losing the support of many local citizens would well serve my cause. The school was, at best, a tenuous arrangement, a conundrum with no easy solution in the foreseeable future.

So I held my tongue and avoided any conversation that centred on the escalating discontent between some in the thirteen Colonies and the Empire. I kept my head down and went about my work, going out of my way to help those in need whenever I had the means to do so, and throwing my efforts into teaching the children.

In time, I managed to reclaim some of the faith I had lost as a result of the public hanging. It is a miracle that the human mind can accomplish such a feat, and while I would never condone the villagers' actions, I did learn to forgive them and prayed that in the future we would search for better ways to handle such disputes.

The school was my one saving grace, and as the children grew and became accomplished in their lessons, I took great pride in knowing that I had been responsible for something special in this settlement. But even amongst my pleasure, there continued the spectre of sadness and dismay.

These relentless adversaries constantly lurked below the surface, waiting for an opportunity to manifest themselves. As is often the case with human suffering, the agonies of tragedy usually chose the most inopportune times to reveal their true intentions. This is how it was with my family.

By 1767, Jonathan and Papa had raised sufficient capital to purchase their own schooner and to hire a full crew of seven deckhands. Jonathan had learned the fishing trade well and was now the youngest captain in the local fleet, with his own vessel to command. It was a glorious ship, fully equipped to sail to the rich fishing grounds further out on the banks, where they said the cod was so plentiful that one could walk across the water on them.

I never saw this for myself, so such talk could have been pure embellishment, but I heard stories of crews throwing their nets overboard and, within a matter of minutes, quickly pulling them back in with a full catch.

There may have been some exaggeration in the tales that circulated through the village, but Jonathan insisted the stories were true, and although he offered on more than one occasion to allow me to sail with them on one of their excursions so that I might see for myself, I promptly, but politely, rejected his offer. Recalling my previous adventures on the high seas, when we sailed from England to the New World, I was not prepared to set foot on another vessel, even a fine ship such as his.

Besides, I was aware of the crew's feelings toward a female sailing with them. It is a strongly-held belief that to bring a woman on board a fishing boat is to invite bad luck and there is no doubt that Jonathan's crew would have been most discontent had I showed up on the wharves prepared to sail with them.

While Jonathan dismissed such talk as baseless superstition, I had no interest in tempting fate. I admired my brother's fine vessel from the docks and, whenever possible, I was there each time he set sail on one of his expeditions.

I shall never forget the last time I saw him. It was a spectacular September morning. The sun had risen bright and warm, bathing the land with its promise of a glorious late-summer day. When the provisions were loaded and the men were eager to depart, I bade Jonathan farewell and wished him Godspeed, praying that he and all on board his glorious schooner would return to us safe and sound.

He chastised me for worrying too much and wondered outwardly what would cause a beautiful young woman such as I to carry so many burdens on her petite shoulders. I shrugged at his compliment and smiled, telling him that it was simply who I am. I reminded him that beauty was purely in the eye of the beholder.

"Do not worry, sister," he said, kissing me gently on my forehead. "You shall develop fret lines on that pretty face and no man wants his wife to look old before her time."

I giggled. "Jonathan, I have no interest in finding a husband. I have better things to do than devoting my life to pleasing a man."

"Perhaps, sister," he answered with an impish grin. "But it is possible that someone has an interest in finding you."

I blushed. "I would be suspicious that any man interested in the likes of me had surely taken leave of his senses. The man's sanity must surely be tested."

"I don't know, sister." He emitted that deep, guttural laugh that I found so amusing and for which I often teased that no such sound should come from a human being. "You may be pleasantly surprised in the near future."

Try as I might, Jonathan would not reveal the true meaning of his words. Perhaps it was simply a matter of sibling teasing, but he certainly implied that he was aware of a fellow in the settlement who might be interested in courting me. If so, I never learned the name of this mysterious suitor. It was most likely a figment of Jonathan's vivid imagination.

"In good time," he said with a chuckle as she stepped from the dock to the deck of his schooner.

"That is simply not fair," I replied.

"There is not much in life that is fair, sister."

He waved before giving the order to his deck hands to cast free the ropes that tethered the schooner to its moorings. As they sailed away, he yelled back, "All my love to you, my dear sister. And to Mama and Papa."

"Goodbye, Jonathan," I called. "Please hurry back, for I shall miss you." And I whispered, "Be safe, brother."

I could not explain the sudden feeling of emptiness that immediately washed over me as I watched the schooner sail out of the bay, but looking back on the next few days, I may have guessed they were an omen of impending doom.

The next evening, as I stood in Mama's kitchen helping to prepare dinner for Papa and Seth and his guest, the dear, sweet Elizabeth Wolfe, I was given a start when I glanced out the tiny window near the door and observed Jonathan casually strolling up the back walkway, heading toward the house.

"Mama. Papa," I called out, darting for the door. I was relieved that he had come home. "Come quickly. Jonathan has returned early. The fishing must have been poor."

Grabbing the latch, I quickly threw the door open and stepped outside into the waning light of the approaching dusk. I glanced around the yard, expecting to discover my brother standing there, his broad smile lighting up the quickly-descending darkness of early evening. I was surprised and alarmed to see no one about.

"Jonathan," I called, fearing that my brother was making a game of his arrival. We had grown accustomed to his pranks, and I was certain he was hiding somewhere in the bushes.

"Jonathan," I called again, putting a stern tone in my words. "I have no time for your childish games. I have stew on the fire for supper and I must tend to it or it shall burn. If you wish to have supper, dear brother, then you will show yourself right this very minute."

I waited to hear his guttural laughter that I so enjoyed, but there was no reply.

"Alexandria?" Mama said, approaching me from behind. "What is going on here? Come back into the house, my dear, and tend to the stew."

"I saw Jonathan out here but a few minutes earlier," I explained, continuing to peer into the diminishing daylight. "He was coming toward the house."

"That is not possible," Papa said, as he joined Mama and me on the back steps. "I am certain that, by this time, his vessel must be nearing the rich fishing grounds on the banks. From down on the docks, I've heard the weather has been clear with strong winds, so he must be making good time with little resistance."

"No, Papa," I insisted. "I am certain that Jonathan was right here but a few moments ago."

"Surely, you are mistaken, Alexandria," Mama reasoned. "If your Papa says your brother is heading to sea, then I am certain that is the case. Perhaps you are just tired, my dear. You have been working extremely hard at the school in recent days. I suggest that, after dinner, you turn in early. Rest is what you need."

I decided that perhaps Mama and Papa were correct. Indeed, I was tired, and it is entirely possible that a combination of weary eyes and fading light had conspired against me to create illusions.

"Come back inside," Mama said, placing her arms around my shoulders.

I was about to do that, but my attention was drawn to a low-hanging branch of the old oak tree that towered over our house. I was alarmed to notice a large, ebony-coloured bird sitting on that branch, hidden amongst the shade of the leaves, and although I could not say for certain, I had the impression that the creature was staring back at me.

My thoughts were immediately taken to when we were sailing to Halifax on *The Rose*. As we were nearing the coastline, a bird of similar size and colour had visited me on the deck. I remembered the crewman's warning about the creature plucking out my eyes if I got too close to it, and I immediately shivered as icy fingers ran up from the lower portion of my back and found their way to my neck.

I could not know for certain the creature's intentions, but from that evening forward, I took note of the bird's appearances. It seemed that it, or perhaps some of its brethren, had taken to following me about as I conducted my business.

In time, I began to wonder if, in fact, the birds had nefarious intentions, or if they were attempting to communicate with me. Whatever their purpose, however, their presence became both a curse and a blessing to me.

We ate dinner and Elizabeth and I helped Mama clean up afterwards while Papa and Seth sat at the wooden table, discussing news of the impending war brewing in New England, and about some of the local men volunteering to fight for the Crown should war be declared. Mama insisted that Seth promise he would not be one of them, and he did so, but reluctantly, I could see.

Once the chores were completed, I excused myself and retired to my room. But try as I might, sleep eluded my eyes that night as that same sense of dread that had embraced me on the dock the day before took hold of me once again.

"Jonathan," I whispered in the darkness, hoping that my words would ride the late summer breeze and magically find his ears. "Be safe, my brother. Come home to us in good health."

Alas, my prayers were not answered. Two days hence, word arrived with the returning ships that a fierce late-summer storm had appeared over the horizon on the fishing banks. The ships were floating targets for its massive waves and gale-force winds.

The crews on the limping vessels that were fortunate enough to avoid being swamped reported valiant stories of survival and tales of tragedy, as three of the local schooners with all hands onboard were lost to nature's fury. It broke my heart to learn that Jonathan's schooner was one of those lost.

The unforgiving Atlantic Ocean had claimed another of my brothers.

XXIV: A heavy cross to carry

The days that followed were difficult to navigate. When Mama heard the news that Papa brought upon his return from the docks, she collapsed in his arms. The only other time that I had witnessed such grief and sadness was when Mama was told Samuel had died. She was simply devastated.

"No. No. No," she moaned, her voice torn apart by grief. "Not my boy. Not another one of my boys."

I struggled to hold back my own grief and put my arm around Mama.

What does one say to a woman who has lost two of her children? I wondered.

"Why couldn't you have answered my prayers, God? Was it too much to ask to save by brother? My mother can't endure the loss of another child," I whispered, though no one was listening.

My father hung on to my mother and turned to me. "They said the storm came on fast, just over the horizon, out on the banks. There was no advance warning. One man told me the ships were easy targets for the huge waves and strong winds."

Mama was inconsolable as Papa continued to speak, his voice hushed, his eyes boring into mine. "Some of the vessels had the good fortune to avoid being swamped and their crew members told me stories of how they managed to avoid tragedy." His voice broke and he cleared his throat. "Three of our schooners and all souls on board them were lost."

He hung his head so that I could not see his tears.

The next few months were difficult for the entire settlement. The town lost twenty-three good men when those three schooners were sucked down to the ocean floor. In some instances, fathers and sons from the same families were lost. Eight of those men were on Jonathan's ship, and we were simply devastated by the reality that our beloved son and brother would never be coming home.

While Mama had somehow, with the grace of God, found a way to come to terms with losing her Samuel during our voyage to this New World, she was never able to recover from the blow of giving up another son, this one her first-born. She had long said that it was an unforgiving God who would take a mother's child before her time here on Earth was complete. The reality that two of her children had died before her became too much to bear.

As the months slipped by, we could see Mama fading into nothingness. She withdrew from her work in the settlement, refusing to assist with the arrival of any more babies. She said she simply could not bear to bring something so innocent into a world where death and suffering had the upper hand.

We worried about Mama's health, as she simply refused to eat. She became reclusive, spending much of her time in her bed. I feared the worst and prayed that somehow Mama would find her way back from this dark place, but my prayers were for naught.

The following spring, Mama passed away as she mourned the deaths of her oldest son and the younger one who had gone before him.

The village physician, Dr. Robert MacIntosh, said Mama died of something called consumption. I, on the other hand, believed she died of a broken heart.

We interred Mama in the burial grounds that had been established on the outer edge of town. We put her next to two graves where she had insisted we bury items that had belonged to Samuel and Jonathan. It was her thinking that, if their bodies were not there as they were at the bottom of the ocean, at least their personal belongings should mark the place where they were to rest for all eternity.

I was never sure if Papa thought that to be a good idea, for he did not voice an opinion on the matter, but he agreed with whatever Mama wanted. I believe that he was hoping that, if he fulfilled her wishes, her burden would be lessened somewhat. It was clear Papa was hurting for her, but, like the rest of us, he was helpless in his efforts to reach Mama.

With Mama and Jonathan now gone and Seth preparing to marry Elizabeth Wolfe and move out to their own residence at The Falls, where my brother worked for Mr. Richard Kempton, our home became a shell of its former self. Papa seemed to spend increasingly more hours at the store. He sank to depths of despair that I had never seen before in him, and he became increasingly more dependent on the devil alcohol, finding solace in the bottle. I was losing him as well, and I was left alone to ramble through the house.

I was thankful to have my work to keep me busy, and for Gabrielle's company, for without them both, I fear that I would have lost grip of my sanity.

A constant state of darkness enveloped me. Since I was a child, I had believed that I was strong enough to take anything that this world could throw at me, and I believed that tragedies were put before me to test my fortitude and faith, but nothing could have prepared me for what was yet to come.

For months, a troubled child who was disruptive in class had challenged me, and on occasion even threatened me with violence. It had become clear that Master Percival Merrick had no interest in studying and chose instead to rise against my authority. Eventually, it reached the point when I had to ask the thirteen-year-old to stay at home until he could learn proper decorum and behaviour.

Both Gabrielle and I felt that we could not teach Percival in his current frame of mind and that he was taking too much of our attention, which meant he was causing the other children to lose precious time from their studies while we dealt with disciplinary issues. We agreed we could not allow this behaviour to continue but, as the head mistress, I decided that I would be the one to deliver the directive to Percival.

It was a cold, damp day in March when I asked Percival to remain after the other children in class were dismissed so that I might speak with him. I delivered my message as kindly, but firmly, as I could, but he did not take kindly to his suspension, and vowed that his father would be to see me.

I had heard of Mr. Luther Merrick, a man who worked on the docks. Although I had not met him, even though I had taught some of his other children, I was aware of his reputation. He was known to be a hateful and tough disciplinarian who ruled his family of seven children by the Biblical verse "spare the rod, spoil the child."

I suspected Percival was correct and that it was likely that his father would, indeed, pay me a visit. If that were to come to pass, I had no idea how I would react, for this was the first occasion since opening the school that I had to suspend a child from his studies.

It had always been my philosophy that every child deserves an education, but I came to realize that in order to be educated, a child must want to learn. In Percival's case, it was painfully clear that the boy did not want to be in school. Even so, I hoped that Percival's words were nothing more than an idle threat.

The next afternoon, March 21, I learned they were not.

"Miss Gorham," the burly and scruffy man barked as he stormed into the schoolhouse. He must have been waiting outside for all the children to be dismissed. "May I have a word with you?"

"Mr. Merrick." I nodded, trying to force a smile to cross my face, but I feared that it would not be sincere, for I was terrified by this brute who was now hovering over me as I sat at the worktable, preparing lessons for tomorrow's class. "Yes, you may," I stammered, knowing from the burning look in his eyes that this was not a happy man. "But we have to be quick about it, as I am expecting another appointment very soon."

"Am I to understand that my son is not welcome in this school?" he quickly began, spit flying from his curled mouth as his nostrils flared in anger.

The dirt from the day's work on the docks was still evident on his face, hands and clothes and I could smell his sweat. I felt cornered and vulnerable, like a caged animal, but I was committed to answering his questions. Swallowing hard, I knew I had to stand my ground.

"I am sorry, Mr. Merrick," I replied. "But that is so. Percival has not learned proper behaviour and, as a result, his actions are extremely disruptive for the entire class."

"Is that right?" he barked. Slamming his hammer of a fist on the table, he spat his words at me as if they were the venom from a poisonous snake. "You are saying I don't know how to raise my son? You are saying he is not good enough to be here?"

"I am not saying anything of the kind, Mr. Merrick," I answered, trying to remain calm while rising to my feet. "Please remain civil. I am simply suggesting that he can return to the class when he learns to control his disruptive ways."

"Why do you get to decide how he should behave? Did I not help to build this place? Did I not spill enough blood and sweat to earn a place in this building for my son?"

"Your contributions were, and still are, greatly appreciated," I said, slowly backing away from the table. "I believe your other children have found great success here and, with them, our debt to you has been repaid many times over."

"I will decide when my debt is repaid, Miss Gorham, not some nobody who thinks she has the authority to control my boy's future."

I watched as his eyes turned to narrow slits, his complexion turning blood-red. I could tell he was quickly losing control.

"Mr. Merrick," I said, "I do not believe you should resort to insults. That is no way to speak to a lady and I would ask that you, sir, refrain from the use of such language in my school. Perhaps it best for you to leave for today and come back at another time when we may discuss this in a more civilized manner. Perhaps you might like to bring Percival with you upon your return."

"I'm here now to talk to you," he barked, lurching toward me with more speed and agility than I would have guessed that a man of his age and large build would possess. "I'm here to settle this."

He grabbed me by my shoulders and forced me back against the wall until I was trapped.

"Mr. Merrick," I screamed. "Please let me go at once. You are hurting me."

"I do not believe you have ever been shown how to fully please a man, have you, Miss Gorham?" He grabbed my dress and ripped it away from my body to expose my womanhood.

"What are you doing? Let me go," I cried. "Please leave at once."

"Be quiet," he commanded, pulling on my under garments and adding to my indignity.

"You must not do this. I mean no harm to you or your son. Please release me at once and we will discuss this matter at another time when you are more composed."

The look in his eyes was that of a madman, and I feared his intentions. Pulling down his trousers, he spit his angry words at me. "I will finish this now."

Under his enormous weight I was trapped and, though I struggled to break free, I was no match for his animal-like strength. The assault was brutal, the pain unlike anything I had ever before experienced in my life.

"Please, Mr. Merrick," I begged and sobbed. "Please stop. You are hurting me."

I do not know the full duration of the assault, but when he was done, he merely grunted, pulled his throbbing body off of mine, picked up my dress and threw it at me as I lay weeping on the planked floor, trying to pull my aching body into a ball to prevent his gaze from falling upon me again.

"We are done," he said, pulling up his trousers. "This is settled. Percival will be in this classroom tomorrow morning and there will be no more talk of this suspension."

I said nothing as he hurried from the school, leaving me hurt, bleeding and feeling deeply ashamed.

Just beyond the door he spoke to someone and I remembered that Mrs. Buchanan had made an appointment to see me about her daughter, Netty, who was struggling with her English. Had she arrived a few minutes earlier, Mrs. Buchanan would have witnessed the assault.

"Afternoon, Mrs. Buchanan," he said, standing in the doorway to block the woman's entry.

"Good day, Mr. Merrick," I heard her respond, and I could tell the woman was surprised by his presence in the school at a time in the afternoon when the men are usually working. From my position on the floor, I could not see Mrs. Buchanan and I was certain she could not see me. "What are you doing here? Shouldn't you be at the docks?"

"I had business here," he said.

"Of course," she answered. "I too am here to see Miss Gorham. Netty needs some extra help with her English lessons and so I'm hoping Miss Gorham will have a few suggestions of how I may help her deal with the challenges."

"I just left Miss Gorham," he said. "I do not believe she is ready to see another visitor at this time. She's been very busy this afternoon."

"I see," the woman answered, and I could tell by her judgmental tone that the speculation had begun.

While Mrs. Buchanan was, indeed, a lovely woman, she was, by most accounts, also known to be one of the settlement's most effusive gossips. Based on the evidence before her, I was certain that she would surmise Mr. Merrick and I had just engaged in some sort of physical interaction, which indeed we had, but most certainly against my will.

"I think it best, Mrs. Buchanan, if you give Miss Gorham some time to herself," he said, leading her away from the doorway. "Perhaps you should come back another time for your appointment."

"Very well," she said, and I could tell the die had already been cast. "But she was expecting me."

"Perhaps tomorrow would be better," he insisted. "As I was taking my leave, Miss Gorham had indicated she was not feeling well."

"All right, Mr. Merrick." It was clear Mrs. Buchanan was not happy about being turned away. "Whatever you think is best."

In hindsight, I should have jumped from the floor and exposed the man for the cruel cad that he was, but the overriding thoughts of guilt and embarrassment prevented me from doing so. Instead, I cowered in the corner and wished for them both to leave.

Minutes later, after I heard the door close and was certain they had gone, I pulled myself off the floor, hurried into my dress, which was now in need of mending, and fixed my hair. If I had gone directly to Papa right then, I am certain Mr. Merrick would have been dead by sunset and Papa would be facing a murder charge.

It is possible that no court would have convicted him but, remembering the brand of justice that had been handed out to that poor woman who had done nothing more than take a loaf of bread to feed her children, my sense of reasoning led me to conclude that Papa would surely have been hanged by the same rope.

Instead, I stilled my emotions and steeled my nerves. Gathering my things, I slipped from the school and made my way directly home, being careful to avoid contact with any others. I did not want anyone seeing me in my condition. Looking back on it now, I realize this one of the many mistakes I had made that day.

The first, and greatest mistake that I had committed was resisting the urge to kill the heathen for what he had done. Surely, no one would have blamed me after the crime he had just perpetrated.

The second mistake I committed was giving in to my fear and keeping his secret, for I know now that such secrets are destructive and deadly. Such a secret becomes a heavy cross to carry.

XXV: Let him without sin be the judge

I told no one about what had transpired that day at the schoolhouse, not even Gabrielle, but I am certain she knew something was terribly wrong with me. After that day, I practically became a recluse, abdicating most of my responsibilities at school, which then fell to Gabrielle.

At home, I avoided my family as much as was possible. Even Papa, who, by now had succumbed to the addiction of the evil alcohol, surmised that something had changed within me, although he was at a loss as to how to help.

I carried the dreadful secret with me for several months, wearing my mask of shame and guilt on the inside, and praying that, in time, the situation would improve. It wasn't until the beastly man's seed started growing inside of my belly that I knew I would have to confide in Gabrielle, for I would not be able to conceal my secret much longer.

By now, however, more than my body had been brutalized by Luther Merrick. As I had feared would be the case, Mrs. Buchanan had spread word throughout the settlement that I was a harlot, an adulteress who had lain with a married man. Such whispers can have serious ramifications, especially when they fall upon the ears of sanctimonious hypocrites who judge without knowing, or caring about, the truth.

As expected, I was shunned and considered an outcast, for in the eyes of these Puritans, being intimate with another woman's husband was a sin. The villagers shunned me as though I had developed some dreadful disease.

Amongst the chorus of detractors, demands arose for my dismissal as head schoolmistress, a position I reluctantly relinquished, but knowing that no amount of denial on my part was going to undo the damage delivered upon me, I stepped down and handed the title to my best friend. Thanks to Mr. Merrick, the life I had carefully constructed was destroyed, and I was left a shadow of my former self.

"Alexandria," Gabrielle cried when I finally confided in the only friend I had left in the whole wide world. "Why have you not spoken of this before now? What a tremendous burden you have been carrying, and all on your own."

"I am ashamed," I admitted. We were sitting at the kitchen table in my home. "I am ashamed for what has happened."

"But why, my friend?" She spoke with soothing words and refrained from judgment, as a true and ever-lasting friend should, nay as a true God worshipper should. "You have done nothing wrong for which to be ashamed. You must tell someone, Alexandria. You cannot keep this secret any longer, for it will surely consume you."

I knew she was right, but I also understood that it was much too late to accuse Luther Merrick of such a dirty and dreadful deed. The time to have done so was four months earlier, when I had sufficient evidence and cause to prove my claim.

But now such an accusation would come down to my word against his, me an accused adulteress looking for someone else to take on my responsibility, and he a working man with seven children to care for. I understand how the system works.

No matter the seriousness of the claim, I would be the one found at fault and should expect no mercy, no sympathy nor support from the other villagers. No, I understood that I faced a bleak and tumultuous future unless I found a way to change things.

"Whatever happens, Alexandria," Gabrielle said, hugging me closely before departing that afternoon, "you must know that I am your true friend. No matter what happens, you can count on my loyalty, to the bitter end. If you need anything, no matter how significant or minor, please do not hesitate to ask. There is nothing I would not do for you, and you must know this to be true."

"I do," I assured her, hugging her firmly. "It is comforting to know that I have a true friend."

"I fear that our society is not forgiving for a woman in your predicament," she replied through her tears. "It is my regret that Mr. Luther Merrick is not made to suffer the consequences for his heinous crimes."

"In time, Gabrielle," I whispered, vowing to remain steadfast in my convictions. "The man shall be judged for his deeds and that judgment will be handed out by a power greater than that of any on earth."

I understood that Gabrielle took a great risk in remaining my loyal friend, as it would not be acceptable for anyone to keep the company of an accused harlot. But my friend had grown accustomed to being shunned by the so-called good folk of this settlement, those same people who claimed to be God-fearing Bible worshippers.

No matter how I felt about the people of this settlement, however, I understood that I must find a way to make this situation right for the child now growing inside of me. Although it was conceived by a violent and hateful act, I knew I would love this child with all that I am, but I also knew that he would not be accepted into this society unless I could affect a change. My child would be labelled a bastard and would carry that title with him for his entire natural life.

So began the formation of a plan that I hoped would be his salvation. Whatever I was forced to do, I knew it had to be infallible. If I wanted my child to have any chance at a normal life, no one must ever know the truth about how he was conceived.

The remaining months of my pregnancy were difficult. Were it not for the love and support of my friend and her generous mother, Mrs. Lewis, whom Gabrielle took into her confidence with my blessing, I would have been alone. Papa had no idea what to do to help me and I do not blame him for his incompetence in such a matter. While I am certain he loved me as his daughter, I understood his embarrassment that he believed he had raised an adulteress.

It also became painfully clear that my struggles were also becoming his problem, as many of his loyal customers at the mercantile began purchasing their goods elsewhere, as if they blamed him for something I may have done. That loss of business resulted in tensions mounting between Papa and Jabez Gorham, whose relationship had already become tenuous at best because of Papa's growing dependence on alcohol. It was plain to see that the partnership was precariously close to ending and my personal plight may have been the final nail in that coffin.

Seth and his future wife, Elizabeth, also felt the sting of my soiled reputation and, in time, it became easier for them to avoid me than to risk being ostracized as if they condoned the actions of his wayward sister. It broke my heart that my personal reputation had put them in such an untenable situation.

It was unjust that my family had to choose between their place in our society and their daughter and sister, but that is how it was for them. While I missed them sorely, I understood and told them so. I wished them nothing but the best of health and undying happiness, which could only be accomplished if I stayed out of their lives.

I had become an outcast in a village where just people claimed to reside, and I became resigned to spending much of my time alone and isolated from the people for whom I had done so much. My once-daily trips to the market became fewer and fewer, and I relied on Gabrielle to bring me the things I required. I had become the one thing that I had feared I would become, a shunned woman.

The days were long, but I managed to keep myself busy. I took to writing daily in this journal, which I hoped, someday, would be passed onto my child when he or she was of sufficient age to accept the truth.

I read from Mama's Bible, the one she had brought with us when we came to this promised land. While it spoke of harsh justice for those who sinned, I found it difficult to accept the words for their literal meaning, choosing instead to believe that God would be more forgiving than the members of his flock who live in this village.

As the days turned from summer to autumn, I toiled out in the back gardens that Mama had first planted and that I had worked to help her maintain, and to which I had devoted so much time following her death. There was a good harvest that year, with an ample supply of root vegetables and potatoes that would see us through the impending harsh winter that, according to all the signs of nature, was going to be cold with lots of snow.

I also busied myself making preserves, just like Mama had taught me, and I worked hard at maintaining the household, although lately I was the only person using the residence as Papa had taken to sleeping wherever he could find a bed, usually collapsing somewhere in a drunken stupor. His fall from the upper echelon of our society was now complete and I, his only daughter, shouldered the burden of blame.

Gabrielle and Mrs. Lewis, God bless their precious hearts, did their best to keep up with me, while carrying out their own responsibilities elsewhere. With my absence, Gabrielle had twice the workload at school, and Mrs. Lewis had five other children and a husband at home to take care of while at the same time carrying another baby in her own womb. But they did the best they could to care for me.

Were it not for their love and the generosity of these special people, God's angels, I do not know how I would have survived, let alone maintained my sanity. To say it was difficult would most certainly not be an accurate assessment of the situation.

As it had become customary for me to spend a great deal of my time in the back garden, tending to the crops and picking the wild berries that grew in great numbers just beyond our yard, I found myself becoming better acquainted with nature and often resorted to speaking with the creatures who visited there. One of my regular visitors was the large, ebony bird that I had first noticed more than a year ago, at the time of Jonathan's death.

I am certain that had anyone overheard my conversations, they would most assuredly have concluded I had taken leave of my sanity and, truth be told, I was not certain that they would have been misinformed. I talked often to the large, black bird, telling it my deepest and darkest secrets, and revealing my hopes and dreams for my future and that of my unborn child. It helped somehow to speak these things out loud even if nobody spoke in return.

I expected nothing from this creature except for a non-judgmental ear, and I received that. I knew I could speak with Gabrielle about my inner-most thoughts, but I feared I had already placed sufficient burden on her delicate shoulders, so this winged creature became my silent confidant.

In time, it was as though we had developed a bond, and it came to the yard daily. I looked forward to the visits with great anticipation. The bird would sit on a tree branch and I would talk as I worked.

I made a trip to the market one day in November, which in fact would be my last ever appearance before the citizens of this community. The treatment I received on that occasion confirmed my belief that the only opportunity my child would have for a normal life would be one that did not include me, but I had no idea how I was going to make that happen.

I should have waited for Gabrielle to carry out my errands, but she was extremely busy, and I wanted to relieve her stress. My brief time at the market came on a cold afternoon as the bitter wind whipped my long red hair around my head and nipped at my face as if it were a rabid dog.

Not a single person spoke to me the entire time I was there. Even those whom I had helped in the past would not acknowledge my presence. Some vendors quickly closed up shop when they saw me approaching and others, while in my presence, openly spoke about the evils of adultery, saying that women who commit such a sin were destined not only to burn in the fiery depths of hell, but also to carry the Devil's spawn. They pointed at me when they spoke.

If only they had known the truth about my predicament, perhaps their treatment would have been different, but I could not be certain of this. The only thing of which I could be certain was that I had not broken any commandment.

With my pride intact, I held my head high and went about my business. I was comfortable in the knowledge that I had nothing for which I should be ashamed.

Upon my return home that afternoon, with the few supplies that I did manage to purchase, I sat about devising a plan that would allow me to escape the confines of the social prison in which I now found myself sequestered by circumstances that had largely been beyond my control. At that point, I knew not what actions I would have to take to secure my escape, but I feared it would require something drastic on my part.

XXVI: Violet

During the days that followed my misadventure at the market, I could think of nothing else but making good on my plan to escape the shackles that now kept me prisoner in this place I no longer considered home. However, try as I might, I failed to devise a workable plan for my unborn child and me.

The idea of securing passage on a vessel to go someplace else was beyond reach, both from a monetary perspective and from a practicality point of view, as a woman in my current condition, alone and with child, was in no shape to endure a long sea voyage.

I had also thought of packing a few things and fleeing to a neighbouring settlement further down the coast, but with no place to call home or anyone to count on for support once I reached that destination, such an idea did not seem practical either.

Eventually I became resigned to the reality that my child was to be born in this house that had, in recent years, been the place of such sadness, and would be raised as a bastard, a child conceived in an act of violence. He or she would be shunned and ostracized as if he, himself, had committed the cardinal sin.

Even though I had not yet met this child growing inside of me, I knew that I would love him and must provide him with the best possible chance to have a normal life, free of societal stigmas that would surely hold him back and create a miserable existence for him.

It was during one of my visits in the backyard, on a late November afternoon, that an opportunity for escape finally availed itself; although, initially, I failed to recognize the invitation for what it was.

I ventured outside only on very rare occasions by this time, and I often went no further than the safety of the secluded backyard, where I could relax away from prying eyes and gossiping tongues while enjoying the fresh air. On this day, I had brought Mama's Bible with me and was sitting on a small, wooden bench on the back stoop, reading a passage, ironically about God's forgiveness, when I discovered I was not alone.

Indeed, as I glanced around the yard, I found that the black bird had returned, and it seemed as though it was trying to win my attention.

The conversation between the bird and myself started off as it normally did, with me telling the creature everything on my troubled mind, while it rested on the barren tree branch, the leaves having long dried up and fallen for the season. The creature listened intently, bobbing its head as if understanding every word I uttered.

However, shortly into my dissertation, it became clear that on this day my black-feathered friend had something different in mind. Furiously flapping its powerful wings and calling out as if trying to verbalize its communications into some sounds I might understand, the black bird flitted from branch to branch, pausing every so often to keep my attention.

As the bird made its way to the edge of the tree line bordering our backyard, it became clear that this majestic creature wanted me to follow it into the woods.

From the early days when we arrived in the settlement, I remembered the warnings about not venturing too deep into the woods because of the dangers that lurked there. I had mostly obeyed those directives over the years, wandering only on occasion into the woods in search of berries and sometimes wildflowers, but always being careful not to stray too far from the settlement.

Other than that, I had no reason to go there, so the thought that I might follow this black bird into the forests on this cold afternoon in the early days of winter seemed like the thinking of a mad woman. But, throwing caution aside, that is exactly what I did.

I felt compelled to follow the black-feathered creature and, strangely enough, I felt safe in the bird's companionship. For reasons that defied logic, I believed that if it wanted me to follow it, then it must have a plan that might ultimately lead to my salvation.

We ventured deep into the woods that afternoon and, as darkness quickly descended over the dense forest, I realized that, not only had I travelled too far to turn back before nightfall, but I did also not know how to go back. I was lost, cold and quickly becoming afraid. I could also feel my child moving about in my belly and I feared that my anxiety might not be good for him.

The bird, which had stayed with me all this while, sprinted from branch to branch and continued to lead the way until eventually I came upon a small opening in an outcropping of rocks. As the night closed in, it became clear that the bird wanted me to take shelter from the elements among these boulders.

I collected some fir boughs to fit over the opening and placed them within reach, then addressed myself to the narrow space. It was a snug fit, but somehow, I managed to squeeze my large belly into the hole. I then pulled the boughs over the opening and made myself as comfortable as I could.

Darkness enveloped my surroundings and the strange noises of the deep forest echoed throughout the night. I found myself praying for salvation from this hell into which I had ventured.

As sleep overtook my weary and aching body, I also wondered if, indeed, I had finally taken loss of my senses. It was not natural that a sane woman put herself in such a predicament as the one in which I found myself.

"For the love of God," I prayed, "rescue me."

As one would expect, I passed a restless night. Snow fell lightly, covering the forest floor with a thin carpet of white.

By daybreak, I was hungry and cold, and afraid that I would never find my way back to the settlement. But I realized that, by the grace of a power greater than me, I had survived the elements. I pulled myself from the hole in the rocks, understanding that it was the bird that had saved me from certain death.

The creature had brought me to this place where I could stay dry and warm, and stayed with me throughout the night, as if it was ready to defend me from any intruders. My guardian was perched on a nearby branch, its dark feathers now covered in a thin coating of white snow.

"Thank you," I whispered.

As I watched the bird shake the snow from its sleek, ebony body, I asked, as if expecting it to answer, "Where to now? Where must I go?"

Suddenly, as if being summoned from somewhere deep within the mysterious forest, I was startled to notice a slender woman appear near the tree where the bird had perched the night before. She was a vision of natural beauty, draped in thick animal fur, her long black hair falling around her shoulders and her dark skin making a strong contrast to the recently fallen snow.

I had heard stories of the First People inhabiting these woods and I had seen them on occasion around the village, but despite the years I spent in this New World, I had never had reason to meet one. Papa said I had no business mixing with them.

"Hello," I whispered, while extending my hand in what I hoped was a friendly greeting. Although I knew not why, I immediately felt safe with her.

I waited for her response, but eventually came to understand that this woman most likely could not understand my language. Pointing to myself, I said, "My name is Alexandria."

She looked at me. I could see she was puzzled.

"What is your name?" I asked, although I realized if she could not understand my language it was unlikely she could know what I was asking.

We stared at each other as the crow remained calmly on the tree branch, watching us both. Finally, it called out as if issuing a command.

The native woman reached out her right hand to me.

"I do not understand," I said, looking into the woman's dark eyes. "What is it you want?"

She gently beckoned.

"You want for me to follow you?" I asked.

It was a subtle nod, but indeed that was her response. Somehow, she had understood my question.

"Very well," I said, stepping toward her.

In my predicament, I had no other option but to follow the woman, and so I did. I followed silently, trying to stay close to her, as we moved deeper into the forest. I remained dubious of the prospects for getting out of these woods, for I had no idea where we were headed or what lay ahead, but I also understood that there was no turning back for me.

I do not know how far we walked or for what duration, but sometime later we cleared the thick underbrush and found ourselves on the edge of a small native village of numerous huts and shelters, and I could see the smoke rising straight up from several fires. I could not explain it, but I instantly felt this place would welcome me.

"Where are we?" I asked, but the woman did not answer. Instead, she made her way past the structures until she reached the fur-covered opening of a small hut. She entered, turned and waved for me to follow.

Inside, there was a fire pit in the centre and several piles of fur around the outer edges. As well, there were gatherings of straw and pelts, which were clearly beds.

The woman motioned for me to be seated on one of the beds. Then she placed something on a piece of bark that resembled a dish and handed that to me. She moved her mouth as if she intended for me to eat the food, and so I did, as I was famished.

Although the texture was foreign to me, I was pleasantly surprised by the taste and, forgetting my manners, I immediately devoured the entire portion.

"Thank you," I whispered, passing the dish back to my generous hostess. She smiled and nodded.

It became clear to me that the black bird had taken me to the place among the rocks so this woman could find me and bring me back to her village.

Although I longed for answers, I resigned myself to accepting my circumstances. If this woman were kindly welcoming me into her home, then I would be a gracious guest and accept her generosity without question or fear.

"Did you come to help me?" I whispered, not really expecting an answer.

"She did."

I was startled by the deep voice of a man who had quietly entered the hut as I was getting settled. Instinctively pulling my body back on the bed, I asked, "Who are you?"

He answered in a language I did not understand, but I immediately found myself speculating that this man was likely the woman's husband.

"Do you speak English," I asked. I was intimidated by his large stature. I found his tall, hulking body and mannerisms more than a little imposing.

"Pieces," he replied as he carefully studied my appearance.

"You learned at the settlement?" I asked while wondering what kind of connection the black bird had with these people.

"Yes," he answered.

"You say she came for me," I continued. "How would she know to come for me and how would she know where I would be?"

"Black bird," he said, backing up to stand beside the woman.

"The black bird told her? How is that possible?"

"Spirits guide her," he explained.

"The spirits?" I was intrigued and I wanted to know more. "What spirits?"

He said nothing but waved his arms through the air.

"The spirits are all around here?" I asked.

"Yes," he said. He was unable to elaborate.

"So, the spirits, through the black bird, sent her to find me and to bring me back here?" I said.

"Yes," is all he said as he turned to leave, but not before he said something to the woman in their language. From her reaction it was obvious he was giving her instructions of some sort.

"What is her name?" I asked as he made his way to the fur covered entrance. "What shall I call her?"

Again, speaking in a language I could not understand, I believe he told me her name.

"I am sorry, but I do not understand," I said. "Ask her if I may call her Violet?"

I cannot explain it, but to me she appeared to me like a violet, a strong wild floor that grows in these woods in great abundance during the spring.

As he did so using their language, she turned to me and nodded.

"Very well," I said, smiling. "Violet it is." Turning back to the man, I inquired, "Now what?"

"You stay," he answered, motioning to the hut. "Stay here."

"I should stay here?"

"Yes," he said as he turned and left.

The woman stoked the dying embers at the bottom of the fire pit and then threw pieces of brush and wood shavings on the glowing ash. Immediately, the flames jumped to life.

"Well, Violet," I whispered. "What do we do now?"

Smiling warmly, she motioned for me to lie back on the bed, and I did as she instructed. The fur and brush were soft under my back, and I suddenly felt extremely relaxed.

I watched as Violet gathered two plush hides from a pile and brought them to me. She knelt beside the bed and spread them over my body. Instantly, wrapping me in a blanket of warmth. I smiled back at her kindness.

As my body relaxed under the warm pelts, and the fire crackled in the pit, I felt my eyes beginning to close. I was not sure how the black bird had arranged this miracle, but I felt safe for the first time in many months. I was content to be in this place and in the company of this generous woman.

I was truly thankful for whatever spirits had brought me to this place.

XXVII: A tiny angel

After that day, I never again called Liverpool my home. I remained with Violet in her village and welcomed her unconditional support.

In time, we learned to communicate with the use of many words from my language that I taught her. I appreciated the care she provided as I was nearing the end of my pregnancy.

I was thankful to be in a place where no one judged or gossiped in the background when I was near; where no one pointed fingers or accused me of cavorting with a married man whose loyalty ought to rest with his family. I had been welcomed into this village of kind and caring people without questions or judgment. I had found peace.

My relationship with Violet was a most beautiful and natural thing, and while I was unable to arrive at any logical explanation as to how I had found this place or why these generous people welcomed me into their fold, after a period of time I stopped questioning the miracle that the crow had somehow instigated.

I learned to accept my situation for the saving grace that it was. In my hour of need these beautiful people rescued me, saving me from God only knows what horrible fate was awaiting me in the forest or, perhaps even worst, in the settlement that I had called my home.

Weeks passed and the winter closed in on this wild land. The snow was deep and the cold unrelenting, but I was never in want for anything. I was well sheltered from the elements with ample sustenance and a mountain of pelts to keep me warm.

Violet's husband was a good provider and took me into his home as if I were part of his family. I never once felt threatened or alone in this mystical land of wonderment about which I had heard so many horrifying things following my arrival in this new world so many years ago.

I determined that those stories were nothing more than that, pure embellishment by those who wished to frighten others or to keep all of these beautiful experiences for themselves. It is also possible that they were truly too ignorant to understand and appreciate these special people whose homeland we had invaded.

Whatever the case, I considered myself to have been most fortunate that Violet had found me that day among the rocks. I was also thankful for the black bird, for it had clearly played a large role in my rescue from my previous hurtful existence. The bird was truly my guardian angel, my saviour.

If I had one regret about never returning to Liverpool, it was not being with my dear friend, Gabrielle Lewis. I missed Papa and Seth as well, but I knew my brother would be making a good life with his darling Elizabeth Wolfe, while Papa was drinking himself into oblivion and was not likely to even notice that I had gone away. If he did notice, I could not be sure that he would even care that I was missing, not with me being such an embarrassment to him. Perhaps he may even be relieved.

But it was Gabrielle I most fretted over, for I feared that, by running away without an explanation, I had left her wondering about my whereabouts and wellbeing. To her, it must be as if I were dead. I regret that I had likely caused her such hardship.

It hardly seemed fair that one friend would do that to another, but I was in no condition to travel back to visit her. I prayed that, somehow, Gabrielle would feel in her heart that I was in good health and, indeed, in good spirits.

Although I had no calendar by which I could keep track of the passing days, I knew by the natural elements that winter had officially arrived and the stirrings in my belly indicated that the blessed event was near.

I had long ago found a way in my heart to forgive Mr. Luther

Merrick. Were I a vindictive woman, I would have held the grudge and taken it with me to my grave. But I feared that such hatred would be unhealthy for my unborn child.

While the child had been conceived in violence, I vowed that he or she would know only love and happiness and, above all, would not know the hatefulness that had compelled the man to assault me in the first place. That truth would come only when the time was right, when the child was prepared to embrace the reality of his conception.

Based on the number of months that had passed since I followed the crow into the woods, I was certain that it was near the end of December when the first of many sharp pains invaded my belly. I knew, as only a woman could know, that it would not be long until my baby drew his first breath.

The following three days of labour were intense, but I thanked God that Violet remained at my side, wiping the sweat from my brow with a damp cloth, holding my hand and guiding me through this experience. She cried when I cried and when I smiled up at her, she returned the warm gesture. She was such a kind and loving soul, a gift from the heavens.

When the time was near for the baby to arrive, Violet left the hut for a moment and returned with her an older woman whom I had never before seen but quickly came to appreciate. The woman's gentle touch and soothing chants—none of which I could understand—helped me through the most excruciating pain I had ever experienced.

It became obvious from the skill and knowledge she displayed that this woman had helped to guide many babies into this world. She reminded me of Mama, whom I had observed on many occasions working with expectant mothers.

It seemed she worked for hours, and when I saw Violet's eyes light up, I knew the baby had finally arrived. And when I saw the tears starting to flow, I knew there was something terribly wrong. I was tossed on a tumultuous sea of emotions.

"Violet," I whispered, as she tried to avoid my inquiry. "What is wrong? Is something wrong with my baby?"

Were she able to put her despair into words that I could understand, I am certain Violet would have informed me that my baby boy was still born.

"Jonathan, my sweet baby boy," I wept. It had been my plan to name my son after my oldest and dear brother, whom I lost almost two years earlier.

I cried for the child and asked God why, after all the hardships that I had already been through, he chose to punish me in such a manner. I was all but ready to surrender myself to the depths of grief, when Violet shook me to full attention.

I had not been aware that I had been carrying *two* babies. The tribal elder worked tirelessly to bring the second child into the world. The pain was excruciating but I asked God to give this child a fighting chance. I prayed to all that is holy to let this baby live, and to allow me the opportunity to experience the pleasure of motherhood once before I die.

I would never outwardly speak the words that I was thinking, but there was no doubt in my mind that, considering all the trials and tribulations that I had been put through in recent years, that I deserved to hold and nurture this baby and to have him love me as a child would love his mother.

In time, my prayers were answered, and my tears of sadness turned to those of happiness when I heard the baby cry. When Violet turned and looked at me with those big dark eyes sparkling with more joy than I had ever before seen in my life, I knew this baby was special. I knew he was the one and he was mine.

"Samuel," I sobbed as Violet took the tiny baby boy from the elder, wrapped him in a small pelt from an animal I did not recognize, and passed him to me.

"Samuel," I cried again as I gently kissed his face and hands. "My baby," I sobbed as my body shook with unbridled joy. At that moment, all the evil and sadness in the world were forgotten. He was perfect.

I thanked God for answering my prayers and, as I hugged the precious little thing to my bosom, I vowed that my baby would never know the depths to which mankind can fall. My child would never know that he was conceived in hatred. Instead, I promised that he would know only peace and contentment and above all, love.

Over the following months, as Samuel grew stronger from the nourishment he drank from my body and our natural bond deepened, I came to appreciate his presence in my life. But I could not escape the growing sense of foreboding that darkness was about to fall again. I recognized the signs. My body was failing me and, by the time spring arrived, I had reached a conclusion.

After carefully considering all the options before me, I knew what I had to do. I bundled Samuel in several layers of pelts and, with sufficient food and water to make it back to Liverpool, I set out from the native settlement.

Violet came with me to the spot near the rocks where we had first met. There, I was amazed and inspired to discover a large, black bird seemingly waiting for my arrival. It was if the spirits knew of my plight and sent the bird to meet me. I could not know for certain if it was the same bird that had led me to this place several months earlier, but I sighed in relief as the bird welcomed me back, not so much with sound, but in how it moved and how it studied me and the precious package I was carrying in my arms.

"Can you lead me back to town?" I whispered.

The bird immediately flitted to another branch.

"I shall follow you," I replied, for it was clear that the bird knew in which direction we should travel.

Before leaving this place at the rocks, I stared deeply into Violet's dark eyes. They were like deep, pools of the darkest water I had ever seen. I could feel her pain and I understood her suffering, but she knew I must do this.

As the bird called, I quickly embraced Violet one last time. "Thank you, my friend," I said as I held her close.

She kissed Samuel's forehead and then turned to leave. Seconds later she disappeared into the thick woods, and I was left wondering if she had ever really been there at all.

Quickening my steps, I followed the bird through the forest as it moved from branch to branch, keeping a slow pace so as to ensure that I did not lose it from my sight.

I do not know how long it took to reach my destination, but it did not seem as though it took any more than an hour to arrive at the backyard that I had left five months earlier.

Watching from the tree line, I kept my distance, for if anyone were in the residence, I did not wish to be seen. I could not know what had become of the place or if Papa and Seth were there. However, I did not want to encounter either of them this day, for I feared if I did, they would demand an explanation of what had become of me and I did not wish to give them one for I would have to divulge my secret, a truth they must never know.

Remaining hidden in the thick underbrush, I managed to skirt the perimeter of the settlement without being seen. Not much had changed in my absence, not that I had expected much development in just five months.

Finally reaching my destination, I remained hidden until darkness fell. I was thankful that Samuel had remained cooperative during this entire time. He truly was a tiny angel.

As light faded into dusk, I made my way to the back door of the modest home that was my goal and I peered through the bevelled glass of the tiny window. To my relief, I saw Gabrielle sitting at the kitchen table. It was clear she was busily preparing the evening's meal for her family.

I feared that my sudden appearance might put her into shock, but the hour was wearing on and Samuel would soon need nourishment. Gently rapping on the heavy wooden door, I pulled back and remained hidden in the advancing shadows. I waited for Gabrielle to open the door.

"Yes?" she spoke softly, glancing around the backyard. Her word was like gentle music to my ears and I understood how much I had missed her in my absence.

"Is there someone out here?" she asked. I was afraid that she would be troubled if I did not speak soon. "Please show yourself."

I swallowed hard and spoke softly, "Gabrielle, my dearest friend, it is I."

It was as though my friend had seen a spirit, for her complexion quickly faded to pale white and I could see her knees weaken.

"Alexandria," she whispered as I emerged from the darkness. "How?"

She caught her breath. "Where have you been all these months? I feared that you had succumbed to the winter elements."

"It is a long story, my friend, and we do not have much time," I answered while advancing toward the door. "I have an urgent matter to discuss with you."

She took my hand and guided me into the kitchen that was awash in a variety of smells that I immediately recognized as rappie pie, a potato-based dish that I had learned to enjoy during many meals with the Lewis family.

"Please do come in," Gabrielle said. "I have missed you so much. Are you well?"

It was at that moment that my baby decided to make his presence known.

"Alexandria," she said, pulling back the fur in which he was swaddled close to my body. "Who do we have here?"

"His name is Samuel," I told her.

I quickly related the story of how the black bird led me to the native woman, the village hidden in the forest, the birth of my sons and the sad loss of my first-born.

"By all that is holy, you have truly had an ordeal," she said when I was done. I could tell by her expression that she considered my adventures as if they were the fanciful imaginings of a mad woman.

"As extraordinary as this may seem," I assured her, "it all truly happened just as I said."

"Of course, Alexandria." She nodded. "I do not mean to doubt you. I am astonished by everything you have said but so very happy that you have returned."

I knew that our bond was a tight as ever. "How are Papa and Seth?" I asked.

"They were devastated by your disappearance," she said. "They searched the forest for weeks, but when the deep snow closed in, they gave up hope for your safe return. They resigned themselves to the tragedy that you were gone. They concluded you had run away from your sorrows and most likely succumbed to the elements."

"I am sorry they had to endure that." I sighed and wiped away my tears. "How are they now?"

"Your Papa is trying to stay away from the demon drink, but I fear he is losing the battle and he is not well. I regret to say that it appears he is not long for this world," Gabrielle said. "Seth and his bride are soon to move into their new home at The Falls. I am sure they will be happy. They will be greatly relieved that you have returned."

"They must never know," I quickly explained. "This visit with you will be my only stop in the village and you must never tell anyone that I returned. You must promise me this."

"But, Alexandria," she protested, "they miss you so deeply and they are profoundly worried."

"It must be this way," I told my friend.

"Why must it?"

"It simply must," I insisted. "Clearly, they knew of my condition and the speculation that came with it cost them dearly. I regret that they paid for my fall from grace. But they know not of my child, and to explain Samuel's existence would mean I would have to reveal the entire secret, including the assault, and I am not about to do that. They must never know that I had returned, nor must they ever know that my baby was born."

"Very well," Gabrielle reluctantly agreed. "I will honour your trust, even though I do not fully understand your reasoning. But what will you do?"

"Thank you, my friend. I know this is difficult, but I do so very much appreciate your willingness to do this for me," I smiled and squeezed her hand. "I have missed you so deeply."

"And I have missed you," she whispered. Then she added, "There has been an occurrence during your absence that may interest you."

"Do tell." My curiosity was piqued.

"Mr. Luther Merrick is dead," she blurted out.

"Indeed." I was shocked. "How?"

"His death occurred under the most unusual of circumstances. It happened before the turn of the new year. I did not see it for myself, but according to the stories, Mr. Merrick was attacked by a flock of large black birds, as many as seven."

"Black birds?"

"Yes." Gabrielle nodded. "Those who saw it say the birds swooped into town with a vengeance. They made their way directly to the docks as if to seek out Mr. Merrick. By all accounts he put up a brave battle, but the creatures were powerful and too many. He lost the effort and eventually succumbed to his deep wounds. They say it was horrific how he died."

"I can only imagine the horror," I replied, as my thoughts wandered to the black bird that had led me into the forests and my salvation.

It was now clear to me that, just as the black birds had brought me to my refuge, they were also meant to exact revenge on my behalf, but I did not share my belief with my friend. Whatever natural forces had brought us together, had clearly worked their magic.

"It must have been a dreadful sight," I said.

"Indeed," Gabrielle said. "After the attack, the black birds reportedly returned to the forest from whence they had come, causing no harm to any other person in town. They say it was like a large black storm cloud had moved in over the docks that day and then quickly dispersed."

"That sounds like a storyteller's embellishment," I speculated.

"It would seem so, yes," my friend agreed. "Were it not for the many witnesses who relayed the same circumstances to all who would listen, I would be inclined to agree with your assessment."

"Then we shall label it as unexplained," I suggested with mixed emotions about what I had just heard. This was the man who had viciously attacked me, but I had also, by this time, forgiven him. Admittedly, I was torn by this news. "Let us move on, shall we?"

"Very well." She paused and studied me. I could tell my sudden appearance had thrown her into a quandary and I understood her confusion. "While I am happy beyond description to see you," Gabrielle continued, "I must ask: why have you now chosen to return from the woods?"

"The hour is urgent," I explained. "In our time together, I have come to accept you as more than a friend. You have become my kin and it is in that capacity that I must ask you to undertake a great responsibility."

"Anything, Alexandria," she quickly replied. "You know that I will do anything for you."

"And I would most assuredly return the commitment. You must know that."

"I do, indeed. Our bond is deep," Gabrielle agreed. "Please tell me what you would have me do."

As the tears welled in my eyes, I pulled Samuel from where I had carried him next to my heart and offered him to the only true friend I had ever known in this settlement. "You must take him," I whispered, feeling my heart break as I spoke the words, although I knew in my soul this was the only way for I feared the time would soon come that I would no longer be able to care for him as the sickness within me was growing stronger.

"Alexandria," she reacted with emotion and shock. "While he is a precious little lamb, I cannot take your baby."

"You must," I insisted. "I trust him with no one else. You must take him and raise him as part of your family. No one must ever know his true identity. You must do this for me."

"I cannot," she said, and I could tell she was overwhelmed with by my unusual request. "You must raise your own child. Your love for him is obvious. Samuel must know his true mother."

"I am afraid that is not possible, as I will soon not be able to take care of him and provide for him the things he needs," I explained. "He deserves the chance to go onto the greatness that I know awaits him and I am certain that, with you as his mother, he will have that chance."

"Why will you not be able to care for him? Are you ill, Alexandria?"

"He needs you," I said deciding not to burden my friend with worries about my condition. "You must agree to do this."

"Why me? Why not your Papa or Seth?"

"They do not know of his existence and they must never know," I said, placing Samuel in Gabrielle's arms. I could see right away the bond that would exist between them. "When he is of an age when he can understand, you may tell him the truth, but until that time, please protect him from the heavy burden."

"How will I explain that I suddenly have a child?" Gabrielle asked.

"I have considered this," I told her. "Is your mother not about to have another child?"

"She is. Within days."

"When that baby finally comes, can you not keep its birth shrouded in secrecy and in due time, reveal the arrival of twins to the town?" I suggested. "Samuel is extremely tiny, and by this coming summer it would appear as though they were twins. As most of the folks in this town pay little heed to your family, I am sure this deception will work."

"I am not sure about this," Gabrielle said slowly. "Mama and Papa would have to be in on the ruse, and I am not certain they would undertake such a hoax. Even though they love you as if you were their own child, they are not prone to such deception."

"You must convince them that this is the only way that Samuel will have a normal life," I cried. "Now, I must be going."

"You are going to leave him?" she asked, still trying to come to terms with my request.

"Yes." I knew this was the only way. "I must."

"Oh Alexandria, my dear, dear friend," she wept, hugging my baby tightly.

"Do not weep for me, my friend, for it is time for me to rest," I whispered. "I have made peace with this. Samuel will thrive in your care. I know this to be true. Please, I implore you, keep him hidden until the time is right."

"I will honour your wishes," Gabrielle assured me. "I will lay down my life for him, you can be sure of that."

"I am. That is why I came to you."

Gabrielle is holding Samuel now, watching me as I finish my final entry in this journal. When I am done, I will give it to her, along with the black, leather-bound Bible that had belonged to Mama, and that I took with me into the woods.

On the Bible's inside front cover, I have inscribed my name, Alexandria Gorham, at the top of the page. Directly below my name I wrote 'Jonathan (deceased) and Samuel', along with their date of birth.

On the next page in this journal, I have written a note to my beloved child. He will see it when the appropriate time comes. Gabrielle will see that he knows the whole story.

And this is the end of what I can write. Gabrielle is Samuel's mother now, and she will care for him as I could have hoped to.

But I am gone.

XXVIII: My dearest Samuel

My dearest Samuel,

I pray that you are having a wonderful life. While you will not remember the short time we had together, I want you to know that am proud to be your mother.

Now that you have heard the truth from my trusted and truest friend, Gabrielle, and you have read my journal, I pray you have room in your heart to forgive me for what I have done. I also hope you understand that I did what I thought was best for you.

It is my wish that, through my sacrifice, you have found joy and peace with the Lewis family, and that they have raised you as one of their own, with much love and affection. I know them to be wonderful people and I am confident they have treated you well.

While it breaks my heart that I will not be with you on your life's journey, I know you have gone on to become a great man. Please know that I have been with you in spirit, and I will keep you forever in my heart.

Sometimes, my precious Samuel, life can be cruel and may visit upon you hardships that will test your resolve, but I am certain you will be brave and strong. Keep your faith. You will persevere, for there are no hardships that you cannot overcome with desire, passion and belief in yourself.

I must impart one more piece of information that will be of great service to you. If you have read my journal, you know of my life's journey, my joys, my trials and tribulations. I must now share with you the power of the crows and how they brought me through the trying times.

Take heed, Samuel, for these majestic and powerful birds are your allies. They are never to be feared, for they will never bring you harm. I still do not know what great power bestowed upon me the special gift that allows me to connect with those black birds on a spiritual level, but I owe my sanity and my very survival to these beautiful creatures, who rescued me in time of need. They pulled me from the deepest, darkest well of despair that one could ever imagine, and we developed a bond that few can ever share, and fewer even understand.

I have passed that bond onto you, for we have made a pact through which I am certain they will watch over you, your offspring and our descendants for generations into the future. Rest assured, my son, that, with the crows to bear witness, you will suffer no injustice or indignity. Somehow, while a logical explanation is not evident, I know this to be their vow to me and I know their bond to be true for they watched over me as guardians, guiding me through terrible times. Do not ask how it can be so, because I do not understand it myself, but, we are somehow miraculously connected.

In turn, I vowed to them to remain with the people of the land who took me in, and to help them as best I can as their world is being invaded. I will remain with them for as long as my ever-weakening body will allow.

Dear Samuel, it would be my ultimate wish to see you one more time before I break free of these mortal chains that have kept me tethered here but I feel my journey is near complete and my life has all but run its course. I would give all that I am to hug you tightly one more time, to kiss your forehead, and run my fingers through your beautiful hair.

I would give my life to gaze upon the great man that I know you have become. With all my heart, I wish for you a long, happy and fulfilled life.

In your hours of trouble, look to the crows and know they are my messengers. Take comfort in their numbers and rejoice in their presence for they are your guardians and your protectors.

Goodbye, my sweet, sweet baby boy.

Crows and Owls

29: Parliament is in session

They listen without making a sound, heads almost completely rotating as if on swivels. They carefully check out their surroundings. Their concentration is intense; their yellow eyes search for their prey.

Perched on wooden posts, the three, large brown and white raptors, their razor-sharp talons ready to strike, knife-like beaks ready to tear their victim to shreds, scan the caged enclosure that holds them and their brethren.

These powerful birds hunt and feed on small animals and other birds. They are equipped with keen vision that allows them to detect and catch prey with their sharp talons and hooked beaks. They usually hunt under the cover of darkness, but they are also known to strike in the daylight.

Zeroing in on their prey, they take position, ready to spring into action.

As the large black crow bounces across the grassy bottom, oblivious that its fate has been sealed, the owls spring from their posts. They are stealthy, gliding silently through the still air.

The trio swoop toward their unsuspecting target. And then, in an instant, they strike.

By the time the crow senses the danger, it is too late. The owls are cunning hunters and there is no escape.

As the crow sends out a distress call to a flock that is nowhere nearby to hear its cries, the largest owl's powerful talons grab its neck, piercing through the layer of black feathers and tearing through flesh until it finds the spinal cord.

The crow is paralyzed. Mercifully, its death is swift.

"That was brutal," the student says to the teacher as the owls quickly devour their kill. "It never gets any easier to watch."

"You should be used to it by now," the teacher snaps, checking the locks on the large enclosure that houses dozens of owls of various species, large and small, gathered over the years from habitats around the world. "You have been observing our friends ever since you were a child, and you know this is part of the natural order of things."

"It may be natural, but I'm not sure I will ever get used it," the student says. "There's so much violence in their kills."

"It's not violent; it's the way things are." The teacher's anger is obvious. "You and I have had this conversation many times, and you know it's their instinct, part of how they survive. The owls must hunt and they must kill."

"Doesn't mean I have to like it."

The teacher glares at his charge. "It is also part of who *you* are, a large part of your inheritance. You must accept it as your birthright."

"But why our family, and why crows?"

"Our feud with the crows goes back centuries," the teacher says. "As I've told you many times, both families of birds are genetically imprinted with an intense and strong dislike of the other. It's instinct. Simply put, crows don't like owls and owls don't like crows. Those black birds are our mortal enemies."

"Is that why we've come to this town? Are we here because of the crows?"

"You know it is." Sighing forcefully, the teacher says, "Crows and owls have been at war with each other since a major wrong was committed against one of our ancestors in this town, when the crows acted as judge, jury and executioner. We have come to make things right."

"Why now?" The student is almost afraid to ask. "Why me?"

"These battles have been fought for generations in many locations, but the war has finally come home to roost. You have seen the book of owls, where all our heroes are honoured. They were the chosen ones. You are the chosen one now, and, in time, your picture will join the others."

"I don't want to be in that book."

"It is an honour to be included among the heroes. You should be proud."

"Not if it means I must attack one of my friends. I can't be proud over that." He pauses and then, taking a deep breath, says, "You say this is all part of a plan, but the timing just seems so—so random."

"There is nothing random about it. Their chosen one was born sixteen years ago in this town and our champion was born sixteen years ago in our former home. This battle is inevitable."

"But I don't want to do this."

"You will. You cannot refuse it, for it is your destiny just as it is his destiny. It is time. The owls have spoken and the crows know we are here."

"I am not ready for this," the younger one says, his voice not much more than a whisper.

"Well, my boy, if you are not ready by now, you never will be ready," the teacher says. "But I pray you are, because the battle is nigh and there is no room for the faint of heart."

30: The morning inquisition

Jesus, Alex thinks, rolling over and blinking his eyes open. *What time is it?*

Facing the window, he can see the sun is shining brightly as the light peeks around the edges of the closed blind.

He slides out of bed and checks his phone, where it has been charging at its station on the desk. He sees that it's 7:27.

Still early yet. No wonder I'm so tired, he thinks, remembering that he had stayed up most of the night reading Alexandria's journal. *My God, I can't believe what that poor woman went through.*

He moves to the window and timidly pulls back the blind. He carefully surveys the backyard and is relieved to see no one there. *If only everyone knew the real story behind Alexandria Gorham, maybe they might reconsider the legend they've heard all these years.*

"She was not a witch," he murmurs, just as he hears a light knocking at his door. "Mom, is that you?" he asks.

Stupid, he thinks. *Who else would it be at this hour in the morning?*

"Yes, Alex." She speaks softly. "I was just on my way downstairs to get coffee and I heard you moving around in there. Is it okay if I come in?"

"Sure."

"Morning, honey," she says, entering the room. She gives him a warm hug. "How are you this morning? Did you sleep well?"

"Not bad, I guess."

"I saw your light was still on a few hours ago when I got up to use the bathroom. Were you okay?"

"Fine," he says, choosing not to tell her that he had difficulty sleeping as he was worried about the note and the man he's seen several times outside the house. "I started reading when I went to bed and I guess I must have fallen asleep with the light on. But I slept okay. How about you? Sleep well?"

"Not really. I tossed and turned all night, but mostly I just stared at the ceiling," she answers, taking a seat on the edge of the bed. "Thank God it's Saturday and I don't have to be at the office, or my ass would be dragging. So, what do you have planned for today?"

"Not much, really. Bree is dropping by before lunch and we're going to meet up with Ozzie. We were thinking that maybe we'd take a hike through Pine Grove this afternoon. We like hanging out there. It's very peaceful. I like how quiet it is."

"That sounds nice. I like it over there, too."

Alex can tell she's studying him and he knows she wants to ask more questions, most likely about his visit with Zoey the night before, but he decides not to push her about it as it's much too early for an argument.

"Remember to take some water with you," she tells him. "It's supposed to be hot this afternoon."

"I will." In an effort to make conversation, he asks, "Hunter up yet?"

"Yes, he got up a while ago and had a shower. I think he's already downstairs getting breakfast. He has to be at the store for nine."

"Right. How about you? What are you going to do today?"

"Don't have a whole lot planned, actually," Samantha says with a shrug. "I've finally got a Saturday where there's not much happening around town and I'm kind of feeling lost."

"I imagine you are. Your Saturdays are usually hectic and filled with all kinds of official functions that require the mayor's presence." He smiles at her and adds, "Maybe you could use this day just to relax? That would do you a world of good. Or maybe you could spend some time with Kate. You haven't done that in a while."

"Maybe." She returns his smile and the room suddenly becomes quiet. "Was thinking maybe we'd swing by the farmers' market this morning. It's been a while since I've had the chance to drop in there and I always enjoy my visits as I get to catch up with a lot of people."

"Sounds nice." Feeling an increase of tension, Alex quickly says, "So, Mom, if we're done here, I'd really like to grab a quick shower before I get something to eat."

"Oh yes, sorry, honey. Didn't mean to slow you down," she answers, quickly jumping off the bed. Making her way to the door, she adds, "Alex, you know if there is anything you want to talk to me about, I'm always here for you. Anything at all."

"Yes, Mom, I do know that," he says, speaking softly. "But I'm okay. Why?"

"I don't know. It's just that I get this feeling you're not being completely honest with me about everything that happened last night between you and Zoey. You know how I feel about that woman and I hope you would not keep secrets from me."

"Come on, Mom. Don't do this already this morning." He exhales and continues, "It's too early. Let's not ruin the day before it even gets started."

"I'm not doing anything, Alex," she says, remaining calm. "I just want you to know that I am here for you, but I can't help if you don't tell me everything. That's all I'm saying."

"And I appreciate that, but there is nothing to tell you."

He joins her at the door and gives her a quick kiss on the cheek. "You will be the first one I tell if I need anything. Now, if you don't mind, Mom, I'd really like to get that shower."

"Of course, Alex." She studies him and adds, "Sorry to delay you."

When she is gone, Alex closes the door and sighs. *She knows something is up, but there is no way I can tell her what Aunt Zoey told me last night or she would lose her mind, and God knows what she'd do.*

Returning to the desk and opening the bottom drawer, he removes the mysterious note that he found affixed to the front door. Quickly scanning the message that reads, "I'm coming for you!" he thinks, *There is no way I can tell her about this or it would really blow her mind.*

Neatly folding the paper in half, Alex places the note inside the backpack that he plans to take with him to the park. *Oliver must see this. He'll know what to do.*

Retrieving a robe from a hook behind the door, Alex makes his way to the bathroom. *Or at least I hope he will.*

By the time Alex arrives in the kitchen, the entire family is gathered there, laughing and eating their breakfast.

"Morning everyone," Alex says, going directly to the fridge to get a glass of milk.

"Morning, Alex," Kate says, grabbing his arm and gently spinning him around. She gives him a hug and adds, "How's our boy today?"

"Good," Alex replies, returning the hug and planting a light kiss on her cheek. "All good here."

"Great." Kate watches as he pours a glass of milk.

"And…?" he asks, his eyes squinting in the bright sunlight that's spilling around her shoulders as it comes in from the window over the sink.

"And nothing," Kate replies. "Just haven't seen you for a day or so." She shrugs. "That's all."

He nods. "Yes, well, everything is going great. Happy that school is out for another year and looking forward to hanging with Bree and Ozzie today."

"Yes, the dastardly duo," Kate says with a chuckle. "How are they?"

"Fine, I imagine." He takes a large gulp of milk. "Haven't heard from either of them yet this morning, but it is only early and it's Saturday, so they may not even be up yet."

"Hmmm, right," Kate says. "Your mom and I were thinking maybe we could have a nice family dinner together this evening. It's been a while since we were all together for a meal, and everyone appears to be free. We can celebrate the start of summer."

"I have to work until five," Hunter answers. "But I should be home by six. Dinner actually sounds nice. Is it okay if I invite Ally? It's Saturday night and we usually do something together on Saturday nights."

Exchanging glances with Samantha, Kate shrugs. "I guess so. We would love to have her join us."

Turning to the younger boy, she asks, "How about you, Alex? Would you like to ask your friends to join us?"

He considers the suggestion and then says, "I'm sure they'll be busy."

"You don't know until you ask, Alex," Kate says. "Is there some reason you don't want to ask them?"

"No." He shakes his head. "I just know they do a lot of things with their own families, especially on the weekends."

"Can you at least ask them?"

"Maybe he's ashamed of us," Hunter suggests. He adds with a wink, "I know I'm ashamed of him."

"Come on, Hunter," Samantha responds. "That's not helpful and it's not funny. You know that's not the case, so smarten up."

"Maybe he's ashamed of his friends, then," Hunter counters. Grinning at his younger brother, he adds, "More specifically, maybe he's nervous to be around Bree. She is pretty cute."

"Just shut up, Hunter," Alex snaps. He knows his brother is just being a pain in the ass, but he doesn't like it when Hunter picks on him.

"Yes, Hunter. Knock it off," Kate adds. "Just be quiet and finish your breakfast. You have to go to work soon."

"Yes, ma'am."

Hunter quickly gulps down the last few mouthfuls of frosted coated, blueberry flavoured mini-wheats, his favourite cereal. Placing the dishes on the counter near the dishwasher, he says to Alex, "Sorry, bro. I was just having some fun. But you have to stop being so sensitive about everything that I say. Lighten up some."

"Hunter." Samantha's tone is sharp. "Please go to work."

"I'm going. I'm going." He laughs, leaving he kitchen. "See you all around six."

"So," Kate says again to Alex. "Will you ask them, or don't you want to invite them?"

"Yes," he sighs. "If it's going to make you guys happy, I will ask them but don't be disappointed if they say no."

"Don't do it for us, Alex," Samantha says. "Do it because you want to spend time with them. We like the pair of them; they're nice kids, but they are your friends. It's up to you, so please do whatever you feel comfortable with."

"I said I'd ask them and I will," he answers. "Now, let's just drop it."

"Okay, Alex," Kate nods. "Moving on. Anything exciting happen with you yesterday?"

Staring at her, he says, "You know what happened yesterday, Kate. I'm sure Mom has told you everything by now."

"She has," Kate agrees, nodding. "I was asking for your perspective so I can get a better understanding of what's been going on while I was away."

"Nothing's going on," he answers, getting frustrated of this constant questioning. "You know the story. Aunt Zoey came back to town yesterday and I met up with her last night where we talked a bit about my family's history. And that's all that happened. Nothing more."

Studying his face, Kate replies, "That's it? That's all that happened?"

"Like I said, that's all."

"You're not holding anything back?"

"No." Alex is trying to remain calm, but he is losing his grip. He finally says, "What is it with you two? Can't you just believe me when I tell you something? It's like you don't trust me."

"Honey," Samantha steps in. "It's not you we don't trust." She pauses to study her son's reaction, then adds, "It's *her* we don't trust."

"I know. I know. You have made that point perfectly clear."

"Come on, Alex. You can't really blame us," Samantha says, "not after everything that has happened in the past."

"Yeah, well, maybe you don't know the whole story."

"The whole story?" Kate asks. "What does that mean?"

"Nothing." Alex fears he has slipped up and may have already said too much. "It doesn't mean anything." He stops short of losing his temper. "Now, can we just please drop it, please? I'm hungry and I want to get something to eat before Bree gets here."

"We just want you to know that we don't like this, Alex," Samantha says, approaching him where he's still standing near the fridge. "We worry about you."

"A little too much."

"That's because we love you and we want you to be safe."

"I know that, and I am safe." Glancing at both women, he shrugs. "Now, can I eat, please? I'm hungry."

Taking Samantha by the arm, Kate says, "Come on, dear. Let's let him get his breakfast."

31: Someone is watching

"Hey, lazy bones," Bree says when Alex opens the front door. "Are you ready to go?"

"What do you mean?" Alex laughs at his friend's declaration. "You're early. It's not even ten-thirty yet." Holding the door open, he adds, "I wasn't expecting you until around eleven, but come in. I'm not quite ready, but it won't take me long."

Leaning out and looking around, he asks, "Ozzie's not with you?"

"Nah, he said he was too busy right now," she answers, pushing past him into the house. "He wants me to text him when we're leaving, and then on our way to the park we have to stop by his place and meet him there."

"Busy? On a Saturday morning? What's he doing?"

Moving to the living room, Bree says, "I don't know and I didn't ask him. Wasn't really any of my business."

"Don't you find Ozzie is being a little bit strange these days?" Alex says, following her.

"What do you mean 'strange'?" Plopping on the couch and thinking about Alex's question for a few minutes, she adds, "I hadn't really noticed anything unusual."

"Strange, you know, as in being evasive and distant, like he's constantly distracted or something," Alex explains as he sits down next to her. "Maybe it's just me, but don't you find he's kind of pulling away from us?"

Bree considers Alex's observations. "I've never really thought about it before, but now that you mention it, I guess he does seem a bit more standoffish than usual. I mean, Ozzie has always been a little off kilter compared to most people, but I find it's his little quirks that I like most about him. I think they make him unique."

"Maybe." Alex nods. Pausing for a minute, he then adds, "But lately, it's more than that. Don't get me wrong. You and Ozzie are my two best friends in the whole wide world, but these days I just pick up a strange vibe around him." He sighs and adds, "I can't really explain it and maybe it's just me."

"Have you talked to him about it?"

"I would, but I don't know what to say and I don't want to upset him," Alex tells her. "How do you start a conversation like that with someone who is a close friend? Do you suppose it's not us that he's having trouble with? Maybe it's someone else, like another friend?"

"He has no other friends, Alex," Bree says. "Besides you and me, there is no one else that he hangs with, so who else would he be upset with? He's pretty much a loner and we are all alike in that way. We don't easily fit in with others."

Alex sighs heavily. "That is true, I guess." He shrugs and adds, "Well if it's not us, then maybe it's someone else."

"Like who?"

"I don't know, like his family?"

"It's just his father and his younger sister, Dani, so I can't image he's having serious problems with either of them, except the normal shit that we all have to deal with when it comes to our families. Really, I don't think I've ever heard him talk about other family members."

"I don't know." Alex pauses and then says, "His dad is more than a little weird, so I wouldn't be surprised if it had something to do with him."

"You've said that before, Alex, but I don't really see it." Bree shakes her head. "I haven't been around his father all that much, so I'm not really sure what you mean, but he always seems nice to me."

"Like I've told you, I can't really explain it. It's just a feeling I have whenever I'm around him." He looks away from her, then adds, "It's this vibe I've always had—like he's watching me, studying me. And it makes me feel really uncomfortable."

"That's creepy, Alex. Have you ever stopped to think it may be all in your head?" Bree stares at her friend and then finally asks, "Has he said something that offended you?" She pauses then adds, "Has he ever done anything inappropriate around you, like made a pass at you?"

"Jesus, Bree." Alex jumps from the couch and stares at his friend. "*That*'s creepy. And no, he hasn't. He hasn't done anything like that."

"Sorry," she whispers. "I didn't mean anything, but you just never know about people. I was just trying to help you figure this out. You're the one who brought it up."

Glancing at the clock on the wall, Alex says, "It's getting close to eleven. I guess we should go. Why don't you text Ozzie and tell him we're leaving in a few minutes? I'll pop upstairs and grab my backpack. By the way, did your mother happen to mention anything about Ozzie's father calling about that barbecue?"

"No." She shakes her head. "Not yet." She studies him then says, "You know, Alex, if you don't want to go to his barbecue, then don't go."

"I think my mom really wants to go, so I don't see that I have much of a choice. Something about her mingling with her constituents, or something like that," he says and shrugs. "I'm not a politician and I don't think I'd ever want to be one. I see how hard mom works and the shit she puts up with. Phone calls at all hours of the day, constant meetings and people yelling at her over stuff they don't even understand. It's just not worth it." Making his way up the stairs, he adds, "I'll be right down."

"May I use your washroom?"

"Sure," he says, his long legs easily taking the steps two at a time, "but you don't have to ask. You know where it is."

By the time Alex comes down the stairs again, Bree is standing at the front door. "All set?" she asks, opening the door.

"I sure am," Alex replies as he goes out ahead of her. "Let's get go—Fuck!"

"What's wrong, Alex?"

"This," he says, pulling a piece of paper from the front door. "Here's another one of these fucking things."

"Oh, my God." Bree recognizes the paper right away and knows that it's just like the note from yesterday. "What does it say?"

"I'M WATCHING YOU!" the note reads in large, red letters.

Alex studies the paper. "Jesus Christ," he says, his mind quickly racing to understand what this message means. He feels like he has just been punched in the gut. Taking a deep breath, he whispers, "What the hell is going on here?"

"I don't understand." Bree reads the note over her friend's shoulder. "I got here less than half an hour ago and there was nothing on the door. I promise you, Alex, there was no note there when I got here," she scans the front yard. "That means whoever put it there might still be around."

"I believe you," he whispers, also scanning the front yard. "What the hell does all of this mean?"

"I don't know," she says, her shaky voice conveying her apprehension. "What should we do?"

"I think we should go back inside for few minutes where it's safe. I need to think this through."

Quickly retreating into the house with her, Alex slams the front door behind them and turns the deadbolt. "There! If someone's out there, they can't get in."

"Now what, Alex?" The concern in Bree's voice is palpable. "Should we call someone?"

"Who?"

"I don't know. Your mom, maybe." Her breath quickens. "The police?"

"I can't call the police, and I don't want to worry my mom," he says, taking a deep breath to gather his thoughts. "This will push her off the deep end."

"You did tell her about the note from yesterday, didn't you?"

"I was going to tell her last night, but she was already upset about Aunt Zoey coming back and I didn't want to make things worse."

"For frig sake's, Alex, you have to tell her."

He knows she is right.

Bree continues, "You have to take this more seriously, or else something is going to happen. Two notes in two days and someone lurking around your house tells me someone is out to get you."

"Maybe the notes weren't intended for me. Maybe I'm just the one who found them first." He looks helplessly at his friend as if grasping for straws. "Maybe it's all just a big joke."

"You know this isn't a joke." Her eyes narrow as she thinks about the note. "And I don't think they're meant for anyone else. If someone is watching the house, as you say there is, then they know when everyone else left and they can put a note on the door without being caught. Clearly, this was meant for you."

"Do you think?"

"I do," she whispers. "And so do you."

"You're probably right," Alex pauses to consider her words, then says, "I think we should cancel our plans for today."

"I think that's a good idea." Tears trickle down her cheek. "I don't really feel much like going to the park anymore. I'm scared and I'm afraid for you."

"Maybe you should go home," he suggests. "Do you think if you called your mother, she would come and pick you up? I don't think it's a good idea if you walk home by yourself right now."

"She would, yes." Bree nods, brushing away the tears.

"Just tell her I wasn't feeling well."

Pressing her mother's number on her favourites' list, Bree says, "And what are you going to do if we don't go the park?"

"I am going to talk to someone who I think can help me."

"Who?" She squints at him as she listens to the phone ringing.

"A friend. Oh, and can you let Ozzie know we're not coming?"

She nods, then, after her mother answers, Bree tells her quickly about the change in plans. "I'll be watching for you to pull up at Alex's, and I'll come right out....Thanks. You're the best."

As soon as the call is done, she turns to face Alex. "Who will you talk to?"

"I can't tell you."

"Can't or won't?" She glares at him. "I'm afraid for you, Alex, but I can't help if you're not fully honest with me."

"It's just a friend," he tells her. "Someone who is helping me with things."

Bree studies him. "I don't like any of this. You could be in real danger. You need to tell someone about this who can really help you find out what's going on."

"I will."

"Like your mother."

"She'll worry."

"Of course, she will, and she'd have every reason to worry," Bree says, the tears still falling. Speaking softly, she adds, "I'm worried and you should be worried."

"Come on, Bree, everything is going to be okay." Pulling his phone from his backpack, he adds, "Just give me a minute until I make this call."

Seconds later he says into the phone, "Hi. It's me. I need to see you right away....Yes, it's urgent. Can you come by and get me?"

He listens to whoever is on the phone and then says, "Twenty minutes? Okay, I will be waiting. Thanks."

"What are you up to Alex? Who was that?"

"Like I told you, it's a friend who can help me figure this out."

Watching for her mother through the window in the front door, Bree says, "You're making a big mistake, but it is your decision."

"Sorry about this afternoon. I was looking forward to hanging with you guys." He smiles, trying to put on a brave face for his friend. "Maybe we can do it tomorrow?"

"Maybe," she agrees. "Just call me later and let me know what you find out."

32: Birds of prey

"Hi Alex," Oliver says as the slender, white-haired teenager opens the door of the red half-ton truck that he uses in his contracting business. He watches as Alex jumps into the cab.

"Hey Oliver," he says, throwing him a quick smile as if to convey the message that he's being brave about all of this. "Thanks for coming right over."

"No problem. You said this was urgent. What's up?"

"It is urgent," Alex blurts out, grabbing the seatbelt, pulling it snuggly around his skinny frame and securing it into place. Looking straight ahead, he adds, "Let's go someplace where we can talk, and no one can see us."

"How about my place?" Oliver suggests. "There's no one there and I typically don't have unexpected guests."

"Perfect," Alex says, remaining focused on the street ahead. "I have a lot to tell you."

"Are you okay?" Oliver puts the transmission in drive and presses the gas pedal. "You don't sound okay."

"Yes," Alex nods, quickly turning his head in all directions as if scoping out the neighbourhood.

Spotting the large black crow circling above his house, he sighs heavily. *Augustus. Thank God*, he thinks, and adds, "But a lot has happened since last night and we have to talk."

"Do you want to talk about it while we're driving?"

"Not really. I'd prefer to wait until we get to your place." He pauses and gathers his thoughts. "I have something to show you."

"This sounds serious," says the man who—if everything Zoey told him last night about his bloodline is true—Alex must consider as his protector. "Should we also involve your aunt in this discussion?"

"Probably. But not right away. I just want to talk to you first."

"We'll be there in about fifteen minutes and then you can tell me everything."

Once at Oliver's place, Alex quickly removes the two notes from his backpack and relates the entire story, including that he has seen someone snooping around the house.

"At first, I thought maybe it was a reporter, because they have just showed up at the house before, looking for the boy who survived the tragedy thirteen years ago," he says. "But the more I think about it, I really don't think so, especially with the messages."

"God damn," Oliver mutters. "You say all of this started yesterday?"

"Yes, in the afternoon."

Turning to face the teenager, Oliver asks, "Why didn't you say something last night?"

"Because," he exhales and then says, "I didn't know if it was something I should worry about or not."

"Oh, Alex, I think it's clear that this is something we should be worried about," Oliver responds. "What did we tell you last night about being prepared for anything and watching out for any possible threats? I think this qualifies as a threat."

"I know." He nods. "I know and I'm sorry I didn't tell you."

"It's no good to be sorry after the fact. If we are going to get you through whatever's coming, we must take everything seriously. We have to be cautious. I know this is all new to you and it's all very scary, but you have to accept it and deal with it straight on. You have to be aware of your surroundings at all times and, like I said, take everything seriously, even if it seems like it's something insignificant. Never let your guard down." His posture becoming stiff, almost defensive, he says, "This threat is real."

"I get it."

Looking the boy straight in the eyes, Oliver asks, "Do you? I'm not so sure you do."

"Yes." Alex returns the glare. "I do get it and I know you're right." He exhales and glances away; "I know you are trying to help me, so, from now on, I promise I will tell you everything."

"Good." Oliver nods. "It's very important that you do."

"Who do you think is doing this?"

"I have no idea, but we have to figure out who sent these notes and who the hell has been lurking around your house." Oliver picks up his phone.

"Who are you calling?"

"Your aunt Zoey. I think it's time we told her about this. She may have some ideas."

In less than half an hour, Zoey is at Oliver's place and listening as Alex relates the events from yesterday and this morning.

"Shit." She pushes her hair back behind her ears. Alex can tell the news has hit a nerve.

"What does all of this mean, Aunt Zoey?" Alex asks. "Do you have any idea who is doing this? And why?"

"Yes." She sighs heavily. "Unfortunately, I do."

"So, tell me, please. I need to know who is out to get me."

Turning to Oliver as if searching for reinforcements, she swallows hard.

He nods and says, "Go ahead, Zoey. Tell him everything. This is not the time to hold back."

"Okay, Alex, I will tell you who I know is doing this and why," she says. "But first I have to tell you something else." She pauses, and then asks, "Did you have chance to read Alexandria's journal yet?"

"I did." He nods. "I read the entire thing last night. It was incredible. I can't believe what that poor woman went through."

"It was something else, that's for sure," she agrees. "Do you remember reading about Luther Merrick?"

"Yes, he was the son of a bitch who attacked Alexandria in the school."

"Exactly." She nods. "This entire story—everything that is happening to you right now and everything that is going to happen in the near future—is connected to him and what he did to her."

"I don't get it." Alex shakes his head. "How so?"

"You will also remember that, in her journal, Alexandria writes that seven crows made Luther Merrick pay for his indiscretions.

They killed him."

"Yes, I remember." Alex nods. "It's chilling to think about that, and I wish I could say I felt sorry for the bastard, but I don't."

"He got what he deserved, but in the process of carrying out their brand of justice, the crows ignited an ongoing feud with the owls that has spanned the generations."

"Owls?" Alex is confused. "I don't understand."

"Yes," Zoey answers. "Why the owls took on the charge for that bastard remains a dark mystery that many of our ancestors have tried—and failed—to unlock over the centuries, but make no mistake, Alex, this feud is real and it has landed at our feet. They say the sons inherit the sins of their fathers. Well, the descendants of Luther Merrick inherited his sins and they have carried this bitter blood feud with them throughout the generations."

"This is too incredible to believe." Alex tries to swallow but suddenly his mouth is dry and he doesn't have any spit. He says, "I really can't wrap my head around all of this. What is the special bond that connects the owls to that family?"

Zoey searches for the words to help him understand. "Just as we embody the spirit of the crows, thanks to the mysterious connection that Alexandria forged with the black birds, the members of the Merrick family embody the spirit of the owls and, as such, we are mortal enemies." Her eyes narrowing, she explains, "Just as crows and owls are natural adversaries in the real word, the conflict between our families is also real. It's been a battle that has been passed down from one generation to the next until, just like you, they have reached their own chosen one—the fiftieth ancestor of Luther Merrick."

Squinting at his aunt and trying hard not to jump to any conclusions, he takes a deep breath and asks, "That would be who?"

Zoey, again, looks to Oliver.

"Go on," Oliver says with a nod. "You must tell him. He needs to know."

"Well, Alex," Zoey says, "It's your friend, Ozzie Merrick."

The words hit Alex like a brick to the head. "Oh no. No way," he says, softly, trying to hide his emotions. "So, you are telling me that

Ozzie and I are, what, mortal enemies?"

She nods. "I am afraid so."

"And what does that mean, exactly?"

Oliver answers. "It means, Alex, that you can't trust him or anyone in his family. No one connected to him in way. It means they are coming after you."

"To do what?"

"To hurt you. Their ultimate objective is to destroy you—to kill you," Zoey answers, going straight to the point. "They believe that if they kill the golden one then they break this centuries-old curse."

"Ozzie would never do that."

"Maybe not on his own." Oliver says. "But it's his sworn duty to the owls and you can be sure his father is behind him, pushing him. I know you think he is your friend, but you can't trust him."

"But—"

"No buts, Alex." Zoey picks up the conversation again. "It's just like Oliver says. You cannot trust him. No matter how well you think you know him, Ozzie Merrick is not your friend."

"But he is," Alex insists. "I've known him for the past couple of years and we have been through a lot together. He would never do anything to hurt me. I am positive about that. I know him."

"You only think you know him, Alex, but the truth is, it has all been an act with him and with his entire family."

"I have to talk to him."

"I know you want to, but you can't," Zoey cautions. "It's best that the owls don't know we've figured this out. Keeping this to ourselves gives us an advantage."

"Do you really think Ozzie would hurt me?"

"I do," she says. "My grandmother, Clara Underwood, told me the whole story, just as her ancestors told it to her, and I've researched this family feud my entire life. It's Ozzie's mandate. He cannot resist, no matter how hard he tries. The instincts are genetic. He has been programmed for this confrontation his entire life and so he is on a mission. What you thought was a friendship over the past few years, has really been him collecting intel about you and your family. He knows your weaknesses and your vulnerabilities. He's been studying you and so has his father."

"I can't believe this."

"Believe it."

"Can we stop them?"

"I hope so, but it will mean that you will ultimately have to confront him. It is the only way."

"You mean fight him?" Alex shakes his head. "I could never do that."

"You will not have a choice, Alex. This die was cast hundreds of years ago when Luther Merrick attacked Alexandria Gorham and now you two are on a deadly collision course."

"I have to tell mom and Kate." Alex exhales after considering what he has just heard.

"You really can't tell anyone, Alex. The thing about secrets is that once they have been spoken, they can never be untold."

"But what if they are in danger?"

"They *are* in danger," Zoey tells him. "The owls will stop at nothing, and they won't let anyone stand between them and you. These notes and this person sneaking around your yard is just them taunting you. They are playing with you, like a predator plays with its prey. It is the owls, that is a certainty."

"How do we fight them, then?"

"Whenever I've been on my trips over the years, "Zoey says, "I've not only been studying crows. I was also studying owls, and that is how I know that the only way to fight them is to meet them head-on. If you cower in a corner, they will keep on coming at you until they finish the job. They will devour you unless we stop them, for, if the legend holds true, only one of you will survive."

"Jesus." He cringes at the thought. "I really don't understand all of this."

"I know it seems like a lot." She pauses to give her nephew time to reflect on what he's heard, then adds, "But remember what Alexandria Gorham wrote in her journal—the crows are with us. They are watching. They will help us and they will protect us."

"But they are only birds."

"They are more than birds, Alex. You know that," Zoey answers.

"Because of the pact Alexandria made with the crows, they have not only been watching over us, her ancestors, but this entire town. As she explained in her journal, no one in this place knew that she sent the crows to be the guardians of her village."

"That was a long time ago," he says.

"It was." She nods. "But the crows have been watching over the people of this town, even though we haven't even been aware of what has been happening. It has been recorded by the keepers that, throughout this town's history, the black birds have fought against evil and oppression, and protected the weak and vulnerable. At times, their cause has been misinterpreted and even misunderstood. They have been shunned as well as feared, but always, their motivation has been to do Alexandria's beckoning and that of the chosen ones, those who are her direct blood line: us."

33: Revelations

Glancing at the call display screen on her phone, Samantha sees it's Cliff Graham. She quickly answers. "Hey, Cliff. What's up?"

"I'm doing what you asked me to do," the retired police officer says. "I'm keeping tabs on one Miss Zoey LaCroix." He is watching Oliver's house and has been staked out for the past forty-five minutes. His truck is hidden around a corner, and he is behind a shed on a neighbour's property. "What are you up to on this fine summer day?"

"Kate and I have just popped down to the farmers' market to pick up a few things for dinner tonight. She took off to look at something, so if she comes back, I will have to stop talking about that woman," Samantha tells him, while scanning the marketplace for her wife. "I haven't told her that I asked you to watch Zoey because she won't like that I did that. I will only tell her when I know you've found something that we should be worried about. Should we be worried?"

"Honestly, Sam, I don't know what I've got," Cliff says.

"So, do you have anything new to tell me since last night?"

"I do," Cliff says. "There's definitely something going on with Zoey and Oliver. I followed her here almost an hour ago and she's still in there."

"At Oliver's house?"

"Yes, and get this." Cliff pauses as he knows this tidbit of news will upset his friend. "Your son is also there."

"What? Are you sure? He told me he was going to Pine Grove with his friends today. I thought he was there."

"Well, I don't know what to tell you, Sam, because I am positive he's here."

"That little bugger," Samantha says. "He lied to me. I thought he and I had reached an agreement that he wouldn't see her again after last night until I could go with him. I am not happy about this."

"Didn't think you would be."

"What the hell is that woman up to, and with Oliver, no less? I still can't believe that he is sucked into some kind of relationship with Zoey LaCroix, and now she's pulled Alex into the mix." She exhales and adds, "This can't be good."

"I wish I could tell you more about what's happening with them, but I can't hear what they're talking about. But I will stay on it."

"Of course, Cliff. I appreciate that piece of information," she tells him. "I'll have to try and figure out some way to bring this up to Alex without pissing him off. He won't take too kindly if he finds out that I have his aunt under surveillance."

"No, I'm guessing he would not be too happy about that."

"So, what now?"

"I'll stick with her until noon, then I have to take off for the afternoon. Carly and the girls are down for the weekend, and I promised them and Julie that I would go to the beach with them." He cringes and adds, "I hate the beach; all that freaking sand and suntan lotion. I would rather stay home and watch the Jays' game."

Samantha laughs. "Oh, Cliff, it's not all that bad. How are Carly and the girls?"

"Good. They are heading home tomorrow so I figured I better spend some time with them."

"As you should. Zoey's crap can wait."

"No, don't worry," Cliff says, his eyes pulled to activity around the front of Oliver's house. "I've got one of my guys lined up to keep a watch. I promised you I would keep tabs on her and that's what I'm going to do....Jesus."

"What's up Cliff? What is it?"

"I'm not sure, Sam," Cliff tells her. "I am going to have to call you back."

"No Cliff, don't cut me off without telling me what's hap—"

He ends the call, cutting off Samantha. He says to no one, "What in the hell is going on over there?"

From his vantage point behind the shed, Cliff watches several crows that have suddenly landed in Oliver's front yard. He quickly counts them, "Six." He exhales and whispers, "What are you guys up to?"

Moving from the side of the shed to behind a nearby flowering lilac bush to gain a better view, Cliff keeps his eyes locked on the crows. *What are you guys doing?*

The crows have circled *something* on the ground. *What you got there, fellas? What is that?*

"Shit," Cliff says. *Is that another bird?*

The six crows suddenly move into action, springing toward the other bird they seem to have trapped. With talons and beaks moving swiftly, the black guardians tear into their quarry without hesitation or sign of remorse.

Come on, guys. That's pretty freaking brutal.

The prey is helpless. The death is swift.

What did you guys just do? Better still, what kind of bird was that?

Grabbing his phone and turning on the camera mode, Cliff points it toward the commotion and zooms in on the circle of crows, hoping he can get a better look at the other bird now lying motionless in the middle of the gathering.

Clearly, whatever that was, you guys didn't want it to get away.

Focusing on the motionless form, he asks no one, "Is that an...owl?"

~

Inside the house, Alex has just learned some dark secrets about his existence and, according to Zoey and Oliver, what awaits him in the near future. Hearing the commotion on the lawn, the trio quickly open the front door.

"An owl," Zoey says, studying the bloodied body that is the crows' handiwork.

"This time of day?" Alex asks. "I thought they only came out at night."

"Typically," Zoey says. "But they can emerge in the daylight if they have reason to, especially if they feel threatened."

"Threatened? By what?"

"Us. Or, more specifically, you," Zoey tells her nephew.

"Why now?" he asks. "What's got them all riled up?"

"I'm not sure." Zoey shakes her head. "But clearly, they've been motivated into action by something—or someone."

"So, what do you think this one was doing here?" Alex asks.

"Spying," Oliver answers. "It was a scout gathering information for the others."

"And for the Merricks," Zoey quickly adds. "Let's not forget that they are the ones behind this."

"Do you really think so?" Alex asks, watching the crows. They remain fixed in their circle, motionless, as if they are awaiting their next command. *Just like obedient little soldiers*, he thinks.

"I do." Oliver nods as a sudden and loud piercing screech cuts through the still air.

"Augustus," Alex says, spying the larger, jet-black crow perched on a nearby tree branch. Clearly, this one is in command. "Man, am I ever glad to see you, Augustus. Did you do this?"

The crow stares at him, its black beady eyes blinking steadily.

"The Seven," Zoey says as the other six crows suddenly spring from the ground and fly off around the back of the house. "If they are here, things are starting to get serious."

The larger crow caws a few times and then it also takes flight, following its brethren, leaving the broken and bleeding body of the dead owl sprawled on Oliver's lawn.

"You and Alex go back inside," Oliver says. "I'll get rid of that thing."

"Come on, Alex," Zoey says, taking her nephew by the arm and leading him back inside. "We need to make a plan."

"A plan?" he asks.

"For when the owls come back," Oliver says, jumping off the front steps and approaching the owl's body.

"You think they will?" Alex asks.

"Oh yes," Zoey answers her nephew. "There's no question about that. They'll be back and in larger numbers. This little one was sent to watch us."

Closing the door behind them, she adds, "The next ones will be warriors and they will be on a mission with one target in mind—you."

~

In his hiding place behind the lilac bush, Cliff is stunned by what he's just witnessed. *What the hell was that all about?*

He retreats to the shed, being careful to remain hidden. Glancing at his phone, he thinks about calling Samantha Henderson to fill her in on the latest.

But what would I tell her? That I just watched a bunch of crows kill a little owl?

He sighs heavily. *That's not news. She'll think I'm fucking nuts. Hell, I think I'm fucking nuts.*

Checking the time on his phone, he sees it's almost noon, which means he has to leave.

Come on, Cliff Graham. Get a god-damned grip. Slipping out from behind his hiding place, he thinks, *these freaking crows are going to be the death of me yet.*

He's been dealing with unusual crow behaviour around this town from as far back as he can remember, and he can't shake the feeling that something major is brewing with those black birds.

I don't know what you're up to, he thinks, sliding behind the wheel of his truck, *but whatever it is, I'm sure it's not good. I'll be watching you guys, but not right now.*

He says to the empty truck, "Right now, it's time for the beach. Oh, yay!"

~

Using a shovel that he's retrieved from a back shed, Oliver scoops up the owl's bleeding carcass and is about to toss it into a compost bin when his phone rings.

He slips the phone from his back pants pocket to see who's calling. *Charlie? What the heck does he want?*

"Hey, bud," he answers. "What's up?"

"Hey, yourself," Dr. Charlie Webster responds. "Not much, just chilling. It's going to be a scorcher of a day, according to the forecast."

"Thanks for the weather update," Oliver replies, "but I could have told you that."

"That's what I like about you, Oliver. No time for small talk; it's straight to the point."

"Sorry, Charlie," Oliver says, tossing the owl's remains into the bin. "How are you?"

"Good. Everything's great."

"How's Rebecca and the kid?"

"We're all fine," Charlie says. "I'm just calling to see what you're up to today. I've finally got a free weekend and Rebecca is taking Liam to visit her parents, so I'm totally on my own. They are staying for the night and, if you're not doing anything this afternoon, I thought maybe we could hang for a bit. Haven't seen much of you lately, and I thought maybe we could grab a few beers and catch up."

"Geez, Charlie." Oliver thinks quickly. "I'd really like to, but I don't think I can this afternoon." Carefully choosing his words, he adds, "I'm kind of busy."

"Busy? When were you ever too busy to pass up free beer?"

"You have a point," Oliver chuckles. Thinking about it further, he adds, "Can you give me a few hours so I can finish up here? How about around three?"

"I can do three," Charlie answers. "Why don't you come by my place? If you're interested in staying for dinner, I could throw a couple of steaks on the barbecue."

Returning to the house through the back door, Oliver says, "You might be able to twist my arm." He chuckles. "Need me to bring anything?"

"Nah, just yourself."

"Okay, sounds good."

Oliver ends the call and, before closing the door, he scans the backyard looking for any more crows—or owls. Then he pulls the door closed and makes sure the locks are secured.

Can't be too careful, he thinks, remembering his earlier warnings to Alex.

He heads back to Zoey and Alex in the living room. *Odd*, he thinks. *I haven't heard from Charlie for weeks and now, all of sudden, he calls with an invitation to hang.*

He can't quite put his finger on it, but for some reason, the call seems out of place today. *Don't get paranoid, Oliver*, he thinks. *You don't need any distractions right now, not with everything that's going on. That kid is counting on me, so stay focused.*

"Well, Alex, that is an interesting question," Zoey is saying as Oliver joins them in the living room. "Hey, Oliver," she says. "Did you get rid of it?"

"It's gone." Turning to Alex, he asks, "What's an interesting question?"

"I was just asking Aunt Zoey about you and your family."

Oliver frowns. "What about me and my family?"

"I'm not sure if Aunt Zoey has ever allowed you to see Alexandria Gorham's journal or not, but there is some very interesting information in there about what I assume must be your family, as I know your ancestors go a long way back in this town, just like mine."

"I've seen the book with her, but since I am not a member of your family, I am not permitted to read it." Turning to Zoey, Oliver asks, "What's he talking about?"

"Don't you think it's time you told him, Aunt Zoey?" Alex pushes. "If, as you've told me, it's best for the truth to come out, don't you think it should *all* come out, including everything that involves Oliver?"

Zoey stalls and studies the pair standing in front of her. Looking for the right words, she finally says, "It's just that I wasn't sure it would serve any purpose at this point."

"Oh, I think it's important," Alex replies. "And I think we should tell him."

"Tell me what?" Oliver asks. "If you guys know something that involves me, then I have a right to know it. If we are going to be a team, then let's be a team and make sure we are all fully informed."

"I agree." Alex takes a stern tone and says to his aunt, "Either you tell him, Aunt Zoey, or I will."

Zoey sighs forcefully, "All right, then. I will tell him." Facing Oliver directly, she says, "Oliver, the truth is that, while you and Alex are not blood relatives, you are kin, connected by the same events that started this battle a couple hundred years ago."

"What are you talking about?" Oliver turns to Alex. "Are we family?"

"Sort of," Zoey says. "You have heard me talk about Alexandria Gorham having a baby boy. His name was Samuel."

Oliver nods. "Yes. I've heard you and Alex talking about it, but what does that have to do with me?"

"Alexandria could not raise her son. She gave her baby to someone to raise for her. That person was her best friend, Gabrielle..." she pauses, as she is not sure how Oliver will react to what she is about to tell him.

Oliver waits, but he is growing impatient. He finally says, "Go on, Zoey. Finish your statement."

Studying the man who is her strongest ally in this ancient battle, the one she and Alex must lean on right now, she finally says, "The parents of Gabrielle Lewis raised Alexandria's baby as their younger son. It appeared to the community as though he was Gabrielle's younger brother."

Oliver finally says, "What the hell are you talking about?"

Alex jumps in. "I am descended from Alexandria's son, Samuel. You are descended from Gabrielle's brother. They were raised together. Although not related by blood, you and I are tethered together by events that happened hundreds of years ago, just as I am tied to the Merrick family."

"Jesus," Oliver says through taut lips, his eyes narrowing to tiny slits. "Why am I just hearing about this now?"

"Because that's not what's really important in all of this," Zoey says. "Other than the fact that you are Alex's protector, your family connection is irrelevant."

"Irrelevant?" Oliver snaps at her. "I'm irrelevant in all of this? Aren't I the one who has to risk my life to protect this kid?"

"Okay. Okay. I'm sorry. That was a poor choice of words," Zoey says, trying to remain calm. "I didn't mean it that way. You know how I feel about you."

"Do I?" Oliver glares at her. "You should have told me about this."

"The important thing is that now you know why the crows chose you to be Alex's protector," she tells him. "Because members of the Lewis family have always been part of the big picture. Your family has been protecting Alexandria's descendants pretty much from the beginning. And you are right, I should have told you about this a long time ago, but knowing that truth doesn't change anything. Your number one priority is to protect Alex, as it is also my number one responsibility."

"It's a lot to digest," Oliver says after a long pause. But after studying Alex for several minutes, he says, "I know my priority and I know what I have to do." Facing Alex directly, he adds, "I will do whatever I have to do to protect you from this threat, Alex, you can be sure of that."

"Thank you, Oliver," Alex says. "I feel safer when you are around."

Oliver nods and turns back to Zoey. "Is there anything else I should know? Have you been keeping any more secrets from me?"

She shakes her head. "No, I promise, that is all. No more secrets."

"Sure," he says. He squints in her direction and sucks a large gulp of air between his clenched teeth. "I'd like to believe you."

34: Lost equilibrium

It's almost two-fifteen by the time Alex returns home, where he finds Samantha waiting for him in the living room. He notices she gives him the cold shoulder when he enters. He knows this isn't like her as she usually greets him with a smile and most times, a series of questions or comments. If she ignored him, then that can only mean one thing—she's mad at him.

Shit, he thinks, joining her on the couch. *This isn't good.*

Taking a deep breath, he says. "Hey, mom. It was so quiet in here, I wasn't even sure if you were home."

"Yes, sir, I'm here." She does not look up from the paper she's reading.

Alex detects something in her voice that tells him he's in trouble. "Where's Kate?" he asks. "I thought you guys were spending the day together."

"She had to run over to Charlie's for a couple of minutes," Samantha answers, still focusing her attention on the report in front of her. "She'll be right back."

"What did you guys do this morning?" He's trying hard to get her full attention, but she isn't budging. He can tell she's not happy with him. "Anything exciting?"

She takes her time answering but finally exhales and says, "We went to the farmers' market and stopped at the café for lunch. Nothing major."

"Well." He sighs heavily, thinking that he should just leave before she lights into him. He's not sure what's bothering his mother, but he can tell she's struggling to keep her emotions under control. "That sounds like a nice quiet Saturday morning."

"Hmmm, it was nice," she says, nodding, but refusing to make eye contact with him.

Finally, after a few minutes of awkward silence, she asks, "And how was Pine Grove?"

"It was nice. We just walked and sat beside the river. You know, just sort of hung around there," he tells her. "It's always quiet there, very peaceful and calm. I was surprised there weren't more people around taking advantage of this sunny day."

"Yes," she agrees. "It was a lovely day."

"Okay then," he sighs again as he starts to rise from the couch. "I guess I'll just pop upstairs. I've got some things I want to get done before dinner."

"Please sit down, Alex," she says, finally raising her eyes to connect with his. "We need to talk."

"Talk about what?" He hates these confrontations, but he fears one is bubbling near the surface and she's about to explode.

"You are lying to me." She exhales with a force. "I know you were not at the park this morning." She stares at him, unblinking, as she does when she is angry. "So, I am going to ask you again and I expect you to be honest with me. Where were you—*really*?"

Plopping back on the couch, he studies his mother's face. He hates that he's been caught in a lie. For as long as he can remember, he's always told her the truth; but when it comes to anything to do with his aunt Zoey, he knows how she will react, so he usually tries to skirt the issue.

"Okay," he sighs. It's clear, this time she knows the truth. "I was with Aunt Zoey, but I didn't want to tell you because I knew you would be mad...and I can tell that you are."

"Oh, you can tell that I'm mad, can you?" She squints and her face turns red. "Well, I am very mad, young man, but I don't know who I'm maddest at—that woman for bringing out this side of you, the side that I don't like; or you for lying to right to my face."

"I'm sorry."

"Sometimes, Alex, sorry isn't good enough," she says. "I thought you had more respect for me than to lie to me. Even if you think something is going to make me mad, I expect you to be honest with me."

"I know 'sorry' sometimes doesn't cut it, but I didn't think you would understand."

Looking directly into his eyes, she asks, "Understand what, exactly? That your aunt doesn't think twice about putting you in harm's way? That she turns you into something that you aren't—a liar?"

"It's not like that," he tells her, trying not to raise his voice, even though he's growing frustrated by her constant attacks on his aunt. He knows she's not perfect, but she is family. "It's just the opposite."

"The opposite? What are you talking about, Alex? Are you in danger? Are you in trouble?"

Jumping to his feet, he looks back down at her and says, "I just can't tell you."

"Sit down, Alex. We're not done. What do you mean, you can't tell me? You know you can tell me anything. If you're in trouble, I can help."

"You can't help me with this."

He decides he must leave the room before his mother gets him to talk. He knows his refusal to answer her questions will only make her angrier, but he has learned over the years that she has the uncanny ability to get him to tell her every secret he has. He fears that if he stays, she'll get this secret from him. He can't risk that—not yet at least. "Some things are better left alone."

"Alex," Samantha says as her son walks away. "You can't leave when I'm talking to you. You have to tell me what's going on. I'm worried about you."

"No," he says, darting up the stairs. "I can't."

"Please come back down here so we can talk," Samantha calls after him.

Closing his bedroom door, he leans against the wall and sighs. *How in the hell does she know where I was?* He wonders if she's somehow tracking him. He's fully aware of the technology out there that would allow her to do just that.

She wouldn't, he tells himself as he makes his way to the window. *Or would she?*

He pauses and tells himself to calm down. *Maybe she would do that if she thought I was in real danger.* He knows this isn't over because once his mother has a bone to pick, she won't let it go.

She's kind of like a rabid dog, that way, he thinks.

Scanning the backyard, he spies the large black crow resting on a tree branch that hangs close to the house. "What am I going to do, Augustus? She is never going to let this drop. She knows something is up, but I can't tell her anything. She won't understand."

He studies the bird's reaction. "Truthfully, I'm not even sure I understand. And Aunt Zoey says if my family finds out about what's really happening, then they'll be in danger. But they could already be in danger."

The bird stares at him, its dark, beady eyes blinking quickly.

"I wish you could talk to me," he whispers, pressing his face against the glass. It's cool despite the outside humidity and he finds it a bit refreshing. "You would know what to tell me." He sighs and adds, "You would know what to do."

The crow freezes and remains still. It stares at him.

Let go, Alex. He hears the voice enter his head. It's like someone is whispering in his ear.

He tries to shake it off.

No. Don't fight it. Feel the warmth of the sun on your skin. Hear the gentle breeze as it rustles through the leaves. Listen to the tiny songbirds as they chirp nearby....Let go of the anger. Let go of the fear....Embrace what you know to be the truth.

The voice echoes, bouncing around in his head.

Closing his eyes, Alex feels his body become light and he drifts as if he is transported to another place; another time. As if by instinct, he embraces the feelings that are enveloping him. He knows, somehow, not to resist.

He sees nothing but light. He hears nothing but silence. Until the voice interrupts his tranquility.

"Alex, I don't want to do this, but I have no other choice," the mysterious male voice reverberates in his head, sending shock waves through his mind as his body tingles with tiny electrical charges.

It is the voice of someone he recognizes.

"I am compelled by them to strike you down," the male says.

And this time, he recognizes the person who is speaking. "Ozzie?" he whispers, as a face comes into view, emerging from the dense fog that seems to be embracing them. "What are you doing here? How did you get here?...Compelled by who?"

"I have come for you," Ozzie answers, but his voice is different. His tone is more firm and cold, devoid of any emotions. His words sound hollow, as if they are an echo. "I cannot fail. I must do this. It is inevitable."

"Do what? What's inevitable?"

"This is our destiny, Alex. Yours and mine. We are the chosen ones," Ozzie says, as dozens of owls suddenly appear from the void and flutter about, hovering near his friend. The birds remain silent, but clearly they are there to protect Ozzie. Alex can sense that they are the warriors.

Alex suddenly feels a rush of adrenaline flow through his body. "It doesn't have to be this way," he tells his friend.

He senses danger and looks around. They could be in a room or maybe not; he can't tell as the fog is too thick. It's a place he does not recognize, a place he has never been before. Wherever it is, he knows he is not safe here and he must find a way out.

"Let me help you. Despite what we have been told, we don't have to do this."

"Yes," Ozzie tells him, remaining emotionless. "It's in our blood; we cannot fight it. It is who we are. It's our destiny."

Feeling drawn toward Ozzie, Alex resists the urge to confront him, but he knows he must defend himself or he will surely die.

"Jesus!" Alex screams.

His eyes snap open. He feels lost, dizzy, as if the room is quickly spinning. He's out of control. *Where in the hell am I?* he wonders.

Grasping for reality, Alex remains still. Resisting the urge to panic, he feels the blood slowly return to his brain and suddenly realizes he's lying on the hardwood floor of his bedroom and staring up at the ceiling.

He takes a deep breath and then quickly exhales. *What the fuck?*

He feels lost. *How in the hell did I get here?*

One minute he was standing in front of the window, talking to the crow and now, he's sprawled on the floor, not able to remember how he got here.

Just breathe. His chest feels heavy, as if someone placed weight on it.

Giving himself a few minutes to regain his bearings, he suddenly remembers his aunt Zoey telling him about how she has visions and how they always seem so real to her. He also recalls her saying that if he hadn't already received visions, she expected he would soon get them, especially in light of what is about to transpire.

Did I just have a vision? he wonders, rolling onto his side. Pulling his knees up to his chest, he turns himself into a ball of human flesh.

Was that a vision? Was it a look at my future? Are Ozzie and I destined to confront each other?

He is confused. *I don't want to fight Ozzie. He's one of my best friends.*

Regaining his balance, he slowly rises to his feet and returns on the window. "Are you still out here, Augustus?" he asks, scanning the yard and trees for his black-feathered friend. Spotting the large bird, he says, "Did you send me that vision? Is that what they are like? Do you really have the power to do that?"

Making eye contact with the crow, he adds, "It was you, wasn't it?" He swallows and the saliva feels like tiny shards of glass as it passes through his constricted throat. "Holy crap. That was wild. What are you trying to tell me?"

Studying the bird's movements as its head bobs back and forth, its eyes blinking as if it's sending Morse code, Alex nods.

"I think I get it," he says. "I understand. You want me to remain focused on the task at hand and not be distracted by anything else—including my mother. My life depends upon it."

The crow bobs its head as if it is agreeing.

"But I know Mom is worried about me and she only wants to help. I hate making her feel this way."

The crow suddenly becomes still, taking on a defensive posture.

"I get it. I get it." He takes a deep breath. "She can't help. There is nothing she can do."

He breaths in and the air makes his lungs burn. "There is no way of stopping this, is there?"

The crow springs from the branch and takes flight, quickly soaring off out of sight. *Probably off to meet up with the others.*

"So, what am I going to do?" he says, even though he is alone in the room. Snatching his phone from the desk, he quickly dials his aunt.

She answers after the first ring. "Hi, Alex, everything okay?"

"Not exactly."

"What's wrong? Are you okay?"

"I am okay," he tells her, struggling to maintain his grip on reality —whatever that is. "Well, physically at least, for now, but my brain can't take much more of this."

"What's going on?" Zoey asks

"I think I just had my first vision," he blurts out. "And now I'm really confused. It was wild—and so real."

"Tell me everything that happened and everything you saw."

"I...," he stammers, then digs deep and continues. "I saw me and Ozzie in a place. I have no idea where we were, but he was surrounded by all kinds of owls that scared the crap out of me. I knew they were there to help him; to attack me."

"Did he say anything to you? Could you hear him?" Zoey asks, adding, "Sometimes I've had visions and I can't hear any sound."

"He told me he was coming after me. He said he didn't want to do it but he had no choice because they were making him do it. Was he talking about the owls, Aunt Zoey? Was he saying the owls were making him do this?"

"Yes, Alex. I would say that is exactly what he was talking about." She pauses, then adds, "The owls and Ozzie's father. Do you know if his father was there? Did you see him anywhere?"

"No. I just saw Ozzie. Everything was kind of hazy, like there was a cloud of thick mist hanging over us." He pauses, still unable to come to terms with this recent development. "It was probably one of the weirdest things that has ever happened to me."

"I know exactly what you mean, Alex," she says, her words becoming less urgent.

"What should I do? If my vision comes true, then that means my friend is coming after me. I can't let this happen. I really don't want to face off against Ozzie. He's one of my best friends." He swallows and, speaking softly, adds, "I don't know what I would do without him and I don't want to see him get hurt."

"Alex, we've had this discussion," she says. "You must do this because, at the end of the day, it will either be you or him who survives. That's just the way it's meant to be; the way it has been foretold for several hundred years. This is your destiny and you have to decide if you're going to rise up and face it, or buckle under the power of the owls. If you do that, you won't survive—we won't survive."

"That's a lot to deal with, Aunt Zoey." He sighs heavily, fighting hard not to cry. *I'm stronger than that. Tears*, he thinks, *will make me appear weak.*

"You were meant for this, and if you work with us, we can get you through it. Let the crows be your guide. Remember, Alexandria made this pact way back then and it's the crows' sworn duty to protect you. Follow their lead. Listen to Augustus. The others in the flock will do whatever he commands and he will make them come to your side. You will never be alone as long as I am with you...as long as the crows are with you."

"I hope you're right, Aunt Zoey," he says. "Ozzie seemed so focused and...determined."

"I am right, Alex," she tells him. "Would you like to meet again and talk further? I would come to your house, but Samantha won't want me there. You could come over here. Oliver is out for a couple of hours so I can't send him but I could come and get you. I prefer you not walk over here alone. Not right now."

"No. I am okay here. I'm safe. No one can get into this place," he tells her. "Thanks to mom, we're locked down tighter than a fortress. I just needed to talk to you."

"You can call me any time, Alex, day or night. Same goes for Oliver. We'll always be very close by."

"I appreciate that."

"Bye, Alex," he hears her say as he ends the conversation.

"Jesus. This is all too much," he says, exhaling with a force. Moving back to the window, he adds, "What in the bloody hell am I stuck in the middle of? Destinies? Pacts? Vengeance? Crows? Owls? What in the fucking hell am I going to—?"

As he gets close to the window, he notices someone as they quickly duck out of sight behind a hedge.

"No fucking way," he says, bolting to the bedroom door and bounding down the stairs, his long legs taking two steps at a time. "Not this time, you fucker."

"Alex?" Samantha immediately springs from the couch. "What's wrong, honey?"

Throwing open the front door, he says, "Nothing. Just don't follow me."

"You're freaking me out," she answers, ignoring his directive.

She follows close behind her son as he heads directly to the hedge where he saw the lurker less than a minute ago. "Where are you going? What are you doing?"

"Nothing," he says. "Please just go back inside."

"Not a chance," she says. "You're scaring me."

Alex stops as he reaches the hedge and surveys the area. "Nothing," he says, breathless. "Not a God-damned thing."

"Alex, can you please tell me what's happening?" Samantha says. "Are you okay?"

After a glance at his bedroom window, he answers, "I am just fine."

"Well, you don't look fine. Tell me what you are doing."

"I can't," he says, turning to go back inside the house.

"Yes, you can and you will," Samantha says. "Right this minute, or you are in big trouble."

"It was nothing, Mom. I just thought I saw a dog out here and, from my window, it looked like he was injured," Alex lies. "I thought maybe it was hit by a car out in the street, but I guess I was mistaken."

"You thought you saw an injured dog from your bedroom window?"

He can tell she's not buying it. "Yes, I guess I was just seeing things."

"I don't think so, Alex, and I don't think you are being truthful."

Making his way back through the front door, he says, "I am sorry if I frightened you. I just wanted to help the poor dog."

"Well, you did scare me, and I have to tell you, mister, I am not buying your explanation." Her frustration is evident in her words. "There was no dog, injured or otherwise."

"Well, I am sorry you don't believe me," he says, making his way back up the stairs. "But that's what happened. Now, if you don't mind, I think I'll take a nap before dinner."

"Alex, please come back down here so we can talk about this. I want to know what's really going on with you."

"I'm fine, Mom. Really. I'll be back down in a little while," he says, quickly ducking back into the sanctity of his bedroom and closing the door.

I just need to think. He sighs, falls onto his bed and closes his eyes. *I need to wrap my head around all of this.*

35: Payback

"Here you go, buddy," Dr. Charlie Webster says, handing his good friend Oliver Lewis a cold beer. These two have been friends for many, many, years.

"Thanks, man," Oliver smiles, accepting the beer and taking a long drink. It's hot this afternoon so the cold liquid tastes good. "That hits the spot," he says, sitting the half-empty bottle on the arm of the wooden Muskoka chair.

Taking a chair next to Oliver on the back deck, Charlie says, "So, what have you been up to?"

"Not much, really, except for work. I've got jobs lined up to at least the end of October and I expect people will soon be calling to book me for some last-minute work before the holidays."

"Geez," Charlie laughs. "Don't even say that word. Summer's just getting started and I don't want to think about the holidays for a few more months yet. But I'm glad to hear work is going so well for you."

"Oh, it is," Oliver says. "If there's one thing about being a contractor, it's that you can always find work. There's always someone wanting something done in their house or around the yard."

"That reminds me," Charlie says. "I have been thinking about renovating the basement. We haven't touched the place since we moved in, and Becca also wants to make some changes in the kitchen, like adding a new countertop. Mostly cosmetic. Think you would have time to squeeze us in? I'd like to tell her we're finally going to do it. She'll be surprised, 'cause she's been after me for a while now to call you about doing it and I've kept putting it off. But you'd be doing me a real solid if you could put us on your schedule."

"Depends on when you want it done."

"I know Becca would love to have the work in the kitchen completed sooner rather than later, but whatever you can do for us would be great. I don't think there's any great rush," Charlie tells him. "As far as the basement goes, I'm not in any hurry, so that work can wait until you have more time on your hands."

"I have no idea when that would be," Oliver says. "My advice is to get it done all at once. That way, you only have your place torn apart one time and you limit the mess."

"I guess that makes sense." Charlie nods and takes a sip of beer.

Oliver pauses and considers his schedule. "As it looks right now, I could probably squeeze you in at the end of August or early September. I've got some other jobs lined up for around that time, but maybe I can push them for a bit. I expect they'll take a while so if you want this work done, you better do it now while I have some flexibility in my calendar."

"That would work for us." Charlie smiles. "I'll let Becca know, and if you can tell us a week or so before you are coming, we will move things out the way so you can have free access."

"Great, and I'll drop by some time when Rebecca is also home so that I can hear what she wants."

"She trusts me to tell you what she wants."

"Well, I don't," Oliver chuckles, cocking his right eyebrow. "Not one freaking bit."

"What? I have good taste," Charlie says. "You wouldn't trust me with renovations?"

"Nope." Oliver shakes his head. "For when I'm sick, yes. For your renovation and design skills, not so much."

"Even after everything we've been through over the years?"

Oliver stands pat. "Not even after everything we've been through."

The two men laugh and take sips of beer. "Okay," Charlie concedes. "You know me too well, my friend. I'll let Becca handle the interior design work."

"Smart move, partner," Oliver says. "But come on, Charlie, while I appreciate the work, is that the real reason you invited me over for beer and steak?"

"Do I need a reason?" Charlie studies the man he's known for as long as he can remember and then says, "We hadn't seen each other in quite some time, and I thought it would be nice for us to catch up."

"Seriously? If you say so." Oliver remains suspicious. "But we've gone for a lot longer than this without so much as a phone call and it never seemed to bother you before."

"Yes, I say so." Charlie's voice and demeanour confirm for Oliver that his friend may be hiding something. "I didn't think I needed any other reason to spend a few hours with my best friend."

"You don't." Oliver takes another sip of beer. He grins, "I like beer and steak."

The two men become quiet. It's an awkward kind of silence, as if they are searching for the next topic of conversation.

A few minutes later, Oliver finally smiles and says, "Okay, friend, so what time are we eating? I haven't had anything all day and I'm starving. I think I could eat a horse."

"No horse," Charlie answers, springing up and ducking into the house. "Just good ol' Grade A beef."

He returns to the deck a few minutes later with a plate stacked high with tenderloins. "Just picked these up this morning, so they're nice and fresh. Still take your steak medium rare?"

"Yes, sir. That's the best way."

"Let's get it going, then," Charlie says, laying the steak on the hot grill. "So, Oliver, what else is new in your world? Seeing anyone special?"

"Nah, I don't have time to date these days."

"Really? Handsome stud like you?" Charlie chuckles. "I thought you would have been snatched up years ago."

"Not interested, brother." Oliver shakes his head and adds, "Not right now, at least."

"You can't work your life away, Oliver. There's got to be more to your existence than that."

"I'm good." Oliver watches his friend at the barbecue, then says. "Why are you so interested in my personal life all of sudden? It's never bothered you before."

Turning around to face his friend, Charlie asks, "And why are you so suspicious all of a sudden, Oliver? I haven't seen you in a bit and I was just curious about what you've been up to. That's all."

Oliver pauses before answering, then says, "Sorry, man. I always get a little cranky when I'm hungry." He pauses and shrugs. "The steaks smell good. Need me to do anything?"

"You could get us each another beer from the fridge, if you'd like," Charlie says, nodding toward the house. "There's also some salad in the fridge, if you want to grab that too. Oh, and I guess we'll also need some plates and forks too, while you're in there."

"On it." Oliver gets to his feet. "Anything else?"

"A couple of knives might be a good idea."

Oliver laughs again as he leaves the deck. "I thought you were ready for company. I'll take a quick leak while in there as well, if you don't mind."

"Not at all. You know where the bathroom is."

Grabbing two beers and the bowl of salad from the fridge, Oliver pauses before returning to the deck. He's known Charlie for as far back as he can remember and he can tell when his friend is nervous, as if he's either got some bad news to deliver or is fishing for information. Since he's pretty confident his friend would not have any bad news for him, he's sure it's the second option.

What are you up to, Charlie? he wonders, deciding he better return to the deck before his friend comes looking for him.

~

Several hours later, Charlie listens to his phone as Samantha's number rings and rings.

"Hello," she finally says. "How are you, Charlie?"

"I was just about to hang up," he answers. "Is this a good time to talk?"

"Well, your sister's in the kitchen working on dinner and I was helping her, but I have a few minutes to talk. What's up?"

"Not much, I'm afraid," he says. "Oliver just left. He was here for a couple of hours and we talked but I'm afraid I don't have anything to tell you about him and Zoey."

"Nothing?"

"No, I casually let slip that I had noticed she was back in town, you know, hoping he would take the bait, but he didn't. Not even a nibble. He just talked right over that little tidbit and quickly changed the subject. I know Oliver would never miss the chance to talk about that juicy bit of gossip, but he seemed very guarded. So, I'm thinking you might be right. There could be something going on between those two. I can't explain it, but it was just very strange. He just wasn't his usual, carefree self."

"It is strange that they are spending so much time together," Samantha says. "What could they be up to?"

"What could who be up to?" It's Kate. With her back to the kitchen door to smother her voice, Samantha failed to notice her wife had entered the room. "What's going on? Who are you talking to?"

"Oh, hey, honey." She turns and smiles. "Nothing. I'm just talking to your brother."

"Charlie? What does he want?"

"Just a minute, honey. I want to say goodbye."

After she ends the call, she says, "He was just calling to tell us he can't come for dinner tonight."

"I was there a little while ago and he never mentioned anything to me," Kate says. "Why didn't he call me?"

"Said he dialed me by mistake." Samantha chuckles nervously. "Anyway, he said he can't make it because Oliver showed up and they had steak so he's not hungry."

"I don't know," Kate shakes her head. "Sounds like my brother's a little screwed up. Maybe Rebecca shouldn't leave him alone too often."

Samantha chuckles again. "Maybe not." Hoping to change the subject, she quickly adds, "How are things coming along in the kitchen? Need my help with anything?"

"Nope. I was just coming to tell you dinner is ready. Do you want to tell the boys?" Kate says. "I'm really disappointed neither of Alex's friends were able to join us."

"He said they were both busy," Samantha says, giving her wife a hug. "I'll go tell them to come down."

"Great," Kate says, heading to the kitchen, "and I'll get the drinks. You want wine?"

"No, not tonight," Samantha answers as she starts to ascend the stairs. "Think I'll just stick to water."

~

Opening her front door, Zoey tells Oliver to come in. "I wasn't expecting to see you here tonight," she says.

"I wasn't expecting to see you tonight either," he answers, going directly to the kitchen.

"What's up?" she asks, following him. "Can I get you anything?"

"No." He shakes his head. "So, I just left Charlie Webster's place."

"How's Charlie?"

"Fine, I guess, but he was acting really odd."

"How do you mean?"

"I don't know," Oliver looks at her. "Strange. It was like he wanted to say something to me or ask me a question, but he just couldn't find the right words."

"That is strange for Charlie Webster," Zoey agrees. "I've never known him to be at a loss for words. What do you think he wanted?"

"I don't know but your name came up a couple of times and I found that kind of strange," Oliver says. "I mean, let's be honest, you're not someone Charlie and I usually talk about."

"That is odd."

"I couldn't shake the feeling that he was fishing for information and, considering everything that's going on right now, I am not leaving anything as a coincidence."

"That's smart." Zoey considers what she's just heard. "But why would Charlie Webster care about me?"

"That's just the thing, he wouldn't. Not unless—"

"Not unless someone was pushing him to ask questions."

"But who would care?"

"Samantha Henderson, that's who."

"Do you really think she could convince Charlie to do her dirty work?"

"I do." Zoey nods. "Everyone around here sees Samantha as a saint, but I have always found her to be devious and sneaky, especially where Alex is concerned."

"She means no harm, Zoey. She's always looking out for Alex," Oliver says. "When it comes to Alex, she's laser-focused on protecting him. And I think you would agree, that's a good thing. Besides, how would Sam know about our connection?"

"Trust me, she knows. She thinks she's being smart, but I've spotted Cliff Graham lurking around, trying to keep his head down, thinking I can't see him. I bet she's hired him to watch me."

"She wouldn't do that, would she?"

"She would. Absolutely—"

Zoey stops mid-sentence when she hears several loud thuds outside. "What the hell is that?"

"I have no idea," Oliver says, rising from the stool. "But I'll go check it out. You stay right here."

"Not a chance," she says, following him to the front door. "Do you think it's safe to go out there?"

"Don't know, but we have to check," Oliver says, slowly opening the front door.

"Jesus," he sighs as the door swings open, and he spots three dead crows that have been placed on her front veranda. Slowly inching forward into the waning light of evening and scanning the front yard for any possible threats, he adds, "What the hell is this?"

"Oh my God, Oliver," Zoey whispers.

Kneeling beside the bloodied carcasses, Oliver whispers, "Hey fellas, where did you come from?" Quickly glancing around the yard, he adds, "Who did this to you?"

"It's payback," Zoey says, kneeling next to Oliver. "Payback for what the crows did to that owl this morning."

"Do you think?"

"I do." Tears trickle down her cheeks. "I also think this is a warning. I hope Alex is okay."

36: More than dinner

"It's too bad your friends couldn't join us," Kate says to Alex, smiling at him across the table.

"They were both busy, but they said to tell you thank you for the invitation and they hope they can do it some other time," he says, messing with the tossed salad in front of him. He doesn't really feel much like eating right now, but he decided he better put in an appearance at the table before his mother came to find him. The last thing he wants right now is another confrontation with Samantha.

"For sure," Kate says. "Anytime. I hope they know that."

"I think they do."

"Besides," Kate adds, "we'll be seeing Ozzie on Monday for his father's Canada Day barbecue."

"Right." Alex nods again and smiles, although it was more like a grimace. "The famous barbecue."

"Is there a problem with that?" Kate asks.

"Nope." Alex shakes his head. "Looking forward to it."

"Okay then," she answers. Turning to the only guest at the table, Kate says, "And, Ally, it's always nice to see you. Glad you could join us. I hope you enjoy the chicken."

"Thank you, Ms. Webster." The petite brunette smiles at her from her seat next to Hunter. "I can't wait to try it," she adds, picking up a knife. "It looks really delicious. My mother can never make chicken so that it tastes like anything. She's usually a good cook, but her chicken is always so dry."

"Chicken can be a challenge to prepare," Kate says. "Samantha is the real chef in this house, but I found this recipe about ten years ago and I've been making it ever since. It's really very simple. The secret ingredient is paprika, and I add little bit of garlic powder for some extra flavour. You can have the recipe if you want it." Winking at Hunter, she adds, "That big brute sitting next to you doesn't like it much."

"Come on, Kate, you know that's not true," he responds. Turning to Ally, he adds, "Don't listen to her. She's just picking on me."

He cuts off a sliver of the baked chicken and shoves it in his mouth. Speaking around it, he adds, "You know I love your chicken, Kate."

"Yes, Hunter," she chuckles. "I know you do. If there's one thing you'll learn about Hunter, if you haven't already," she tells Ally, "it's that he likes to dish it out, but he's not very good at getting it back. But I guess he's not so bad in the long run."

"No." The young woman giggles, taking his hand under the table and squeezing. "It's alright. I think I'll keep him."

"Oh," Hunter says to her with a grin. "You do, do you?"

"So, Ally," Samantha speaks up. "How's the job going? I don't know if I could handle a room full of screaming kids every day, especially in the heat."

"It's awesome," Ally says. "And the kiddos aren't that bad. I actually love spending time with them. They are so funny and always make me laugh, no matter what kind of day I'm having."

"You better like spending time with them," Hunter pipes up, "if you're going to be a teacher."

Samantha adds, "You were lucky to land a summer job in your field of study. I wish Hunter had been so lucky to find something in engineering."

"What?" Hunter says with a shrug. "I like it at the grocery store and they've been good to me over the years, giving me a job every summer and letting me work there on holidays when I'm home. There'll be enough time later on for me to be stuck in an office somewhere."

"I was just saying that it would look good on your resume if you could list a few years of experience in something closer to your profession while you were a student." Samantha sighs. "That's all."

"Geez," Hunter says. "Someone's a bit testy this evening." Looking directly at Samantha, he adds, "Did you have a bad day?"

She forces her answer through pursed lips. "I had a lovely day, thank you very much."

Alex suddenly interrupts, "May I please be excused?"

Kate looks at him. "But you haven't touched your chicken. Are you feeling okay?"

Staring at his mother from across the table, he adds, "Yes, I'm fine. I'm just not hungry."

"You should try to eat something, Alex," Kate tells him. "You usually like chicken done this way."

"Let him go, Kate," Samantha says. "You know how stubborn he is. If he doesn't want to eat, don't force it."

"Fine," Kate says while shooting a sharp glare at her wife. To Alex, she says, "You may go, Alex, but I'll save it and you can have it later."

"Thanks." He nods, pushing himself away from the table.

"Alex," Samantha says. "We're not done. We have to talk about what happened earlier today."

"No, we don't," he snaps. "There's nothing more to discuss."

"Oh, yes there is," his mother insists. "And I will be up to see you later."

"Don't bother," Alex says as he bolts up the stairs. "I don't want to talk anymore. I'm tired."

"What was that all about?" Kate asks her wife.

"Not now, Kate," Samantha says, pushing herself back from the table and walking away. "Thanks for working so hard to prepare dinner, but I'm not hungry either."

"Well," Hunter says. "So that's dinner at the Webster-Henderson household. Wasn't that lovely."

"Don't, Hunter," Kate snaps. "Please just eat your dinner." To Ally, she adds with a sigh, "Sorry about that. It's not usually like this around here."

Slamming his door and flopping on his bed, Alex considers his predicament.

What am I going to do? I want to tell Mom what's going on, but Aunt Zoey says it's not safe for her or anyone else. The less they know, she says, the better it will be for them. He rubs his eyes. *I can't handle this. It's way too much; it's all coming at me way too fast.*

He's staring at the ceiling when his phone snaps him out of this trance. He sees it's Ozzie calling.

"Shit," he says. *I don't want to talk to you right now.*

Hitting the *dismiss* button, Alex stares at the blank screen as he expects Ozzie to call again. If there is one thing he's learned about his friend over the past few years, it's that he's persistent.

Seconds later, just as he expected, the phone rings again and Alex knows he can't avoid Ozzie this time because it may tip him off that he knows something.

"Hello," Alex reluctantly says into the phone.

"Hey Alex. What's up?" Ozzie asks. "Did you cut me off just a few seconds ago?"

"What? No way." He lies. "This is the first time my phone rang."

"Really? No shit. Oh well, something must have happened the first time I called." He pauses and Alex waits for him to speak. "So, what's happening?" Ozzie finally asks.

"Not much." Alex tells himself to remain as aloof as he can. He knows his friend is pretty smart and if he's not careful, he knows Ozzie will trip him up.

"I didn't hear from you after Bree texted and cancelled this morning," Ozzie says. "She said something about you not feeling well. How are you feeling now?"

"I'm okay. I figure it must have been something I ate, or maybe it was the heat getting to me. Not really sure what it was, but I'm feeling pretty good right now." Searching for the right words, Alex finally asks, "So, what did you end up doing today?"

"Not much." Ozzie's words don't convey any type of deception that Alex can detect. "I just played some Minecraft and then my father wanted me to help him with the pool this afternoon. Said he had to get it ready for his big Canada Day shindig that he's planning. I guess you guys got invited?"

"We did."

"I hope you're coming. I can't handle these things, so I need you here."

"Mom wants to come."

Ozzie hesitates, then asks, "Don't you want to come, Alex? It sounds like you don't want to."

"Oh, no—no. I want to come, for sure. It's just that…"

"What, Alex? It's just that what?"

"Well…"

"Just say it, Alex."

"Okay, I'm just thinking it's too bad that Bree isn't going to be there. It'd be fun having her there with us."

"She can come," Ozzie tells him.

"Are you sure? She says her family didn't get an invitation and I don't think she'd want to crash the party. Your father probably wouldn't appreciate that."

"Shit, man, I can fix that. I'll call her and make sure she knows she can come. In fact, I'll tell my father he needs to invite her whole family."

"Jesus, Ozzie, you don't have to do that. I don't want to make him mad at me for talking you into pressuring him to invite more people."

"Fuck that," Ozzie says. "He won't get mad at me. He probably just didn't even think about inviting them. It won't be a problem."

"Well. If you're sure it will be alright."

"It will be fine. Don't worry about it." Ozzie pauses and Alex can hear him breathing. His friend finally adds, "You like her, don't you?"

"Who?"

"Come on, man. You know who I mean." He chuckles. "Bree. You like her. Admit it."

"Of course, I like her, she's always been a great friend to me. You both have."

Ozzie pauses again, then says, "You know, Alex, the thing about friends is that they can turn on you pretty quick. You always have to watch your back even with people you think you can trust."

"What are you saying, Ozzie? That I can't trust Bree?"

"Hell, no, man. I think Bree feels the same about you as you feel about her. I don't think you will ever have to question her loyalty to you."

"Well, what then? What did you mean I have to 'watch my back?'"

"Nothing. I didn't mean anything. As usual, I was just talking bullshit." He laughs and Alex can tell his friend is nervous. "Just kidding around. You know me."

Do I, really? Alex thinks, but says, "I guess. It just seems like an odd thing to say."

"I guess maybe it is true, then, what people say. I am odd." Ozzie laughs but Alex senses there is something off about him.

"You're not odd, Ozzie. Let's just say you're different. We're all different, you, me and Bree. I think that's why we're such good friends." He sighs and adds, "I hope that never changes."

"Why would that change? I plan on us being good friends for the rest of our lives."

"Me too, Ozzie. But you just never know. Things do change and people change, often because of outside stuff they can't control."

"I don't know what you mean, but you're freaking me out, Alex," Ozzie replies. "I don't see anything that would make me stop being your friend."

"I feel the same way, but you know what? We should just stop this bullshit right now and agree that we are going to be best friends for the rest of lives—and Bree, of course."

"Of course. I agree," Ozzie says. "So, what you got planned for tomorrow? Want to do something?"

"Not sure. Tomorrow's Sunday so I'll probably just lay low," Alex answers. "Take it easy, you know?"

"Yeah, me too, I guess. My father has already told me he'll need my help to get things ready for the barbecue the next day, so I imagine he'll keep me pretty busy."

"Well, you go ahead and have fun with that," Alex says with a laugh. "I'm sure we'll be talking again tomorrow at some point."

"For sure," Ozzie says. "Gotta run. Talk soon."

"See you," Alex answers, pressing the button to end the conversation.

Now that was just weird, he thinks. *Weirder than usual, and that's saying something when it comes to Ozzie.*

Finding Bree's number, he presses talk.

"Hi Alex," she quickly answers. "How are you?"

"Okay, I guess."

"You guess? What's wrong?"

"Oh, nothing serious. Just having a little tiff with my mom."

"Are you guys going to be okay?" Bree asks. "You usually get along really well."

"Yeah," he says. "I hope so, but you know that as long as Aunt Zoey is in the picture, Mom is not going to be happy. She just wants her out of my life and for good. If she had her way, I would never see Aunt Zoey again, ever."

"You can't really blame her, Alex. Not after the last time your aunt was here. It was pretty clear that she was trying to drive a wedge between you two."

"I didn't see it that way, but I guess it must be true because you and Mom keep telling me that." Alex pauses then says, "Anyway, let's not argue over that. One argument is enough for one day."

"Agreed." In her usual calm tone, she adds, "Other than that, how are things?"

"Not good, there's a lot of shit going on right now." Alex exhales with a force. "If you're free tomorrow I could really use a friend and I thought maybe we could hang for a bit? I want to check out something at the old cemetery. There's someone buried there—I think—that I want to locate. I wondered if you'd like to help look for the grave marker."

"Who?"

"An ancestor I just found out about. I'd like to know more about my family roots," Alex tells her. "It's really fascinating."

"Okay, that should be interesting, and then will you finally tell me about everything that's going on with you?" Bree pauses and he can sense she is upset. "I'm really worried."

"I'll tell you what I can," he says. "What time can you be ready? I want to get out of here as early as possible before Mom attacks me again."

"How does nine sound?" she suggests. "I could be ready to go by then."

"Perfect. I'll be at your place by nine."

"I'll be waiting," she tells him. "See you then."

Thanks, Bree, Alex thinks as he ends the call. *I can always count on you.*

Moving to the window, he searches the yard for anyone lurking about and spots the large, black crow on the nearby tree branch.

"Hey Augustus," he whispers. "I can always count on you, too. You're like my guardian angel or something."

The crow's head bobs back and forth, its eyes occasionally blinking.

"Whatever is coming, I feel better knowing you'll be there with me. I'm scared, Augustus. I just wish I knew what was going to happen."

The crow stares at him, sometimes blinking. They are connected in a way that few would understand. Human and crow. Bonded for life, each destined to protect the other from whatever threat is lurking in the shadows.

"We can do this," Alex says as the crow maintains eye contact. "Or at least I hope we can."

37: A walk in the past

"Where do we start?" Bree asks, as she follows Alex through the rows of weather-beaten headstones of various shapes and sizes that mark several thousand graves spread over the sprawling tract of land at the edge of town. Many of the region's original settlers are buried in this historical cemetery that was declared a provincial heritage site several years ago. "There's just so many of them."

"My guess is that we should look somewhere around where my mother's family is buried," Alex says while carefully weaving around the graves, many of them showing years of neglect.

"Tell me again, who we're looking for. You know, I heard somewhere that it is bad luck to step on a grave," she adds, while very carefully choosing where to place her feet.

"I heard that too," Alex says with a chuckle. "But I don't believe it. Just like a lot of other stuff I heard growing up, I think that's an old wives' tale. You know how superstitious people are around here. Believe me, I've been to this cemetery many times and I bet I've probably stepped on hundreds of graves—"

"And what?" Bree cuts him off. "You don't have any bad luck?"

Alex stops short and turns to her. "Good point. Maybe I should reconsider what I was just about to say."

"Do you think?" she giggles.

Alex enjoys the way she laughs. It's just one more thing he likes about her.

"Yuppers," he says, resuming the trek. "It's this way."

Pointing to several ancient markers that vandals have recently knocked over, he says, "Assholes! Just be careful right here. I don't want you to trip."

"Why would someone do such a thing?" she asks, manoeuvring

around the fallen markers. "Isn't it kind of sacrilegious or something to destroy these things?"

"You'd think that, wouldn't you? But some people don't care, and they don't respect anything—even dead people. I guess they have to get their jollies somewhere."

"That's just perverted, if you ask me. I mean, how much pleasure can you get in destroying something so important?"

Stopping and scoping out the area, Alex says, "Right over there is where my mother, father and brother are buried. We'll start there."

"It must make you sad to come here, Alex," Bree observes as he makes a beeline to the graves he visits as often as he can.

"You'd think that, wouldn't you? But the truth is, I actually feel better every time I come here. No matter how low I'm feeling, it's like I can find a connection with them when I'm here. It's quiet, which makes it an excellent place to clear your head. And once I do that, I can think more clearly."

"I guess maybe I can see that," she says as the pair reach the graves adorned by the bouquet of multi-coloured lilies Alex had placed there two days earlier. He's glad they haven't wilted yet.

"Those are pretty, Alex," Bree says, taking a position beside him and checking out the headstone. "And they're lilies. That's appropriate. I love lilies."

"Yes." Alex nods and stares at the grave marker. Bree remains quiet to give Alex whatever space he needs to deal with the moment. "Lilies were her favourite flower," he whispers, his voice so soft she can hardly hear his words. Finally, he adds, "Okay, let's see if we can find those other graves."

"Tell me again, who are we looking for?"

"We're looking for Samuel Gorham...There," he says, pointing to a cluster of headstones at the northern end of the family lot where a lone crow has perched. "That's Augustus over there. He's showing us where it is."

"The crow is showing us where the grave is?" Bree asks, following closely behind Alex as he weaves around the markers in his path. "I know you have a way with crows, Alex, but how—?"

"I just know," Alex says. "Trust me."

As the pair approaches the marker, the crow takes flight, springing from the granite stone where it had been perched. As it climbs into the warm summer air, it emits several soft caws.

"Thanks for the help, Augustus," Alex calls after the crow.

"That's such an unusual name," Bree says. "How do you know his name is Augustus?"

"I'm not really sure." Alex shrugs. "I can't explain it. Besides, don't you think he looks like an Augustus?"

"I don't know." She also shrugs. "I honestly don't know what an Augustus should look like."

"No?" Alex laughs and points to the crow as it soars off to an unknown destination. "Him," he adds. "It looks like him."

"I guess so," she giggles. Turning to the gravestone in front of them, she asks, "So is this the one you're looking for?"

"Yes," Alex answers after quickly reading the markings on the stone. "Yes, this is him—Samuel Gorham."

"Who was he?"

Kneeling and studying the stone more closely, Alex says, "This man, my dear Bree, was Alexandria Gorham's one and only child, and he is my direct ancestor."

"No way," Bree says. "That is so cool."

"Yes, very cool. And listen to this." Alex points to the grave marker. "The headstone does not give his date of birth, because obviously no one knew for sure when he was born. But it says here he died on March 12, 1821."

Bree pulls out her phone and takes pictures of the stone. "What else does it say?"

"It says Samuel Gorham wed Annabeth Wentworth on June 25, 1789," Alex reads from the stone. "And it looks like she died a month before Samuel, on February 14, 1821."

"On Valentine's Day. That's romantic," Bree says. "They are together for all of eternity."

"You think so?" Alex looks at her, carefully considering her comment. "I never would have seen it as romantic in any way, but maybe so."

"Trust me, Alex. It is romantic." Glancing at the nearby graves, she adds, "There's a lot of headstones right around here in this cluster. I wonder who they are for?"

"Let's have a look," Alex says, springing to his feet.

Moving to a nearby stone, he says, "Abraham Gorham, born December 25, 1780. I wonder if this is Samuel's son."

"Here's another right here," Bree says, inspecting a nearby marker. "It's for Barnabus Gorham. What was that date of birth again on the that one you just read? This one says December 25, 1780."

"These two gentlemen must have been twins," Alex says. "Samuel was a twin. His brother Jonathan was dead when he was born."

"That's sad," Bree says. "How did you know that he had a dead twin?"

"It's in Alexandria's journal. What's even more interesting is that the same thing happened to me." Glancing at her as if trying to gauge her reaction, he adds, "Did I ever tell you that I was a twin, and my brother was dead when he was born? His name was Andrew."

"No, I'm sure you never did. I'm sure I would remember that," Bree says, staring into his eyes where she can see his vulnerability. Taking his hand, she says, "I'm very sorry about that, Alex."

"It's okay, really." He shrugs and turns his head. "I never knew him, so I'm used to him not being here. But sometimes I still find myself missing him. It's kind of odd, really, when you think about it. How can you miss someone you never knew?"

"I am sure you do." She gives him a few seconds to regain his composure, then adds, "And I'm sure it hurts."

"Yes, but there isn't much we can about those things, is there? But I do sometimes wonder what it would have been like to have grown up with a brother, other than Carter and Hunter, of course. It would been interesting to have a twin to share my life with."

"You know, whenever you need to talk to someone about this, I'm always here for you, right?"

"Yes, I know that and I appreciate it." He smiles and adds, "Now, let's get back to business."

"Okay, then. So when did these guys die?"

"It looks like Abraham Gorham died June 17, 1839," Alex reads from the stone.

"And this says Barnabus Gorham died November 3, 1841," Bree adds. "Looks like they were pretty close to each in age when they died."

"And,"—he motions toward the grave markers—"it looks like they are pretty close in death."

"The others in this group must be their families."

"Probably," Alex agrees, quickly scanning the markers. "Look at this one that's right next to Samuel and his wife's grave. It's for Beatrice Gorham. Says she was born September 9, 1785, and died April 26, 1789."

Standing beside him, Bree says, "That's very sad. She was so young when she died. I wonder what happened. She was probably their daughter."

Bending closer to read the carving that is slowly being lost to the ravages of time and the elements, Alex reads, "Let the little children come to me, and do not stop them; for it is to such as these that the Kingdom of Heaven belongs. Matthew 19:14." He pauses. "I believe the early settlers were very religious, so I'm not surprised to see inscriptions like this."

"So that's three children born to Samuel and Annabeth," Bree observes. Looking about she asks, "I wonder if there are others?"

"Here's one for an Evangeline Gorham Cooke. She could have been Samuel's daughter. Says she was born July 27, 1783 and died May 15, 1841."

"All your ancestors, your family," she says. "You should see what else you can discover about them. For instance, Evangeline was married to someone named Cooke. What was his first name and did they have any children? They'd be part of your family as well. And why is she buried here with her mother and father and not with her own husband and children? Now you've got me wondering."

"This type of research is addictive. I hear once you get bitten by the genealogical bug, it's hard to pull away from it," he says. "But you are right, all of this raises a whole lot of questions about who I am—questions, but no easy answers."

"Well," she tells him. "Let's see if we can find some."

"Where would I even look?"

"I'd start at the museum in town," she says. "I'd suggest that we'd go tomorrow, but it's Canada Day so it would be closed. By the way. Ozzie's dad finally called my mom last night and it looks like we're also invited to his barbecue after all."

"That's awesome." Alex is relieved to hear the news. "Mom really wants to go, but I hate those kinds of gatherings so I'm glad to hear you're going to be there to help get me through it."

"I don't think it's going to be as bad you think," Bree says. "Now, getting back to why we're here, I have a question. How did you know about Samuel Gorham in the first place?"

"Just like the part about him having a twin brother. Everything was in Alexandria Gorham's journal. I read it last night. There's some fascinating stuff in there and it really helped me to get a better understanding of who I am. It gave me some information about my family tree, but no details about the family after her death."

"That's really great, Alex. I know you've been curious about your family roots for a long time, so I'm glad you're finally getting a few answers," she says. "You really have to let me read that book. It sounds very interesting."

"Sure, you can read it when I'm finished with it. Just give me a couple more days. I want to check on a few more things before I lend it to you."

"Great," Bree smiles. "That's the book you got from your aunt Zoey, right?"

"Yes, the same night that started all of this stupid stuff between me and mom."

"You were going to tell me what's going on with you two," Bree says. "Want to talk about it?"

"Not really, but it is bothering me." Alex sighs. "Mom and I are usually very close, and I hate that we're fighting. But she just refuses to understand that, for me, spending time with Aunt Zoey is kind of like spending time with my real mom. In a way, it gives me a connection to her. She just doesn't get it."

"Have you told her this?"

"I have, but she is determined to keep me away from Aunt Zoey, and it's just not fair." He sighs, resisting the overwhelming urge to show his anger. "In fact, I got out of the house early this morning to avoid her, because I knew what she was going to be like. I just can't take it."

"I know it seems that way, Alex, but do you think that maybe the real reason why your mom doesn't want you to see your aunt is because she feels threatened by her? Maybe she doesn't want you to see Zoey because she thinks your aunt will try to take you away from her. I mean, Zoey is your blood relative, after all, so maybe your mom might fear that bond that you obviously have with her."

He considers Bree's suggestion and then says, "Aunt Zoey would never do that. She knows how much I care for Mom. I would never let Aunt Zoey or anything else come between us."

"I know you wouldn't, but have you told your mother that?"

Bree raises a good point, he thinks.

She continues, "Maybe she just needs you to reassure her that you'll never leave. Sometimes, people need to hear things, even things that we take for granted. You can't assume that she knows how you feel."

"Aunt Zoey is important to me, but so is my mom." He pauses, thinking about the situation. "Mom has been there for me through a lot of things over the years. I know how much she's done for me and I would never turn my back on her, but she has to understand that I have questions about who I am, and I believe Aunt Zoey can help me find some answers. It's killing me to think that this has upset Mom so badly, but I need her to understand that I just can't walk away from who I am."

"Well, then, I suggest you tell your mother how you feel about all of this, but..."

"But what?"

"But you don't always listen to me, Alex."

"Yes, I do—most of the time."

"No, you don't." Bree shrugs. "I keep telling you that you need to tell your mother about the threatening notes and about someone lurking around your house but I'm pretty sure you still haven't done that yet. Have you?"

He hesitates but finally shakes his head. "No. But it's for her own safety."

"That doesn't make sense. She'd be safer if she knew what was going on, instead of being caught by surprise if something happened to you or someone else in your family." She stares at him. "You can't keep this from her, Alex. It's very serious. And maybe she can help."

"She can't help," Alex shoots back. "I have to deal with this by myself."

"Yourself? You could be in danger. I mean, no one sends notes like that if they weren't intended to be threats."

"I know you are right, Bree, but you have to trust me on this."

"I like you, Alex—a lot. I think you're smart and brave, considering everything you've been through in your life, but sometimes you're also stupid and pigheaded. Sometimes, there are things you can't deal with on your own, and this is one of them. You need to get help before it's too late."

As he's about to answer, a loud squawking noise pierces the tranquility of the cemetery, cutting through the morning air as if it is sounding an alarm.

Augustus? I thought you had left, he thinks and says, "What the hell?"

He quickly scopes out the area, searching the grounds and trees for his black-feathered friend. He shivers despite the heat, as if there is danger nearby.

"What is it, Alex?" Bree asks, inching closer to her friend. "What was that horrible noise?"

"That was Augustus," he says, pulling her closer to him. "He's warning us that something is wrong. He wants us to leave."

"What? How do you know that?"

Alex can sense the fear in her voice. "I just know it. Come on," he says, pulling her with him. "We've got to go right now."

"Okay but how do you know we are in danger?" Following closely behind him, she adds, "Danger from what?"

"I don't know."

He feels that someone—or something—is watching them, but he can't locate the source of the possible danger. "But we really do have to go."

"Okay, Alex," she answers, breathlessly as she's broken into a steady lope to keep up with him. His long legs make him exceedingly quick. "But you are going way too fast for me."

"Sorry, Bree," he says, slowing his pace a bit in order to allow her to stay with him.

"I am really scared. Whatever that sound was, it didn't sound human to me."

"I know what that was," he says, staying close to her as he can feel her fear. "It was the crows telling us to get out of here. I'm more afraid of whatever threat is hiding around here, stalking us."

"Oh my God, Alex, what are you saying?" She cries. "It sounds like you're saying we're being hunted."

"We are." He hates being blunt because he knows his answer will scare Bree even more than she is now. "But I don't have time to explain right now."

As they leave the outer edge of the cemetery, he adds, "You just have to trust me that we aren't safe."

38: A secret yet to be told

"I don't know, Sam," Cliff says into his phone as he watches Samantha Henderson pull up and park in front of Zoey LaCroix's house. He's been observing the house since early this morning and all seems quiet. "Do you really think it's a good idea for you to confront her right now? I mean, we really don't know what she's up to."

He can see her speaking into her phone as she turns off the ignition.

"I don't think I have much of a choice," Samantha says. "I have to know what's going on with her and Alex. Since he refuses to talk to me about it, I have to ask her. I know this will not be pleasant."

"He'll be pissed at you if he finds out that you have talked to Zoey."

"I have to take that chance. How long have you been here?"

"Close to two hours. It's been pretty quiet. Not much activity around here this morning. It's actually more like a ghost town."

"Well, it is early on Sunday morning and people are at the cottage or wherever it is they go in the summer. I sometimes wish I had a summer get-away that I could escape to."

"You and me both," Cliff agrees. "Although having a cottage also means you have more work to do and, honestly, I don't have time to do everything I have to do right now at the house, so I really don't think I could add anything else to my list. Besides, Jewels wouldn't like it. She'd rather spend her time at home or at the beach." He sighs and adds, "I hate the beach."

"Come on Cliff," Samantha says with a chuckle. But he can tell she's nervous because of what she's about to do. "You need to make time to enjoy yourself, especially now that you're retired."

"Yeah, right," he laughs, waving at her from this truck. "Does this look like I'm retired?"

"Good point." Sam smiles then asks, "So, have you seen anyone around the house today?"

"Not a bloody soul. I think maybe she might still be sleeping. I haven't seen any movement inside."

"It's ten-thirty. I am sure she's up by now. And no sign of Oliver this morning?"

"Haven't seen him."

"What about crows?"

"There have been a few but nothing too major," he says. "But those god-damned birds did cause quite a commotion at Oliver's yesterday while I was there."

"What do you mean?"

"It was pretty freaking weird. A bunch of crows attacked this little owl right on Oliver's front lawn and they actually killed it. But then again, it's not the first weird thing that crows have done around this town."

"No, it is not, but," remembering the dead owl that hit her living room window the other night, she adds, "Kind of weird that you saw an owl, though. It's only been the last few days that we've seen owls showing up around here."

"Right," Cliff agrees. "That's why I found yesterday's attack to be kind of odd."

"I wonder what's up with that?" she asks.

"Whatever was going on, that poor little owl didn't stand a chance against those crows. They tore him apart."

"That sounds gruesome."

"It was," Cliff tells her.

"Well"—Samantha sighs and Cliff sees her open her car door—"I guess if I am going to do this, I should go and do it."

"It's not too late. You could just drive away and she wouldn't even know you were here."

"I have got to do it for Alex's sake," she says.

"Okay, but I'll be out here if you need me."

"I hope I won't need you, Cliff. I can't imagine anything getting so bad that I'll have to call on you for help, but it is good to know you're here if I do."

Ending the call, Samantha slips her phone into her purse, leaves the car and closes the door. Looking at the house again, she takes a deep breath. *Okay, Samantha, you can do this*, she thinks, entering the yard and heading toward the veranda. *You have to do this for Alex's sake.*

She's just about to knock when the front door swings open.

"Sam," the slender redhead greets her. "I wondered if you were going to come in or if you were just going to sit out there in your car all day."

Samantha is caught off guard. "I didn't even have a chance to knock."

"Yes, well—come in. I know you're here to talk to me." Zoey turns and walks back toward the kitchen. "About Alex, right?"

"Yes," Samantha answers, slowly stepping inside the dimly-lit house and closing the door behind her. Hearing it click closed, she suddenly feels like she's trapped even though she knows she can leave whenever she wants to.

"I thought as much," Zoey says. "I'll get you something to drink. Something cold maybe? Iced tea perhaps?"

"No thanks. I'm fine," she says, following the voice. "I am worried about Alex and I need to know what's going on between you two. I can tell something is really bothering him."

"Did you ask Alex about it?" Zoey asks, taking a seat at the kitchen counter and motioning to her guest to be seated.

Samantha declines as she thinks she'll have a better vantage point if she remains standing. "I did. But he won't tell me anything."

"Maybe there just isn't anything to tell you, Samantha."

"Come on, Zoey. I don't buy that. He's been on edge ever since you showed up at the cemetery two days ago, and I can tell he's keeping secrets. More importantly, he's lying right to my face."

"And you assume that has something to do with me?" Her eyes squint as she glares at Samantha. "Or that I'm to blame for him lying to you—if he is lying."

"His personality changes whenever you're around, so it wouldn't be the first time that Alex has lied to me to hide his relationship with you." Staring at Zoey, Samantha asks, "What are you up to?"

"Me? I'm not up to anything except for trying to spend some quality time with my nephew. Or did you forget that he's my nephew?"

"I didn't forget anything, but it seems like it's a point that you forget quite often, what with all your travels and the disappearing acts that you've pulled over the years."

"So, I travel. So, what. Is that illegal? Does that mean I can't spend time with my nephew when I come back home?" Zoey pauses and then adds, "Have you ever stopped to think that maybe he *wants* to spend time with me?"

"I know he does, and that's the problem."

"Why is that the problem?"

"Because he's not safe with you, and you know it," Samantha says, glaring at the other woman. "You always bring trouble with you when you come back to town, and you always manage to throw Alex right smack in the middle of it. I won't let you do that to him this time."

"I don't know what you think you know, Samantha, but I would never intentionally put Alex in harm's way."

"And that's really the crux of it right there, Zoey. You would never do it intentionally, but you always end up doing it," Samantha says. "It's strange that you can't see that he's never safe when he's around you."

"Is that what you think? Honestly, I think he's very safe," Zoey answers, staring at her visitor. "In fact, he's safer when he's around me than he is with you."

"How can you say that after everything you've put him through? All the far-fetched stories that you tell him about his so-called 'destiny' and all the crap you feed him about his 'calling,' whatever the hell that is."

Samantha is pissed that this woman would have the audacity to make such a claim. "I've been by his side since the beginning. I've always been here to help him pick up the pieces every time you leave. I've been the one who has hugged him, wiped away his tears and made him feel better when he's had a rough time. Not you. You run away every time he needs someone, so don't give me this bullshit that he's better off with you than with me."

"Come on Sam, enough with the drama. I'm not saying that you haven't been there for him or that you haven't cared for him, because you have been there, and I can't take that away from you. I don't *want* to take that away from you, but you simply don't know the whole truth."

Samantha is fuming. "There you go again with this whole 'truth' shit. What in the hell do you mean by that?"

"I can't tell you," Zoey says. "I won't tell you because, if I do, you'll be in more danger than you're already in."

"What kind of bullshit are you talking about. Danger? What danger?"

"It's real, Samantha, and that's all I can say."

"This is getting me nowhere fast," Samantha says, her anger about to break free. "If you won't tell me what's going on, then I guess I have no choice but to forbid you from seeing Alex."

"You can't forbid me from seeing him," Zoey fires back. "I think he may have something to say about that."

"You're trying to drive a wedge between us just like you did the last time," Samantha says, resisting the urge to raise her voice. "You have never been happy that Lily left her son with me to raise instead of with you. I get it. You thought Lily should have chosen, you so you've done everything you can over the years to pull me and Alex apart."

"You have no idea what you're talking about. You only see what you choose to see," Zoey says. "The truth is, someday soon Alex will become the person he's destined to become, and no matter how hard you want to fight it. You cannot stop that progression. That reality was carved in stone many years ago and if you try to get in his way, he will just go around you. I promise you that."

"This was a waste of time," Samantha says, spinning on her heels to leave. "You'll never be honest with me. Just do me a favour and stay away from Alex."

"I'm not the one you should be telling but before you go flying off the handle at Alex, I would urge you to carefully consider your next move."

"Is that a threat?"

"Not at all," Zoey says. "I'm trying to tell you something for your own good. I know you love Alex and you only want to do what's best for him, but you have to understand that his true purpose may be different from the one you envision for him. If you confront him with this, you confront him at your own peril."

"I didn't come here to get advice from you on how to deal with Alex. I've been doing just fine for all these years, thank you very much."

"Yes, you have." Zoey nods. "But be careful how you treat him. These are precarious times for him, and he does not need another problem from you right now. If you push him too hard, he will shut you out."

"Jesus, Zoey, you never stop."

"I'm just trying to warn you."

"So, I'm warned, now leave him alone."

Opening the front door, with her back to Zoey, Samantha adds, "You know, Zoey, someday all these problems you cause will come back and bite you in the ass. The day will come when you will regret the things you do."

As the door closes behind her, Samantha leans against the wooden surface and sighs. *That was a waste of time. But really, what did I expect from her?*

She's just about to step off the veranda when she notices several large crows have suddenly lined up along the stone walkway, three on each side, sort of like an honour guard. But she knows it's nothing like that. She feels intimidated by the presence of these black birds. She's been down this road before and she doesn't like seeing them here like this.

"Okay, fellas. Easy does it," she says, proceeding slowly with tiny steps. Carefully monitoring the crows as she goes, she hopes her presence will startle them away. She knows this is not typical crow behaviour. Usually, they fly off whenever any human is around.

"I don't know what you want, but I am not going to hurt you or

Zoey, if that's what you're afraid off," she tells them as she cautiously makes her way along the path.

Cliff, having seen the crows, is standing at the head of the walkway to the house. "Easy, Sam," he says. "Just one tiny step at a time."

"Don't come any closer, Cliff. They might feel threatened by you," she says, her voice hardly a whisper. "I don't think they want to hurt me."

"You can't be sure. Besides, I'm not worried about those ones on the ground." Pointing toward the roof of the veranda, he adds, "I'm worried about that big one up there."

Slowly turning and looking up, she exhales. "Jesus, Cliff. He's a god-damned monster."

"I sure as hell wouldn't want to tussle with him," Cliff says. "Come on, Sam. You're just about here."

"Jesus," Samantha sighs, reaching the end of the walkway and rushing onto the street as Cliff reaches out and grabs her. "That was scary."

Turning to watch the crows as they stare her down, she adds, "I've never seen anything like that before. What do you think they want.?"

"You're asking me?" Cliff says. "I have no idea, but there's seven of them. Remind me again. What does seven crows mean?"

She thinks a moment, and a shiver goes through her. She whispers, "Seven crows a secret yet to be told."

39: Rubber mallet

Samantha is exhausted. She feels both mentally and emotionally drained. All she wants to do is relax and enjoy what is supposed to be a day of rest.

Yeah, right, she thinks, driving down the street lined with elm trees where she's lived for the past two decades with her wife and two adopted sons. She thinks about the work that awaits her when she gets home. *As if that's ever going to happen.*

I should have listened to Cliff, she thinks. *I'll never be able to get through to that woman.*

Approaching her modest, but comfortable home, she is surprised to see a red half-ton truck parked in the driveway, with the words "Oliver Lewis Contracting" emblazoned on a magnetized sign that's secured to the passenger side door.

Shit. What does he want? Her mind immediately recalls the conversations she's had with Cliff and Charlie about the unusual pairing of Oliver Lewis and Zoey LaCroix. *I wonder if he's found out I was asking about his relationship with Zoey? But how?*

She shrugs it off. Whatever it is, she knows better than to underestimate this man. She's known Oliver for many years, and she's seen him talk his way out of some pretty tight spots.

He's a sweet talker, that one. Better be careful with him, she thinks, parking beside the truck.

The last thing she needs right now is to have a run-in with Oliver. Reaching into the backseat and grabbing the bag of groceries she picked up on her way home from Zoey's, Samantha wants to just jump back into the car and go for a nice long drive—somewhere...anywhere.

She exhales and looks to the clear, blue sky as if searching for strength. *But you can't do that Samantha.*

Entering the house through the front door, she finds Kate and Oliver seated in the living room. "Hey Oliver," she says, trying to sound sincere.

It's not that she doesn't like him, it's just that she wasn't prepared to see him when she got home. In fact, she likes him very much and she's worried about him. "What a pleasant surprise. We weren't expecting you, were we?"

"Hey, Sam," Oliver quickly replies with a friendly smile and, noticing the bag she's carrying, springs to his feet. "Let me get that for you."

"No," Samantha says, heading directly to the kitchen. "I've got it. I just have to stick the milk into the fridge and then I'll be right back."

As if she owes him an explanation, she adds, "Grocery stores are closed tomorrow for the holiday, and we needed a few things. Kids, you know? They drink a lot of milk."

"Okay," Oliver says, returning to this seat and smiling at Kate. Raising his voice as Samantha disappears into the kitchen, he adds, "Well, they are growing young men."

Kate smiles. "But we love them just the same."

"So, as I was saying this is an unexpected surprise," Samantha says to Oliver after returning to the living room. "What brings you by on a Sunday morning?" She sits beside Kate on the couch.

Kate says, "He came by to pick up a rubber mallet."

Samantha looks at her, puzzled. "What?"

"Yes," Oliver says. "I've got a tiling job coming up this week and I'll need the mallet for that. When I was getting my tools lined up for the job, I remembered that I had loaned it to Charlie about a month ago. I don't really know what he needed it for, but when I dropped by his place yesterday to pick it up, he couldn't find it. Says he thinks he lent it to you guys, but he wasn't one hundred percent positive." Grinning, he adds, "You know how absentminded good ol' Charlie can be."

"Yes, well, good ol' Charlie is mistaken," Kate answers, shaking her head. "My brother did not lend us a rubber mallet or any other tools, for that matter. What would we need a rubber mallet for?"

"Not really sure, Kate." Oliver smiles. "Charlie was obviously mistaken. I'll have another look around my place when I get home, and if I can't find it, I'll just buy another one. They really aren't all that expensive."

"Sorry we couldn't help you," Kate says. She's puzzled. "Not really sure why Charlie would think he loaned us a rubber mallet, of all things. That would be a pretty strange thing for us to borrow." She grins, rolling her eyes at Samantha. "After all, neither of us is very handy with tools."

"Yes. Well. There's a lot of strange things going on these days," Oliver says. "But really, that's okay. It's not a big deal."

"Yes," Kate agrees. "A lot of strange things."

"So, Oliver. Did Kate offer you a drink or anything?" Samantha speaks up after surmising all of this talk about a rubber mallet was just a decoy. She senses that Oliver is here for a totally different reason. "Can I get you a coffee or maybe something cold? It's only early, but it's already hot out there."

Quickly glancing at his watch, Oliver says, "No, thanks, Sam. I really didn't plan on staying. Just came by for the rubber mallet."

"Okay," she says. "So, what have you been up to lately? It seems like we haven't seen you in forever." She smiles at him and asks, "Keeping well?"

"Yes," he nods. "I'm keeping well. As for doing anything exciting, the answer is no, unless you call work exciting. It's been pretty steady, but I'm not complaining."

"That's good." She nods and then, after careful consideration, adds, "So, guess who I saw yesterday?" She pauses to give him time to answer.

"I have no idea." Oliver shakes his head and looks her directly in the eyes. He shrugs and asks, "Who?"

Keeping her tone casual because she knows Kate will not like her discussing this subject with anyone outside of the family, she says, "Zoey LaCroix."

"What?" Kate reacts first, a not so-subtle message to her wife telling her not to go there.

"Yup." Samantha nods, ignoring Kate's message. "I had to look twice, but I saw her walking down the street yesterday when I was on my way into town hall."

"Are you sure it was her?" Kate asks.

"I am."

"What the hell? I thought she was out of town."

Samantha can see Kate feels blindsided by this revelation.

"Why didn't you tell me yesterday that you actually saw her? That's a pretty important piece of news, don't you think?"

"Don't know." Samantha says. *She's pissed,* she thinks, then says, "It slipped my mind, I guess. Probably because of everything else that's been going on."

Oliver speaks up. "I heard somewhere that Zoey was back in town."

I bet you did, Samantha thinks, but says, "I wonder when she got back."

"I don't know," Oliver answers. "I haven't heard anything other than the fact that she has returned."

"Well," Kate sighs and Samantha can detect the frustration in her wife's voice. "This is *not* good news."

She shoots Samantha an angry look and Samantha wonders if she has made a mistake bringing this up. *Oh well, nothing I can do about it now.* She shakes her head and says, "No, not good news at all."

Turning to face Oliver she continues to probe. "I wonder what she's up to this time."

"Don't have any idea," Oliver says. "I guess we will all have to be on our toes. But maybe she will behave herself this time."

"Do you think?" Samantha says.

"I don't," Kate adds. "If she's back in town, then she's up to no good. She always causes so much shit whenever she's around. I don't trust her as far as I can throw her."

"You know, Kate," Oliver says, "people do change."

"They don't change that much," Samantha says. "I'd like to think that she can change, for Alex's sake, but I'm not holding out much hope for that."

Rising to his feet, Oliver says, "All I'm saying is that maybe we should give her a chance." Turning to leave, he adds, "It's possible that maybe she learned her lesson after the last time. I mean, everyone was pretty pissed at her but maybe we should all just get over it."

"It's easy to say that, Oliver," Samantha says. She also stands up. "You didn't have to pick up the pieces after she left."

"I understand," he says with a nod. "Charlie told me Alex took it pretty hard when he heard the truth about what she was doing."

"That's a bit of an understatement," Kate suggests as she and Samantha walk with him to the front door. "Alex was devastated when he found out that Zoey was going behind our backs to try and have his adoption revoked. She didn't have a chance, legally, because the agreement is iron-clad, but he was shocked that his aunt would try and do something like that. And for what purpose? Money? Maybe, because he does stand to inherit a fortune when he turns twenty-one, but I've always been under the impression that Zoey didn't need money."

"I don't know, Kate," Oliver says, reaching the door, "but sometimes people are motivated by things other than money."

"If it wasn't for money, what then?" Kate asks. "She's always had access to Alex because she is part of his family. We've never prevented her from seeing him whenever she wanted to, but now we have to be careful about her seeing Alex even with one of us in the room. We just don't trust her."

"Don't know, then." With a smile he adds, "I think it's time that I've got to go. It may be Sunday, but I've got a busy day lined up. Lots to do around my place."

"For sure," Samantha replies. "It was nice to see you, Oliver." She smiles and adds, "I hope you find your rubber mallet."

He grins. "It's no big deal, really. I'm sure it will turn up somewhere."

"Sorry that Charlie sent you all the way over here on a fool's errand," Kate adds, opening the door for him. "But you know you are always welcome here and you don't need a reason to visit."

"Not a problem," he says, stepping out onto the doorstep. "It was a pleasure catching up with you both. See you soon." He darts down the steps without looking back.

Kate closes the door and sighs heavily as she turns to face Sam. "Well, that was odd." She grimaces. "Interesting, but odd."

"It sure was," Samantha says as she walks away.

"Wait a second." Kate says. "I'd like to know why you didn't tell me that you saw Zoey yesterday. And don't tell me you forgot. You would never forget something that important."

"I wasn't keeping it from you," Samantha says. "I just didn't want to tell you until I knew what she was up to."

"The question, Sam, is what are *you* up to?" She studies her wife's face. "I know that you will do anything to protect Alex."

"Yes, I will," she says.

"So, what's happening, then?"

Returning to the couch, Samantha says, "I know you told me to wait, but the truth is that I've been having Cliff Graham run surveillance on her for the last two days."

Kate can't believe what she's just heard. "You didn't think to talk to me first before you did that? Do you know how much trouble this could cause if Zoey finds out that you've been watching her?"

"It's too late. I'm sure she already knows." Samantha knows she is digging herself a deeper hole, but she continues. "Cliff's a good cop and he knows what he's doing, but he's a big guy and it's difficult for him to lay low. I think she's probably seen him around her place. Besides, she always seems to know things before they happen. It's kind of weird."

"Jesus, Sam." Kate sighs, her anger obvious. "What makes you think she knows?"

Samantha hesitates but she knows she has to tell Kate everything because keeping the truth from her will only make matters worse if she ever finds out. Telling herself to remain calm, she swallows and says, "Because of something she said when I saw her this morning."

"You saw her this morning? For Christ's sake, Sam." Kate's reaction was predictable. "What are you doing?"

"I was just trying to find out what she was up to."

"Didn't you learn anything from the last time we tangled with that woman?"

"I know. I know. I screwed up but I was just trying to protect him."

"Protect me from what?" It's Alex. The women had been so busy with their conversation that they had not heard their son enter the house through the back door and then come into the living room by way of the kitchen. Now he's standing in front of them.

He asks again, "What are you protecting me from?"

"It was nothing," Samantha says. "We were just talking about Oliver and your uncle Charlie. Like I said, nothing serious. There's nothing to worry about."

"So, you weren't just talking about me?" It's clear he heard their conversation.

"No," Kate shakes her head. "We were talking about your uncle's bad memory and just kidding around about how we have to protect him from himself."

"I don't think so," Alex responds, glaring at the two women who raised him. "It didn't sound like you were discussing Uncle Charlie."

"Yup, we were," Samantha says and, in effort to change the subject, she quickly adds, "You were out early this morning. Where did you run off to?"

"Just went for a walk. I needed some fresh air to clear my head."

"How are you doing?" Kate asks. "Did it work? The fresh air, I mean. Did it clear your head?"

He answers politely, but it is clear he is annoyed. "It was a nice walk, but it's getting a little stuffy out there so I'm glad I went early."

"Yes, it's a good idea if you have to go outside this time of year to do it early before the humidity sets in," she agrees. "So, what are your plans for the rest of the day?"

"Absolutely nothing. I think I'll just relax and unwind for the rest of the day."

"I think we may take a drive down along the coast after lunch and maybe stop at the beach for a while," Samantha says. "Why don't you come with us? It will be fun."

"No, I don't think so," Alex answers, starting to ascend the stairs. "I'm not in the mood for the beach."

"Well, if you change your mind, just let us know," Samantha calls after him. "We would love to have your company."

"Thanks for the invitation, but I think I'll pass."

Upon hearing Alex's door close, Samantha asks, "Do you think he believed us?"

"Would you?" Kate walks away.

"Where are you going?"

"Outside for a bit. I just need some space."

"Are you mad at me?" Samantha asks.

Continuing toward the kitchen and the back door, Kate replies, "What do you think?"

As she hears the back door close, Samantha whispers, "I think you're both mad at me."

40: It is written

"She definitely knows something is going on," Oliver tells Zoey as they drink iced tea away from prying eyes in the seclusion of his back deck. "I can't tell you what she knows, but she suspects something, and it's not just about you and Alex. I'm sure she knows something about us."

"I'm not surprised," Zoey says, drawing in a mouthful of hot, humid air. "She's been snooping around for the past few days, and she's had Cliff Graham doing her dirty work for her. I didn't see him when I got here, but I bet he's out there right now."

"He wasn't," Oliver says. "I checked before you arrived and he wasn't anywhere in sight, or at least his truck wasn't. It's kind of hard to hide something like that on my street, where there is very little traffic. For a guy with such a good reputation for police work, you'd think he'd drive something more discreet when he's staking out someone's place."

"That doesn't mean he's not out there," Zoey observes. "I think he's better at his job than we give him credit for."

"He's always been a good cop and he's a very nice guy. I've always liked him." Oliver pauses, then asks, "The bigger question is, what do we do about Samantha?"

"I don't know that there's anything we can do," she says, turning to face him. "We knew she would eventually find out that I was back. This town is too small to hide anything like that. Too many people sticking their noses where they don't belong."

"True enough," Oliver says. "And, honestly, right now, I'm more worried about what we can do for Alex."

"Me too. He's my number one concern. I can sense that the owls are getting riled up, and their numbers are growing by the hour. I think they are getting ready to strike and we know that Alex is their ultimate target."

"Is he ready?" Oliver asks. "Are we ready?"

"We have to be, Oliver. For his sake," she says. "I think he is slowly accepting the truth, but it's a lot for him to digest. I still have a hard time accepting it after all of this time and I've had many years to put it all into perspective. If only Sam and Kate would have given me more access to him over the years, he would have been better prepared. I could have made sure he was ready instead of just throwing him into all of this."

"The poor kid," Oliver says. He gulps down some of the cool liquid. "He must think we're crazy. I mean, when you think about it from his perspective, all of this must seem far-fetched, yet we're expecting him to accept it as if it was gospel."

Zoey glares at him, her nostril flaring. He can sense that he has hit a nerve with that last comment. The minute the words left his mouth, he wished he could have taken them back. *But once it's spoken, there's no taking it back.*

"It is gospel, Oliver," she tells him. "You, of all people, should know that. Alexandria and the crows put these events in motion a long time ago all because of the actions of one evil man, Luther Merrick. Now, we have to deal with it—you, me and Alex. He's counting on us. They will come for him, soon."

"If it is going to happen soon, maybe we should take him and get out of this town," Oliver suggests. "Let's go tonight."

Zoey looks at him, but says nothing.

He gives her a moment to think about his suggestion, but when she doesn't respond, he adds, "Give me an hour and I'll be ready. I don't need much."

"It's not that easy, Oliver." She sighs, then adds, "Alex can't run and hide from his destiny because the owls will find him. If I thought that would work, I would have done that a long time ago, but the best place for him right now is right here, in this town where it all began. He has to stand his ground right here, where the crows are best equipped to protect him."

"Can they?"

"Defeat the owls, you mean?"

"Yeah."

Zoey takes a deep breath and then exhales forcefully. "Yes, they can." She pauses, then adds, "But it won't be easy and some of them will die in the process."

"Jesus. Really?"

"Yes." Turning to look him squarely in the eyes, she says, "And they won't die alone."

~

Ozzie Merrick, the scrawny, bespectacled teenager with the tousled brown hair, approaches the enclosure where the parliament is in session. He doesn't know why, but he feels compelled to be there.

"You summoned me?" he says to the larger owl perched near the front of the mesh cage, its round, yellow eyes observing his every move.

The owl emits a series of high-pitched screeches as if calling out to its kin and, as if on command, six other owls of various sizes and different shades of greyish-brown immediately take perches around the first raptor. They are its allies, but clearly not its equal.

"The time has come, hasn't it?" Ozzie whispers, addressing the owls.

The raptors grow silent and stare at him, their gaze so intense that he feels as if he is their prey. He can almost feel their powerful talons ripping into his flesh, their razor-sharp beaks tearing the skin from his bones. He shivers at the thought.

Ozzie swallows and the saliva feels like razor blades as it makes its way down his throat. He exhales with a force and the owls, wings flapping and beaks snapping, prance on their perches as if they are startled by his breath.

"I know my father has told me that I have no choice but to do this." He pauses and allows the owls to settle down. "But I really can't. Alex is my best friend, and I cannot hurt him."

The owls grow silent again. They glare at him, and he feels their eyes burning holes through his skin, almost like they are trying to reach his soul. Their power is awe-inspiring. Ozzie knows he cannot resist them. *But I have to try.*

"This is just very hard for me to wrap my head around," Ozzie tells the owls, and they listen when he speaks, like he has power over them. He is sure they understand everything he is saying—maybe even his very thoughts.

"Alex and I are alike in so many ways," he whispers. "How can you expect me to hurt him?"

The lead owl squawks. Ozzie has no idea how it happens, but when the owls address him, he can understand their message. He has been communicating with the owls ever since he was a young child.

"Yes. I get it," he says. "This feud goes a long way back and he, just like the crows, are our mortal enemies, but the truth is, Alex has never hurt me." He maintains eye contact with the lead raptor. "Hell, in the years that I've known him, he's never even said a nasty word to me. Other than Bree, there isn't anyone else in this town that I can call a friend. This just isn't right."

The owl squawks again.

Ozzie nods. "Yes. I have been told this is my destiny, but I believe destinies can be changed."

"No, Ozzie, they cannot. Not this one."

Spinning around, Ozzie sees his father, Myles Merrick, glaring at him. "Geez, Dad, you were so quiet that I didn't hear you coming," he says, avoiding eye contact. He knows his father does not like when he resists his ancestral obligations. "If you hadn't spoken, I would never have known you were there."

"That's how it's done, Ozzie," Myles says. "Silence is your best ally, other than the owls themselves, of course. If you sneak up behind Alex, you will have the element of surprise and you will have the upper hand. You can strike him down before he even knows you are there."

"I can't do that." He exhales and says through gritted teeth, "I don't want to do that."

"You can and you will," Myles says, his voice stern. "The owls demand it and you cannot resist them."

Ozzie sighs heavily and, taking a deep breath, says, "I still don't get it. Why do the owls have so much power over us? Why do we have to do whatever they command?"

"Because that is how it has always been for our people. I know this is difficult, but as I have told you many times, Ozzie, it's ancient history. Centuries ago, well before modern civilization, our ancestors regarded owls as the gatekeepers of the underworld. They helped protect the souls of those who unintentionally strayed into this land. They were seen as auspicious symbols of courage, higher assistance and supernatural wisdom," Myles explains, as he has done many times in the past. "They are our spiritual partners. That's how it has been for generations and that's how it will continue. You will see to that."

"How?" Ozzie asks, resisting the urge to cry because he has learned over the years that his father does not tolerate any show of emotions. "By destroying my best friend?"

"Yes," Myles says, putting his arm around his son's shoulder and pulling him close. "Right now, the crows are becoming too powerful, and it is time to restore things to their natural balance, so you will meet your destiny. The time is upon us."

~

Placing his face against the glass, Alex steadies his breathing. He steels his nerves. *Still*, he thinks. *I must remain still...and quiet.*

"I don't know, Augustus," he whispers. "None of this seems right to me."

Somehow, he is connected to the large crow perched on the tree branch that stretches close to his bedroom window. The two, crow and human, maintain eye contact.

"I understand what Aunt Zoey has told me. I know she and you expect me to do this, but I'm not built for this." He sighs and swallows. "I don't like confrontations. Besides," he exhales and pauses, gathers his thoughts. "I could never hurt Ozzie. He is one of the only two true friends I have in this town. How can you expect me to kill him?"

The crow blinks and Alex understands.

"I know. I know. It is my duty, my responsibility and I owe it to your flock to protect you. I trust you, Augustus, and I trust Aunt Zoey, but you are asking a lot of me. Until a few days ago, I didn't know about any of this stuff; about my obligation or my destiny," he says, as he watches the crow's head bob up and down. "You have always been there for me, Augustus, for as long as I can remember. I have never understood our connection, but I get it now. If what I read in Alexandria Gorham's journal is true, then we are linked by what happened all those years ago. But, honestly, don't you think this feud between the crows and owls has gone on way too long?"

He hears the crow cawing through the glass and he can see the bird has become agitated.

"I know crows and owls are mortal enemies and I know that if they have gathered here in such large numbers then it means they are coming after you and your family, but does it really have to end with bloodshed? What you are asking me to do is to kill my best friend—to commit murder."

The crow blinks several times and Alex remains quiet. He closes his eyes and listens. It's as if he can hear the bird's thoughts: *It is a matter of survival. The owls embody all that is evil. Their chosen one will manifest that evil and he will draw upon them for his power. He will become strong, and he will strike you down. That is their way. He will follow his destiny.*

"No," Alex whispers, his eyes remaining tightly closed. "Ozzie won't do that."

He will, and you must be ready.

Opening his eyes and staring at the crow, he says, "I will never be ready to do what you're asking."

You will.

The crow suddenly springs from its perch and soars high, making several loops over the house and yard before it flies off.

"I wish I could just fly away, like that," Alex says, turning from the window just as his cellphone rings. Glancing at the screen he sees that it's Ozzie calling.

"No," he sighs. "I can't do that right now." He lets the phone ring several more times before it goes to voicemail.

"Jesus Christ," he sighs again, flopping onto the bed and staring up at the nondescript gyprock ceiling with its white paint. He says to the empty room, "What in the hell am I going to do?

I know Aunt Zoey and Oliver and the crows—especially the crows—expect me to do this but even if I am the 'chosen one,' I am not a protector. I am not a fighter, and I will never be able to hurt Ozzie, even though they all tell me that is exactly what I must do. They tell me it's my destiny, but that destiny was set in motion several hundred years ago when times were different. I can't do this. How can I even be thinking about doing this?

He's tired. He needs rest to recharge, to gain a different perspective. Closing his eyes and hoping that sleep comes quickly, he says, "Give me strength, Augustus. Give me strength, my friend."

~

As dusk slowly gives way to evening darkness, the edge of light on the horizon exhibits its full beauty.

Oliver says to his companion sitting next to him in the other Muskoka chair, "That's a lot to put onto the shoulders of two young men."

The pair are on his back deck, enjoying the picture-perfect sunset, the various hues of colour giving way to the blackness that will soon envelop them.

"I know," Zoey agrees. "But it is decided. We cannot stand in the way, and we cannot alter the course of their fate. All we can do is be there for Alex."

"Do you know when this will happen?" Oliver asks, staring at the first star that suddenly appears in the evening sky, twinkling obliviously to the fates on earth.

"She grasps his hand and squeezes, her grip gentle and soothing. "Within days."

"I see," Oliver nods and turns to face her. "I will be there for him."

"I know you will be," she says and smiles. "I know. As will I. It is written."

41: Sunshine, barbecues and so much more

"You have a lovely home, Myles," Samantha says. She and Kate are sitting on one side of the glass patio table, across from their host. Soaking up the beautiful landscape, she adds, "I just love your backyard. I wish we had a pool."

It's a hot day and she thought the kids might be in the water, but they have disappeared inside the sprawling four-bedroom, three-bathroom home.

"Yeah, right," Kate smiles at her wife. "Like we have time to use a pool or even take care of one."

"Thank you, Mayor Henderson," the tall, slightly balding man answers with a crooked smile. Beaming with pride from the compliment, he adds, "I can't believe this is actually the first time you've visited since we moved to town two years ago. Clearly, I should have invited you over much sooner."

"Please, Myles, call me Samantha or Sam," she tells him. "I'm not much for formalities."

"Good enough," he says. "Then Sam it is."

Kate speaks up. "So, Myles, now that you've been here a few years, how do you like our fair little town?"

"I just love it here," he says. "When my wife died, I knew I couldn't stay in our former home. There were too many painful memories. Besides, it's very cold in northern Ontario. When I accidentally came across a listing for this home one day, I immediately fell in love with it. I knew right away it would be the ideal place for me and Ozzie and his sister, Dani. When we moved here, I worried about them making friends, but they have done really well here. I am really glad that Ozzie and Alex have become such good friends."

"Yes," Kate agrees and smiles. "Ozzie is a nice kid. Kind of shy, but a great young man."

"Dani," Samantha adds. "That's such an unusual name for a girl, but I really like it."

"Truthfully, it's short for Dannielle," Myles answers. "But Dani suits her much better."

"It's cute," Samantha nods. "Kind of conveys strength."

"Yes, well, she is a firecracker, that one, but I wish she would impart some of that strength to her older brother," Myles says.

"What do you mean?" Kate asks.

"Nothing really. It's just that Ozzie is sixteen—the same age as Alex—and I'm worried that he's not going to be ready to tackle the hardships of the world," Myles answers. "There are times when he seems a bit lost."

"Everyone has their own strengths and weaknesses. I remember when I was sixteen, I had no idea where I was headed in this world," Samantha says, just as the doorbell rings, "so Ozzie's lack of direction seems pretty normal to me. I'm sure he will find his way."

"Yes, well, I hope he soon figures it out because I'd like for him to have a plan. Now, if you will please excuse me," Myles says, rising from his chair, "I think a few more guests have arrived."

Kate says, "Is there anything we can do to help you get things ready?"

"No thanks," he says, as he moves away from the table. "Everything is all set." Turning, he says with a smile, "True confession time. I actually had the food catered, so whenever we're ready to eat, all I have to do is put the burgers and steak on the barbecue and take everything else out of the fridge." He laughs, "Please don't hold that against me, but I just figured it would taste much better than anything I could have made. I'm not much of a chef. Can I get either of you another cold drink while I'm in the house? It's pretty hot out here."

"Not for me, thanks," Kate answers. "Not just yet, anyway."

"Me neither," Samantha says, raising her glass so he can see she's hardly touched the first one he gave her when they arrived.

"I'm good for now."

When Myles is gone, Kate whispers, "Nice guy," to her wife.

"I don't know," Samantha whispers back, squinting into the bright sunshine that's spilling over Kate's shoulders. "It's probably just me, but something seems a little off about him."

"Off?" Kate looks puzzled. "How so?"

"Like he's trying a little too hard to make a good impression on us. I know, weird, right?" Samantha shrugs. "But for me, I've always been a little suspicious of people who think they have to impress me. Just doesn't seem sincere."

Kate shrugs. "If there's one thing I've learned about you over the years, honey, it's that I should always trust your instincts."

"I don't know a whole lot about him, but it seems like he's a bit of a recluse," Samantha says while scanning the back patio and yard. "That's why I found his invitation to this barbecue to be a bit strange. Why now?"

"That is true, but what else did we have planned for Canada Day?"

"Well, don't forget that tonight we have to be at the waterfront for the fireworks. Being the mayor, I would never live it down if I was a no-show."

"What time is that, again?"

"Dusk," Samantha reminds her wife. "But I would like to go down before it gets too late so we can take in some of the celebrations at the park."

"You mean, so you can put in a campaign appearance," Kate says with a laugh. "I know you haven't forgotten this is an election year. But you don't have to worry, Sam. I think you're a shoo-in for re-election."

"I never take anything for granted," she replies. "And for the record, if I am voted back in, I promise this will be my last term. I'd hang it up now, but there are a couple of important developments coming along that I've been working on for years and I'd like to see them through. After that, I am done."

"Okay." Kate smiles and Samantha is relieved that they have managed to get beyond their disagreement from yesterday over her obsessing about Zoey LaCroix. "I will hold you to that."

"You can do that," Samantha smiles and reaches across the table to take her wife's hand. "It's a promise. I will even put it in writing."

"Not necessary," Kate says with a chuckle. "Verbal contracts are just as binding."

"Oh, hi, Sam and Kate," Lisa Hamilton says as the short, but stylish, woman walks onto the patio, followed by her two daughters, Bree and Lauren.

"Hi, Lisa," the couple answer in unison.

Acknowledging the girls, Samantha adds, "Nice to see you, too, Bree and Lauren. The boys are off somewhere in the house."

"Yes," Myles says, coming up behind the trio. "Bree, I think you probably know where to find Ozzie and Alex as you've been here before. They are in the den." Addressing the younger Hamilton child, he says, "Lauren, why don't you come with me, and I'll help you find Dani. I'm not sure what she's up to, but I think she's in the living room."

"What a gorgeous day," Lisa says, joining Samantha and Kate at the table as Myles and her daughters disappear inside the sprawling house. Taking a chair next to Kate she asks, "How have you guys been? Seems like I haven't seen you in forever."

"I know, right?" Kate says. "Probably the last time we saw you was maybe two months ago, when we were at the ER with Alex's twisted ankle."

"I think you're right." Lisa nods. "I have to admit that I was a bit surprised when Myles invited us over for a barbecue. Kind of caught me off guard, as he's never done that before and it all seems so—I don't know, right out of the blue."

"I was thinking the same thing," Samantha agrees.

"Don't get me wrong," Lisa says. "I think it's a nice gesture that he called, and I appreciate the invitation. We didn't have any plans for today anyway, as Warren is working." With a hearty chuckle, she adds, "Saved me from coming up with something to keep the girls occupied for the day. Probably would have just gone to the beach."

"I was just going to ask where Warren was," Kate says.

"Police officers, you know," Lisa answers. "Seems like he's always working. Truthfully, though, he wasn't supposed to be on duty today but one of the other officers got called away for a family emergency so they asked the off-duty guys if one of them could come in and take the shift. You know Warren," she says with a shrug. "He was the first one to volunteer, but that's why I love him so much."

"He is one of the good ones," Samantha tells her. "He's always thinking of everyone else."

"He sure is," Lisa agrees. "But that's okay because even if Warren hadn't been working, we would have probably just puttered around the house for the morning and then, like I said, gone to the beach."

"Well, ladies," Myles says, returning to the patio. "Don't let me interrupt your conversation, but can I get anyone anything?"

~

When Bree arrives in the den, she finds Ozzie and Alex sitting at opposite ends of a leather-bound sofa, playing a video game. It seems to her as if they are engaged in quite the battle.

"Hey guys, what's up?" She asks, sliding past Alex and taking a seat in the middle of the sofa between her two friends. She waits for an answer, but the boys remain quiet. The tension is so thick she can almost taste it.

She asks again, "What's going on, guys?"

"Not much," Alex finally responds, quickly glancing at her. It seems more like a grimace to her than a friendly greeting. "Just playing a game."

"I can see that," she says. "I was expecting you would be out in the pool seeing as it's so hot. I brought my bathing suit if you'd like to check out the water."

"I don't feel much like going in the pool right now," Ozzie says. "But you guys can go in if you want to. I'm just going to stay here for a while longer where it's nice and cool."

"Are you okay, Ozzie?" Bree asks, studying her friend's face. She thinks he looks a little flushed. "You sound a little, I don't know, a little upset or miffed or something. Did you guys have an argument?"

Keeping his eyes glued to the screen, Ozzie says, "Nope. We're fine. Just want to finish kicking Alex's ass."

"You only think you're kicking my ass," Alex fires back. Remaining focused on the game, he adds, "You will never beat me."

"Oh, I don't know about that," Ozzie answers, his fingers flying over the game controller. "I think I've got you figured out."

"You think so, do you?"

"Okay, guys," Bree says. "I see what's going on here. You're both trying to impress me with your skills, but you already know I don't care all that much about video games."

"Nope," Alex tells her. "It's not about the video game at all."

"Really? Then what is it?" She asks, glancing quickly from one to the other and waiting for an answer that doesn't seem to be coming from either of them. "Because something is definitely going on between you two."

Ozzie says, "It's between me and Alex."

"Okay, Ozzie," Alex says, dropping his controller. His frustration is clear to Bree, which actually surprises her because Alex is usually fairly level-headed. "I've had enough," he continues. "Let's call it a draw for now and we'll just walk away."

"Never," his opponent responds as the game erupts into a series of loud explosions, flashing lights and noises. "I just killed you."

"Yup," Alex says, rising from the sofa. "You sure did. Looks like you kicked my ass after all." He exhales forcefully. "I think I'll go outside for a bit. That pool sounds like a good idea after all. Coming, Bree?"

"Sure thing," she says.

"No, you can't," Ozzie tells them, quickly springing from the sofa. "Not yet, anyway. I want to show you guys my collection first. I'm sure you've never seen anything like it."

"Collection of what?" Alex asks. The two have been friends for several years and Ozzie has never before mentioned that he collected anything. "What are you collecting?"

Looking at him coyly, Ozzie smirks then blurts out, "Owls."

"What?" Alex is surprised by his friend's sudden declaration, but he knows he should not have been, not considering everything he knows now about Ozzie's family history. "Owls? Dead ones? Live ones?"

"Live ones, course," Ozzie tells him.

Of course, Alex thinks.

"Come," Ozzie motions for Alex and Bree to follow him. "I'll show you."

"No, I don't think so," Alex responds.

"This sounds really interesting," Bree speaks up. "I'd like to see them. I knew you liked owls, Ozzie, but I didn't know you collected them. That's taking your passion to whole new level, isn't it?"

"They are my father's, really," Ozzie tells her. "They have been in the family for a really long time. We got them from all over the world. I guess you could call it more of an obsession than a hobby."

Heading toward a side door, he says, "Come on. You can see them. They are pretty awesome. I think you'll be impressed."

Tugging on Alex's arm, Bree says, "Come on, Alex, let's go see them."

"No, I don't think so," Alex resists. "I really don't want to."

"What's wrong, Alex?" Ozzie asks as he opens the heavy door. "You don't have to be scared. They are in a cage so they can't hurt you."

"I'm not scared," Alex fires back. "I just don't have any interest in owls."

"That's too bad," Ozzie says, stepping through the door. "They are beautiful birds, and they are extremely powerful creatures. They are well suited for hunting—and fighting. They always get their prey."

Glaring at Alex, he says, "Come on, then, Bree. If Alex doesn't want to see them, I'll show you."

Pulling on Alex's arm again, she coaxes, "Come on, Alex. What can it hurt?"

He sighs forcefully and looks at her. "I really don't want to....But okay, Bree. I will come see the freaking owls, but only because you are asking me to."

"Thank you," she says, leading him through the opening to the room into which their friend has suddenly disappeared.

It is dark in the room, with only a few dim lights, and a distinctive, musky odour hangs in the thick air.

"Wow!" is all Bree can say as she stares in amazement at the large, wire-mesh enclosure that practically fills the room. She marvels at the idea that something such as this could be kept here. "This is amazing; freaking awesome."

"If you say so," Alex says, trying to calm his breathing so he doesn't panic.

"Don't you think it's beautiful?" Bree asks, stepping closer to the enclosure and pulling Alex with her.

"If you like that sort of thing," Alex says as he feels the icy fingers of fear tapping on his spine much like a piano player tickles the keys. His eyes quickly scanning the enclosure, he sees trees, rotten stumps, a water source that looks like a small make-shift lake and owls—lots of owls swooping around within the confines of the mesh. He can tell it took a lot of ingenuity and money to build this structure.

"But these creatures don't belong in captivity," he says. "They should be out in their natural habitats. They deserve to be free, not held here like prisoners."

Approaching the mesh, Bree says, "From the outside of the house, you would never know this section was back here."

"I think we should go, Bree," Alex says, turning away from the enclosure. "I really don't want to be here."

Pulling away from his friend, Alex is surprised when Ozzie suddenly appears from the shadows. Stepping close to Alex, he asks, "Going somewhere? What's the rush? Don't you like my owls? They are my friends."

Alex stares at him and then answers, "I just find it stuffy in here. I need some fresh air."

"I don't know what you mean," Ozzie says. "The environment is fully regulated in this room for the sake of the owls. It's not too hot or too cold and they get lots of food. I think it's just right, don't you think so, Bree?"

"I don't mind it," she answers. "But you go ahead outside, Alex, if you want to. I will be out in a minute. I just want to watch the owls for a little," she says, observing the birds as they swoop within the enclosure, some of them occasionally emitting a low-pitched screech. "They are pretty amazing; so graceful in flight."

"Okay then, you stay here. I'm going outside," Alex says.

He notices Ozzie is now standing in the doorway, blocking his only exit. He says, "Can you please move, Ozzie, so I can get out?"

"Sure, but I think you should really stay a bit longer," Ozzie tells him. "You've hardly seen my owls and I want you to get to know my friends a little better."

"I know them well enough," Alex says, as he comes toe to toe with Ozzie, the person he thought was his friend but all of sudden seems intent on keeping him trapped in this place. "I just want to get out so can you please move out of the way?"

"Come, Alex," Ozzie taunts as Bree notices the owls are suddenly starting to behave differently, as if they are becoming agitated. "It's almost time for them to hunt. I want you to watch them in action. You'll get a kick out of this. They are elite killers."

"No, I don't think so." Alex is starting to lose his temper with his friend, and he hates how he feels. "I don't want to watch anything." Their faces dangerously close to each other, Alex says to him, "I just want to get out of here."

"You can't get out, Alex," Ozzie says to him. "You know we can't get out. We are trapped, caught in this cycle. We are in this together."

As the owls grow more excited and their screeching becomes more intense, Bree backs away from the enclosure. "Ozzie, it looks like something is getting your owls worked up. I think I want to leave, too."

"See what you've done, Alex," Ozzie says. "You've got the owls worked up and now you've got Bree all upset. What is wrong with you?"

Through clenched teeth, Alex says, "You know what's wrong with me."

"Do I?"

"You do." Alex studies him and then whispers so that Bree can't hear him. "I know it was you and your father. I know you were the ones who put those notes on my door. And I am pretty sure that it is your father who has been snooping around outside our house the past couple of days. I know what you want. But if you are trying to scare me, it's not working."

"Well, my friend, if you know so much, then you know that we are destined to do this regardless of what either of us may want." Ozzie glares at Alex and adds, "And you should be scared."

"I guess we are," Alex says as Bree moves next to him.

She asks, "What are you guys talking about?"

"Nothing important," Alex answers while maintaining eye contact with Ozzie. "Are you ready to get out of here, Bree? It's time to leave."

"I am," she says, seeing that her friends seem to be locked in an intense stare-down. "Let's all just go back by the pool," she suggests, taking Alex's arm. "I think we all need to cool off."

"No," Alex answers, pushing past Ozzie, their shoulders brushing as he goes by. "I think I'm just going to go home. I am not really in the mood for swimming or a hamburger—or company."

"I'll go with you," Bree says, following close behind. To Ozzie she adds, "What is going on with you guys?"

"I have no idea what you're talking about, Bree," Ozzie says. To Alex he quickly adds, "Thanks for coming, Alex. We will see you soon."

He whispers as he watches his friends leave the den, "Very soon, and I hope you are ready."

42: When owls call

As Alex walks home along the town's deserted main street, he thinks about the way Ozzie was at the owl enclosure. He is sad that his friendship with Ozzie had apparently been a ruse perpetuated by the owls, an elaborate lie carried out for years to gather information on him and his family. He feels betrayed that his connection to Ozzie was part of a devious scheme leading toward a confrontation with deadly consequences.

It seems like Ozzie has accepted the truth. Maybe it's time that I accepted it as well.

It's a holiday Monday and it's hot. People are out at their cottages for the last day of the long weekend or soaking up the sun at the beach, while many are gathered down in the town park for celebrations to observe Canada's birthday, and where there will be fireworks later this evening. He's supposed to meet Bree there around seven, but now he isn't sure he should go. He knows Ozzie is coming after him. *It might not be safe.*

I don't want to do this, he thinks, glancing at his reflection in the large windows as he strolls past the empty storefronts. *But I don't think you are going to give me any choice. I hate it that this is what our friendship has become.*

He wishes he could have told Bree the real reason he had to leave the barbecue. After all, he was the one who wanted her there in the first place, and he's the one who pushed Ozzie to make sure his father invited her family.

She didn't understand why I had to leave. And why would she? But she wouldn't understand even if she knew the truth. How could she? Hell, I don't even know that I understand.

Turning the corner to the narrow street that will eventually lead to his neighbourhood, he remembers the warnings that he has received from Oliver, his protector, and his Aunt Zoey—always know your surroundings, always be aware, always be ready to defend, and don't show your fear, for the owls thrive off of fear.

"Watch your back and be prepared for anything," he remembers them saying as he quickly scans his surroundings. "Be ready and take nothing for granted."

I don't know that I will ever be ready for any of this.

"Trust your instincts," his Aunt Zoey told him. "And, most importantly, trust the crows, because they are your strongest ally."

Where are you, Augustus? He thinks, his eyes bouncing from tree to rooftop, from tree to yard and then searching the sky.

"I could use you right about now," he says, glancing upward again as the sky quickly grows darker. He is shocked, but also relieved, to see dozens of crows, large and small, have suddenly appeared and are now swooping overhead, gliding and dipping on the warm air currents.

"Thanks guys," he whispers, picking up his pace as he fears that the sudden appearance of so many crows around him could also mean that danger is nearby.

"Are you here, Augustus?" he asks the flock.

A loud, piercing caw cuts through the hot, humid air, confirming the presence of his feathered friend.

"I am glad to see you," he says as the large, jet-black crow, its ebony feathers reflecting a purplish-green glow in the afternoon sunlight, quickly drops down from the crowded sky and swoops near his head before taking a perch on an overhanging branch of a maple tree.

The others in the murder light on nearby trees, power lines and rooftops, taking a defensive position around the teenager and their leader.

"I saw them, Augustus," he says, coming to a stop so that he can address the bird. "The owls."

The powerful crow caws softly.

"There were a lot of them. And some of them were big." He exhales. He's afraid and he believes the crow knows it. "Some of them are much larger than even you."

The crow flaps its wings.

"Sorry, my friend, but it's true. They are big and I can tell that some of them are very powerful," Alex says. "I'm afraid, Augustus. Now that I've seen them, I know all of this is real. I'm also afraid that, if we have to fight, we won't be able to take them. I am not a fighter. You are the warrior, but I am not ready."

The crow remains silent as if considering everything he just said.

"I know I am supposed to do this," Alex says, "but is it too late to change directions? Maybe there is some other way."

The crow caws softly.

"I know. I know," Alex answers. "But whatever this thing is—this fate or curse—it has really changed Ozzie. He was so intense, and he seemed very angry. I have never seen him like that before. He is not the guy I used to know, but he is still my friend."

The crow prances back and forth on the branch while emitting a series of low, guttural caws.

"I know I can no longer trust him," Alex says reluctantly. "I know the owls have taken control of him, but he's my friend, somewhere deep inside, and I can't believe that he would ever hurt me."

The familiar red half-ton truck suddenly pulls up to the curb and Oliver says through the open window, "Alex, what in the hell are you doing out here by yourself like this? Not a good idea, my friend."

"I am not by myself," he says, pointing to the dozens of crows that are stationed nearby. "Can't you see them? I have protection."

"I see them, Alex, but you are still a walking target," Oliver says, leaning over and opening the passenger-side door. "Get in. I'll take you home, or wherever you want to go. Zoey's, maybe?"

"No, home will be fine," he answers while climbing into the cab and pulling the door shut behind him. "You know, Oliver, Augustus would not let anything happen to me."

Putting the truck into gear and pulling away from the curb, Oliver says, "I know that he will do whatever he can to protect you, but he won't be able to keep you safe if you pull stunts like this."

"Stunts like what? Walking?"

"Exactly," Oliver says. "You weren't being smart. You may as well paint a target on your back and say come and get me."

Alex asks, "Do you think someone would really have attacked me right on the street?"

"I don't know, but why give them the opportunity?" Oliver answers. "You may not be able to see them, but you can be sure that there are owls all around here and they are watching you."

Alex can see that Oliver is upset with him. His words conveying an urgency he hasn't heard from him before.

Oliver says, "You are their constant focus, you can count on that. You have to understand that you are their prey."

Considering his friend's warnings, Alex finally says, "I'm really scared, Oliver. I saw the owls this afternoon and they are freaking powerful-looking. They are fucking big birds. With their talons, they could rip those crows to shreds in a heartbeat."

Oliver throws Alex another glance and exhales. "Don't underestimate the power of the crows. In battle, it's not always about brute force, Alex," he answers, speaking softly in an effort to calm the boy's nerves. "There's also strength in numbers. Look at all those crows back there, and that's just a small sample. They are your defence."

"But we don't know how many owls are around, do we?"

"No." Oliver shakes his head. "We don't, but your friend Augustus, he can command an army of crows if he has to. I've lived in this town for a long time, and I've seen them come here in mass numbers in the past. If he thinks there is a need to summon them, he will. His goal is to protect you, and he will use everything in his arsenal to do that."

"How do you know that?"

Oliver pulls his truck over to the curb in front of Samantha and Kate's house. "I just know. I assure you that your feathered friends will meet the challenge. You can count on them, and you can also count on me and Zoey. We are with you."

"I am grateful for that," Alex says, staring at the empty street and the shimmer of heat rising from the pavement. "It's that Ozzie has changed so much over the past couple of days that it's freaking me out." He exhales and adds, "And his father is just plain-ass creepy. I can't say I've ever really liked the man all that much, but I am really sad to see what all of this has done to Ozzie."

"I know, Alex," Oliver says. "He finds himself in the same position you're in, only he's the enemy, and you have to see him in that light. You have to stop seeing him as your friend." He looks directly at Alex and adds, "Your life depends on it."

"Jesus." Alex sighs. "I wish I could go back in time and change all of this. I would stop Luther Merrick before he ever had chance to attack Alexandria Gorham and put all of these events in motion."

"Me too, but time travel isn't possible," Oliver answers. "But wishing for things to be different won't make it happen. So, we have to brace for what's coming. We have no other choice."

"Will we survive all of this, Oliver?" Alex asks.

"If I had a crystal ball, I could see how we make out. But I'm afraid that we're stuck in this moment, and we have no choice but to deal with whatever fate throws at us." He smiles. "Now, what are you doing for the rest of the day?"

"Nothing much, right now," Alex says. "This evening we're all going down to the park for the fireworks."

"I don't think that's a very good idea," Oliver says after some consideration. "I think you should stay home and lay low. I will come by to watch the place. We know the time is close, so let's not give the owls any openings."

"No, I can't do that. My moms are both already pissed at me for leaving the barbecue this afternoon and they will never understand if I don't go with them tonight."

"They'll be more upset if you get hurt or killed, Alex. From a strategic point of view, going to the park this evening where it's going to be dark, and with large crowds, is not a smart move. The owls maneuver better than crows in darkness and they will take advantage of the opportunity to strike at you. I know that's what I would do if I was hunting you."

"Jesus, Oliver, that's a creepy thing to say."

"That's the point, Alex. You'd be making yourself a target again.

You have to be careful here and think strategically. Think like your enemy would think."

"If I give in to them and change my entire routine, then they win," Alex says, grabbing the handle and pushing open the truck door. "I hear what you're saying, and I appreciate your advice, but I have to do this Oliver."

"All right, Alex," Oliver says with a sigh. "But I will be around, too, and I'll do whatever I can to protect you. But do me a favour. When you're there tonight, stay with the crowd. Don't put yourself in a position where you'll be alone, like you were just now, and don't hang with Ozzie."

"I hear you, and I will do my best to avoid him," Alex says as he slides from the cab. "I am curious about one thing though."

"What's that?"

"How did you know where I was just now?"

"I just knew," Oliver says with a shrug. "It was just instinct, I guess. You never know when the owls or their proxies are going to strike, so I have been watching."

"I think there's a lot of that going around these days," Alex replies. "People going on instinct, I mean."

"Hmmm." Oliver nods. "True enough." He pauses, then adds, "Be on your toes and don't trust Ozzie. Do not let your guard down, and please call me if anything comes up. I will be close. Now you go inside and make sure everything is locked. I'll stay here for a few minutes."

"I'm okay, Oliver. You can take off now." Alex nods with a reassuring smile. "Thanks for the lift."

Oliver is about to answer when a strange, screeching noise cuts through the hot afternoon air.

"Fuck," Alex says, coming to an abrupt stop. He feels like he's just been punched in the gut. He knows that is not a noise any crow makes.

Quickly glancing around the yard, checking out the trees and his surroundings, he can't locate the source of the sound, but he can feel he's being watched—hunted.

Also hearing the cry, Oliver jumps out of the truck and sprints around the vehicle to Alex. "What the hell was that? It didn't sound like any crow that I've ever heard."

"It wasn't," Alex tells him, struggling to catch his breath. "It was definitely an owl."

"Just breathe, Alex," Oliver says, taking him by the shoulders and staring into his yes. "Take long, deep breaths. Come on, let's get you inside."

"It was an owl," Alex manages to say between gasps. "It was a warning."

43: Battle on the bridge

Despite Oliver's warnings, Alex finds himself roaming through the town park as the sun begins to dip below the horizon, one of hundreds of people gathering there for the annual Canada Day fireworks. The show will start once darkness sets in, in about half an hour.

Are you out there, he wonders, scanning the trees, grounds and rooftops, looking for any clues that owls may be lurking somewhere, hidden in the shadows. *Stay sharp*, he tells himself. *They could be here...and they could be anywhere.*

"What happened to you this afternoon?" Bree asks as she hurries to keep pace with him. She is almost jogging to match his stride.

Alex has been trying to avoid his parents all evening and welcomed the reprieve that his friend provided, but he knows he isn't out of the woods yet. He will soon face an inquisition from his moms, not only for leaving the barbecue earlier today with a very weak excuse, but also for everything that has been happening over the past few days. Samantha and Kate are smart, and he's sure they know something is up. And to top if all off, now Bree wants an explanation.

What am I going to do? If I can't tell my moms and Bree the truth about the crows and owls, as Aunt Zoey says it will put them in even greater danger, what in the hell am I going to tell them? How am I going to explain why I've been acting so weird for the past couple of days?

"Can you please slow down, Alex?" Bree pleads. "I've told you before that when you move that quickly I can't keep up with you, and I really want to talk. You left so quickly this afternoon before I could ask what was wrong, and I got the feeling that something happened between you and Ozzie. Please tell me what's wrong. Let me help."

"You can't help," he tells her. "Speaking of Ozzie, do you know if he and his family are here?" Alex asks. "I haven't seen them yet."

"I don't think so," Bree answers. "He said something about helping his father clean up after the barbecue, so maybe they aren't coming. We had fun in the pool, and you missed some great food."

"I wasn't hungry," Alex says, maintaining his steady pace.

"I don't think that was it," Bree says. "I can tell something is wrong. You have been avoiding Ozzie and now you don't even want to talk about him. You guys usually get along very well. What's going on?"

"It's nothing."

"Come on," she pleads, and he can detect the concern in her voice. "You and Ozzie are friends and now you won't even talk to him. What gives?"

"Like I said, it's nothing," he fires back at her while weaving in and around the boisterous crowd that has gathered in the park. *Everyone seems to be happy*, he thinks, observing people as they laugh and celebrate the arrival of summer. *Why is this happening to me? Why am I the one who has to fight for his life?*

"Please slow down," Bree asks again, quickening her pace. "Where are you going? We've passed a couple of good spots back there where we can get a clear view of the fireworks. Let's go back and check them out."

Alex keeps pushing through the people, all the while scanning the surroundings for any sign of owls or Ozzie and his father. He finally says, "I've always wanted to watch the fireworks from the old train bridge. I'm going there, but I think you should stay here."

"What? Why? We can get a good view of the fireworks from here." He can tell she is disappointed in his sudden proclamation. "That's quite far up the river, Alex. It's almost dark and I'm not sure we can make it there before the fireworks start."

Alex knows that Oliver and his aunt Zoey would not approve of his decision that will make him more vulnerable. He knows he is likely putting himself in serious danger from the owls, *but honestly, I have to end this tonight. If this is going to happen, then let's just get it over with. I can't take this anymore.*

"You can get a better view from the bridge and there are fewer lights to interfere with the fireworks. But you should go back with your mother and Lauren."

He knows his decision will upset her, but he doesn't want her there if something happens. *It's for her own good*, he thinks, refusing the urge to look back at her. He doesn't want to see her disappointment.

"Alex," she begs, and he pulls further from her. "Please wait for me."

He says nothing more as he disappears through the crowd.

I just can't do this any more. All the secrets. All the lies I've had to tell my mothers. They don't deserve that. It has to stop before something happens to them.

If this is my fate, then so be it, he thinks ten minutes later, as he stands on the old train bridge that has traversed the fast-flowing river for more than a century. It is now part of a popular walking trail since the train no longer runs through town.

He wonders, as he leans on the railing, why more people don't come here to view the fireworks display. The place is pretty much empty tonight, except for him and the occasional passerby.

"Okay you bloody owls," he says, his voice carrying down the river. He swallows hard in an effort to suppress his nerves. "I'm right here. Come and get me."

He's not sure they've followed him to the bridge or if this is even the night that they are coming for him, but, while he is scared to death by the mere thought of their eventual arrival, he hopes they will come. A part of him knows the time has come to face the demons.

"If you want me so badly, then here I am," he says, standing firm on the wooden decking of the bridge. "I am ready."

"Are you sure?"

Spinning around, Alex is startled, but not surprised to see Ozzie standing there.

"You should not be so quick to meet the owls," his friend says, as he slowly moves closer. His voice is like a void, hollow and lacking any emotion. "They are not going to take it easy on you just because you and I are friends, and they won't stop until they get your blood."

"So, you say, Ozzie." Alex stands pat, feet planted on the bridge. "Where are they, these so-called warriors of yours?"

"They are here," Ozzie tells him. "Why are you in such a rush to meet your doom, Alex?"

"If this is my fate, then so be it," he replies, not really sure if he believes what he just said. "If this is going to happen, let's get on with it."

"They will strike, when they are ready," his adversary says as a series of low, guttural screeches shatter the warm evening air. "Hear them, Alex? They are calling for you. They are coming for you, and they grow excited. They smell their prey. They can sense your fear. They want your blood."

"Yes, well, you should know that I am not alone," Alex says, as seven large crows swoop down and land on the bridge railings next to him. As if forming a battle line around their charge, they move into defensive position.

"That's it?" Ozzie asks, almost with a chuckle. His confidence in what the owls are capable of is clearly evident. "We are not afraid of a few crows, Alex. The owls will make mincemeat out of them."

Watching as several of the owls now circle above Ozzie's head and then land on the railing next to him, Alex says, "I guess we shall see."

"Yes," Ozzie says with a nod. "We shall see. But at the end of the day, Alex, you should know this is not personal. I still like you very much, but I have no choice. I have to do this. I know you're in the same boat."

"If we are going to take each other out, then I want you to know that I hold no grudge against you." Alex pauses and then, speaking softly, says, "I will always consider you a very close friend no matter what happens here tonight or what comes afterwards."

"Well, then," Ozzie says, stepping forward as the owls begin to beat their wings as if telling him to advance, "let's do this."

"I'm ready," Alex says. "Augustus, it is time," he whispers, as the largest crow of the seven which had been positioned next to him on the railing sends out a very loud and urgent call. Within seconds dozens of crows descend from the darkening sky and light on the old train bridge to form a barrier around the boy.

Going on the offensive, the owls take flight. Others emerge from the trees along the riverbank. Alex can see that Ozzie has also brought reinforcements. There are too many owls for him to count.

Very clever, he thinks, as he watches crows and owls meet in mid-flight, claws cutting through feathers and beaks snapping. *Be careful my friends. Augustus, save as many of your kin as you can.*

"They are all going to die, Alex. Every last one of them. I'm coming for you," Ozzie tells him, pushing his way through the flocks of crows that are attempting to block his path. Somehow, he's managing to repel them without suffering major injury.

Standing firm, Alex tells him, "I'm right here, Ozzie. I'm ready."

"Are you?" Ozzie sneers and Alex can see that his friend is wielding what appears to be a large hunting knife. "Say your prayers."

Augustus breaks from the flock of crows and swoops in, making Ozzie his direct target. The boy is too slow in raising his arms to fend off his attacker.

The strike is brutal. Alex cringes as the large, powerful crow latches onto his friend's face, ripping a large chunk of flesh from his cheek.

"Fuck," the boy screams in pain as the blood pours from the wound. Dropping the knife, he puts both hands to his face to protect his eyes.

Falling to his knees, the blood gushing from the wound, he cries out, "You god-damned fucking crow, look at what you've done. You will pay for this. Athena, strike!"

A large, powerful owl breaks from the battle overhead, where owls and crows are entangled and the dead from both sides drop toward the river below the bridge.

Alex cringes as the sound of combat echoes through the evening air. "Fly, Augustus," he whispers.

The large owl has set its sights on Augustus, who is swooping in for another attack on Ozzie. "Turn back, Augustus," Alex screams. "That owl is coming for you!"

He watches in horror as the owl that Ozzie called Athena finds its mark, meeting Augustus in mid-fight. Screeches and cries fill the evening air as the first of the fireworks erupt into an array of bright colours further down the river.

"It's game over for that crow," Ozzie says. "Athena won't stop until she kills him."

"Augustus!" Alex screams as the crow becomes locked in a battle for its very life. "Fly away. Get out of here. Save yourself!"

"There's no getting away from Athena," Ozzie says. He grabs the railing and pulls himself to his feet, the blood pouring down his cheek and dripping onto his chest, his white T-shirt turning red.

"There has to be another way to settle this," Alex says. "Let's put an end to all of this and talk about it."

Retrieving the knife from the planks, Ozzie fires back, "There is no other way."

As Ozzie raises the knife to strike, Alex sees dozens of crows break from the main fight and descend on the attacker, knocking him to the planks at Alex's feet, pinning him there and rendering him harmless. The knife skitters away, out of reach.

Alex bends and says to him, "It's over. Tell your owls to leave and we can end this before any more of our birds are hurt. I am not going to fight you, Ozzie. I refuse to hurt you."

"You won't have to worry about fighting him, Alex." Another voice rises through the cacophony of crow and owl calls that, with the sound of fireworks, fill the air. "Because I am going to take you out."

Alex is surprised to see Myles Merrick emerging from the flock of owls. "You?"

Myles stoops to retrieve the large knife. "Useless," he jeers at his son. To Alex, he says, "I knew Ozzie doesn't have the fortitude for this, so I followed him here. I will finish his job."

"Augustus," Alex cries out, knowing he is no match for Myles Merrick. "I need your help."

As Myles moves toward him, dozens of crows swoop in to defend Alex. Forming a black wall in front of him, the crows flap and flutter, beaks snapping. Ozzie crawls away from the fight, hoping to escape with his life.

"Fucking crows," Myles curses. "Athena," he calls. "I could use you."

The powerful owl breaks from its battle with the large crow, and Alex watches as Augustus flies off into the darkness. He can tell his friend is badly injured. *Go on, my friend. Be safe.*

"Alex, are you okay?" A new voice has suddenly entered the confusion.

"Oliver?" Alex should not be surprised by his sudden appearance on the bridge. "I'm okay. How did you know where I was?"

"I just knew," Oliver answers, moving to the boy's side and remaining focused on their adversaries. "I told you not to make yourself into a target, so I guessed you would do just the opposite."

As Oliver steps toward Myles Merrick, Alex cautions, "He has a knife."

"Get out of here, Alex," Oliver commands without looking back. "Get to someplace safe. I will take care of this."

The large owl swoops in, flapping fiercely around Oliver's head. He swings his fists until he makes contact, sending the owl back toward the railing, where it lands on the planking next to Ozzie. "Go on, Alex. Run while you have time."

"Oliver Lewis, the protector. I expected you to show up. You can't stop this," Myles says, charging forward. "That boy has to die tonight."

"Not if I have anything to say about it," Oliver says, grabbing Myles' arms as he swings the knife.

The blade slashes into Oliver's right forearm, but Oliver manages to pin Myles' arms and force him back to the railing. He moves with a speed and agility that Alex didn't know the man possessed.

Oliver effortlessly picks up Myles Merrick and throws the helplessly flailing man over the railing.

Myles disappears into the darkness below.

"Dad," Ozzie screams. He springs to his feet and rushes Oliver from behind, catching him off guard.

Watching in horror, Alex sees Oliver struggling to maintain his balance. "Alex," he cries, "get out of here! Go now."

He loses his balance and tips over the railing, also plunging into the darkness.

"Oliver!" Alex calls out as his friend disappears from view.

Ozzie looks down at the river, then starts to climb the railing.

"Stop, Ozzie," Alex cries. "You don't have to do this."

"Dad!" Ozzie yells hurling himself towards the river rushing under the bridge. "I'm coming!"

"Ozzie," Alex screams into the dark below. He can hardly see the water. "Oliver! Where are you?"

They are gone. He listens as the owls quickly retreat from the bridge and disperse. They have lost this battle.

"Augustus," Alex calls out. "If you can hear me, wherever you are, call your kin. Tell them they can leave. I am safe now. The battle is over."

"Alex?" He recognizes the voice. "Oh my God, Alex, are you hurt?"

"Bree," he says, spinning around and seeing her standing at the end of the bridge. Her white complexion and wide eyes tell him she is in shock. "What are you doing here?"

"I wanted to make sure you were okay," she says, rushing toward him. "What happened here?"

"Did you see anything?"

"Yes," she cries. "I saw them all go into the river. The birds? The owls and the crows? Why? I don't understand."

"It's a long story, Bree," he says.

"Are they okay?" she cries as she rushes to him.

"I don't know." He turns back to scan the river below, but it is too dark. "I can't see any of them. Can you please call 911?"

44: Picking up the pieces

"Alex, honey," Samantha says, lightly knocking on her son's bedroom door. "Are you okay? Can I please come in?"

When he doesn't answer, she taps again. "We have to talk, Alex. I know you're still very upset over everything that's happened, but it has been seven days and we need to talk."

"I don't want to talk," he finally says from the other side of the door.

"But, honey, there are so many questions that need to be answered and while I know it's hard, we do need to discuss everything that happened that night," Samantha says. "Warren, Bree's father, was here a little while ago and I have an update.

She waits for an answer, then adds, "Please, may I come in?"

When he doesn't answer, she taps again. "Alex?" She speaks softly. "I need to know you're alright."

"Okay. Okay," he finally answers. "The door isn't looked. You can come in."

"Hey, honey," she says, opening the door just wide enough to slip into the darkened bedroom. Moving toward the bed where her son is laying, she adds, "How are you doing?"

"I'm fine," he sighs, but he refuses to look at her because he knows that if he makes eye contact, he will lose it. Instead, he stares at the ceiling.

"Are you hungry? I can make you some lunch. You just tell me what you'd like, and I'll get it for you."

"I don't want anything," he tells her. "So, what did Bree's father say? Is there any news on Oliver?"

"Well, not much actually," Samantha whispers. She can see that her son is in a lot of pain, but she knows there isn't anything she can say that will make him feel better. "The divers have been searching the river and they still haven't found any sign of him. They figure his body got caught in the currents that run under the old train bridge and was pulled out to sea. You know the currents are strong in the middle of the river. There have been a lot of drownings there over the years."

"So, now what? What does that mean? Are they going to keep looking?"

"Well, honey, that's the thing," she pauses, hesitating to tell him. "Warren says they have made the decision to call off the search."

"What?" Alex bolts upright. "Are you fucking kidding me? They can't stop looking. Oliver is out there somewhere. He might still be alive. He might be injured."

"Honey, after all this while, the chances of anyone surviving are pretty slim."

"That doesn't mean it can't happen."

"True," she says with a nod. "But it is very unlikely. If Oliver had made it to shore somewhere further down the river, I am sure we would have heard something by now. They've had searchers scouring both riverbanks for days and have found no sign of him."

"What now, then?" Alex asks, trying hard not to show any tears that are close to breaking through the dam he's built around his emotions. "We can't even have a funeral for him if they don't find a body."

"No, I'm afraid there won't be any funeral. But there is talk of holding a memorial service for him," Samantha says. "That would give everyone a little bit of closure at least."

"That's not the same thing," Alex says, wiping away the tears that are now trickling down his face. He knows he's lost this battle. "This is so unfair. They found the other two bodies right away, so why can't they find him?"

"I don't know, honey, but they have been searching around the clock." She sighs and continues. "Speaking of the other two, I've heard there will be services for Ozzie and his dad this coming Saturday. I will be attending, as will Kate. You are welcome to join us, but only if you feel up to it."

"I don't want to go." His answer is quick.

"I'm sure and I understand, but there's still lots of time if you change your mind."

"I won't."

"Okay." She nods and says, "Whatever you wish. I am not going to push you on that."

"I just can't." He blinks to fight back more tears. He knows that if he starts crying, he may never stop.

"That's fine," Samantha reassures him. "It is your decision. I still don't know what happened on that bridge and how you all ended up there in the first place. I thought you were going to stay in the park with Bree."

"I can't talk about it now."

She studies him and then adds, "The police still want to talk to you about that night. They have lots of questions about how all of this happened. Kate and I have been putting them off, with Charlie's help. We've been telling them you are in shock, and you are much too upset to talk about it, but they keep insisting they need information soon. I'm not sure how much longer we can keep stalling them. Warren didn't come right out and say that this morning, but he certainly implied as much."

"I'll tell them what I know but it isn't much. For some reason, Ozzie's dad just attacked me while Bree and I were watching the fireworks from the bridge." Speaking almost as if he's in trance, Alex adds, "It's like the man went crazy. Oliver tried to stop him and they got into a fight. They went over the side and Ozzie jumped in to try and save his father. That's all I know."

"There are just so many questions." Samantha chooses her words carefully. "Like, what were you doing on the bridge in the first place? What was Oliver doing there with you? How did Ozzie's father end up there? Why would Myles Merrick attack you, of all people? We hardly knew him."

"Maybe he had some kind of mental break or something? I don't know." Alex shakes his head. "It all happened so fast. It's kind of a blur."

"Yes, well, I should tell you that I went to see your Aunt Zoey two days ago. I figured that she must have been involved somehow, and if there was anyone who would know what went on there, it would be her."

"And, what did she tell you?"

"Honestly, not a lot. But this has her name written all over it." She pauses, takes a deep breath and continues, "At some point Alex, you will have to tell me everything and, like I said, the police want to know the circumstances. Right now, like you said, they are saying Ozzie's dad had some sort of mental break or a psychotic episode, but I don't buy that. We had just seen him only a few hours earlier that day and he seemed perfectly fine. I don't know what it is, but there is something more sinister behind all of this and you will have to tell us everything that you know."

"I can't do this anymore," he says, and rolls over with his back to her. "If you don't mind, I want to get some sleep."

"Okay, Alex. I am going to be right downstairs whenever you want to talk." Heading to the door, she adds. "Kate and I want you to know that we love you very much and we are here for you, no matter what."

She gives him a few moments to answer. When he doesn't respond, she slips out of the room and closes the door behind her.

"All you have to do is ask," she whispers.

Trying to force the images of that night out of his head, Alex knows that the time is soon coming when he will have to tell his parents everything that happened, but he will put it off for as long as possible.

They will never understand, he thinks, rolling onto his back again and staring at the ceiling. *Shit! I don't even understand it, for Christ's sake, and I lived through it. The whole thing seems too far-fetched, like some sort of god-damned story concocted by someone with a warped imagination.*

But, he sighs, remembering the sacrifice Oliver Lewis made to protect him, *it was real. It did happen.* Wiping away tears, he sighs. *Jesus, Oliver, where the hell are you?*

He wishes he could just go to sleep and when he wakes up all of this would turn out to be a bad dream. *Oliver and Ozzie are gone, and it was all my fault*, he thinks, as his phone screen lights up.

When he sees that it's Bree calling again, he dismisses the call. He hasn't spoken with his friend since that night and he's still not ready to talk to her. He knows she saw everything that happened on the bridge, but clearly, she hasn't told anyone about it or the police would surely be knocking down his door.

I should talk to her. She deserves answers, he thinks, scanning his favourites list. *No*, he tells himself, laying his phone on the bed next to him, *I just can't. Not yet anyway. She will think I have lost my mind if I tell her the whole truth.*

He closes his eyes tight and takes a deep breath. *Maybe I have lost my mind. Maybe none of this is real....But it is,* he tells himself as his phone rings again.

Scanning the phone screen, he sees the call is from his aunt Zoey.

"Hello," he says, answering on the first ring.

"Hi Alex," she replies.

"Am I ever glad that you called. Where have you been for the past three days? I've been crawling out of my own skin over here. I need some help," he tells her. "I don't know what to do. My moms and the police want answers, and I don't know what I should tell them."

"If you tell them the truth, Alex, they will not believe you," she says.

"I know and that's why I haven't told them anything, but they want to know what happened."

"I expect they do, Alex, but you tell them the truth at your own peril," Zoey answers. "My advice is to be as aloof as possible and to skirt the truth. They won't understand. When it comes to the crows and what they do, discretion is the best policy."

"That won't be enough for them," Alex says. "I'm trying hard to not lose my grip on reality, but you know my mother will not drop this until she knows everything."

"I know," Zoey says. "She came to see me yesterday, but I didn't tell her anything. She really is worried about you, but it is your decision whether you want to tell her the whole truth."

"I know," he agrees. "And I will do it when the time is right."

"How are you really doing?" she asks.

"Other than losing my mind, I guess I'm doing okay. But this isn't easy."

"I know it's hard, but you are strong, and you will get through this," she tells him. "There will be questions and there will be suspicions. We knew there would be. But I believe in you, Alex, and I know you will make it."

"Yes, well, I am not so sure about that."

"You will," she tells him. "So,"—he can detect the hesitation in her voice—"I have one other thing to tell you."

"What's that?" He's almost afraid to ask.

"I am leaving town." Her answer seems blunt to him. "I wanted to tell you that I have to go."

"Why?" He pleads, "I need to see you."

"There isn't time to explain, Alex. I am leaving tomorrow, and I have a lot to do before I go. Besides, if I see you now, it will only raise more suspicions, especially for Samantha. You can do this. I believe in you. More importantly, the crows believe in you."

He fights the urge to cry. "And what about Oliver? We can't give up on him.

"You don't need me, Alex." She suddenly seems distant to him. "You have everything and everyone right there in your life. You have a strong support system from people who love you. Lean on them, Alex, and you will be all right."

"And Oliver?"

"He's gone, Alex." She is blunt. "You have to accept that and move on."

"But why?

"Because he did what he had to do."

"Why are you leaving right now, after everything that's happened?"

"I just have to go."

"Where are you going?"

"Away," she says. "But I will call you when I reach my destination and get settled."

"I don't understand."

"I know you don't," she says. "But it is for the best. You will understand someday. Now, I do have to go. I have lots to do before I leave but I wanted to say goodbye."

"Please, Aunt Zoey," Alex pleads as she ends the call.

He quickly hits her number, but it goes straight to voicemail.

"Great," he says, tossing his phone back on the bed. "Now that I really need you, you're leaving town. Maybe Mom was right about you after all."

Pulling a pillow over his face, Alex feels lost, like he has been set adrift on the wide, open ocean. Up and over the waves he goes. He feels like he's about to drown.

"Augustus," he whispers. "Where are you? I need you."

He hasn't seen the largest crow since that night on the old train bridge and he doesn't even know if Augustus survived the fight with the lead owl. He could see the attack was brutal and the owl was vicious, powerful. He could tell Augustus was badly injured, but he had no way of knowing just how badly—or even if he's still alive.

The two, human and bird, are kindred spirits. They are connected in a way that no one would be able to explain. He dreads the thought that his feathered friend may be dead.

"Augustus?" he says, after suddenly hearing several light taps at his bedroom window.

Rushing to the window, he quickly pulls back the curtains and rolls up the blinds. He is relieved to see the crow perched on the nearby tree branch.

"Holy shit," he says, leaning on the glass. "Holy fucking shit. It's you. You've come back. Augusts, am I ever glad to see you, my friend."

As the black bird prances back and forth on the branch, like it is doing some sort of ritual dance, Alex adds, "Are you okay? Are you hurt?"

The bird stops, becoming perfectly still and, staring at Alex, it connects with him on a spiritual level.

"Yes," Alex nods. "I know we defeated the owls, but it cost us a lot. Oliver is gone, and could be dead, and how many crows did we lose?"

The boy listens as if he can comprehend the crow.

"Yes, I understand that they all made the ultimate sacrifice for the greater good, but it was a steep price to pay and I'm not sure I was worth it," he says. "All in the name of saving me."

The crow blinks quickly.

"Yes, I understand that we all have a role to play in life, and that I have more to do," Alex says. "But I am only one person, and my life isn't any more important than anyone else's. Why did Oliver have to die so that I could live?"

The bird's head bobs and it continues to blink, quickly.

"More to the story?" Alex asks as the crow suddenly springs from the branch and takes flight, heading off to some mysterious destination that only crows know about. "I don't understand what you mean by that, Augustus. What more could there be?"

Epilogue

July 2

"Mister," the petite, dark-haired woman says to the strange man she's found sprawled on the rocks along the riverbank. She can't be any more than twenty-five years of age.

Giving him a gentle nudge she adds, "Can you hear me, mister? Are you okay?"

She's lived in this town her entire life and doesn't recognize him as anyone from around here.

He's still breathing, she thinks, placing her ear on his chest. His clothes are wet, which tells her he just crawled from the river. While she can tell he's badly injured, he somehow managed to make it up over the rocks.

What happened to you?

"I don't know who you are, mister," she says, "but you are one lucky fellow to still be alive. That water is pretty rough today."

Scanning his badly-battered body and then checking along the shore for any boats or for signs of anyone else, she adds, "I wonder where you came from."

Did someone attack you and throw you in the water? she wonders, pulling her cell phone from her pocket and preparing to dial 911.

"No," the man suddenly says, reaching out for her as he tries to sit up. "Please don't."

"What?" she says, pushing him back down. "Just stay there and be still. You could be badly injured. I need to get an ambulance."

"No," he says again, trying to push her hands away. "I don't need an ambulance."

"Listen, mister, stop moving around," she tells him. "You need to be still until we can have you checked out. You could have a head injury. Who are you? What is your name?"

Remaining quiet, as if considering her questions, the man then says, "Honestly? I don't know."

"You don't know? That's interesting. Do you know where you are or where you came from?"

Considering her questions again, he then shakes his head. "No. I have no idea," he says, speaking so softly she has to strain to hear him.

"So, either you won't tell me or you can't tell me," she says, studying the mysterious man, the cool water lapping at his feet. "Either way, I think you need to see a doctor. Please remain still while I call someone."

"I am fine," he tells her, pushing her hands away again and moving into a sitting position. "See," he says, "I can get up."

"Can you?" She nods. "I see that, but just don't try to stand up."

"Why not?"

She observes as the man tries to pull himself up to his feet and then stumbles. She helps him sit back down on the rocks to keep him from falling.

"Because I told you not to," she says. "I can see you're injured and you obviously need medical attention. I will call my father. He will know what I should do."

"How will he know what to do?" The man reluctantly returns to a seated position. "I'll just sit here for a few more minutes and catch my breath."

"Because he's a doctor and maybe you will listen to him."

"You are a pushy thing, aren't you?"

"That's what they tell me." She grins.

"Well, you should believe them."

She chuckles. "What would you know about me?"

"Clearly not very much," he answers, scanning his surroundings. "Can you tell me where I am?"

"Liverpool," she answers, pointing toward the opposite shore. "Just go around the head over there, and you'd be right in the bay. The town is right there, on both sides of the harbour."

"Really?" He is surprised. "Liverpool?"

"Indeed," she nods. "My hometown. I was born and raised here. I came back to work after I finished university."

He's just about to ask her another question when a familiar, low-pitched cackling noise catches their attention. Looking around, they notice that several large crows have perched on the rocks not far from where he had crawled up on the shore.

"Crows," he says.

"Yes," she nods. "There's lots of them around here."

"There certainly are," he says, keeping his eye on the ones that have gathered close to him. "Can you do me a favour and tell me how many there are in that flock?"

Doing a quick count, she tells him, "Eight. There are eight crows in that murder right there."

"What does that mean?"

"A wish," she tells him. Smiling, she adds, "Eight crows for a wish."

"Right. A wish. You seem to know a lot about crows," he says.

"It's a thing."

"A thing? I see." He studies her face, then adds, "You look awfully familiar to me. Have we met before?"

"I don't know." She shakes her head. "But I don't think so and I am pretty good with faces. Besides, let's not forget that you apparently can't remember too much, so it's best not to put a lot of faith in your first impressions. You probably have me confused with someone else you know. I'm sure it will come to you."

"Maybe," he whispers as he continues to scrutinize her features. Finally, he asks, "What did you say your name was?"

"I don't believe I told you," she says with a smile, and he suddenly feels as if he's with someone he can trust. "But it's Sydney. Dr. Sydney Goodwin."

Acknowledgements

As you can imagine, creating a book is a major undertaking, and while the writing often takes years and is usually done in isolation, there are always numerous people who play a key role in completing the process. It's appropriate, then, to acknowledge a few of those people who helped bring *Seven Crows a Secret Yet To Be Told* to fruition.

First, I must extend my deepest gratitude to publisher Brenda J. Thompson and my extraordinary editor, Andrew Wetmore. They are the driving force behind Moose House Publications. This has been an incredible journey. Thank you for your support and guidance throughout the process.

Thank you as well to my friend and fellow dreamer Marci Lin Melvin for her many years of unwavering support, advice, insights and gentle prodding. Her never-give-up attitude and creativity played a major role in helping to shape this book. I could not have done it without her. Saying thank you hardly seems like enough, but thank you.

I must also extend my deepest gratitude to graphic artist Rebekah Wetmore for the amazing cover design. Capturing the essence of an entire book in one image is no easy assignment, but Rebekah delivered an image so compelling that it is simply stunning.

Another person I must acknowledge is my very talented photographer friend, Heidi Jirotka. To say she is creative and innovate would be an understatement. Thank you, Heidi, for going above and beyond to make me look good. You rock!

Another heart-felt thank you goes to the book sellers and bookstore owners for their unwavering support over the years. Those of us who dare to think we can make it as writers would flounder without the support of such outlets. You are a vital piece of the equation, so I applaud you.

I've saved my last thank-you for my most important supporters, my family, especially my wife, Nancy. She has been my rock through the many years I've been chasing this dream of becoming a published author. She is always the first one to give an insightful word of advice and a gentle prod when it is needed. To say I could not have done it without her is an understatement. There are not enough words to say how much I appreciate her.

As always, I want to send a huge shout-out to the fans of these books. Thank you for being supportive throughout this extraordinary journey. This would not be possible without you. It is my hope that you find the story is every bit as intriguing and suspenseful as you hoped it would be.

Now that the secret has finally been revealed, stay tuned for *Eight Crows for a Wish.*

About the author

Vernon Oickle was born and raised in Liverpool, Nova Scotia, where he continues to reside with his wife, Nancy, and their family.

Growing up in a small town in rural Nova Scotia, Vernon always wanted to pursue a career as a newspaper reporter. After completing high school in 1979, he attended Lethbridge Community College. He graduated in 1982 with an honours diploma in Journalism and returned to Liverpool to work at the local newspaper, *The Advance*. His community newspaper career spanned 33 years.

In addition to his long list of newspaper awards and honours, in 2012 Vernon received the Queen Elizabeth II Diamond Jubilee Medal, recognizing his contributions to his community, province and country, and in April 2015 he received a Distinguished Alumni Award (Community Leader) from Lethbridge College. He was inducted into the Atlantic Journalism Awards Hall of Fame in the spring of 2020.

As a testimony to his outstanding career, in 2014 the South Queens Middle School in Liverpool announced the creation of the Vernon Oickle Writer's Award, to be given annually to a student who excels in the art of writing, either fiction or non-fiction.

Seven Crows a Secret Yet To Be Told is Vernon's 34th published book.

9 781998 149209